BLINDSIDED

ALSO BY CLYDE PHILLIPS

Fall from Grace

BLINDSIDED

A MYSTERY

CLYDE PHILLIPS

WILLIAM MORROW AND COMPANY, INC.
NEW YORK

It is the policy of William Morrow and Company, Inc., and its imprints
and affiliates, recognizing the importance of preserving what has been written,
to print the books we publish on acid-free paper,
and we exert our best efforts to that end.

Library of Congress Cataloging-in-Publication Data

Phillips, Clyde.
Blindsided / Clyde Phillips.—1st ed.
p.   cm.
ISBN 0-688-17154-0 (acid-free paper)
I. Title
PS3566.H4764B58   2000
813'.54—dc21   99-44732
CIP

Printed in the United States of America

First Edition

1 2 3 4 5 6 7 8 9 10

BOOK DESIGN BY OKSANA KUSHNIR

www.williammorrow.com

For Steven Foster, childhood friend . . . still

ACKNOWLEDGMENTS

I want to express my gratitude to my agent, Helen Breitwieser, for her faith and grace. She was always there, pulling for me.

Deepest thanks to my editor, Claire Wachtel, for her tireless advocacy and advice. She was always there, pushing me.

Gillian Foster, dear friend, opened her Martha's Vineyard home to my family. It was there, swans drifting on the pond outside my window, that I wrote this book.

Stan Berkowitz sat with me, hour after hour, and listened, over and again, as this story took form. It was with his help that it finally found its shape.

Heidi Wenzel, my researcher, turned my vague questions into reliable answers.

—–—

My wife, Jane, made it all possible.

My daughter, Claire, made it all worthwhile.

BLINDSIDED

1

His first fix of the day bloomed like a slow explosion in his chest.

Skip Lacey, a desolate sixty-year-old with a body ravaged by decades of hard drugs, leaned against an abandoned watchman's shack in the Union Pacific rail yard. Driven outside by San Francisco's worst heat wave in decades, he sat watching the trains come and go, screeching steel on steel.

Fighting back the pain of his chronically aching teeth, he took an Oreo from his jumbo bag and let his head fall back.

As Lacey floated on the rolling wave of his high, he closed his eyes, the image of who he used to be appearing like a ghost behind his eyelids.

He opened his eyes, not sure if he'd fallen asleep, and noticed a man crossing the tracks. Heading toward him. At first Lacey thought it might be a yard cop coming to roust him. He considered trying to stand, to stumble away. But his brain couldn't quite get the signal to his legs.

As the man got closer, Lacey could see that he wasn't a cop. Just some guy carrying a cardboard box. Probably looking for a place to flop.

When the man finally reached the shack, he squatted in the shade. Lacey noticed that, although he was dressed in a clean white shirt and chinos, he was barefoot.

Lacey shaded his eyes from the halo of sun behind the man's head. "You got a candy bar?"

The man set his box down by the rock circle of Lacey's dormant cooking fire. His face still in silhouette, he stripped off his shirt.

Lacey squinted at the man's body, sweat-streaked and powerfully sculpted. "Hot, huh?"

"It don't bother me," the man said, his voice low. He unbuckled his belt and let his pants and underwear fall to the dirt next to the rocks.

"Then why the fuck you taking off your clothes?" Lacey said, irritated that the sweet privacy of his morning fix was being interrupted. He pried another Oreo apart and scraped the white sugar filling across his lower teeth. They pulsed with a dull aching throb.

The man squatted down next to him and jutted his face in close to Lacey's. "Because I don't want to get blood on my new clothes."

Somewhere in the recesses of Lacey's drug-soaked brain, a primitive flight instinct was triggered. His hips twitched in response, but that was all.

The man reached over to the fire circle and picked up a large jagged rock. Lashing out, he cracked the rock against Lacey's temple.

Before Lacey could understand what was happening to him, the man smashed the rock into his face again, shattering his cheekbone.

Lacey fell over on his side, his hands flailing to protect his face. "Why?" he screamed. "Why are you doing this to me?"

"Because," the man spit as he caved in Lacey's nose with another blow, "I am Jacques Carpenter."

Lacey blinked at him. "I don't know what that means." He struggled to prop himself up on his elbow. "Do you have any idea who I am?"

"Only who you used to be." Carpenter kicked out Lacey's elbow, sending him thudding back onto the dirt. He swung the rock into his jaw, splintering his teeth.

Lacey lay still. His face split and bloody, he drifted in and out of consciousness. The blazing sun was in his eyes, but he couldn't manage to close them.

Carpenter dropped the rock and opened his cardboard box. He removed his shoes and put them on top of his clothes. Then, reaching deep into the box, he came up with a grey metal spoon.

He glanced over to Lacey's chest. It rose and fell as he moaned in pain.

Good, Carpenter thought, he's alive.

He'll feel this.

Carpenter ran his thumb over the razor-sharp edge of the spoon. He had stolen it from the prison mess six months ago and had sharpened it every night since. Methodically scraping it on the floor of his cell, he had read aloud from his Bible to cover the scratching sound of metal on concrete.

Stepping over to Lacey, he put his bare foot on the injured man's forehead and bent over.

"Lacey!" he hissed. "Lacey!"

Skip Lacey stirred, blood from his broken mouth streaming down to his ear.

"It's time," Carpenter said.

He brought the blade of the spoon close to Lacey's left eye.

A powerful survival reflex erupting within, Lacey bucked his body, his back arching. In one brutally swift motion, Carpenter dropped his knee onto Lacey's chest, pinning him, and plunged the spoon into his eye socket. With a hard twist of his forearm, he gouged the eye out of his head.

Lacey screamed, his voice pitching higher and higher in his agony. His cries were lost beneath the squealing of the railroad cars as they clattered out of the yard.

His hands bloodied and the anticipation of the kill rising in his throat, Carpenter steadied Lacey's head with his other knee. He jammed the spoon into the right socket and yanked out his other eye. Then, before Lacey could even gasp, Carpenter brought the rock down with the full force of his pent-up rage. It cratered deep into Lacey's skull.

Wheezing a crimson mist, Lacey died in the bloodstained dust.

Carpenter stood and held his hands before him. Then he urinated on them, washing the blood away.

Never taking his eyes off Lacey's devastated face, he slowly dressed himself. He put his shoes, the spoon, and the rock into the box, and lifted it up. Then he walked back the way he had come.

The dusty wind of a passing train curled over him and he knew that revenge is what would keep him alive.

2

————

JANE CADIOTTI AWOKE, sweat-drenched and hot, thinking of the man she had killed.

She drew in a breath of recognition, and understood that she'd had the dream again.

The air, even this early, was thick and warm; and she knew there would be no relief from the heat wave. Stretching the sleep from her body as she sat up, Jane suddenly remembered that today was the day.

And she smiled.

————

Jane pulled her thick black hair into a ponytail and appraised herself in the bathroom mirror.

She was the seamless blending of both her parents' physical virtues: her mother's olive skin and slim frame and her father's high cheekbones and deep brown eyes.

In the past, the thought that this was the year she would turn forty would bring a clutch of regret that her life was somehow unfulfilled. But not this day. Her lips creased into a little grin and she nodded thankfully at her reflection.

On the bedroom television, a weatherman droned on about even more days of triple-digit temperatures. Jane sat at the foot of her bed and pulled on her tennis shoes. Then she took her mug of tea from the lowered ironing board that for years had served as a makeshift dining table. Sipping her tea as she rose, Jane thought about all the dinners eaten here alone.

She put the mug on top of the TV and stooped to upend the ironing board. It squeaked as if in protest when she collapsed it.

Squatting down, she lifted the ruffle out of the way and slid the ironing board under the bed. She stood up, retrieved her tea, and crossed to the door. Turning, she looked back into the room.

This, she thought with some satisfaction, was how a bedroom should look.

——

Jane sat in the front window seat and contemplated her home. The living room was spacious and bright. Overstuffed pillows she and her aunt Lucy had made from antique floral fabric adorned the two couches framing the fireplace.

The kitchen, merely adequate when she had bought this house after the earthquake, had been transformed into a true workplace for serious cooking. And Jane Candiotti was a serious cook. There was a soft yellow reading chair in the corner where she often scanned the *Chronicle* before heading to her job as a homicide inspector in the city's Nineteenth Precinct.

The hallway leading to the two bedrooms had always been a little dark. But, Jane decided, there was a coziness in that. The Parsons table near the front of the hallway was topped with dozens of photographs of her huge Italian family. Her eye was drawn to the tallest one in the center of the mismatched group of frames. Her father, Poppy, alone now for so many years, looked back at her, his large dark eyes shining in a candid moment at one of his backyard barbecues.

This house had been Jane's sanctuary for almost ten years. She had passed her thirties here. The parties and the solitude, the lovers and the loneliness, had all brought her to this day.

Shifting on the cushion, tucking her feet beneath her, Jane turned to look out the huge bay window.

Across the way, the American flag on the Harbor Office hung limp against its pole, as if in submission to the coming heat. A brown pelican waddled along the crest of the roof and hunched into its repose on the waterside edge.

The bare masts of the sailboats in the Marina stood like sentries, occasionally swaying in unison on a gentle swell. Two women in shorts and T-shirts speedwalked across Marina Green, talking and laughing as they went.

Cito, a homeless man who had been sleeping in this neighborhood for almost a year, shuffled by with his greying Labrador retriever. Jane watched as he, the back of his hand always touching the fur of his dog's shoulder, stopped at the corner and listened. He crossed the street and made his way, Jane supposed, to the duck pond at the Palace of Fine Arts a few blocks away.

Cito was blind.

Jane looked across the waters of San Francisco Bay. Three fishing boats, their nets dry and ready, plowed the surface toward the Golden Gate Bridge. Seagulls swarmed around them, frenzied at the prospect of food. As the boats neared the bridge, its roadway defining the horizon, Jane turned away.

There was still too much pain associated with the bridge.

The portable phone rang.

Jane picked it up. "Hello."

"Good morning," Kenny Marks said, his voice tinged with excitement.

Jane smiled. "Hey you."

"Hey yourself. Truck's all loaded. I'm on my way."

"I can't wait."

"Me, too. See you soon." He hung up.

Jane switched off the phone and looked up the street. Waiting for Kenny.

This was the day she had been anticipating for months. The day Kenny Marks moved into her house. Into her life.

The day the loneliness ended.

3

THE SEARING HEAT drove the people of the Tenderloin out of their stifling tenements. This crumbling district, north of Market Street, had long been home to a colony of drug addicts and dealers, prostitutes and ex-cons . . . and their children.

Someone had cranked the cap off a fire hydrant on Ellis. A young black teenager, Marco, held a trash-can lid against the torrent of escaping water, creating a cooling spray that shot out to the middle of the street. Black kids, white kids, and Vietnamese kids—all of them peers in this melting pot—stomped and squealed in the showery mist. Marco laughed as he maneuvered the trash-can lid back and forth, making sure everyone got wet.

And making sure his beeper stayed dry.

A wiry Vietnamese man, twenty years old with slicked-back black hair and a silver wire earring in his left ear, sat on the roof of the building across the way. Smoking a cigarette, he watched the kids playing in the water and remembered the days when he was younger and had time for such things.

His name was Tran Nguyen, but in the Tenderloin he was known as Punky-Boy. He was, as he liked to consider himself, a businessman.

Drawing deeply on his cigarette, he let the smoke fall out his nostrils. Then he looked to the right and saw a man trudging up the hill past Marco's primer-grey Camaro. He carried a single cardboard box in his muscular arms. When the man reached the fire hydrant, he paused to look at the kids. Then he turned and climbed the steps to number 82 Ellis.

A con, Punky-Boy thought. Fresh meat.

He flicked his cigarette over the side and rose. He knew that this man would be coming to see him as soon as he had enough money. Punky-Boy smiled and shifted the .45 in his waistband.

He could always use new customers.

—--—

"Those two go in the guest room and that one's for the kitchen," Kenny said to the moving men. The men nodded, dark patches of sweat broadening on the backs of their shirts, and lugged two more cartons down the hall.

"You actually have something to contribute to a kitchen besides an appetite?" Jane teased as she sat on the floor and rummaged through a large unmarked box. She was in a great mood, thoroughly enjoying the day.

"Hilarious." Kenny gently tugged on her ponytail until she stood up. He was just over six feet tall, and although he was in his mid-thirties, his handsome boyish face and ready smile made him seem five years younger.

Jane pressed into him, a perfect fit, and he kissed her hair.

"You okay with this?" he asked.

"Perfectly."

" 'Cause, ready or not, here I am."

Jane stood on her toes and touched her nose to his. "Please stop worrying. We'll be great."

"It's just that, given our history . . ."

"It's our history," Jane said, "that got us to this point. I wouldn't trade any of it away."

The moving men reappeared and crossed to the front door. The older one glanced over to Jane and Kenny and smiled. "Hot enough for ya?"

"Plenty," Kenny said as the men headed back to their truck. Then he put his forearms on Jane's shoulders and gently bumped his forehead against hers. "I'm a lucky guy."

"Why's that?"

"The girl I love, loves me, too." He pulled her into a loving kiss.

On the porch, the moving men stepped aside as Bobby Farrier, Kenny's fifteen-year-old nephew, came in carrying two guitar cases. Dressed in baggy black shorts, a sleeveless yellow T-shirt, and a backward baseball cap, he stood in the doorway, shoulders slouched, eyes on the floor.

Kenny noticed him and broke off the kiss. "Great, Bobby, you found 'em!" His enthusiasm was met with Bobby's habitual cheerless silence. Kenny turned to Jane. "Guest room?"

"You love those guitars," Jane said. "Let's keep them up here in the living room." She smiled at Bobby. "What d'ya say, Bobby?"

Bobby leaned the guitar cases against one of the couches. "Whatever," he said, and shambled back outside.

Jane could see the worry in Kenny's face as he watched Bobby go. Not wanting this day to be compromised in any way, she reached into the box and pulled out a picture of an old acoustic guitar in a filigreed silver frame. "Don't tell me . . ."

Kenny shrugged. "My first guitar."

"You framed a picture of your first guitar?"

"Call me sentimental."

"And this?" Jane asked, holding up a plastic bag stuffed with cotton balls.

"From the insides of aspirin and vitamin bottles."

Jane fought back a smile.

"Hey," Kenny protested. "How often do I need cotton?"

"God, you're cute."

Kenny snatched the bag from her hand. "Why do I suddenly feel like I'm trapped inside an episode of *Mad About You?*"

"Where you want this?" came a voice from the doorway.

Jane and Kenny turned to see the moving men with an old, beat-up refrigerator. "You brought that thing?" Jane asked.

"Sentimental, remember?" Kenny nodded to the moving men. "How 'bout the garage?"

As the men muscled the refrigerator back down the steps, Jane asked, "And we need two refrigerators because . . . ?"

"Look at it as an opportunity for more grocery shopping. You know how you love to shop."

"No, that's you."

Kenny was about to respond when he spotted Bobby sitting on

the top step of the porch. At first it seemed like he had stopped to watch the kids playing soccer on the green. But then he stooped his head and lit a cigarette.

Kenny blew a long frustrated sigh and started toward Bobby. Jane put a gentle hand on his forearm. "Not today, Kenny," she said softly. "Please."

——

Jacques Carpenter pushed open the door and stepped into his new home. After sixteen years in a cell, this grimy one-room apartment would suit him just fine.

He dropped the cardboard box next to the hot plate on the cracked blue Formica countertop. Rats, startled at the sound, scurried behind the wall. Their chittering squeaks mingled with the bass-booming rap music and the yelling of the kids outside.

Somewhere a baby was crying.

Carpenter peeled off his shirt, his prison-pumped back muscles glistening with sweat. He lifted open the air-shaft window, merely because opening a window was something he hadn't been able to do in half a lifetime.

Turning from the window, he unfolded the top flaps of the box and began to remove his possessions. A pair of jeans and a pair of chinos. Two thrift-shop white shirts and two changes of underwear. A razor, toothbrush, and soap. A carton of Marlboros. An alarm clock. A loaf of bread and two packages of bologna. A six-pack of Bud. And his Bible.

The rock and the bloody spoon he had used on Skip Lacey were already at the bottom of San Francisco Bay. The boys in the joint had been right. Lacey had fallen a long way from the old days.

With a derisive snort, he tossed the Bible out the window and listened as it fluttered and fell, landing among the detritus at the bottom of the air shaft.

4

I'VE NEVER SEEN so many Joni Mitchell CDs in my life," Kenny called out to Jane. "Did you know you have two *Ladies of the Canyon?*"

Jane took a yogurt from the refrigerator. "That, sir, is a classic." She had to speak loudly over the music Kenny was playing on the stereo as he unpacked his CD collection. "And who, I'm afraid to ask, are we listening to?"

"Lightnin' Hopkins, blues god."

"So this is my life, huh?" Jane asked. "Blues and the toilet seat up?"

"I'll work on the toilet-seat thing. But the blues are here to stay." He turned to Bobby, who was absently surfing through the TV channels with the sound off. "Right, Bobby?"

Bobby nodded indifferently, never taking his eyes off the screen.

Kenny was about to take the remote from him when the phone rang. Jane answered. "Hello."

Cheryl Lomax, the dispatcher at Precinct Nineteen, was on the line. "Hey, Inspector. It's Cheryl. Sorry to bother you on moving day."

Jane shot Kenny a look. "How'd you know?"

"The whole station knows," Cheryl said. "Looks like you and Inspector Marks are giving new meaning to the word 'partners.' " A heavyset black woman in her late twenties, Cheryl Lomax touched up the lavender polish on one of her very long fingernails. "Anyway, we're a little shorthanded and the lieutenant asked me to call you. He apologizes for busting up your big day, too."

Jane rolled her eyes. "What's up?"

"We got a nasty one over at the Union Pacific rail yard," Cheryl said. "Can you roll on it?"

Jane looked at the mountain of cartons waiting to be unpacked. "We're there in twenty."

"What's up?" Kenny asked as she rang off.

Glancing toward Bobby, Jane said softly, "Duty calls."

"Shit," Kenny said, looking around. "Where's my stuff?"

"I put your gun and badge in your nightstand."

Kenny smiled. "Really? That's so . . . domestic." He hustled down the hallway to the bedroom.

Jane laughed and grabbed up her bag. After double-checking that her service revolver was inside, she slung it over her shoulder.

Kenny came back up the hall, strapping on his shoulder holster. "Bobby," he said as he stood between him and the TV, "Jane and I have to go to work for a couple of hours. Will you hold down the fort for us?"

Bobby nodded slightly.

"He lives!" Kenny joked, and he and Jane hurried out the door.

— —

"You see the bruise on his shoulder?" Jane asked as Kenny jammed on the accelerator of his black Explorer and tore away from the curb.

"Yeah. I'm gonna talk to him about it when we get back." Kenny threw the car into a hard right at the Safeway. "If fuckin' Lonnie laid a hand on him again, I swear to God . . ."

"What's your sister doing with a yo-yo like him anyway?"

"She just couldn't stand being lonely anymore, I guess."

"I'm gonna call in," Jane said. She reached for the microphone, Kenny's words still in the air, and she thought of the mistakes she had made in the past, all in the name of loneliness. Not trusting her instincts. Believing that unchangeable men would change.

And then, almost four years ago, Kenny had come along.

Less than a year after he moved up to Homicide, they had become lovers. But Jane had wanted children. Kenny had hesitated, and she had broken it off.

Not long after, Lieutenant Spielman made them partners and,

after a while, they became good friends. Kenny remained loyal and committed to her, unwavering in his affection.

Then he saved her life on the Golden Gate Bridge, almost losing his in the process, and Jane finally understood that she loved this man.

"Don't forget," Kenny said as they raced by the Safeway parking lot. "We gotta go shopping later."

"I won't forget." Jane put her hand on his leg. "Slow down a little, will ya? We're not in a hurry."

Kenny eased up on the gas. "Habit. Sorry." He looked over to her. "You okay?"

"Not exactly how I wanted to spend my day."

"Look on the bright side," Kenny said.

"And that would be?"

Kenny smiled, his eyes twinkling. "Bobby's probably going through your underwear drawer right now."

"Not likely. That would require actual movement on his part."

"Good point," Kenny said as he passed a slower car and blasted up Franklin Street.

5

POLICE ACTIVITY WASN'T unusual in the Union Pacific rail yard. This was where stolen property frequently turned up or where high-speed chases ended, often televised by local news helicopters. A kidnapped six-year-old boy was found here in the spring. Barely alive in a reefer car headed for Salem, Oregon.

But this was different.

More than a dozen squad cars and forensics vehicles were parked around the abandoned watchman's shack where Skip Lacey's body lay under a yellow plastic sheet. A huge black crime-scene van pulled up next to the coroner's wagon. On its side was a poster of a handsome young uniformed policeman with the slogan SFPD, WATCHING OUT FOR YOU.

Two yard workers, shirtless in the heat, approached Sergeant Oswaldo Castillo. They were lugging a large metal watercooler.

"Cold drink?" the younger one offered.

"You bet," Ozzie said gratefully. He filled a paper cup with ice water. He was in his late forties with a full head of thick grey hair and the genuine kindness of someone who loved his job. "Thanks, guys."

"My little brother's a cop," the other worker said.

"Where at?" Ozzie asked as he refilled his cup.

"Detroit."

"Tough town."

The younger worker nodded toward the yellow plastic sheet, the contour of Lacey's body pressed beneath it. "So's this."

"Sometimes," Ozzie acknowledged. "You guys see anything out of the ordinary this morning?"

"Nah, we got here after it all hit the fan." They were bending down to heft the cooler again when the Explorer tore through the yard, fans of dust trailing in its wake.

They watched as Kenny slid to a stop behind the crime-scene van and he and Jane opened their doors.

Ozzie started forward. "Thanks again for the drink."

"You bet," the older worker said as he and his buddy muscled the watercooler over to a couple of patrolmen near the chain-link fence.

Jane and Kenny stood in front of the Explorer for a moment, absorbing the scene.

A frail young woman with wispy blond hair sat in the maw of the crime-scene van, talking with a policewoman. Her hands trembled as she lit a fresh cigarette with the stub of the one she was smoking. A boy, maybe ten years old, sat on the step below her, munching on Oreos from a blue jumbo bag. He looked like a softer, less weary version of the woman.

"Sister and brother?" Kenny asked.

"Maybe. Or mother and son."

"Hell, in this city, they could be husband and wife."

They moved forward, weaving their way through the numbered evidence markers on the ground. Lieutenant Aaron Clark-Weber, the extremely thin leader of the forensics team, knelt beside the body.

"Hey, Aaron," Kenny said. "How's the diet?"

Aaron finished putting a paper bag over Lacey's left hand and fixing it in place with a rubber band. Wincing slightly against the pain in his arthritic knee, he rose to greet Jane and Kenny.

"Morning, Inspectors. Sorry to drag you in on your big day."

Jane glanced at Kenny as she moved around Lacey's body. She stepped over two upside-down Styrofoam cups. "So, what do we got?"

"Your basic John Doe junkie," Aaron said. "Older than most mainliners maybe, but still really dead."

"Cause?" Kenny asked.

"Looks like blunt force. Repeated blows to the head."

Jane squatted down. "Weapon?"

"Probably a rock," Aaron said. He pointed to a gap in the fire circle. "Wouldn't be surprised if it came from there."

"Your guys find it?"

"Not yet."

Jane started to reach for the plastic sheet.

Aaron shot a look to Kenny, then said to Jane, "Uh, Inspector."

Jane looked up.

"This is one of the bad ones and you might want to—"

"I can deal with it, thanks, Aaron." She took the edge of the sheet in her fingertips just as Kenny knelt down next to her. Pulling in a sharp breath, Jane lifted the sheet.

"My God," she whispered.

"This poor fucker really pissed somebody off," Kenny said as they stood up.

"Aaron, where are his eyes?" Jane asked.

Aaron gestured with his foot toward the overturned Styrofoam cups.

"Motherfuck," Kenny said under his breath.

"Wanna see 'em?" Aaron asked.

"We'll take your word for it, thanks," Jane said. "Any prints?"

A forensics tech, dusting the side of the shack, shook his head at Aaron. "No fingerprints yet," Aaron said. "No tire prints either. But there's something weird turning up."

"What's that?" Kenny asked, still looking at the Styrofoam cups. They were covered with a light dusting of beige from all the dirt that had been kicked up.

Aaron nodded to the numbered evidence markers. "There's footprints everywhere. Not shoe prints. Footprints. I'm talking about someone, probably the killer, was barefoot. And he's a big guy, too."

Kenny and Jane looked at each other. Then Jane's eyes went to the woman and boy in the back of the crime-scene van. "They the ones found the body?"

"Yeah." Aaron took out a notebook. "Penny Kinsella and her kid, Randy."

"Mother and son," Jane said as she and Kenny started toward them.

"And I had my heart set on husband and wife."

Penny Kinsella tugged on Randy's shoulder. He scooted up next to her, leaning in close, when Jane and Kenny arrived.

"Hi," Jane said. "I'm Inspector Candiotti and this is Inspector Marks. Can we ask you guys a few questions?"

"They going to take us away?" Penny asked, her voice surprisingly mature for such a young woman.

Kenny looked to the policewoman.

"Social Services is on the way," she said.

He turned back to Penny. "Help is on the way."

"We don't want no help," Penny Kinsella said.

"Yeah!" Randy said defiantly. He clutched the bag of Oreos to his chest like a stuffed toy.

"Where do you live?" Jane asked.

Penny stared off across the yard, watching a train swaying as it changed tracks. "Around."

"Around where?"

"Around here."

Jane motioned for Kenny to take notes as she went on. "Was it you who found that man?"

Penny nodded, lighting another cigarette.

"Did you know him?"

"Nope."

"Then why were you here?"

" 'Cause it's too hot where we live."

Kenny leaned forward. "And where's that?"

Penny's eyes flashed with anger. "I told ya, around."

"Do you have an address?" Jane asked.

Penny looked away. "Not exactly."

Jane turned to the boy. "Randy, what grade are you in?"

He shifted on the step. "I don't know."

"Okay, did either of you see anyone else in the area? Anyone who might have done this?"

"Nah," Randy said. "He was already dead a long time before."

"How do you know?"

" 'Cause, the flies."

"What about them?"

"There were millions of them," Randy said without looking up.

Penny peered over the top of her son's head as a cream-colored sedan drove up. "Social fuckin' Services."

Jane followed her gaze. "Are you afraid they'll take your stuff away from you?"

"No, you idiot!" Penny said shrilly. "I'm afraid they'll take my baby away from me."

The sedan pulled in next to the Explorer and a young black woman, about thirty years old, got out. Shielding her eyes with a clipboard, she quickly surveyed the area and spotted Penny and Randy.

They tensed like animals in a cage as she walked over to them.

"Hello," she said, forcing an unfelt enthusiasm into her voice. "I'm Mrs. Welch from—"

"We know where you're from," Penny Kinsella said. She nudged her son and the two of them climbed down from the back of the van. "Let's just go."

Jane brushed the back of Kenny's hand with hers as Penny and Randy Kinsella got into the back of the Social Services car.

Mrs. Welch turned to Jane and Kenny. "I'm not the bad guy here, y'know. I didn't make her have a baby. I didn't put them out on the streets."

Jane looked directly into her eyes. "Why don't you try not thinking about all this in terms of yourself?"

Mrs. Welch started to say something, her lips parting in anger. Then, embarrassed, she wheeled around and strode to her car. She got in, slammed the door, and started the sedan.

Penny Kinsella lay her head on the back of the seat, smoking her cigarette as Mrs. Welch drove out of the rail yard. Randy looked out the window at Jane and Kenny. He twisted an Oreo apart and put the two disks over his eyes.

"My God, what that kid has seen," Jane said.

"And I thought Bobby had it rough."

"Social Services?" someone asked.

Jane and Kenny turned to see Hank Pagano, a homicide cop in his early fifties. Tall, fit, and handsome, Hank had the bearing and jawline of a marine officer. In fact, he was a decorated Vietnam veteran and still wore his hair in a military buzz cut.

"Hank!" Kenny said, his eyes shining. "Thought you were off this week."

"Lieutenant called me in. Things are getting a little hairy with the heat wave. Plus . . ." He smiled. "You guys were busy with the move and all."

"Never too busy," Jane said.

Hank took off his coat. "God, it's hot." He looked to Jane. "So how'd the move go?"

"It's still going," Jane said. She noticed the coroner's deputies lifting Skip Lacey into a black rubber body bag. "You check out the deceased yet?"

"Goin' to now," Hank said.

Hank wove his way through the other cops, nodding and shaking hands as he went. He'd transferred over to Homicide from Robbery after losing his wife three years ago, and was well liked by the men and women he worked with.

The coroner's deputies were just hoisting the body onto the gurney when he arrived. With a nod from Aaron Clark-Weber, they stepped back and Hank unzipped the bag and peeled back the sheet to get a view of Skip Lacey.

Jane watched as Hank drew in a long slow breath, his chest filling with air. Then he exhaled slowly through his nose. He zipped up the body bag and, shaking his head, came back to Jane and Kenny.

"Jesus," he said, his voice subdued. "Theories?"

"Could be the work of a completely insane dope fiend," Kenny offered.

Jane looked across the dusty clearing as the coroner's deputies loaded the gurney into the back of their wagon. "Or we might have an extremely smart—and brutal—killer who knew exactly what he was going to do, and did it."

Hank looked at her quizzically.

"The murder weapon, the rock, is gone," Jane explained. "Whatever the killer used for the mutilation isn't here either. No tire tracks. No shoe prints . . ."

"Yeah," Hank said. "But doing this to a homeless junkie? Why?"

Jane closed her eyes and raised her face to the sun. Then she turned back to Kenny and Hank. "When we catch this guy, you can be the first to ask."

6

JANE FINISHED THE REPORT on the rail-yard murder and pulled it from her typewriter. She read it over, signed it, and entered her badge number. Then she slid it under her stapler so the wind from the half-dozen electric fans wouldn't blow it away.

She looked around the bullpen. The other police officers were using everything they had, including their guns and handcuffs, to keep their paperwork in place. The air-conditioning had broken down on the first day of the heat wave, and for the past two weeks, the station personnel had improvised whatever they could to keep cool.

Hank was on the phone, two desks away from Jane. From what she overheard, she figured he was trying to pry a lead out of one of his many street informants.

Officer Mike Finney emerged from the bathroom. In his late twenties, Finney was too overweight for a beat cop. Lieutenant Spielman had temporarily reassigned him to desk duty as the communications liaison officer a year ago, and departmental inertia being what it was, he had just stayed there. The guys called him Moby, but Jane couldn't bring herself to use the nickname.

"Hey, Mike," she called as he walked by, his habitually unfinished crossword puzzle under his arm.

Finney slowed to a stop like a ship at sea. "What's up, Inspector?"

Jane held up her report. "When you get a chance, could you make some copies? Standard distribution."

"You bet," Finney said. Then he spotted Jessica, the sandwich lady, setting up next to Cheryl's dispatch desk. He walked away without taking the report.

Jane had long ago stopped trying to make sense of Officer Finney's existence on the force. She stuck the report back under the stapler and was about to call Social Services to check on Penny and Randy Kinsella, when Kenny came up, a small stack of papers in his hand.

"That computer's old, but she sure is slow." He sat on his desk across from Jane.

"What'd you learn?"

"Twenty-two mutilation murders of all flavors in Northern California the last five years." He smiled. "We could take turns reading them out loud tonight. Who knows what might come up."

Finney walked by with two submarine sandwiches, two Cokes, and a large bag of nacho chips.

"Hey, Moby," Kenny said. "Glad to see you're cutting down."

"Thanks, Inspector," Finney said.

Hank hung up the phone and swiveled in his chair. "You make that call?"

"Yeah, I did," Finney said. He idolized Hank and was always proud whenever Hank talked to him in front of the other cops. "And I got the job. I start this afternoon."

"As what?" Kenny joked. "A barn?"

"Nope. Security guard," Finney answered, Kenny's joke whizzing by harmlessly.

"Mike's wife is pregnant and they could use a couple of extra bucks," Hank said. "I had him call an old friend of mine and . . . looks like it worked out."

"Another mouth to feed," Kenny said.

"I finished writing up the John Doe," Jane said. "Can we split and get back to our first day of living together?"

"Let me get my stuff. Then we're outta here."

Jane watched him go over to the lockers and noticed an older Hispanic woman in the waiting area. She sat forward on the edge of a light green Naugahyde chair, nervously twisting the strap of her purse.

Patrol Officer Sally Banks emerged from the evidence room carrying a brown paper bag. A single woman, Sally had a thick, but not heavy body and dirty blond hair she kept in a tight bun. The Hispanic woman stood up as Sally approached and handed her the bag—the personal effects of some loved one. Clutching it to her chest, the woman tearfully thanked Sally and pushed the button for the elevator.

Sally turned to Cheryl Lomax and shook her head. Then she caught Jane's eye and the two of them shared a silent appreciation for what had just happened.

Sally broke off from Jane and headed toward the stairwell for a cigarette.

Jane turned to Hank and saw that he was staring at a framed photo next to his phone. She saw his mood darken and knew that he was thinking of his wife, Irene, who had died of cancer a few years ago after a long, depleting struggle.

Kenny returned, his coat hooked on a finger over his shoulder.

Jane took her bag from the back of her chair and retrieved the report. "Let's go," she said to Kenny, her eyes still on Hank. "See you later, Hank."

Without looking up, Hank gave a little wave.

"Irene?" Kenny whispered.

"Yeah."

"Poor guy."

As they headed for the stairs, Jane dropped the report into Finney's in-box. He looked up, his body filling his work cubicle, as Jane said, "One for the lieutenant, one for Inspector Marks, one for me, and one for the files."

Finney nodded, unable to speak with half a salami-and-cheese sub in his mouth.

"And tell your wife we're very happy for her."

"Ank oo," Finney mumbled as they walked away.

Kenny held the stairwell door open for Jane. She paused to look out at the flagpole on the small lawn in front of the station. The flag hung flat against the pole, like a wilted flower.

Sally Banks stood against the standpipe on the first landing, smoking a cigarette. Recently, Jane had noticed, something was fading in Sally; her energy, the light in her eyes. Jane recognized it as a surrender to loneliness, a relinquishing of hope.

Sally looked up as Jane and Kenny rounded the stairs. "How's the—"

"Move's going great, Sal," Kenny said. "Thanks for asking."

Jane stopped and smiled. "How're you doin'? Vanilla still being a good kitty?"

Sally dropped her cigarette to the floor and stubbed it out with her heel. "Yeah," she said, looking away. "She's my best little girl." She started up the stairs, the keys on her utility belt clinking as she went.

Jane watched her go, then joined Kenny on the last flight of stairs.

7

JACQUES CARPENTER TUCKED a clean white T-shirt into his chinos and rolled the sleeves up over his biceps. A pressure rose in his chest, an urgency to keep moving. He raked his fingers through his hair, lit a cigarette, and left his apartment.

The jabber of a half-dozen televisions tuned to different stations filled the corridor as Carpenter passed his neighbors' doors. Sweet, faint aromas drifted from the stoves of their kitchens. He descended the stairs, drawn by an inner sense of purpose that had been gestating for years.

Opening the building's front door, Carpenter squinted in the glare of the harsh midday sun and stepped onto the narrow porch. The children were still drenching themselves in the water from the hydrant, a different kid directing the torrent with a trash-can lid. Two young black women, each with a baby, sat on the steps, fanning away the heat. Carpenter slipped by them, the women grudgingly shifting their weight to let him pass, and turned left back down the hill.

Marco, the teenager who had been spraying the kids earlier in the morning, was changing the plates on his soft-top Camaro when he saw Carpenter approaching. Ex-con, he thought to himself, sizing up a potential buyer. He played out the menu in his head: maybe crack, maybe smack . . . definitely weed.

"Hey, bro," Marco said, putting on his best smile. He stood up to greet Carpenter, his hand extended, ready for the soul-shake.

Carpenter didn't respond, didn't look at him or acknowledge that he even existed. He simply walked on.

"Nice talkin' to ya," Marco said under his breath as he sat

back down. He looked at his watch. In an hour it would be time to head for the playground. The kids he had been showering from the hydrant would find their way there by then and he knew he could move some stuff.

Carpenter turned right at the bottom of the hill, a metallic taste of excitement in his mouth. He spit into the gutter and drew on his cigarette.

He needed money. Money to buy a gun.

——

Jane looked through the computer printouts while Kenny drove.

"Anything?" Kenny asked.

"Lot of sickos in this city."

"Without them, we're out of a job."

"Most of these," Jane said indicating the pages, "are already solved. And the others don't fit the MO."

"You mean the thing with the eyes?"

"Creeps me out," Jane said. "I don't like this one, Kenny."

"It's not your garden-variety wham-bam murder. But we'll get this guy."

Jane put her feet up on the dash. Once Forensics sent over the fingerprints, she knew, they most likely would get a name to go with the body. Until then, there was little they could do.

She turned to Kenny. "Timmy called while you were on the computer."

Kenny passed the Safeway and turned left onto Marina Boulevard. The sun, low in the sky, sent splinters of silvery light off the bay. "Let me guess. Can we get to your dad's barbecue a little early to help set up?"

"How'd you know?"

"Because you gave him two hundred dollars last week. So I figured he wasn't calling about money."

"Excellent deduction, Inspector," Jane said. "Did you tell Bobby about it?"

"Yeah. Guess what he said."

"Too easy. He said"—Jane let her facial muscles go slack— " 'whatever.' "

Kenny sighed. "I don't know what to do about that kid."

"Just go easy on him," Jane said as Kenny pulled up in front of the house. "It's a lot of work trying to save someone's soul. You can't do it all in one summer."

Kenny switched off the engine and touched her face. "Thanks."

— —

Bobby was sitting on the couch watching *Cool Hand Luke* with the sound off. He turned to his uncle, his eyes red and glassy. "Paul Newman's an actor?"

"Yeah, he's an actor," Kenny said as he took off his shoulder holster. "What'd you think?"

"I thought he was a salad dressing."

Jane leaned into Kenny and whispered. "I think he's stoned."

"He is. The little fucker."

"You're on your own with this one," Jane said as she headed for the kitchen. "I'm going to make a call."

Kenny flopped down on the couch next to Bobby. "*Cool Hand Luke*. Classic, huh?"

Bobby zapped the TV off with the remote. "I wasn't really payin' attention."

"Remember that barbecue at Jane's dad's on Sunday?"

"Yeah."

"We're going a little early to help set up. So I'm gonna come by for you around ten." Kenny turned to face him. "Think you'll be up by then?"

"Sure. Why not?"

Frustrated at not being able to get Bobby to engage, Kenny started to put his hand on his shoulder. Bobby jumped to his feet.

"Hey, what's the matter?" Kenny asked as he rose.

Bobby looked away, his feet fidgeting in place. "Uh, I gotta go." He started for the door. "Don't want to miss my bus."

"Bobby," Kenny said softly.

Bobby stopped and turned around.

"How'd you get that bruise?"

"Skateboard," Bobby said, unable to look at his uncle.

"And this is you telling me you're sure Lonnie didn't hit you again?"

"Nah," Bobby said with a nervous laugh. "It was just me bein' stupid on the skateboard."

"Try to be more careful, then, will ya?" Kenny stepped a little closer to him. "And Bobby?"

"Yeah."

"I need you to lay off the dope, okay? I mean, I'm a fuckin' cop. What am I supposed to do here?"

Bobby opened the door and stepped onto the porch. "I'm cool, Uncle Ken."

"Thanks for helping with the move," Kenny called after him, but the door was already closing.

Kenny went to the bay window and watched as Bobby crossed the street. Lighting a cigarette, he turned right, brushed past Cito and his guide dog, and was soon out of sight.

Enervated, Kenny sat heavily in the window seat. He picked up the CD remote and zapped the changer. *The Sky Is Crying* by Elmore James filled the room.

"Ah, the blues. How appropriate," Jane said as she came out of the kitchen, her face drawn with worry. Kenny patted the seat next to him. "You check on the Kinsellas?"

Jane nodded tightly. "Social Services already transferred them to a shelter."

"So they'll be on the streets in like . . ."

"An hour ago." Jane slumped next to Kenny and laid her head on his shoulder. "That poor kid doesn't even know what grade he's in."

Kenny put his arm around her. "Some fuckin' day, huh?"

"Some fuckin' day."

They sat there, each lost in thought. Then Kenny gave Jane a little kiss and stood up. "Look at all this shit. I can't even begin to unpack."

"Let's blow it off and do your favorite thing," Jane said, taking his hand as she rose.

Kenny grinned. "Here? Now?"

"I meant grocery shopping."

"Oh." Kenny's grin broadened into a smile. "That's my second favorite thing."

—–

Jane piled six dozen eggs into the already brimming shopping cart. Kenny came toward her from the dairy case, a carton of orange juice in his hand. "You entering the cholesterol Olympics?"

"I'm making a frittata for Poppy's barbecue. Besides, one dozen is for us."

"Ah, a mere sixty-egg frittata then. Good thing we have two refrigerators." Kenny leaned into the cart and pushed it toward the front of the store. Jane slipped a finger into one of his belt loops as they walked past the produce section.

"Wait!" she said. "Onions." She grabbed up a bag of yellow onions and found a place for them amid the avalanche of groceries. As they moved on, Jane looked around the store. It was crowded, a cool well-lit oasis from the heat.

A woman in sandals and a backless rust-colored sundress carried a fidgety two-year-old boy on her hip. In her other hand was a basket with Cheerios, bananas, Children's Tylenol, and disposable diapers.

Kenny steered their cart to the checkout stand. Jane picked up the new *People*. "Isn't this fun?" she said as she started to help Kenny unload.

"Time of my life," he said with a smile. "But, I think we're gonna have to steal a shopping cart to get all this stuff—"

He was interrupted by the high-pitched shriek of a child. Jane and Kenny, and everyone else at the checkout stands, turned toward the woman with the young boy. She was standing at the end of the express line, her child writhing on her hip. Exasperated and embarrassed, she dropped her basket and hugged her son in close. She cooed gently into the baby's ear, but the child continued to wail.

An elderly man in a red Forty-Niners cap wiggled his car keys in front of the little boy. "He has a fever," the woman said to him as the baby kept howling, his body contorting.

Kenny hurried over to her, picked up her basket, and put a hand on her back. "Come," he said, his voice just above a whisper.

Jane pulled their cart out of the way and Kenny set the woman's basket in front of the grocery checker.

"I got two little ones myself," the checker said as she rang up the Cheerios, bananas, Children's Tylenol, and diapers. "That's nine-eighty."

The woman shifted her baby on her hip and fumbled with her purse.

Kenny reached in and put a ten-dollar bill on the scale.

"Oh no, I have money . . ." the woman started to protest.

"It's only ten bucks. You just get your baby home and don't worry about it, okay?" Kenny's eyes were so sincere that the woman bowed her head in acceptance.

"Thank you, mister," she said as she took her bag and adjusted her crying son higher on her hip. She looked to Jane. "That's quite a man you got there."

"I know," Jane said, her face warming with the certainty that she and Kenny were meant for each other.

8

J ACQUES CARPENTER LIT a cigarette as he came out of the convenience store. Tucking a newspaper and a bottle of Smirnoff under his arm, he crossed the parking lot in a half-dozen strides. When he reached the sidewalk, he leaned against the traffic light and waited.

It was what he did best.

Waiting.

He finished his cigarette, flicking it into the middle of the street, and rolled the sleeves of his T-shirt up to his shoulders. His heavily muscled arms, exposed and dripping with sweat, were a source of pride to him. Hour after hour, year after year, he had sculpted them with free weights in the prison gym. And now they were perfect.

A Jeep slowed.

Its driver, a college boy, leaned over to get a better look. Carpenter moved his eyes, not his head, and stared back at him. If he was going to get into someone's car tonight, he wanted to make sure that whoever it was had the balls to go all the way. The college boy hesitated, then decided to cruise someplace else. He touched his foot to the gas and the Jeep slipped away.

Carpenter lit another Marlboro. A drop of sweat fell from his eyebrow onto the cigarette, making a wet grey spot on the white paper. He let the match fall into the gutter and looked up as a new set of headlights came his way.

A white LeBaron pulled up.

Stopping at a green light, Mickey Title, a bald and paunchy schoolteacher in his mid-fifties, lowered the electronic passenger window. He was miles from home. Miles from where anyone could possibly know him. "You a workingman?"

Carpenter bent over and blew a lungful of blue smoke into the car. "Three hundred."

"Jesus," Mickey said. "What do I get for three hundred dollars?"

"A guarantee."

"Of what?"

Carpenter flexed his arms, watching Mickey Title's eyes as his muscles tightened and bounced. "That I'll not only fuck your brains out . . . you'll come back for more."

Mickey Title caught his breath and swallowed. He clicked the automatic door lock. "Get in."

——

Jane was still awake long after midnight.

She lay in bed, on her back, with her hands together on her chest, listening to the blues Kenny had left on the changer in the living room. Kenny slept on his side, facing her. His breathing was steady, slightly nasal. The sheer white curtains stirred against the open window. It was less a breeze than an errant murmur of air on this hot, still night.

She looked to the dresser. Kenny had placed the picture of his guitar in the antique silver frame next to the cigar box where he kept his wallet, keys, and loose change. Jane smiled. She loved these stupid boy things about him.

Jane tugged gently at the sheet covering Kenny's body. It fell away, revealing a jagged round scar near his sternum.

A bullet wound.

As if in a waking dream, Jane remembered back to that day over a year ago on the Golden Gate Bridge. She had been taken at gunpoint to the top of the South Tower. Forced up there by a man she thought she had loved.

She had been moments from death when Kenny, injured and in pain, had struggled up the main bridge cable and reached the tower's summit. The man shot him in the chest and Jane, using Kenny's gun, was able to kill the man.

Lieutenant Spielman had granted Jane a leave of absence and she nursed Kenny back to health. Changing his bandages, irrigating the wound, guiding him through his physical therapy.

And they had fallen in love. Or rather, Jane had finally allowed herself to fall in love with him.

Kenny had always loved her.

Jane rolled over and put her face next to his. She could feel Kenny's warm breath on her cheek. Then she snuggled down and brushed her lips across the scar.

He opened his eyes.

"What're you doin'?"

"Kissing you."

"That would be a good thing." He touched her hair. "Now come up here and kiss a guy for real."

Jane rolled on top of him and he wrapped his arms around her. Propping herself up on her elbows, Jane kissed Kenny deeply, needing to give herself to him.

Kenny responded, sliding his hands down to her pelvis and lifting her onto him. Jane gasped, a shiver rippling deliciously across her back. She began to move her hips rapidly against his, pulling him inside with each thrust. Her breath quickened to a series of tiny sighs.

"Hey," Kenny said, "let's take our time here." He drew her face to his and kissed her eyes. "I'm not going anywhere."

"Shh," Jane moaned as she quickened her grinding.

Kenny put his hands on her shoulders and, raising himself slightly on his heels, pushed even harder. Their bodies slapped together, sweat mingling, until Jane could feel the ember of an orgasm glowing deep inside. She dug her nails into Kenny's chest and pumped even harder.

"Oh God," she said.

——

"Oh God!" Mickey Title screamed. "Oh God! Oh God! Oh God!"

He lay facedown on the bed in Carpenter's apartment. The rolls of fat on his pasty body trembled with each of Carpenter's angry thrusts.

Carpenter dragged his fingernails down the schoolteacher's fleshy white back as he slammed his penis harder and deeper into his anus. Thin streams of blood welled in the nail tracks and ran down his sides.

Wanting to, needing to, inflict pain on this pathetic man, Carpenter intensified his pumping.

"Don't hurt me anymore," Mickey Title begged, his voice hoarse and weak.

"Shut up."

"Yes. Yes. Okay. I'll shut up."

Carpenter rammed his penis hard up his ass.

"Oh God! Oh God! Oh God!"

In prison, there were those who gave and those who took. Jacques Carpenter learned early on that he had to give the best or he would be devoured. After fifteen years of butt-fucking those who had asked for it and those who hadn't, Carpenter was utterly, completely in control.

He fell forward onto Mickey Title's back, his elbows on the bed next to the teacher's ears, and jammed his cock home to the hilt.

"Oh . . . my . . . God," Mickey whimpered.

Carpenter came without a sound. There was a quick tightening of his loins, a brief moment of sensation, and then he withdrew. He peeled off his bloody rubber and tossed it on the floor. Mickey, panting heavily, his breasts heaving, rolled over.

"Jesus," he rasped. "When . . . can I see you again?"

"Anytime you got three hundred dollars, you can see me."

Carpenter padded to the refrigerator and took the bottle of Smirnoff from the freezer.

He pulled a hard swallow from the bottle, wiped his mouth with his hand, and said, "Get out."

9

CALIFORNIA DEPT. OF CORRECTIONS
BOARD OF PRISON TERMS
PAROLE REVIEW HEARING REPORT

SUBJECT: Jacques Yves Carpenter
CASE NO.: 0231870-9B
INMATE NO.: 421899

Subject was convicted for possession of and intent to sell one (1) ounce of marijuana in 1983. This was his third arrest and first conviction. He was sentenced to eighteen (18) months at Wolliston Medium Security Facility by Judge Marilyn Hotchkiss of the Alameda Superior Court, District 3.

Nine (9) months into his sentence, Subject's wife died and Subject subsequently became a disciplinary problem. Repeated consultations with Dr. Thomas Straw, Wolliston staff psychologist, proved unfruitful.

Subject attacked a fellow inmate, causing him to be hospitalized with numerous broken bones.

For this action, eighteen (18) months were added to Subject's sentence.

Two additional violent incidents resulted in the extension of Subject's sentence by another five (5) years.

During that time, Subject assaulted Mr. Norris Kennedy, a California State correctional officer. Officer Kennedy was hospitalized with a fractured skull and other injuries. Ten (10) years were added to Subject's sentence and he was transferred to the maximum security facility at San Quentin.

While at San Quentin, Subject's propensity for violence dissipated. He enrolled in a Bible study program and has, in his words, "seen the light."

Subject has now lived harmoniously among the prison population for the last eight and one half (8 1/2) years with no incidents that have caused any problems for either the other inmates or the prison administration.

Attached to this report are statements from Dr. Adam Schwartz, Assistant Warden at San Quentin, and Dr. Ruby Sibbett, prison psychiatrist. Each attests to Subject's exemplary behavior over the past several years. Each recommends Subject's early release taking into account sixteen (16) years time served and good behavior.

CONCLUSION: It is the unanimous finding of this Parole Review Board that Subject, Jacques Yves Carpenter (Case No. 0231870-9B), has been rehabilitated by the California Criminal Justice System.

— —

Senior Parole Officer Larry Schultz placed the hearing report on the credenza behind his chair. He'd do his filing after lunch. He always did his filing after lunch. He was a tidy man. Some in his department would call him fastidious. But not to his face.

Larry hated that word.

Punctual and neatly dressed, he was always respectful of the seventy-five to ninety parolees under his charge at any given time. As long as they were respectful to him.

A new bird had been released from the cage yesterday. He had until noon today to check in with Larry. This guy was another diesel from the joint—convicted under the state's Determinate

Sentencing Law or DSL. His jacket showed that he was a hardcase con with an extra fifteen years tacked onto his original sentence for violent incidents while incarcerated.

You fuck up in the can, you pay the man, Larry always said.

Larry Schultz looked at the small travel clock next to the picture of his wife, Enid, and their identical twin sons, Louis and Lawrence Jr. It was 12:03. The diesel was late. But Larry was a reasonable man. The new parolee could have been slowed down by any of a number of unforeseen scenarios, what with the heat wave and all.

He'd give him until 12:05.

He adjusted the little electric fan on top of his bookcase and thought of how some of his colleagues might handle this. A lot of them would go to the new bird's house the first day out. Kind of get him acquainted with the system. Start him off on the right foot.

That wasn't Larry's style. As far as he was concerned, these cons still had an unpaid debt to society.

And he was society's bill collector.

Pay on time, just by keeping a simple appointment, and everything would be fine. Go delinquent on those payments and society would call in the no-bullshit collection agency.

Twelve-oh-five. The Diesel was now a PAL—Parolee at Large.

Larry Schultz pulled open his bottom right-hand drawer and took out a form. He turned in his chair, adjusting his back cushion, and rolled the form into his typewriter. After checking the correct spelling of Jacques Yves Carpenter's name, he began to type out a warrant for his arrest.

Nobody fell through the cracks on Larry Schultz's watch.

—–

The flag at the Police Academy parade grounds hung as still as if it had melted to the flagpole.

About one hundred and twenty friends and family members rose as a scratchy recording of "Pomp and Circumstance" played over the loudspeakers. Forty-one cadets in their Class-A uniforms marched down the center aisle. Their relatives videotaped and photographed them as they peeled off to either side and found their seats in the front rows.

The presiding captain stepped to the microphone and led all assembled in the Pledge of Allegiance. When they finished, Kenny whispered to Jane, "Play ball!"

Jane elbowed him. "God, were we ever that young?"

Hank leaned forward and said, "Not me."

The cadet commander barked, "Cadets be seated!" They sat in unison, their Class-A hats with the shiny black brims in their laps.

Lieutenant Spielman and his wife, Mary, sat in front of Jane, Kenny, and Hank. Balding and in his mid-forties, Ben Spielman ran his squad room on the principle that everyone was worthy of two things: respect and a second chance. Mary, fanning herself with her program and occasionally snapping a photo, seemed unsettled.

As Chief of Police Walker McDonald, a no-nonsense bull of a man with short grey hair, droned on about "protecting the weak, innocent, and peaceful," Kenny turned to Hank.

"We should sue the city for cruel and unusual punishment."

"I know," Hank said out of the side of his mouth. "I feel like a damn POW out here."

Jane was about to shush them when a baby cried somewhere behind them. She turned to see a young Chinese mother clamber past the others in her row and hurry to the back. A cadet, hearing the baby cry, turned around to peek, and Jane could see that he was the father.

The time finally came for the cadets to receive their stars. As they rose, Lieutenant Spielman and a female patrol sergeant were escorted to the stage. It was a long-standing tradition that parents on the force present their children with their stars.

The cadets were called up, one by one. The formality of the prior proceedings fell away as family members cheered and hooted and ran forward to take pictures.

Benjy Spielman was a twenty-three-year-old version of his father, with wispy brown hair, kind eyes, and soft full cheeks. When he reached the top step, Mary, in spite of herself, pushed forward with her camera.

Beaming proudly when his son's name was announced, Lieutenant Spielman presented Benjy with his SFPD star and shook his hand. Benjy took it and stepped back.

Then, breaking with form, he saluted his father.

— —

Everyone gathered in the shade of the academy's main building for a reception of cake and sodas.

Lieutenant Spielman, his arm around Mary, said, "Thanks for coming out. We really wanted to share this with you guys."

"It was a privilege, Ben," Kenny said. "Thanks for the invite."

"So, Mary," Jane said. "How's it feel?"

Mary looked away, unable to force a smile. "It's one thing that Ben's a cop. But my baby? I don't know."

Hank touched her arm. "Don't worry. I'll watch out for him."

"Thank you, Hank," she said, grateful tears pooling in her eyes. "That means a lot to me."

"Ah, I love that boy."

"Me, too," Mary said. "You coming for dinner this weekend?"

"Wouldn't miss it."

Jane felt Kenny brush against her and she knew what he was thinking: Ben and Mary Spielman have been helping Hank fill his nights since Irene died.

Benjy came up after a round of picture taking with his classmates.

Lieutenant Spielman pulled his son into a vigorous hug. Mary kissed her boy, only the slightest hint of tears still in her eyes. Benjy mistook them for tears of pride and gently wiped them away with his fingertips.

Hank reached in to shake his hand. "Way to go, Benjy."

"If I had any brains, I would have joined a class that graduated in the winter. Goddamn, it's hot!"

Jane kissed Benjy on the cheek. "We're all so proud of you."

"Rumor has it," Kenny said, "you're coming over to the Nineteenth. How'd you pull that off?"

Benjy smiled at his father. "Friends in high places."

Cameron Sanders, an immaculately dressed black man in his

early thirties, approached with a photographer. "Excuse me, Lieutenant. This a good time?"

"Sure is. Benjy, this is Cameron Sanders from the *Chronicle*. He wants to do a story on us."

"Y'know, kind of a father-son, two-generation thing," Sanders said. "Okay with you?"

"You bet. But what about Sergeant Ziffren and her son? You gonna do them, too?"

"Already have," Sanders said. He turned to the photographer. "All yours."

Jane and Kenny stepped away as the photographer clicked off picture after picture of Lieutenant Spielman and his son.

Mary went up to Hank. "What you said about watching over Benjy? Hank, I want you to do that. Okay?"

Hank gave her a little kiss on the forehead. "I'm always there for you, Mary. You know that. Now stop worrying and enjoy all this."

The photographer finished his roll and walked away. Cameron Sanders shook hands with Lieutenant Spielman and Benjy. "I won't take up any more of your time today. With your permission, sir, I'll call you at the station and we can do a phoner."

"Thanks, Cameron. Anytime."

Sanders nodded to the others and crossed the field to his car.

"Okay, guys," Lieutenant Spielman said. "Drinks are on me."

Kenny put his arm around Jane's shoulder. "Just pour a diet Coke over my head, would ya? Jesus, it's hot."

— —

From high in the eucalyptus groves that fringed the academy parade grounds, it looked like a nice little party going on down below. The sounds of people laughing floated on the updraft.

A baby cried.

Jacques Carpenter snuffed out a cigarette with his fingers and squatted on his haunches. He rocked back and forth, humming tunelessly as he shielded his eyes with both hands.

Scanning the crowd, even from this distance, he felt a surge rise in his chest. Soon it would begin.

10

A STALLED TRUCK had traffic at a standstill as Jane and Kenny left the Police Academy.

"Great," Kenny said. "We'll just sit here until we overheat. Tell me again why I don't live in Montana?"

"Because, Inspector Marks, you now officially live with me."

"Change of address; the whole deal, huh?"

"For better or for worse."

Kenny stole a quick glance at her, and Jane realized that he thought she was talking about marriage. The truth was, she didn't know.

Kenny picked up on her discomfort and decided not to press it. "I vote for better."

"Me, too."

Kenny's police radio came to life: "3P118 to 3H61."

Kenny grabbed the microphone: "3H61. Go, Moby."

"Uh, we just got a preliminary report from the coroner on that John Doe from the railroad yard. I looked it over and there's something interesting here."

"Same-day service from Officer Finney?" Kenny said to Jane. "This is too scary." He clicked the mike again. "What is it, Moby?"

"They took some prints and ran an ID on the guy. And . . ."

Jane took the transmitter from Kenny. "And what, Mike?"

"Guy's name was Steven Joseph Lacey. Age sixty-two. Born, Texas. Moved, San Francisco, 1960. Social Services has him in and out of shelters the last—"

"Wait a minute," Jane said. She sat forward in her seat. "I know that name. Steven Lacey? As in Skip Lacey?"

"Affirmative," Finney replied.

"Who was he?" Kenny asked.

Jane put her hand on Kenny's forearm. "A cop."

"That's the part I thought would be interesting," Finney said.

Kenny took the mike. "I never thought I'd say this, but good work, Moby. 3H61, out."

"Thanks, Inspector. 3P118, out."

Kenny put the mike on the console between the seats. The traffic cleared a bit in front of them and he rolled the Explorer forward. "So, who is—was—this guy?"

"Skip Lacey was a narcotics cop," Jane began.

"SFPD?"

"Yeah. I was just coming up when he got caught ripping off dealers he'd busted and keeping their money and drugs for himself."

"Bad boy."

"It was this enormous scandal at the time." Jane blew a long sigh. "Turns out he was an addict."

"A junkie narc? Talk about the fox guarding the henhouse."

Jane nodded. "Anyway, he used the fact that he'd gotten hooked on drugs while protecting the citizens of San Francisco as his defense, and he walked. He was dismissed from the force. But he didn't do any time." She shook her head. "And this is how he ends up. Alone, fucked up, and butchered." She leaned her head against the window and sighed.

Kenny looked over to her. "Hey, what's the matter?"

"How does it happen?" Jane asked. "I mean, what brings someone who wants to be a cop, who goes through the academy and does all the rookie shit jobs, to end up like that?"

"Combination of things, maybe. Bad luck, some sort of personal history, too much temptation." Kenny pushed the Explorer through the light traffic. "Or all of the above."

They rode along in silence, Jane looking out the window, lost in thought. After a few minutes, she turned to Kenny. "How many friends do you have that aren't cops?"

"I dunno. A couple. Why?"

"When I got out of college, I had a ton of friends. Different kinds of people in different kinds of jobs." She turned the air-conditioning up a notch. "Then I joined the force and, gradually, they all drifted away." She shifted in her seat. "Civilians don't understand us, what we do for a living. They think we're weird, so they keep their distance. And we just sort of all gravitate together, perpetuating the isolation."

Kenny started to make a joke, but pulled it back. He looked over to Jane. "You feelin' okay?"

"I don't know. I'm a little moody, I guess. Maybe it's seeing how far a cop, anyone, can fall."

"Or maybe it's seeing how worried Mary was about Benjy taking his star today."

Jane looked out the window at an electric bus, its umbilical reaching to the grid of overhead wires. "Yeah, that kind of got to me."

The bus pulled away revealing a black-and-white squad car parked behind a maroon Lexus. A black teenager was sitting on the curb, his hands cuffed in back, while a patrol officer talked on his police radio.

"Isn't that Ozzie?" Jane said.

"Sure is." Kenny cut across the near traffic lane. "Let's say hi."

They pulled up behind the black-and-white and climbed out. "Hey, Oz," Kenny said. "Everything cool?"

Ozzie held up a finger signaling them to wait a second while he spoke on the radio. "Got it. 3P40, out." He turned to Jane and Kenny. "Nothing's cool in this city, guys. It's a million degrees out and my AC's shot."

Jane looked into Ozzie's car, his home away from home eight hours a day. There were Milky Way wrappers on the dash. Behind the passenger seat was a box of pink teddy bears for the distraught children of domestic calls. A picture of his wife, Laura, was clipped to the sun visor.

Ozzie took his pad from his shirt pocket and started to write. "How was Benjy's graduation?"

"Stimulating and refreshing," Kenny said.

"Yuh, right." Ozzie laughed, his white teeth gleaming.

"What's happening here?" Jane asked.

Ozzie looked to the black kid, who sat studying the dry gutter. "Our friend here was just getting into this fifty-thousand-dollar automobile when I happened to notice he was doing it without the benefit of car keys. So I pull over and he tells me it's his car."

Jane glanced at Kenny, then sized up Ozzie's captive. Things like this were potentially delicate. The Lexus could turn out to belong to the boy, or to his parents. A good cop like Ozzie didn't want to make any racist presumptions, but he still had to go on instinct.

Kenny moved closer to the kid. He was about Bobby's age. No way this car belonged to him. "What'd you learn when you called in?"

"That this lovely car belongs to Marvin Shimelman."

The kid looked up defiantly. "I'm Marvin Shimelman."

The absurdity of this statement somehow eluded him.

"*Rabbi* Marvin Shimelman?" Ozzie said, his eyes bright with amusement.

The kid shook his head, his shoulders slumping. "Aw, man, I'm all flustrated from the heat."

Ozzie grabbed his wrists and helped him to his feet. "Let's take a ride, Rabbi."

Kenny opened the back of the squad car. Ozzie was just putting his hand on the back of the kid's head to guide him inside, when his radio crackled. "3P40."

Ozzie reached inside and picked up the mike. "3P40. Go, Cheryl."

"Oz, we got a hostage situation at Clark Elementary. Shots fired. Injuries. One apparent death. Other units and an ambulance on scene. Can you supervise?"

"On my way. 3P40 out." Ozzie tossed the mike into the car and unlocked the kid's handcuffs. "Your lucky day, Rabbi. Keep the faith."

Jane looked to Kenny. "Do the math: shots fired, plus a death, equals a homicide. Who's rolling number one?"

"Should be Hank," Kenny said, already moving toward his car. "We're rolling backup."

"Then let's back him up!" Jane said, her adrenaline rising.

"See you there!" Ozzie said. He jumped into his squad car and, siren whooping, tore away.

Jane and Kenny scrambled back to the Explorer and climbed in. "Pop the cherry," Kenny said as he cranked the engine.

"Oh, grow up." Jane pulled the red-domed light, the cherry, from under the dashboard and clamped it onto the roof. "Seat belt," she said as Kenny stomped on the gas and sped away from the curb.

The kid watched them go, dust and exhaust settling around him. He waited a minute to make sure they weren't coming back. Then he jimmied open the door of the Lexus and hunkered under the dash. In a moment, the engine purred to life.

He adjusted the rearview mirror, turned on the CD player, and drove away in Rabbi Shimelman's car.

—·—

11

KAREN YIN WASN'T supposed to work this day.

Another teacher had come down with the flu and Karen was called in to substitute. She had left her children with her sister and hurried off to teach a summer session at Clark Elementary.

Her body lay on the hot black tar of the playground, a pool of blood spreading like an oil slick beneath her head.

Caitlin Sprague couldn't look at her. When the crazy man who was holding a gun to her head ran into the school yard, Mrs. Yin had sent the kids scrambling away. But Caitlin was at the top of the jungle gym and couldn't get down fast enough.

Then the police cars had raced up and the crazy man shot Mrs. Yin in the face. Caitlin had tried to run, but he caught her; and now he had his arm around her throat and a gun pushed into her hair. She had lost a shoe when the man grabbed her, and the pavement, baking in the sun, was burning her foot.

She watched as more and more squad cars came sliding to a stop on the other side of the chain-link fence. A big black van with a poster of a policeman on its side drove up onto the side-walk.

Caitlin could see the policemen squatting behind their open car doors with their pistols and shotguns pointed at her and the crazy man. The muzzle of the man's gun was scratching her scalp and the bottom of her foot was burned and Mrs. Yin was dead.

Overwhelmed, she began to whimper.

"Shut up!" the crazy man shouted into her ear. A white man in his mid-twenties, he had the look of someone who knew he had gone too far. Fear flowed through him like lava and his entire body was clenched like a fist. "I told you to shut the fuck up!"

He shook Caitlin hard and she stopped crying.

She saw a black Explorer skid up to the curb. A man reached under the seat and brought up a shotgun. Then he and a woman jumped out. She watched as they ran in a crouch to another man with short grey hair who had been here almost since the beginning.

"Jesus, Hank," Jane said as she joined him and Ozzie behind Hank's car. She took in the scene, the tension palpable in the heat. She noticed Hank's dry cleaning hanging in the backseat.

"This is a circus," Kenny said, gesturing to the swarm of police cars around them.

Hank, never taking his eyes off the man and his hostage, said, "Oz, I need you to set up a secure perimeter. Evacuate the houses to the north and east, and get all the bystanders out of here."

"You got it." Ozzie tapped two young cops on the shoulder and the three of them ran off.

Jane took her service revolver out of her bag. "Situation?" she asked as she thumbed off the safety. She glanced at Kenny. He held the shotgun at his side, chambered and ready.

"The shooter's a lowlife I used to know from the streets," Hank said. "Tyler something, something Tyler. He tripped a house alarm during a B and E. Couple of patrols responded and chased him here. He shot that lady teacher, then snatched that kid."

"A little burglary goes south," Kenny said, "and it all turns to shit."

Hank nodded. "Tell me about it."

"What's he want?" Jane asked.

"The usual. To make it all go away."

Jane looked across the playground. The heat waves shimmering off the pavement gave the scene a dreamlike quality. "Hostage team?"

"They're all at some fuckin' seminar up in Marin." Hank glanced at his watch, then trained his eyes on the man and girl in the school yard. "Last report has them here in fifteen."

"Hank! Hank Pagano!" Tyler yelled. "You still there?"

"Yeah, Tyler," Hank called as he stepped out from behind his car. "I'm not going anywhere."

Tyler, his eyes wild with confusion, lifted Caitlin Sprague off the ground. "I need help, Hank! Who's gonna help me?"

"Help's on the way!" Hank shouted. "You gotta stay calm for me, okay?"

"Fuck that shit!" Tyler whipped around and fired off a shot at the school building, shattering a window and sending a flock of seagulls into startled flight. Caitlin shrieked and Tyler tightened his grip around her neck. The front of her pale green shorts darkened as she began to urinate.

A KGO news truck arrived outside Ozzie's perimeter, its satellite arm telescoping upward before it came to a complete stop. A female reporter and a cameraman ran forward. "I'm Becka Flynn, KGO news. This is Zach. Who's in charge?"

Becka Flynn had hair the rosy color of a new brick and pale green eyes. Connect her freckles, Poppy would say, and you'd have the map of Ireland. Jane tilted her head toward Hank. "Inspector Hank Pagano."

Zach switched on his camera. "Go."

Becka Flynn held out her microphone. "What can you tell us, Inspector Pagano?"

Hank shot her a look. "I can tell you this: Back off. Now!"

Kenny put his hand on the cameraman's shoulder. "We don't want to shut you down. So, why don't you guys set up over there?"

Zach tugged at Becka Flynn's sleeve. "C'mon. Let's let these people work."

Becka Flynn reluctantly followed her cameraman to a vantage point next to the ambulance. Getting down on one knee, Zach nodded and she began her remote report.

—–—

Lieutenant Spielman sat down in a tall chair next to Cheryl Lomax's dispatch console to monitor the radio traffic from the hostage crisis.

Cheryl turned to him. "Hank's been on scene maybe twenty minutes. Ozzie just got there to secure the perimeter. Jane and Kenny, too."

Ben Spielman nodded grimly. "Thanks." He pressed his fingertips to his temples and concentrated as other units reported in. "Everyone be careful," he said softly. "Everyone come back."

Roslyn Shapiro, an elderly civilian volunteer, escorted a young woman past Lieutenant Spielman. When they reached the elevator, she pushed the button and said, "Just go up two floors and tell the man there about your car."

She waited until the elevator doors closed. Then she turned and headed back to the reception area. When she passed the lunchroom, she noticed that the small television on top of the refrigerator was on.

On the screen, a female reporter was crouched next to an ambulance, a man holding a gun to a little girl's head in the background. The word LIVE floated in the bottom right corner.

Roslyn Shapiro gasped and ran into the bullpen. "Lieutenant, come quick! It's on TV!"

——

"Oh shit," Jane said, looking past Hank and Kenny to just inside the perimeter tape on the sidewalk.

Kenny and Hank followed her gaze. Benjy Spielman and two of his classmates huddled behind Ozzie's squad car, watching in wild-eyed amazement.

"Must've picked it up on the scanner," Jane said.

"Welcome to the SFPD, boys and girls," Kenny sniffed.

"Hank, goddamn it!" Tyler screamed, the veins in his neck bulging. "This fuckin' kid just peed all over me!" He cocked his pistol and jammed the muzzle into Caitlin's left ear.

"I'm sorry, mister," she said, her voice a tight squeak. "Please don't shoot me."

Tyler grabbed her hair and yanked back on it. "Hank! Make something happen here!"

Kenny started to rise from cover. "I'll go."

Jane caught her breath, a conflict of emotions welling in her chest. She was both proud of Kenny's courage and fearful of the danger he might put himself in.

"No, Ken. This one's mine." Hank stood out of his crouch and called, "Tyler! I'm coming out!" He held his pistol up for the gunman to see. Then he put it on top of his car, the silvered barrel glinting in the sun. Without turning to face them, Hank whispered to Jane and Kenny, "Don't let this asshole kill me."

"That isn't gonna happen," Jane said as she drew a bead on Tyler's forehead.

"Take it slow, brother," Kenny cautioned as Hank started into the playground.

Becka Flynn and her cameraman inched forward. "You getting this?" she asked.

"Yeah," Zach answered, his voice hushed with excitement.

— —

"How far away is the hostage team?" Lieutenant Spielman asked.

Cheryl Lomax looked at her watch. "Nine, ten minutes."

They stood in a huddle in the lunch area watching the tiny TV set; Mike Finney and Sally Banks and Roslyn Shapiro and the others.

"Oh God, Hank," Sally Banks said. "Please be careful."

Mike Finney swallowed hard, his heart pounding, as he watched Hank place his weapon on the car and start walking toward the gunman.

In another part of the squad room, the fax machine whirred to life and Larry Schultz's warrant for the arrest of Jacques Carpenter curled out. As required, it had his mug shot, release photo, and a brief physical description. The page rolled onto the stack of other faxes and fell, unnoticed, into the recycle bin.

Lieutenant Spielman glanced around and saw officers and civilians standing on chairs and desks, all riveted to what was happening on the television.

"Say a prayer for a brave man," he said quietly, and turned back to watch.

— —

Benjy Spielman and his classmates started to close in for a better look.

"You guys stay put!" Ozzie hissed at them.

Jane watched as Hank, sweat staining the back of his shirt, closed the gap between himself and Tyler.

"Stop!" Tyler commanded. "Turn around."

Hank, his arms outstretched, turned in a circle. When his back was to Tyler, he caught Jane's eye. He gave a half shrug of his shoulders and came around again to face Tyler and the little girl.

"You okay?" he asked Caitlin.

She shook her head. "No. Please make him stop."

Hank looked to Tyler. "Let her go," he said softly, modulating his voice to stay calm. "Let her go and take me. No way anyone's going to shoot at you if you have a cop."

"Any way you look at it, I'm fucked," Tyler said, sweat streaming into his eyes. "I already wasted that teacher."

Kenny knelt behind Hank's car, frustrated. "I hate this shit."

"I know. Me, too." Jane turned as Scott Hicks, the SWAT team leader, hustled up.

"We'll be deployed in one minute, Inspector," he said. He had the face and complexion of a college boy, but he was a capable and ruthless police officer.

Jane saw the elite black-helmeted sharpshooters fan out to take their positions. She noticed that each of them had tiny lipstick-size video cameras attached to their helmets. Everything they saw was beamed back to the SWAT vehicle. From there, the SWAT commander had the advantage of a dozen points of view, one from each of his men.

Jane nodded to Hicks. "Anything bad even begins to happen to Inspector Pagano, take that fucker out."

"You got it, ma'am," Hicks said. Fastening the chin strap on his helmet and switching on his camera, he scurried away.

Kenny shot Jane a look. "Ma'am?"

Tyler pointed his pistol at Hank. "Pull up your pant legs."

"What?" Hank asked. "Why?"

"I wanna see if you're packin' a drop."

A blue Chevy pickup squealed to a stop and a man in jeans

and a white T-shirt jumped out. Frantic, he pushed past Ozzie and wove his way through the maze of police cars.

Caitlin's eyes widened as she saw her father running between the cars. Now, she knew, everything would be okay.

Becka Flynn tapped Zach on the shoulder, wanting him to get a shot of this civilian who had bulled his way past all those cops. "That's my baby," she had heard him say.

But Zach didn't move. "I'm staying with the money," he said.

"Do it! Now!" Tyler shouted. "It's too fuckin' hot out here and I'm feeling really unstable, man!"

"Okay," Hank said. "Whatever you say." He grasped his pants legs and began to lift them.

As Hank's cuffs rose above his socks, Tyler spotted the telltale bulge of his second gun in its ankle holster. He moved his pistol away from Caitlin's head and started to point it at Hank.

"Daddy!" Caitlin Sprague shouted as she ripped herself free from the gunman.

In that instant a number of things happened simultaneously: Tyler whirled to shoot at Caitlin as she darted across the playground. Hank, in one agile motion, threw his body between the little girl and Tyler while reaching down into his ankle holster and tearing his spare pistol free. Hicks, the SWAT team leader, gave the "go" signal. Manny Mantilla, the lead sharpshooter, centered Tyler's head in the crosshairs of his bolt-action Remington 700 and blew out two quick breaths. Jane and Kenny instinctively started forward, their fingers tightening on the triggers of their weapons. Just as suddenly, they stopped. Years of training had taught them that this was now a SWAT situation and they had to stay clear of the firing lanes.

Back at the precinct, Mike Finney found himself unconsciously unsnapping the safety strap on his holster. Cheryl Lomax squatted down in front of the television, unable to look. Lieutenant Spielman put his hand on her shoulder and leaned forward to watch.

Ozzie left the perimeter tape and raced toward Hank's car, Benjy and his classmates following. Becka Flynn and Zach, both moving in a crouch, hustled forward for a better angle.

All of the players in this drama watched in fascinated horror as Hank yelled, *"No!"* and pushed Caitlin to the ground. He fired his pistol three times in rapid succession. Two of the bullets caught Tyler in the torso and the other struck him in the hip, sending him stumbling backward.

Hank landed on Caitlin and, continuing to shield her with his body, turned to face Tyler. The gunman stood there, his arm waving the pistol in wild arcs. He was opening his mouth as if to ask a question when the SWAT sharpshooter blew a hole the size of an apple in the side of his head.

Already dead, Tyler's body crumpled to the steaming blacktop.

— —

"That is the bravest thing I've ever seen in thirty years on the force," Ozzie said as Hank was escorted to the shooting team supervisor's car. Becka Flynn and Zach trailed close behind.

"I know," Benjy said, too awestruck to fully comprehend what had just happened.

Jane came up to Hank as he got into the car.

"How's the girl?" Hank asked, his blue eyes distant and unfocused.

"Scared to death, but she's fine, Hank. How 'bout you?"

Hank looked at her, his voice trailing off. "It's a big thing, y'know . . . ?"

"I know." Jane squeezed his arm. "You did what you had to do and you were great."

Hank gave her a weak smile as a uniformed officer closed the door. He patted the top of the car and it started to drive away.

"My cleaning," Hank said to Jane through the open window.

"Don't worry. I'll get it," Jane said. "I'll write this one up for you, Hank," she went on, walking beside the slowly moving car. "See you at the station. Don't let them make you crazy. You did the right thing."

Two patrolmen parted the crowd of police, news crews, and neighbors as the shooting-team car pulled away.

The rumble of a fire engine caught everyone's attention. Its air brakes sighing when it stopped, its crew jumped down to the street.

"What's up with them?" Benjy asked.

Ozzie waited until the ambulance carrying Caitlin Sprague and her father, and the coroner's wagon with the bodies of Tyler and Karen Yin made it to the street and drove off.

"They've come to wash away the blood."

"Oh."

Kenny caught up with Jane at the curb. "Got all the statements and star numbers. We outta here?"

Jane watched the shooting-team car, Hank's head silhouetted in the rear window, turn left at the corner and disappear. "Yeah, we got some paperwork waiting for us."

Kenny put his hand on her back and guided her to the Explorer. Jane stopped to look at him, both of them sliding down the back side of their adrenaline high.

"Forget what I said earlier," she said. "Today, I'm glad to be a cop."

"Today," Kenny said as he looked around, "I think we all are."

12

JANE READ HER INCIDENT REPORT over a second time. Even the unemotional language the department required of its officers couldn't disguise the fact that something remarkable had happened on the playground of Clark Street Elementary School. A proud smile coming to her lips, she signed the report and entered her badge number.

She looked up to find Finney. He was in the kitchen area standing in front of the open refrigerator door. He's either cooling himself down, Jane figured, or contemplating his next meal. Since he'd started moonlighting on the job Hank had gotten for him, Finney's appetite had somehow grown even more voracious.

Jane tried to imagine his home life: two jobs, a pregnant wife; a cop made forever anonymous by his own passivity. She rose, crossed to Finney's cubicle, and put the incident report into his in-box for distribution.

The door to Lieutenant Spielman's office opened and the officer-involved shooting team stepped into the bullpen. Hank remained in the office with Kenny while Lieutenant Spielman shook hands with the plainclothes investigators. Lou Staley, the older of the two, said, "The whole city saw what happened on TV. I don't see any problems here."

"Shouldn't be," Lieutenant Spielman said. "I'm just worried about Hank. It's a bitch, what he had to do."

"It's the big one," Staley agreed.

"That's one hell of a cop you have there," John Liroff, the other investigator said.

"Thanks, guys." Lieutenant Spielman motioned for Jane to come into his office as the shooting team headed downtown. They were going to the Hall of Justice to debrief Manuel Mantilla, the SWAT sharpshooter who had fired the headshot that killed Arthur Tyler.

Jane followed Lieutenant Spielman into his office. Hank sat quietly in the corner of the couch, the fingers of his left hand absently rubbing at his knee. Catching Kenny's eye, Jane wrinkled her forehead, silently asking about Hank. Kenny closed his eyes for a second and, with the slightest motion, shook his head.

"Report's done," Jane said softly.

Hank looked up to her, his eyes vacant and lost. "Thanks," he said in a whisper.

Jane squatted down in front of him. "Hank, listen to me. It's a terrible, terrible thing killing another human being. I know. I've been there." She glanced at Kenny, then turned back to Hank. "But here was the choice: kill a junkie scumbag like Tyler, or let him blow that little girl away." She rose and put her hand on his shoulder. "No, I'm wrong. There was no choice. You responded as any cop—hell, any civilian—would have and we're all so proud of you."

"I know, thanks," Hank said hoarsely. "It's just so . . . humbling."

Jane saw Kenny's posture stiffen and she looked out into the bullpen. Everyone was watching them. Sitting at their desks or standing against the wall among the electric fans, all of the cops in the squad room were focused on them. There was someone signing in at Roslyn Shapiro's desk. That's what Kenny had noticed.

Lieutenant Jason Bloom had been a police officer for eighteen years, ten of them in Internal Affairs. He had a reputation for being thorough, relentless, and, at times, almost inhuman.

"What the fuck's he doing here?" Kenny said under his breath.

"Is it Bloom?" Hank said without looking up.

"Yeah," Jane responded. "How'd you know?"

"If there's blood in the water within a thousand miles of me, that prick shows up."

Jason Bloom strode through the bullpen, oblivious to the icy stares of the other officers. He was in his late thirties, trim and fit. A serious runner, he came in second in last year's Police Marathon. He approached his work the way he approached his running: with total and inexhaustible commitment.

Lieutenant Spielman intercepted him at the door. "Afternoon, Lieutenant."

"Ben." Bloom shook his hand. "Mind if I have a word with Inspector Pagano?"

"C'mon, Jason. Can't you, just this once, back off?"

"No, I can't." Bloom pushed past Lieutenant Spielman and entered the office.

Kenny nodded politely. Jane stood against the bookcase, her arms folded over her chest. Hank straightened his body, as if Bloom's presence were bringing him back to life.

"Hello, everyone," Bloom began. "Forgive the intrusion. I know it's been a rough day and I'll keep it short."

Jane started to respond, when Kenny touched her foot with the side of his shoe. She noticed Bloom glance down and was sure he had seen it. This guy, she thought to herself, probably knew Kenny was moving into her house even before she did. The tension in the cramped room was so thick, Jane felt she could push against it.

"Hank," Bloom continued, "I saw the KGO tape of the incident and I gotta say you reacted superbly."

Tilting his head to one side, Hank looked at him from the corner of his eye.

Bloom turned to Lieutenant Spielman. "Ben, are you aware that Hank had a prior relationship with the perp?"

"Hank told Inspectors Candiotti and Marks on scene that he knew Tyler from the streets. He subsequently informed me and the shooting team that Tyler had been a sometime informant for him in the past."

Bloom nodded. "Interesting."

Jane pushed away from the bookcase. "What is, Lieutenant?"

Sweeping the room with his eyes, making sure that all of them were listening, Bloom said, "Inspector Pagano deliberately puts himself in harm's way, possibly endangering the lives of the hostage and his fellow officers, rather than wait another ten minutes for the negotiating team."

"You weren't there!" Jane said, stepping forward. "The situation had reached critical mass and something had to be done."

Jason Bloom grinned cryptically, sucking at his upper teeth. "Maybe."

"Jason, goddamn it!" Lieutenant Spielman seethed. "What the hell are you implying?"

"I don't imply," Bloom said quietly. "I merely observe."

Frustrated, Lieutenant Spielman backed off.

Hank rose and took a step forward. Jason Bloom was the same height as him, and equally ready for a confrontation. Jane tensed, worried that Hank might lose his temper. But he said calmly, "It's okay, Ben. I'm used to it. Let him ask his questions. Let him . . . observe . . . all he wants. As usual, he's got nothing to say, and he's saying it anyway."

Jane saw Bloom's right eye twitch with a sudden flash of anger. Then he sniffed a little laugh and shot his cuff to look at his black runner's watch. "Maybe today's not the day, Inspector." He put his hand on the doorknob. "See you around."

"I'd expect nothing less," Hank said.

Bloom pulled the door open and left just as Finney came in with a tray of sodas. " 'Scuse me, Lieutenant. Thought you guys could use some cold drinks."

Jane took the tray from him. "Thanks, Mike. We could."

Finney, never taking his eyes off of Hank, backed out the door.

Lieutenant Spielman grabbed a ginger ale. "Anybody wants something stronger, I've got—" The phone rang. He picked it up. "Spielman." He listened. "Yes, I'll hold."

The others stood there watching him, sipping their drinks. "Hello, Chief. Yes, I know. We're all very proud of him." Lieutenant Spielman sat on the edge of his desk. He listened to Chief Walker McDonald for a moment and his face lit up in a broad smile. "Yes, sir. I'll tell him. Thank you, sir. Goodbye." He hung up the phone and walked over to Hank.

"The City Council and the Police Commission have just unanimously approved a resolution awarding you the Medal of Valor!"

"Oh Hank!" Jane threw her arms around him. "That's fantastic!"

"Way to go!" Kenny said, clapping him on the back.

Stunned, Hank sat down on the couch. He shook his head slowly and said, "Shit."

13

I KNEW YOU'D BE UP," Punky-Boy said. "I know everyone moves in on Ellis and I can always tell who's gonna be a customer."

He popped the latches on an oversize suitcase and opened it. Handguns of all types gleamed in the sun. Jacques Carpenter let a stream of cigarette smoke slip between his lips as he appraised the weapons.

They were on the roof of Punky-Boy's tenement house. The sounds of children playing bounced between the buildings as Carpenter picked up a small pistol.

"A twenty-two?" Punky-Boy said, shaking his head in disdain. "Don't you want something's got more kick than that? I got a Magnum here could shoot a hole through a Jeep engine."

"This'll do."

Punky-Boy pulled his own gun from his waistband. "I wouldn't be caught dead with nothing smaller than a forty-five."

"This is all I need. How much?"

"Well, the serial number's been washed away with acid, so it's untraceable and—"

"It's too fucking hot for a sales pitch," Carpenter said, cutting him off. "How much?"

"Two hundred with a box of shells."

They both knew this pistol wasn't worth half that much. They also knew that an ex-con doesn't have much leverage when it comes to buying untraceable handguns.

Carpenter took a wad of bills from his pocket and peeled off ten twenties.

Punky-Boy slipped the money into his sock. "You see that thing with the cops today?"

"Heard about it."

"Everyone's a fuckin' hero, huh?"

Jacques Carpenter bent over and grabbed a box of .22-caliber ammunition. He looked up to Punky-Boy, squinting into the sun. "Not to me."

Rising, he put the pistol and shells in the pockets of his chinos, stubbed out his cigarette, and walked toward the roof access door.

"Hey!" Punky-Boy called.

Carpenter turned around.

"You need more ammo or a bigger piece, you come see me. I'll do ya righteous."

Carpenter yanked the door open. The faint smell of marijuana wafted up to him from somewhere in the building. Without answering, he stepped inside and closed the door.

Punky-Boy covered his weapons with a black cloth and folded his suitcase shut. "You'll be back, asshole."

14

THE LATE-AFTERNOON SUN was shining directly into the west-facing windows of Precinct Nineteen. Roslyn Shapiro moved along the wall, drawing the shades closed so the cops in the bull-pen could work.

Jane and Kenny sat at their desks catching up on paperwork. The door to Lieutenant Spielman's office opened and he and Hank came out. Mike Finney followed them, carrying Hank's dry cleaning.

Everyone in the squad room stopped working as they passed, the humming of the electric fans filling the room.

Hank's eyes were focused on the floor as he walked toward the stairwell door.

He stopped next to Jane's desk and, barely able to look at her, said, "Can I see you guys later? I need to talk to you."

"Sure, Hank," Jane said softly. "Anytime."

"Six at Dighby's?"

"We'll be there."

Hank nodded and moved on. When he reached Cheryl Lomax's dispatch console, she leaned forward and whispered, "God bless, Hank."

He turned to her and gave a half smile. Then, without looking back, he opened the door and he and Lieutenant Spielman and Finney went out.

The noise level in the bullpen rose again, like a breeze pushing through the room.

Jane sat, still watching the door. She was thinking that Hank, after one of the most profound days of his life, was going home to an empty house. She looked over to Kenny. He had his elbows propped on his desk, his chin resting on his hands, as he read the ME's report on the Skip Lacey killing.

Feeling her eyes on him, he looked up. "What?"

"Nothing," Jane said. "Just looking at you."

"You're entitled." He came around, the pages in his hand, and sat on the edge of her desk. "What do you make of this?"

"You've got a junkie killed in the dirt of a rail yard." She sighed. "Ordinarily it would fall into the great unsolved morass. But the mutilation—"

"And the fact that he was a cop."

"Yeah. There's something about this one that I know is going to come back to haunt us."

"C'mon," Kenny said. "Let's go use the blackboard."

Jane followed him into the interrogation room. Kenny erased the notes from the morning briefing and started to write, the chalk clicking on the slate. "Here's what we have: a name, Steven 'Skip' Lacey. An age, sixty-two. Hair, brown. Eyes . . ." He glanced at Jane.

"Please don't," she said.

"Okay, we'll leave that blank. Height, six feet. Weight, one forty-five. Pretty good for a heroin addict."

Jane looked at her sheet. "Marital status, never married. Offspring, none. Surviving family, one sister in a nursing home in Lubbock, Texas . . . Alzheimer's." She shook her head. "A totally wasted life."

"Only if old Skip can't help us find his killer," Kenny said. "What's it say about scrapings?"

"No traces of anything interesting under his fingernails. Not surprising, considering that he had enough dope in his bloodstream to fuck up a moose."

"Probably too stoned to defend himself."

Jane leaned against the one-way viewing glass. "Okay, let's mention the unmentionable."

Kenny drew an oval on the blackboard. Then he quickly sketched in a nose and mouth, leaving the place for the eyes empty.

Jane read from the report. " 'Victim's eyes appear to have been gouged out of the orbital sockets with an extremely sharp spoon-shaped instrument.' "

" 'An extremely sharp spoon-shaped instrument'? What the hell is that?"

"I don't know." She continued reading. " 'The violence and force of the action suggest an exceptionally strong assailant.' "

"Makes sense. Aaron said the footprints he found indicated that the killer was a big guy."

"Well," Jane said, "you know what we have to do."

"Return to the scene of the crime?"

"Yup." Some movement in the bullpen caught Jane's eye. Ozzie Castillo was walking by with the kid who had stolen the Lexus.

Jane and Kenny stepped back into the squad room. Benjy was in the far corner, talking excitedly to a couple of younger cops.

"Hey, Oz," Kenny called. "What is this, police harassment?"

"Not hardly." Ozzie laughed. "Seems like the good rabbi here never heard of Lo-Jack."

"He has now," Kenny said as Ozzie nudged the car thief into the elevator.

Over by the windows, Benjy went into a crouch with an imaginary gun. "Then it's all like Bam! Bam! Bam! Medal of Valor, thank you very much!"

The other young cops looked past Benjy to the stairwell door. Lieutenant Spielman stood there watching his son. "Two people died today, Benjamin," he said quietly.

The squad room was gripped in silence. Then Cheryl Lomax said softly, "Lieutenant, there's a Cameron Sanders from the *Chronicle* on line two."

Lieutenant Spielman nodded tightly and strode across the bullpen toward his office.

Benjy looked after his father, waiting for his door to close. Then he turned to his friends. "You know what? My dad's right. I'm a jerk."

Jane and Kenny looked at each other.

"This kid's good," Kenny said under his breath.

Jane caught Benjy's eye and he came over to them.

"Must be hard," Kenny offered, "having a cop for a father."

"Nah, it's okay. I just want him to be proud of me is all."

"Just be careful. This can be a serious business we're in," Jane said. "Or does that sound too much like your mom?"

"Sounds like both of them." Benjy grinned. "And don't worry, I'm gonna be Mr. Careful." He looked around to see if anyone was listening. "Uh, can I ask you guys something?"

"Sure, Benjy," Jane said. "What's up?"

"Well, we all saw what Hank did today," Benjy began, finding his rhythm. "It was amazing."

"Sure was," Kenny said.

"Then how come that guy from IA was all over his case?"

"Your dad never told you?"

"He doesn't really talk shop at home. My mom gets upset."

Jane turned back toward the interrogation room. "Step into our office."

Benjy followed her and Kenny inside and closed the door. He noticed the blackboard. "That the guy with the eyes?"

"Without the eyes," Kenny said.

"We heard about that at the academy. Gruesome."

"Pretty ugly," Kenny agreed.

"Okay, here's the deal with Hank and IA," Jane said. "It's public knowledge around here, so I don't think your father would mind us telling you." She sat at the table and rocked back in her chair. "When Irene was first diagnosed with cancer, Hank and she decided to get aggressive about using alternative medicine along with the regular routine of chemo and radiation."

"It was really hard on both of them," Kenny said. "Back then, insurance wouldn't cover anything other than mainstream medical costs and Hank needed money."

Jane picked up the story. "Hank had a friend who owned this restaurant-slash-bar over on Gough Street. Hank bought it from him under the table. He put in some extra hours working the grill at night, and it started making pretty good money."

"But I thought it was illegal for a cop to own a place that serves liquor," Benjy said.

Kenny nodded. "We're getting to that."

"So Hank starts taking Irene down to Mexico for some cure

they have there," Jane continued. "He even took her to Paris once to meet with a specialist in her particular kind of cancer."

"And along comes IA," Kenny said. "Somehow they found out about the bar and Jason Bloom came down on Hank like a ton of bad news."

"He told Hank he'd have to sell the bar," Jane said. "The laws are very specific and there could be no exceptions. Hank filed an appeal citing special circumstances and was denied. Then he offered to quit the force and Bloom told him that since he had bought the place illegally, he'd have the liquor-license people shut him down anyway."

"What a prick," Benjy said.

"Hank was out of his mind with desperation," Jane said. "He went to see Bloom; found him in some Chinese restaurant where he was eating with his wife. And he actually begged him to let him keep the bar as long as Irene was alive. Just so he could have some extra money to help keep her comfortable."

"Imagine someone like Hank begging a weasel like Bloom," Kenny said.

"What happened then?" Benjy asked.

"Bloom completely stonewalled him," Kenny said. "Wouldn't answer him; wouldn't even look up."

"Finally," Jane went on, "Hank said something to Bloom's wife, asking her to help . . . he was that nuts. The wife turned away and Hank did something like put his hand on her shoulder; just to get her attention. And—"

"And Bloom coldcocked him," Kenny said. "Sent him sprawling on his ass in the middle of the restaurant."

"Jesus," Benjy said. "What'd Hank do?"

"He knew better than to get into a fight with someone from IA," Kenny said. "So, he picked himself up, brushed himself off, and . . . just walked away."

Jane shook her head. "Can you imagine the pain, the humiliation?"

"I can't even begin to," Benjy said. "Did the alternative stuff help Irene?"

"Actually, no," Kenny said. "But it gave Irene something

she hadn't had before the money from the bar started coming in . . . hope."

Jane rose and crossed to Kenny. "Bloom never did cut Hank a break and Irene died ten days later."

"A week after the funeral," Kenny said, "Hank gets a notice to sell within thirty days."

"He was still paying off all those medical bills," Jane said. "So he requested through channels to be able to keep the bar just till he could catch up."

"But Bloom wrote a memo to his superiors," Kenny continued, "strongly suggesting that they turn down Hank's request . . . and they did."

"Man!" Benjy said. "What was Bloom's problem?"

"He kept saying that it wasn't personal. That, if he cut Hank a break, he'd have to do it for everyone," Jane said. "And pretty soon the Uniform Code of Ethics would be useless."

"But why's he still on Hank's case after all this time?"

"After Hank sold the bar, he sued Jason Bloom in civil court for assault stemming from the incident in the Chinese restaurant," Jane explained. "He didn't win, but he accomplished what he set out to do."

"Which was?"

"Bloom's performance jacket now had a lawsuit in it," Kenny said. "A pretty serious matter for an ambitious piece of shit like him."

"And his career just stalled," Jane said. "He was a rising star, one of the youngest lieutenants on the force. But since the lawsuit, he's been passed over for a captaincy every year."

"His wife left him soon after that," Kenny said. "And now Bloom's alone and childless at this stage of his life."

"Just like Hank," Jane added.

Benjy whistled.

"So now it's open warfare between Hank and Bloom," Kenny said, opening the door. "C'mon, let's get out of here. It's too hot."

"Hank sued an IA guy!" Benjy said.

"Yeah," Kenny said. "Here was his wife dying of cancer, and he's completely distracted by all this bullshit IA stuff. He's always believed that Irene could have had a better, more dignified death if it hadn't been for Jason Bloom. He simply wouldn't take their shit and he fought back."

Jane stepped into the squad room and turned to Benjy. "Hank was a hero to a lot of us long before what happened in that school yard."

15

THIS IS ONE SHITTY PLACE to die," Jane said.

She and Kenny stood on the patch of dirt where Skip Lacey had been murdered. Pieces of yellow police tape clung to the debris like tiny flags around the watchman's shack. In the rail yard below, a long freight train was just beginning to move, one car at a time, until the whole line of carriages rumbled forward like a giant centipede.

Jane squatted down next to the rock fire circle and studied the ground. It had been trampled flat by the squadron of police personnel that take over a murder site once it's been released by homicide. "Y'know," she said, "I'm here, in the heat and dirt, trying to get a feeling for what Skip Lacey's last moments on this earth were . . . and I can't."

"That's 'cause he probably couldn't feel it either. You said it yourself: he was stoned out of his mind."

"Still . . ." Jane rose and went to the shack. Like all railroad structures, it was built to last forever. She reached out to try the latch on the heavy wooden door, when it was suddenly whipped open from inside.

Kenny ripped his pistol from his shoulder holster, and pushed Jane to the side. He peered into the shack.

Penny Kinsella stepped from the shadows into the shaft of dusty light. "You can't throw me out of here!" she said in her husky voice. "I got my amendment rights!"

Jane held out her hands. "We're not here to give you any grief, Penny . . ."

"That's a first."

"There's a system in this city," Kenny said, putting away his pistol, "that can help you out. If you want, we can—"

"I don't want. Okay?" Penny held her hand flat in front of her eyebrows, like a salute, to shade her eyes. "Just leave me alone, is all I want."

"Okay, we will," Jane said. "Where's Randy?"

Penny's body inched back, retreating to the safety of the darkness behind her. "School."

Jane and Kenny shared a look. "Which one?" Kenny asked.

"Eisenhower."

"Penny, Eisenhower's in Oakland," Jane said softly. "Where's your boy today?"

"Gettin' us some money." Penny leaned against the door frame and took a pack of cigarettes from the pocket of her yellow sundress. "I sent him to the cable-car turnaround at the Wharf." She struck a match and lit up. "He's a great little talker, that one," she said proudly. "Sometimes he can get us forty bucks a day in the summer." She blew a puff of smoke and smiled. "Tourists."

Jane smiled back at her. "Did you know Skip Lacey?"

"He the guy was killed?"

"Yes."

"I didn't know his name, but he was the cocksucker come up here and threw me and Randy out on our asses." Penny looked past them, down into the yard. Randy Kinsella was climbing the hill, a grocery bag under one arm. "This was our place," she went on. "We had it fixed up nice. Roof didn't leak. Sometimes the railroad guys would give us food . . . half a ham once. Then that junkie comes and chases us out of here, all violent and everything." She spit into the dirt. "I'm glad he's dead. Got my house back."

Jane touched Kenny's arm. "Thank you for your time, Penny." She took a card out of her purse. "You ever want to talk or anything, gimme a call, okay?"

"Thanks again," Kenny said, tipping an imaginary hat.

He and Jane crossed the dirt patch and climbed into the Explorer. As Kenny started the engine, they watched Randy climb the hill. He was kicking a partially deflated soccer ball he'd scavenged from somewhere, little explosions of dust churning at his feet.

When he crested the hill, he spotted Jane and Kenny. He stooped down to pick up the ball and held it in the crook of his arm. "Hi," he said, his dirt-streaked face cracking into a grin.

"Hi, yourself," Kenny said. "Hot enough for ya?"

"What d'ya mean?"

Kenny shook his head. "Nothing. It's just something people say on hot days."

"Oh." Randy saw his mother in the doorway and started toward her. Then he stopped and turned back to Jane and Kenny. "Can I ask you something?" he said, his voice thin and high like a girl's.

"You bet," Jane said, leaning over Kenny so she could see him better.

"What'd they do with that dead guy's eyes?"

Kenny let his head fall back to the headrest. "All yours," he said out of the side of his mouth.

"The doctors put that man all back together and he's in heaven now," Jane said.

"Oh," Randy said as if this were explanation enough. "Cool."

"Hey, Randy," Jane called. "Do you need anything?"

Randy Kinsella held up his grocery bag. "Nah, we're doin' great!"

— —

Kenny crossed the last set of tracks, the Explorer shuddering over the rails, and pulled onto the street. "I know what you're thinking."

Jane turned from the window. "What am I thinking?"

"You're thinking: 'How can we save those two? What's going to happen to them when the weather turns?' " He switched on the air conditioner. "If it ever turns."

"How'd you know?"

" 'Cause I was thinking the same thing," Kenny said as he gunned the engine and raced through a yellow light. "Maybe after we unpack, we can bring them some clothes and stuff."

"That's also what I was thinking."

"I know." Kenny reached over and slid his hand under her left leg.

"It's been a long day," Jane said. "Let's go see Hank."

"What do you think he wants?"

Jane looked over to him. "Not to be alone."

"Yeah." Kenny nodded. He revved the Explorer past a slower-moving car. "Afterward, I want to go home and put a dent in all those boxes."

"You got it," Jane said. "Besides, I've got a frittata the size of a manhole cover to make for the barbecue."

Kenny's face warmed into a broad smile.

"What?" Jane asked.

"Nothing. I just love all this domestic shit."

Jane unfastened her seat belt and snuggled into him. "Me, too," she said. "And I love you."

"Thank God."

16

BARRY BONDS HIT a sharp single to left; scoring two and keeping the inning alive.

No one watched.

The TV above the bar in Dighby's was showing the Giants-Cardinals game, with the sound off.

There were eight people in the dark, smoky barroom. All men. All cops or ex-cops.

Hank Pagano sat in a corner booth, his back to the television. He was nursing a drink while absently turning the pages of a tattered *Esquire* someone had left behind.

The front door opened. Hank raised his eyes to the mirror over the booth.

Jane and Kenny stood in a square of white sunlight. They spotted Hank and, drawing the door closed, entered the bar.

A man swiveled on his bar stool and followed them with eyes dulled by days and nights in darkness. He hacked a wet cough, wiping at his mouth with the soiled handkerchief he kept in his left hand.

When Jane and Kenny passed, he turned back to the bar and, staring at his reflection, lit a cigarette.

Hank closed the magazine as Jane and Kenny slid into the booth.

"Hey, guys," he said. "Thanks for coming."

"How you doin'?" Jane asked.

Hank finished his drink, chewing on the ice, before he spoke. "It's all . . . bigger than life, y'know?" He sniffed a short laugh. "Killing a man is bigger than life."

"It's as big and as shitty as it gets," Kenny said.

The bartender, a thick slab of a man with huge hands and kind eyes, put a fresh drink in front of Hank.

"What's your pleasure?" he asked Jane and Kenny. His voice was feeble, broken-down.

"Diet Coke," Kenny said.

"Beer," Jane said. "Whatever's cold."

"Comin' up," the bartender said, pushing the words out. He returned to the bar.

"Throat cancer," Hank said softly, tilting his head toward the bartender. "Diagnosed last March."

"Poor bastard," Kenny said. He picked up the *Esquire,* looked at the cover, and put it back.

"Look," Hank said, "the reason I asked you to come by is I need to tell you something."

Jane glanced at Kenny, then turned to Hank.

"The two of you have been so great since I came over to Homicide, I wanted you to hear it from me personally." He sipped his drink. "Y'know, I look at Benjy and how happy he is, just coming up. And I think, 'Where'd that happiness go for me?' I don't know the answer, but I do know one thing . . . it's gone." He leaned forward, his voice just above a whisper. "This January it'll be thirty years . . . and I'm gonna hang it up." He looked away. "Heh, I feel like some old pitcher announcing his retirement, then he breaks down on TV."

"Oh, Hank," Jane said. She reached across the table and took his hand. "What you've been through today."

Hank shook his head. "I'd been thinking about this way before what happened today." He squeezed Jane's hand and pulled his away. "I'm gonna be fifty in October. Too old for this. Too old and too tired." He shook his head. "And too angry."

The door opened and a man on crutches hobbled in. He sat heavily on the nearest stool and the bartender put a glass of beer in front of him.

Hank looked from Kenny to Jane. "I don't want to be the angry guy anymore."

He took a long pull from his drink and gestured to the room. "Look at this place."

Jane and Kenny followed his eyes. Weary men with nothing to do and nothing to say. Some of them smoking. All of them drinking.

"This isn't the same kind of cop bar we went to as rookies. Places with loud talk and loud music and pool tables. Cops coming off their shifts still flushed with the day. Trading stories and lies." He looked back to the bar, to the men sitting on the stools watching the day pass in the mirror. "This place is a fuckin' waiting room," Hank went on, "where cops come to die." He pushed his drink away. "I gotta get out before I become one of them."

"Does Ben know?" Kenny asked.

Hank nodded. "Told him today. He said he understood, but I think he was upset. We go way back, Ben and me." Hank chewed on the end of a thin red straw. "As I'm sure you know, Ben greased my transfer over to Homicide after Irene died. He said he needed the help, but it was really just to keep an eye on me." He pulled his lips into an awkward grin. "And you guys were there for me . . . a new family just when I needed one." He looked away. "You saved my life."

They sat in silence for a moment, the ballgame droning on the TV.

"Hank," Jane finally said, "sorry, but I have to ask you this. How much has the whole Jason Bloom thing affected your decision?"

"I can't lie to you," Hank said. "It's a factor, a big one. Look what happened today. I . . ." He lowered his voice. "I killed a guy. By all accounts, a completely clean shooting . . . and that vindictive son of a bitch is *still* all over me."

The bartender came over with Jane and Kenny's drinks. He put them on the table and looked to Hank. Hank nodded slightly to indicate that the drinks should be put on his tab. The bartender took an empty glass from the table and left.

"Everyone always said that a lesser man than me would have cracked long ago under the pressure—hell, the harassment—from Bloom." Hank put the twisted red straw in the ashtray. "Well, what everyone doesn't know is that I go home . . . alone . . . every night . . . afraid to answer the phone or open my mail because it might be something else from Bloom or one of the lawyers. I change my clothes, grab something to eat, and then I come here." He shook his head. "Yeah, I'm some hero cop."

Kenny started to speak, but Hank cut him off. "Speaking of lawyers, do you have any idea what all that cost me? Them coming after me and me going after them?"

"No, Hank," Jane said, "we don't."

Hank dropped a twenty-dollar bill on the table. "Everything," he said. "It cost me everything."

Kenny's beeper went off. He pulled it from his belt. "Bobby."

"The nephew?" Hank asked.

"The same," Kenny said.

Hank wiped at the table with a cocktail napkin, not wanting to make eye contact. "You guys should go. Thanks for listening to an old cop grouse."

Kenny finished his soda. Jane realized she had never touched her beer. She nodded to the drinks. "Any chance we can get this?"

Hank looked up and smiled. "None," he said. "See you Monday."

Jane and Kenny rose.

"You need us," Kenny said, "give a call."

Hank nodded.

Jane bent across the table to give Hank a kiss on the cheek. "You take care," she whispered.

Kenny took her hand and they walked back along the length of the bar.

The man on the stool coughed into his handkerchief again and watched them pass in the mirror.

The door opened just as they reached it and a man, younger than the rest, but no less dissipated, brushed past them.

Kenny held the door for Jane. "Jesus, I had no idea."

"Me neither," she said as she stepped back into the harsh sunlight. "Nobody ever knows what someone's going through inside."

Jane, wanting to talk about her own demons, started to say more, but Kenny was already across the sidewalk and opening the door of the Explorer for her.

"Nobody knows," she said to herself, and got in the car.

——

Silk Cullen used to be a DJ.

Somewhere in the Midwest; or so he said.

His voice still had a distinctive resonance, only partially ruined by cigarettes, booze, and drugs. He prided himself on having kicked the jones; but, like so many junkies, he fell back hard on the booze.

A life of almost constant self-abuse had left him broke and on the streets. Now he picked up a few bucks here and there selling the streets' secrets to Hank and other cops.

That's why he was in Dighby's.

He waited for the lady cop and her partner to leave. Then he approached Hank. "Saw you on TV, man."

Hank looked up. "Where'd you get a TV?"

"Stole it," Silk Cullen said. "Wanna buy it?"

"What else you sellin'?"

Cullen knew better than to sit down without being asked. "What else you need?" He slowly reached over for Jane's untouched beer, ready to pull his hand away if Hank said anything.

Hank let him take it. "Only new thing I got going is an ex-cop named Skip Lacey getting himself killed. Hear anything?"

Cullen drank the beer in two swallows. "Lacey, huh?" He put the glass back on the table. "Ain't heard nothin'. But I'll ask around."

Hank slipped him a folded five-dollar bill. "You do that."

Cullen pocketed the bill quickly, as if Hank might take it away. Then he backed up a few steps, turned, and headed for the door.

Hank watched him go in the mirror.

Another casualty.

17

WE HAVEN'T HAD a good night's sleep in weeks," Kenny's sister, Andrea, said.

She was the same age as Jane, but looked ten years older. The combination of a bad marriage and too many bad relationships had taken its toll. "This damn house gets so hot, we almost checked into a motel last night." Andrea took a pitcher of iced tea from the refrigerator.

Jane glanced inside and saw a shelf filled with cans of Miller Genuine Draft. Lonnie liked his beer.

"Why didn't you?" Kenny asked as he poured some tea for Jane and himself.

"Usual. Money."

"Isn't Lonnie working?"

"Not steady."

Kenny leaned against the counter. "Andy, the last time we talked, you told me one of the reasons you were still with him was he helped with the rent."

"One of the reasons," Andrea said, glancing first at Jane, then out the small window box over the sink.

Jane followed her gaze and saw Lonnie come into the cement patio from the garage. He sat in a cheap chaise longue, broken strips of plastic hanging. Sipping a beer, he began to read the newspaper. After a moment, he shifted his seat so he could get more sun.

"He can be an asshole sometimes, sure," Andrea said. "But he can also be very sweet to me." She put her hand on her brother's chest. "I just don't want to be alone anymore, Ken. I can't."

Kenny saw Lonnie dragging the chaise into the sun. "I'm gonna go say hi."

As Kenny went out the kitchen door, Andrea turned to Jane. "Bein' alone's the shits."

Jane found herself looking away. "Yeah, I know."

"But now you got Kenny living with you. How's that going?"

Jane watched Kenny as he approached Lonnie, loving his familiar, confident walk. Then she brought her eyes back to Andrea. "It's everything I ever wanted."

Lonnie noticed Kenny coming toward him. He put the paper down and swung his legs around. "Hey, Ken. What's happening?"

"Came by to pick up Bobby." Kenny sat on a white wrought-iron chair. "A barbecue on a hundred-degree day. What are we, nuts?"

Lonnie was thirty-two years old with long brown hair. A big man, he had the belly and the glassy eyes of someone who drank too much and worked too little. "Should be fun," he said. "Meet the family and all." He took a deep swallow from his beer. "It's good that you're taking Bobby. Keep him out of trouble." He laughed at what he thought was a joke.

"Speaking of Bobby, you know anything about those bruises?"

Lonnie put down his beer and leaned forward, as if to stand. "Bruises? I ain't seen any."

"All you've got to do is look, Lonnie," Kenny said. "He told me he fell off his skateboard."

"Then that's what happened."

From his upstairs bedroom window, Bobby watched as his uncle rose and put his hand on Lonnie's shoulder. Bobby turned his baseball cap backward and left the room.

Lonnie tried to stand, pushing up against Kenny's hand. Kenny held fast. "If I ever find out that you hit my nephew," Kenny said evenly, "I'm going to pay you a visit, a very serious visit."

Lonnie sucked in a deep breath, calling on courage that wasn't there. "Hey," he protested. "I love that kid."

"So do I," Kenny said, releasing Lonnie and stepping back. "And I'm the one who's gonna be in his life forever."

Lonnie, filling with purpose, started to rise.

"Don't," Kenny said firmly. "Just pick up your paper and your beer and go back to sunning yourself. I'm gonna go to my barbecue and we're both gonna remember our talk." He turned and started for the house.

Jane noticed Kenny coming toward the kitchen, Lonnie behind him flushed with anger. She finished her iced tea. "Thanks, Andrea. That was great."

"Anytime. Thanks for taking Bobby to your dad's. He'd never say it, but it means a lot, the way you treat him."

"I'd never say what, Mom?" Bobby asked as he came into the kitchen.

"Ah, nothing. We're just girl-talkin'."

Kenny pushed open the door. "Everyone ready?"

"Still waiting for you," Jane said as they headed for the front door.

Kenny caught up to Bobby and drew him into a playful headlock. "You carrying?" he whispered into his ear.

"Nah," Bobby said, trying to squirm away.

Kenny held on. "Good. I'd really hate to get pulled over by one of my cop buddies 'cause my jerk-off nephew's carrying marijuana."

"I'm cool, Uncle Ken," Bobby said as they stepped outside.

18

— —

KENNY DROVE THE EXPLORER, Buddy Guy on the cassette deck, across the Bay Bridge. Less famous and less glamorous than her sister bridge, the industrial-grey Bay Bridge always reminded Jane of going home.

When they got to the quiet streets of San Leandro, Kenny, as if in respect, turned off the music. Bobby sat in the backseat absently adjusting the air-conditioning outlet with the toe of his tennis shoe. The church where Jane had gone to parochial school came up on the right, its flag hanging flat in the windless morning.

Jane, filling with a flood of distant memories, touched Kenny's arm.

"Almost home," he said. They turned onto Oak Street and slipped past the houses of Jane's childhood.

Neighbors, many of them new to her, looked up from their lawns and their driveways as the Explorer went past. Toward the middle of the block, on the left, was her father's home. A tire still hung from the oak tree in the front yard, waiting now for Poppy's great-nieces and -nephews.

Jane saw her younger brother's Toyota parked in front. "Timmy's here."

"Good," Kenny said as he bumped up into the narrow driveway. "I hope he can carry his weight in eggs, 'cause we're gonna need the help."

They climbed out and lowered the back gate of the Explorer. "This is just the small frittata." Jane laughed as Kenny and Bobby maneuvered it out of the car. "Wait'll you see the one Aunt Lucy brought." She started up the walk, drawn to her father's house by the whispers of her past.

"Hey, Bobby," Kenny said as he closed the tailgate. "Let's just have a good time today. No felonies or anything, okay?"

"Real funny, Uncle Ken."

——

Jacques Carpenter loaded his .22 in the dark, squalid basement of his tenement building. Slapping the clip home, he chambered a round, smooth greased metal sliding.

Across the room, lit only by a single bare bulb hanging from the ceiling, a honeydew melon rested on an old workbench.

Carpenter closed his eyes, steadying his breathing. Then, as sudden as a surprise, he raised the pistol and squeezed off two quick shots. Rats scurried behind the walls, squealing in confusion.

Carpenter crossed the room, pushing his way through the blue cordite smoke that swirled around the lightbulb.

The melon had two holes in it, side by side, about two inches apart. If this were a man's head, the shots would have slammed through the flesh precisely where the eyes would be. Carpenter turned it over. There were a pair of thumb-thick exit wounds, bits of meat and juice oozing.

He reached into a large cardboard box, grabbed another honeydew, and propped it on the table. Then he crossed the room, a little farther away this time. He closed his eyes again, regulating his thoughts, his movements, his breathing, like a predator the moment before the kill.

Opening his eyes, he pulled back twice on the trigger. *Bam-Bam.* The roar of the pistol and the *thuck-thuck* of lead penetrating melon were virtually simultaneous.

Carpenter, with all the time in the world, slowly walked across the room and inspected his target. Pleased, he tossed it away and replaced it with another melon.

He turned and strode to the far end of the room. Closing his eyes once again, he drew a deep breath, the acrid smell of the cordite stinging him high in his nostrils. He smiled, opened his eyes, and fired again.

Pulling a fistful of bullets from the pocket of his chinos, he flipped the cylinder open and started to reload.

Jane was concerned at how tired her father looked. He was seventy-four, with a beautiful head of lush white hair. But the preparation for the barbecue and the excitement of the day itself had finally caught up with him.

He sat on the porch swing, making silly faces for one of the babies. But it was more a routine than anything else; something he'd always done.

"I'm worried about Poppy," Jane said to her aunt Lucy. "He looks . . . well, old I guess is the word."

Lucy looked across the yard to her last surviving brother. Children chased each other, squealing in delight, around the tilting gazebo Poppy had built for his wife all those years ago. "I know," she said. "Everything about him is slower now."

Jane nodded, her eyes hooded with the weight of understanding. She spotted Bobby and Tony, her cousin Elissa's son, disappearing around the side of the house. Probably going off to smoke a cigarette, she thought.

The screen door opened and Jane's cousin Rosemary came out. Nine months pregnant, she sat awkwardly next to Lucy.

"My God, Rosemary!" Jane said. "Are you ever gonna have this baby?"

"He's the father all over again." Rosemary laughed. "Late for everything."

Jane kissed her cousin's belly, her lips feeling the hard, firm skin. "You look beautiful."

"I feel like a house. Danny says I'm eating for two . . . and one of them's Roseanne."

She and Jane collapsed into giggles. They sat there laughing, their foreheads touching, the way they had when they were girls.

"Where's Kenny?" Rosemary asked when she caught her breath.

Jane nodded to the barbecue, where Kenny and a couple of the older cousins were cooking sausages, chicken, and corn. From the gestures he was making as he talked, she could tell that he was telling the story of Hank at the playground again. Everyone, it seemed, had seen it on television, and they had been asking him and Jane about it all morning.

Rosemary glanced at Jane and they shared a quiet moment of connection. These barbecues had forever been the province of Poppy. He loved doing the shopping, the marinating, the cooking—sending up clouds of steam with a spritz from his water bottle. This was the first time he had allowed himself to sit back while others did the work.

"Things change, huh?" Rosemary said.

"Yeah," Jane agreed. "I guess they do."

— —

The two young teenagers, initiates into the Eddy Street Mobsters, turned as the sound of gunfire reached them from somewhere down below. But the echo was indistinct and they couldn't figure out exactly where it was coming from.

Shrugging it off—someone firing a pistol in the Tenderloin wasn't all that unusual—they peeled off a handful of hundred-dollar bills. Punky-Boy took the money and slipped it into his sock.

The boys hefted their new pistols, dull black 9-millimeter Glocks. Feeling as bold as men, they made shooting sounds as they walked to the roof access door.

Punky-Boy closed his suitcase. The gun fired again, *Bam-Bam,* one shot on top of the other. He smiled. He knew it was his .22.

That big ex-con was getting ready for something serious.

— —

Jane sat with her father at the picnic table, Aunt Lucy, Rosemary, and a couple of other cousins across from them. Kenny brought a tray over from the grill. "Okay, everyone, here's platter number two. Say the word and I'll go to the market for another sixty or seventy pounds of sausage."

Jane cleared a place for him. "Any excuse to go shopping, huh?"

Kenny kissed her on top of the head. "I'm gonna go find Bobby before he hot-wires Uncle Rocco's Lincoln." He waved to everyone at the table. "See ya in a bit."

Aunt Lucy watched him go. "Look how much he loves you, Janie."

Jane smiled. "Ain't it grand?"

"He's the one you shoulda been with all these years."

Poppy took a piece of corn from the platter. "So when . . . ?"

"Soon, Poppy. No way I let him get away." She put her hand on her father's knee. "How you doin'?"

"Ah, sometimes good," he said. "Sometimes not so good. To-day's fine, though."

Jane felt Aunt Lucy's foot touch hers. She glanced over to her and nodded.

"Poppy," she began, feeling her way along. "Do you think maybe this house is too big for you now? I mean, another winter in this place and—"

"Honey," Poppy said, light rising in his eyes. "I know you and Lucia been talkin' again, and you're right. This place is too big for me now that I'm by myself." He smiled warmly. "Me and my brothers built this house brick by brick, board by board. Using stuff we couldn't even afford. Heh, I think the back porch and the garage were made with wood your uncle Dante stole from the docks."

"I know Poppy," Jane said softly.

"I took your mother here the day we were married. We had our honeymoon in this yard. It's the only house she ever lived in her whole life." He looked up to the second floor. "You and Timmy were conceived in the same bed I slept in last night." He shook his head. "I can't leave this house, Jane."

Jane put her hand on his shoulder. "It's okay, Poppy. I won't ask you again."

Poppy bent his head and kissed his daughter's hair. As he did, Jane's brother came up and took their picture. "I want one of those, Timmy!" Jane called after him.

"You got it," Timmy said.

Jane looked after him as he moved off to prowl for more photo opportunities. Timmy had turned thirty the month before, but to her he was still a boy. He lived by himself in a studio apartment, did something with computers that Jane didn't quite understand, and seemed, she had to admit, always just a little lost.

Jane felt her father's hand brush hers. Thinking he wanted to hold hands with her, something he'd taken to doing since her mother died, she opened hers. Poppy put something against her palm and closed her fingers over it.

Curious, Jane brought her hand up and peeked inside. Her mother's wedding ring, old and silver and tarnished, lay against her flesh. Tears coming, she looked to her father.

"For when it's time," he said.

"Oh, Poppy," Jane said, and she wrapped her arms around him, holding on like a child.

"Do you have room for another old man?"

Jane turned at the voice.

Jacob Turner, one of her father's dearest friends, sat next to her and put a plate heaped with food on the table.

"Ach, all these kids, all this food, all this heat," Jacob said, his voice tinged with an Eastern European accent.

"Hi, Jacob," Jane said, kissing him on the cheek.

"Hello, sweetheart." Jacob smiled. "I saw your fellow cooking before. Like one of the family, eh?" He cut a piece of chicken and lifted it to his mouth. When he did, his sleeve—even in the heat he wore long sleeves—fell away. Jane looked, as she had all her life, at the numbers tattooed in blue on the inside of his right forearm.

Jacob had been born in Poland and had been captured during the Warsaw ghetto uprising. Through sheer will and courage he had survived year after year at Auschwitz.

He and a younger brother were the only ones in a family of thirteen to live out the war.

He had come to America, following a cousin to San Francisco, and carried on the trade his father had taught him. Now, seventy-six with failing eyesight, Jacob was a wealthy man. He had made his fortune in the diamond business, taking risks and living on the edge from deal to deal—much the same way he had made it through the war.

"Lucy, your Dante's gone. My Goldie's gone," he said in his wonderful teasing voice. "When are you going to marry this old Jew?"

"Oh"—Lucy laughed—"someday I'll surprise you and say yes."

"Don't wait too long, darling." Jacob laughed. "I may only be around another twenty or thirty years."

Poppy stood up, his napkin falling to the grass, and kissed Jane on the cheek. With a little smile for the others, he turned and walked toward the house.

"Nap time," Jacob said.

Jane watched as her father slowly climbed the stairs. "I'm worried about him."

"I can't lie to you, honey," Jacob said. "So am I. It's like he's giving out." He put his hand on Jane's back and stroked her hair. "Did he give it to you?"

Jane looked at him. "The ring?"

"Yes. He's been talking about it for weeks. You know I sold him that ring forty-five years ago." He smiled at the memory. "He couldn't afford it, and I couldn't afford it." He paused as Poppy opened the screen door and went inside. "But, somehow, we made it work."

Jane opened her hand and studied the ring. The tiny diamond caught the sun and winked.

"You should bring it by. I'll have it cleaned and sized for you."

Jane looked around. Her great extended family filled the yard like people at a fair. Some were laughing, some dozing, some kids were running, constantly in circles. Rosemary stood, leaning back to keep her balance. Her husband, Danny, rose quickly and, putting a hand on the small of her back, lovingly guided her to a seat in the shade.

"I will, Jacob," Jane said. "I'll come by." She looked for Kenny, wanting to connect with him, but she couldn't find him.

"Come tomorrow, before the moment passes."

"Okay. I'll come before Hank Pagano's ceremony."

Aunt Lucy leaned forward. "The hero?"

Jane nodded. "He's getting the Medal of Valor tomorrow."

"Did you know," Jacob said, "that Hank used to work for me? Years ago."

"That would be Hank," Jane said. "Always trying for a little extra." She started to say something about Hank's plans for retirement, but held it back.

"Terrible about his wife," Jacob said.

They all turned at the sound of a commotion coming from the side of the house. Jane's cousin Tony came tearing across the yard and raced up the steps to the back porch. He whipped open the screen door and ran into the house.

Then Kenny appeared, his hand tight around Bobby's wrist. He gave Jane a quick nod and she rose. Kissing Jacob on the forehead, she said, "Gotta go. I'll see you in the morning. Where's the showroom these days?"

"Clay and Montgomery."

"Across from the Transamerica Building?"

"No, *in* the Transamerica Building."

"Got it," Jane said. She blew a kiss to Aunt Lucy and hurried across the lawn.

"They were smoking pot," Kenny said when she got to them, his voice quaking with frustration.

"Oh, Bobby," Jane said. "You gave that stuff to my cousin?"

"You promised me you weren't carrying," Kenny said.

Bobby leaned back on his heels and ripped his hand out of Kenny's. "I wasn't," he said. "Did it occur to you guys that the shit might have been Tony's?"

He turned and ran to the gate. Slamming it open, he rushed to the Explorer and climbed into the backseat.

"Damn it," Kenny said, kicking the ground. "Now what do I do?"

"Go talk to him. Maybe even apologize for jumping to conclusions." Jane took his hand. "But don't let him off the hook. Even if the stuff wasn't his, he was still smoking dope."

"You're right," Kenny said as he started toward the gate. "Sorry about ruining your party."

"All in the family," Jane said, liking the way it sounded.

"What're you gonna do?"

"Tell Elissa about her son," Jane said. "No way around it."

"Say goodbye to your father for me."

"Okay," Jane said as she started for the backyard.

She knew Poppy was already upstairs, already asleep.

19

Jacques Carpenter pushed open the front door of 82 Ellis and stepped onto the porch.

The street was empty, hushed in pre-dawn silence. Carpenter lit a cigarette and looked at the sky. Clear and grey, there was a faint amber glow to the east. Another scorcher coming, he thought. The guys in the joint must be getting pretty pissed off.

He went down the stairs to the sidewalk and turned left. Reaching into the pocket of his chinos, he pulled out a switchblade and flicked it open. When he came to Marco's Camaro, he plunged the knife into the convertible top and sliced a six-inch gash above the driver's-side window.

He thrust his hand into the hole and unlocked the door. Climbing inside, he plucked the ignition assembly out with a screwdriver, freeing the steering wheel lock. Then Carpenter hunched under the dash and hot-wired the engine. He knew that once the Camaro was out of the Tenderloin, it was his. Marco wasn't going to report the theft of a car he had stolen himself.

Carpenter slipped the car into neutral and let it roll down the hill. At the bottom, he pushed it into drive and gunned the motor. It responded with a powerful roar.

He turned right, the first low rays of the coming sun fragmenting along the cracked windshield.

He smiled to himself. He was armed and mobile.

Ready for the hunt.

—·—

The Transamerica Building, built in 1972 and climbing over fifty stories, including its monumental spire, rose above San Francisco like an architectural exclamation point. People in the city had taken to calling it the Pyramid.

Jane got out of a taxi at Clay and Montgomery. She hurried up the steps, passing over a mosaic of shadows cast by the building's cement support grid. Looking up, she saw the flag of the Transamerica Corporation drooping in the windless morning. She pushed against the smoke-grey glass door and passed from the harshness of the heat wave into the sublime coolness of the air-conditioned lobby.

She paused to get her bearings. A steady stream of delivery people—FedEx, UPS, bicycle messengers—bustled in every direction. A well-dressed woman about Jane's age walked by. She spoke rapidly to a flock of young executives trailing in her wake.

Jane let her gaze drift to the paintings on the far wall, the sculptures along the windows, the plush carpeting; everything about the Transamerica Building whispered opulence.

She went up to a security guard by the elevator bank. He was a short black man with a shaved head and a tiny receiver in his left ear. "What floor is Jacob Turner Fine Jewels on?"

The guard smoothed his navy blue blazer. "Check in at the desk," he said without smiling. He nodded to a security console.

Jane approached the security desk. A burly man in his early forties was on the phone. She noticed the serpentlike tail of a tattoo peeking out of the cuff of his blazer. His name tag identified him as LEWIS PARKER, CHIEF OF SECURITY.

"Good morning, Mr. Parker," Jane said when he hung up the telephone. "Could you please tell me . . ."

Parker turned his back on her and made a note on a clipboard. When he came around again, Jane resumed her question. "I'm looking for . . ."

Without acknowledging her, Parker picked up a walkie-talkie. "Twenty-one fifty." Someone responded into his earpiece. He clicked the transmission button. "Got it."

When he put the walkie-talkie back in its battery cradle, Jane said, "I really just have a quick . . ."

Lewis Parker turned his back on her again and adjusted one of the color security monitors. Jane was just about to lose her temper when she heard, "Inspector Candiotti, what are you doing here?"

Jane turned to see Mike Finney in a navy-blue blazer. "Mike," she said, surprised. "This is your other job?"

"Yeah," Finney said proudly. "Just another cop moonlighting in security, but . . ." He swept his arm across the lobby. "Look at this place. Pretty nice, huh?"

"Sure is. Any chance you can tell me where Jacob Turner's showroom is?"

"You bet." He leaned over the console. "Mr. Parker, I'm gonna take my friend up to forty-five."

Lewis Parker regarded Jane coolly, then nodded slightly.

"This way," Finney said, leading her to the elevator bank. "She's with me," he announced to the guard near the call buttons. Standing back, he gestured for Jane to enter the elevator first. He followed and pressed "45."

"So, this is the job Hank got for you," Jane said as the doors slid closed and the car began its ascent. The beads of the small chandelier in the mirrored ceiling clinked gently as the car swayed.

"He made the call," Finney said. "But I did the rest. I guess it didn't hurt that he worked here, too, way back when." The elevator clicked past the first ten floors, then accelerated as it went into express mode. "I love this thing." Finney beamed.

Jane realized that this was the most time she had spent alone with Finney. "How's your wife?"

"She's doing great. Thanks." He paused, searching for something else to say. "Where's Inspector Marks this morning?"

"Home. He thinks I'm at the doctor's, but I'm really here as a surprise for him. So let's keep this a secret, okay?"

"My lips are sealed, Inspector."

Jane smiled, thinking that Kenny would have a field day with a straight line like that. The car slowed, then stopped. The doors parted and they stepped out.

The vistas were spectacular in every direction. Another security guard stood in front of a thick glass partition, taking a UPS delivery. Through the glass, Jane could see several jewelry showrooms. A man and a woman, very wealthy from their appearance, were in the first showroom. They were sorting through dozens of diamonds spread before them on a black velvet cloth.

Finney went up to the guard. "Hey, Mitch," he said as he signed the register. "She's with me."

Mitch buzzed the door open. As they passed through, Finney tapped the glass. "Bulletproof." When the door closed behind them, he held out his hand. "Welcome to Jewelers' Corner, the largest collection of fine gems in San Francisco." He shrugged. "I'm supposed to say that. It's in the manual." He started down the corridor. "Mr. Turner's at the end."

"Morning, Michael," a merchant called as they walked by.

"Hey, Ahmet," Finney waved. He turned back to Jane. "He's from Egypt."

Jane looked into Ahmet's showroom and noticed the power forward for the San Francisco Warriors standing over a display of gaudy, but very expensive necklaces. "Isn't that . . . ?"

"Sure is." Finney nodded. "Neat, huh?" He walked ahead, smiling his greetings to the other merchants as he went.

As she followed him, Jane saw that working in this building was a very different experience for Finney compared to his life at Precinct Nineteen. Here, he was respected, perhaps even considered elite by the merchants because he was a real cop. She noticed the confident way he strode past the showrooms, nodding and waving to the customers and jewelers. Jane found herself smiling, happy for him.

They arrived at Jacob Turner's large corner suite and were buzzed in.

"Ach, Jane," Jacob said as he came around the counter. "Welcome, my dear." He kissed her on both cheeks. "So." He tilted his head. "What do you think?"

"This is amazing, Jacob. But the rent must be—"

"Worth it. This is one of the safest buildings in the city." He smiled at Finney. "Thanks in part to Officer Finney here."

Finney blushed. "I'm gonna get some breakfast, Inspector. See you at the ceremony."

"Thanks, Mike."

They watched him go. "Sweet man," Jacob said as he sat on a high leather stool at the counter.

Jane noticed a small television, the *Today* show playing with the sound down low. "All the comforts of home."

"Can't live without my Katie Couric." He patted the stool next to him. "Come sit."

Jane joined him. She looked at the gleaming display cases, at the rows and rows of diamonds of every cut and size. "Wow."

"My babies," Jacob said. "There are nine other showrooms up here, but I've got the prettiest babies." He held out his hand. "You brought it?"

"Yes. Yes, I did." Jane opened her bag. At the bottom, next to her service revolver and her badge, was a small velvet jewel box. She took it out and opened it. Her mother's wedding ring with its tiny speck of a diamond seemed like a poor relation in a showroom of so many larger stones.

Jacob took the ring from the box and slid it onto the tip of his index finger. He picked up a jeweler's loupe and, with a motion as familiar to him as breathing, put it to his eye. "I've always loved this ring, it's authenticity," he said as he held it to the light. "Your father wanted nothing but the best for his bride." He looked at her. "Give me your hand."

Jane held out her left hand and Jacob slipped the ring onto her third finger. As he did, Jane heard herself catching her breath. She became aware of an unexpected pounding in her heart, a pulsing in her temple. To her surprise, she recognized the beginnings of an anxiety attack.

She watched as her fingers began to tremble and felt a fine film of perspiration coming to her face. Suddenly hot and uncomfortable, Jane pulled her hand away. Trying to cover, she turned her wrist and looked at her watch. "Uh, I've got to get across town for Hank's thing." She rose and dropped the ring into her purse. "I'll call you later and we can set something up."

Jacob put the loupe back on the counter. "I know this is a big step, honey," he said, patience and kindness in his voice. "I'm just a phone call away."

Jane reached over and kissed him goodbye. "I'll call."

She hurried back down the corridor, past the other showrooms with their diamonds and gold. Mitch, the security guard, saw her coming through the thick glass and buzzed her out.

Crossing to the elevators, Jane pushed the button and waited.

Her back was to the windows, the magnificent view going unnoticed.

The elevator arrived with a soft ping, and Jane entered, grateful that is was empty. She pressed "lobby" and stood against the back wall as the car began to descend.

Jane tried to calm her shallow breathing. Here she was, on the verge of having everything she thought she had wanted, and she was having an anxiety attack.

Was it second thoughts about Kenny? About living day to day with someone, both intimate and exposed, for the first time in her life?

No, she told herself. She was ready; and Kenny was the right man for her.

Was it turning forty?

Maybe.

Was it her uncertainty about her career?

She'd known for a while that she was on the brink of some sort of professional crisis. Hank announcing his retirement had affected her in ways she hadn't been ready for.

And Poppy.

Someday the phone would ring and . . .

She clamped her eyes closed and drove the thought from her head.

The elevator car passed the twentieth floor and went into express mode. Its rapid gliding descent caused the small chandelier to vibrate. Jane opened her eyes and looked up.

She saw her reflection in the mirrored ceiling.

She seemed, she thought, small and lost.

Like a child.

——

20

HANK LOWERED HIS HEAD and Chief Walker McDonald draped the Medal of Valor around his neck. Then, his blue eyes glistening with emotion, Hank approached the microphone.

"I know the only reason you're all here," he said to the crowd in the main auditorium of the Hall of Justice, "is the air-conditioning."

Jane and Kenny, sitting in front, laughed. "How'd it go at the doctor's?" Kenny asked.

"Routine girl stuff," Jane fibbed.

Kenny looked up to Hank. "Think he's going to say anything about retiring?"

"Nah," Jane said. "Not his style."

Lieutenant Spielman, sitting on the stage, shot a look at them and they quieted down. Looking behind, Jane saw that the place was nearly filled to capacity with cops, politicians, and members of the Police Commission and school board. She noticed Ozzie Castillo and Sally Banks standing together by the California flag.

Standing in the rear was a gallery of civilians. Probably office workers on their break, Jane guessed. She was about to turn back when she spotted Benjy and Finney leaning against the wall in the far corner. They listened intently as Hank spoke, pride shining on their faces.

"I'm very grateful for the privilege of serving the citizens of San Francisco," Hank went on. "I love this city." He stopped and looked down at the faces looking up at him.

"But, I'm not a hero. The real hero is Karen Yin, the school-teacher who gave her life to buy some time for her pupils to get away. The real hero is Caitlin Sprague, who at nine years old has already been through more than most people go through in a lifetime." He nodded to Caitlin, sitting in the third row with her parents and classmates from Clark Street Elementary School.

The double doors at the back of the hall opened. Jason Bloom walked in and stood against the door frame, his eyes fixed on Hank.

Drawing a deep calming breath, Hank went on. "The real hero," he said, looking directly at Jason Bloom, "was my dear wife, Irene, who fought so bravely and so long against cancer . . . And even when she knew she was losing, still woke up with a smile on her face, always grateful for just one more day of life." He touched the medal at his chest. "I would trade this in a second . . . for just one more day with her."

Jane, tears pooling, shifted in her seat to see what Hank was looking at and saw Jason Bloom standing stone-faced next to the local news cameras.

"What's he doing here?"

Kenny turned and followed her gaze. "All the cops in this room, he probably figured he'd catch somebody doing something wrong."

"The guy's a bottom feeder," Jane said as she turned back to listen to Hank.

"So I share this medal," Hank concluded, "with all of them . . . and all of you. Thank you very much."

He stepped back from the microphone as enthusiastic applause surged through the crowd. Hank turned and saluted Chief McDonald. Then he faced the auditorium and saluted his admirers. With a cheer, they rose to their feet, Jane and Kenny in front, and their clapping thundered into a crescendo.

At the back, standing among the secretaries and police clerks, Jacques Carpenter cheered with the others. As the celebration peaked, then ebbed, and people began to file out, Carpenter studied their faces.

Like a lion stalking the herd, he picked out the one he would take.

—-—

Kenny pulled the Explorer into the Union Pacific yard.

"You get the stuff," Jane said. "I'll let them know we're here."

They arrived at the shack and got out. Jane went to try the door while Kenny opened the tailgate. "Doesn't seem like anyone's around," Jane said.

"Randy's probably in school," Kenny joked. He took two boxes from the back, a football and a pair of hockey skates on top, and joined Jane.

"Hockey skates for a homeless person?"

"Maybe they can trade them for something."

Jane knocked on the door. "Good point."

They heard motion from inside and smiled at each other. Someone was home.

The latch lifted and the door was pulled open. Two pairs of eyes stared at them from the darkness. Men's eyes.

"The fuck you want?" one of the men said as he stepped into the light. A tall and muscular black man in his early twenties, he had a long scar across his right cheek. He squinted in the sudden glare of the sun, his right eye drooping. Dressed only in boxer shorts, he had the look of someone who had just been awakened from a nap and wasn't happy about it.

"How you doin'?" Jane said.

"The fuck you want!" the man demanded again.

Kenny slowly lowered the boxes, freeing his hands. "We're just looking for some friends of ours."

The black man looked to Jane, then to Kenny, then down to the boxes. "Ice skates?" he said. "The fuck is this?"

The other man, an even bigger black man in a torn T-shirt and swimming trunks, joined his friend. "Ice skates? You sellin' ice skates in a heat wave? Boy, you is one stupid motherfucker."

From the chemical smell in the shack and the faraway look in their eyes, Jane and Kenny could tell they were crackheads.

"We're looking for Penny and Randy," Jane said.

"Don't know no Penny and Randy," the bigger man said.

"Penny's a white woman, blond, maybe twenty-five," Kenny offered. "And Randy's her son."

The two men looked at each other. "Oh, them," the first one said. "We 'victed them from the premises."

"You evicted them?" Jane said. "Why?"

" 'Cause, bitch," he spit, "we wanted it and we bigger." He smiled, revealing a gap in his upper teeth. "An' now we got it."

"Law of the jungle," the other man said. "Know what I'm talkin' 'bout?"

Kenny stepped forward, his jaw bouncing. "You two big bad motherfuckers threw a tiny woman and her little kid out on their asses?"

"Yeah, boy," the bigger man said, his eyes widening as he sensed a threat. "An' it was sweet, too. They was all cryin' and bemoanin' and shit."

Jane put her hand on Kenny's arm. "Do you have any idea where they are now?"

"Don't give half a fuck where they is."

Without warning, Jane lost her temper. "You assholes! You big, brave crack-smoking assholes!" she yelled. "You throw two innocent people out on the streets so you can smoke your shit and piss in their beds?"

Kenny saw the men beginning to clench, flexing for a fight. He reached over and took Jane's wrist. She yanked it away. "Okay, tough guys, you're fucking with the wrong people on the wrong fucking day!" Out of the corner of her eye, she saw Kenny slip his hand inside his coat and unsnap his shoulder holster.

"Here's the deal," Kenny said, opening his coat just enough for them to see his pistol. "The bad news is, we're cops. The really bad news is, this place is going to be swarming with other cops in about six minutes. Squad cars, helicopters, SWAT, the whole bit."

"And then, assholes, *you're* gonna be 'victed!" Jane shouted.

Kenny picked up the boxes, and he and Jane started back toward the Explorer. "They following us?" he asked out of the side of his mouth.

"I sure as hell hope not."

"3H61!" Cheryl's voice came over Kenny's radio.

Jane and Kenny looked at each other. Cheryl sounded distraught. Jane snatched up the mike while Kenny threw the boxes in the back. "3H61, go, Cheryl." The two men stood glaring at her from the doorway.

Kenny climbed into the driver's seat as Cheryl, her voice catching, said, "Jane . . . the lieutenant needs you." There was a moment of static, then Lieutenant Spielman came on. He spoke softly, almost in a whisper.

"Jane, Kenny?"

Concerned, they glanced at each other. "Yes, Ben," Jane said. "What's the matter?"

"There's been a shooting."

Kenny looked to Jane. "We're not rolling backup. Why's he calling us?"

Jane started to shrug. Then it dawned on her. She pressed the mike. "Who is it, Ben? Who's been shot?" There was a long pause on the other end and she closed her eyes, waiting for the answer. Wanting time to stop.

"It's Ozzie."

21

KENNY BROUGHT THE EXPLORER to a skidding stop outside Jennie's Bride-To-Be bridal shop on Polk Street.

He and Jane jumped out and ran to the sidewalk where Hank stood talking with Aaron Clark-Weber.

"How bad?" Jane asked.

Hank glanced to Kenny, then said to Jane. "He's gone."

Jane leaned into Kenny. The crime-scene van, its huge poster smiling down, pulled up next to an ambulance. Other black-and-whites, having heard the officer-down call, began to arrive, parking at all angles in the middle of the street.

Jane noticed a sergeant motioning to a couple of younger patrolmen to set up a yellow tape perimeter. Just as Ozzie would have done, she thought.

"What do we know?" Jane asked quietly.

"At this moment," Aaron said, "only that he's dead."

"We just got here ourselves," Hank added.

Jane looked to Kenny and saw that his eyes were fixed on something at the mouth of the alley next to the bridal shop. A squad car was parked halfway up the driveway. At first Jane had thought it was another unit responding to the call. But then she recognized it as Ozzie's black-and-white; the candy wrappers on the dash, the picture of Laura on the visor.

Next to it, partly hidden by a corner of the brick wall, was Ozzie's body under a yellow plastic sheet. His left hand lay exposed, his wedding ring throwing off tiny sparks of sunlight.

Kenny went to him, weaving through the photographers and forensics people. He went down to one knee and lifted the sheet.

Jane saw his back tense with a shiver of shock. He gently lowered the sheet and, his face ashen, returned to Jane.

Drawn forward, needing to see Ozzie for herself, Jane started to go to his body. Kenny stopped her. "You don't want to do that."

"C'mon, Ken," Jane said quietly. "It's Ozzie. Besides, I've seen worse."

Kenny blocked her path with his body and put his hands on her shoulders. "No, you haven't."

"Tell me."

Kenny kept his hands where they were, struggling to find the words. "Please . . ."

"Tell me!" Jane snapped. "Kenny, I've know him for fifteen years."

Glancing around, seeing that Aaron and Hank and the others were watching, Kenny sighed and dropped his hands. "Ozzie was shot in the eyes."

"Eyes? As in plural?"

"Yeah. At close range."

"Oh my God." Jane stared at the sidewalk for a moment, pulling her thoughts into line. Then she looked up, her eyes set. "Two murders, two cops. Both with . . ."

She turned from Kenny and strode toward the bridal shop's entrance. As she passed the display window, she saw the reflection of the crowd of bystanders in front of the ATM machine across the street. She turned to look at them, the blank faces of strangers standing in the heat, drawn by the magnetic pull of death. Kenny caught up to her and they went inside just as Benjy arrived in his squad car.

Hank saw Benjy pull up and said to Aaron Clark-Weber, "I don't want him seeing Ozzie."

"Right."

Benjy stepped up onto the curb. "Is it true?"

"Yes, Benjy, it is," Hank said.

"Who did it?"

"We don't know yet." Hank took his arm. "I need you to do something for me."

"C'mon, Hank. Don't put me on yellow tape patrol."

Hank nodded to the throng of bystanders. "I need you to interview the lookie-loos. See if you can learn anything."

Benjy, filling with a sense of purpose, took out his notebook. "I'm on my way."

"Names and addresses," Hank reminded him.

— —

"I heard something. Like firecrackers—there's a lot of Chinese kids around here. Then there was the sound of someone running. And I got kind of curious 'cause I should have heard Ozzie's car start by then. So I go outside and see his car still in the alley. And I went over and there he was . . . and I saw him . . . and oh God . . . he was such a lovely man."

Jenny Nardolillo couldn't go on. She was in her early forties, slender with long brown hair. Her tear-streaked face still retained the vestiges of the beauty she once was. She dabbed at her eyes and looked up as Kenny asked, "Had there been anybody hanging around here? Anybody you felt uncomfortable about?"

Jenny shook her head.

"Had Officer Castillo mentioned anything to you about any cases he was involved in? Anything he was worried about?"

"No. He was like he always was, just happy and sweet."

An officer brought Jenny a cup of water. Kenny joined Jane at the front window. "Looks like a hit-and-run."

"Doesn't make any sense," Jane said as still more police cars pulled up outside. "Ozzie, of all people." She turned to Kenny, her eyes set. "I want this shooter, Kenny."

"Me, too," Kenny said, touching her arm. "We'll get him."

— —

Benjy finished interviewing a young couple who had been making a withdrawal from the ATM when they heard the shots. They had turned around, but all they had seen was the bridal-shop lady running out of her store.

After adding their names and addresses to his list, Benjy approached the man next to them. He was sitting on a fire hydrant, tapping down a pack of cigarettes.

" 'Scuse me, sir," Benjy said. "Can I ask you a couple of questions?"

Jacques Carpenter peeled the cellophane off the package of Marlboros and let it flutter to the street. He looked to Benjy. "Shoot."

"First off, can I have your name and address?"

"Sure, Officer. I'm Ted Kirkland and I live in Las Vegas, Nevada."

Benjy made a note. "Vegas, huh?"

"Yeah," Carpenter said as he lit a cigarette. He blew out a long stream of smoke and turned to Benjy. His eyes fell to the name tag over his left breast pocket and Carpenter nodded to himself. Spielman, he thought. Good. "How can I help?"

"A police officer has been shot and we need to know if you saw or heard anything that could help us."

"Sorry," Carpenter said as he rose from the fire hydrant and started to walk away.

Benjy was about to go after him, when the husband of the young couple tapped him on the shoulder. "Isn't that guy over there"—he pointed at Hank—"the hero cop from that thing in the school yard?"

"Sure is," Benjy answered. He looked around for Carpenter, but he had disappeared into the crowd. "Shit," he muttered. "Didn't get an address."

An unmarked police sedan pushed slowly through the crowd. The driver gave the siren a short whoop. Reluctant bystanders parted and the car came to a stop behind the crime-scene van.

Benjy watched as his father, red-eyed and haggard, got out and walked over to Hank and Aaron Clark-Weber. Hank pointed to Ozzie's body and Lieutenant Spielman went to it.

Benjy saw his father bend down and lift the sheet. A shudder convulsed his body. Lieutenant Spielman put his hand on Ozzie's chest and said something Benjy couldn't hear. Then he rose, wiping his eyes, and looked around. When he spotted his son, he nodded.

Benjy crossed the street to be with his father.

--

Jane stood looking out the window. She had seen Lieutenant Spielman go to Ozzie's body and the look on his face when he stood back up. As he spoke quietly with Benjy, Jane turned to survey the crowd.

Her experience told her that something or somebody out there might have the beginnings of a clue to what happened. A stranger in the neighborhood. A car speeding away. Someone seen running.

As the uniformed patrol officers continued to work the crowd, the first of the television news vans arrived. Jane recognized Becka Flynn and her cameraman getting out of the KGO truck. Kenny came up behind her. "I think we got all we're going to get out of Miss Nardolillo for now."

"Ken," Jane said softly.

"Yeah?"

"Look."

Kenny turned in the direction she was facing. "The people?"

"Past them."

And then Kenny saw it, too. "The ATM machine!"

"Right. Get someone to—"

"I'm on it!"

He hurried to the door. "Aaron! Hank!"

Aaron and Hank ran up to him as Jane joined them in the doorway.

Kenny pointed across the street. "Aaron, get someone over to that ATM—"

"Have them pull the tapes from the security cameras," Jane continued, "and bring them downtown."

"Consider it done," Aaron said.

"Hank, we'll see you back at the station," Jane said. "We're gonna need your help."

"You got it, guys."

Kenny took Jane's arm and guided her through the throng. Jane, unable to help herself, looked over for one last glimpse of Ozzie. The breeze from a passing police car had blown the bottom of the sheet back and she could see his shoes.

"He woke up this morning," Jane said when they got to the Explorer, "and he pulled on his shoes, and then he tied them.

Like every day." Her lip quivered as she fought the impulse to cry. "He kissed Laura while she was still sleeping and went off to work . . . and . . ."—she whacked the roof of the car with the flat of her hand—"someone fucking killed him."

Kenny held the door for her as she got in. He touched the back of his hand to her cheek. "Seat belt," he said gently. He closed the door and hustled around to the driver's side. Scanning the gathering of cops, he caught Benjy's eye.

Benjy nodded and excused himself from his father. Then he went to the middle of the street and held out his hands, clearing an opening in the crowd for the Explorer.

Jane stared out the window, her head against the glass, as Kenny drove past Benjy. A grey Camaro stopped to let it slip into traffic. Kenny waved his thanks and guided the Explorer away from the scene.

Jacques Carpenter waved back.

Benjy watched the Explorer move down the street and was about to return to Lieutenant Spielman, when he saw the fire truck turning the corner.

Coming to wash the blood away.

Just like Ozzie had told him.

—•—

JANE STOOD IN Interrogation Room One, looking out through the large glass window.

She watched Cheryl Lomax and Sally Banks talking quietly at the dispatch console. Cheryl dabbed at her eyes and Sally gave her a tissue. Roslyn Shapiro was at the outside window, staring off to the horizon.

Looking to her left, Jane saw Mike Finney, his lip trembling, unspool yellow police tape around Ozzie's cluttered desk. Across the bullpen, Kenny had unplugged one of the electric fans and was bringing it toward her.

No more looking through glass, Jane thought to herself. Time to jump in and get my hands dirty.

Kenny entered and plugged in the fan. It whirred steadily, not so much cooling the air as moving it. Jane turned away from the window.

"Cheryl said that Ozzie didn't call in a traffic stop. Jensen and Melvoin, first on scene, said there was no sign of a struggle. His gun was still in his holster and the holster was still strapped." She paced, unable to settle. "Basically, Ozzie was assassinated."

"It's no way for a cop to die." Kenny sat on a metal chair and leaned it back against the wall. "Especially a good one."

Jane watched the cops in the bullpen as she roamed the room. They were moving slowly, as if underwater. "Every time Ozzie was offered a promotion, he turned it down. He was afraid of wasting his life at a desk and then having a heart attack or something." She looked to Kenny. "He felt safer on the street."

Lieutenant Spielman walked by the interrogation-room glass. He glanced inside, and he and Jane exchanged a knowing look.

Nodding almost imperceptibly, he went into his office. Jane shook her head. "He's going to call Laura."

"Christ."

Hank came in, his jacket off and his tie loosened. "The bank will have the security videos copied. Aaron said he'd stay and hand-carry them to us."

"Thanks." Jane went to the blackboard. "Okay, guys, here's what we know." She picked up the chalk. "Ozzie was murdered, gunned down in an alley." She wrote MOTIVE on the slate.

"Old grudge?" Kenny offered.

Hank dropped his coat over the back of a chair. "Some fucked-up gang initiation thing?"

"Or"—Jane turned to them—"it could have been random." It was the word homicide cops hated most because it had no link to anything. No history, no logic, and the highest probability of going unsolved. " 'Random' isn't going to do us any good, so let's not go there."

"What about that kid?" Kenny suggested. "The one that Ozzie busted for stealing that Lexus."

"Worth a look," Jane said. "Let me float something here." She made two columns on the blackboard. Then she wrote OZZIE CASTILLO at the head of one and SKIP LACEY at the top of the other. "We've got two murders in one week."

"Yeah," Kenny said. "And both were cops."

"I don't know," Hank interjected. "One active-duty cop. And one junkie ex-cop."

"Granted," Jane said. "But let's keep sniffing around this."

"Just playing devil's advocate," Hank said.

"Right," Jane said. "Now both murders were particularly brutal, and both of them involved the eyes."

"But the MO in one is inconsistent with the MO in the other," Kenny offered.

"Plus, the Lacey eye mutilation wasn't the cause of death," Hank went on. "And in Ozzie's case it was."

"I agree," Jane said. "But let's keep it alive until we're sure it's the wrong tree. Kenny, I know it's a long shot, but see if Ozzie and Lacey were ever involved in the same case."

Kenny made a note on his pad. "Got it."

Lieutenant Spielman stuck his head in. "Anything?"

"Just theories, Ben," Jane said. "You talk with Laura?"

"Yeah."

"How'd she take it?" Kenny asked.

"Kind of quiet, I guess. The police chaplain was already there. And her sisters." He started out the door. "I've got to report to the deputy chief and then I'm going over, too."

"We'll see you there," Jane said. "And, Ben . . ."

Lieutenant Spielman looked to her, his face pale.

"I want this case."

"It's yours, Jane," Lieutenant Spielman said evenly. "Ozzie was my training officer." With a nod to Kenny and Hank, he walked out.

Kenny let his chair fall forward, a little put out that Jane hadn't consulted him before asking for the case.

Hank stood up. "I'm gonna go beat the bushes. Maybe try out the gang initiation angle with some of my yakkers." He picked up his jacket. "If you want, I'll follow up on the Lexus kid, too."

"Thanks, Hank," Jane said. She turned to Kenny as Hank left. "Let's check out Ozzie's desk. Maybe it'll tell us something."

Kenny followed her into the bullpen. The other cops watched as he and Jane stepped over the yellow tape and began exploring the contents of Ozzie's desk.

"Pretty much routine," Kenny said.

Jane was looking at the photographs of Laura that Ozzie had taped to his gooseneck lamp. Laura's eyes were eager, shining, filled with expectation as she smiled for the camera.

Kenny opened the bottom drawer. "Box of Milky Ways." He pulled the drawer farther out. "Prayer cards, Forty-Niners schedule, model police car." He ticked off the contents of each drawer as he inspected it. "Business cards, condoms, Walkman, batteries, toothbrush, tube of Colgate." He pushed the middle drawer closed. "I don't know."

Jane had been going over Ozzie's desktop. She turned to Kenny. "Did you say condoms?"

"The man's entitled."

"Read to me again the part where that bridal-shop lady talks about Ozzie."

Kenny took out his notebook and flipped it open. "Name's Jenny Nardolillo and she said, 'He was such a lovely man . . . always happy and sweet.' "

Jane took the pages from Kenny and quickly scanned them. " 'Always' implies more than once. What's Ozzie doing repeatedly going to a bridal shop? What's he doing with condoms in his desk?"

"He's a married man. Why can't he have condoms?"

"Kenny, Laura's in a wheelchair."

"God, you're right! The earthquake."

Jane motioned for him to keep his voice down. "Ozzie was having an affair with . . ." She glanced at the notes. "Jenny Nardolillo from Jenny's Bride-To-Be."

"Shit."

"We need to go talk to Laura right away," Jane said.

"Why?"

Jane hesitated, not wanting to give voice to the awful possibility she was contemplating.

Kenny answered his own question. "You think Laura might have something to do with this."

Jane stepped over the tape and went to her desk. "Let's take the fact that Ozzie was our friend out of the equation." She picked up her bag. "A man is murdered and we discover evidence that he was having an affair."

"Suspect number one," Kenny said as he got his coat, "has to be the wife." He looked to Jane.

"She could have hired someone. Stranger things have happened." They crossed to the stairwell. "Some job we have, huh, when we have to think like this?"

"Tell me about it." Kenny held the door open for her.

Jane looked outside before going down the stairs.

Below them, on the small lawn in front of the Nineteenth Precinct station house, Officers Mike Finney and Benjy Spielman were lowering the flag to half-mast.

23

Because of all the cars in front of the Castillo house, Kenny had to park the Explorer a block away.

He and Jane walked along the tree-lined street, her arm around his waist, her head on his shoulder. It was late afternoon and people sat on their porches, driven outside by the heat. They watched silently as visitors went up Ozzie and Laura's driveway with flowers and foil-covered dishes.

Jane and Kenny came to Ozzie's house and, nodding to people they didn't know, walked up the wheelchair ramp to the front door. "Ozzie built this for Laura," Jane said as she and Kenny went inside.

The drapes in the living room were drawn against the late-day sun. Friends sat in clutches of two and three, talking in low voices. A priest, a young Mexican man, sat with Ozzie's parents by the fireplace.

Laura was in the kitchen, her wheelchair up against the chrome table. One of her sisters sat with her, folding laundry and sipping tea. They spoke to each other in Spanish, their eyes wet and red. Laura looked up to see Jane and Kenny in the doorway. She motioned for them to come in.

They kissed her on the cheek and sat on blue vinyl chairs. "You remember my sister, Isabel, don't you? From the picnics?"

"Of course," Jane said.

Laura tucked a pair of men's black socks in on themselves and dropped them into a basket. "His clothes were in the dryer when they called."

Jane looked to Kenny. He was focused on the breakfast nook. It was set for two.

Jane took Laura's hand. "We're so sorry."

"We loved Ozzie," Kenny said.

Laura glanced at Isabel. She rose with the laundry basket and left the room.

"Everyone loved my Oswaldo," Laura said. "Twenty-seven years. How will I go on?" She squeezed Jane's fingers. "Do you have a fellow now, Jane?"

"Yes. Yes, I do."

"Do you love him?"

Jane smiled. "Very much."

"Then get off the force," she said with surprising firmness. "Don't take the chance of someone you love having to feel the way I do now."

Jane felt herself flush. Kenny shifted in his chair.

"Tell you the truth," Jane said, "I've been having a little midlife crisis lately."

"Listen to it, dear."

"Maybe," Jane agreed. She leaned forward, her forearms across her knees. "Laura, can we ask you a couple of things? About Ozzie?"

"Yes. Of course."

"Well, when something like this happens, we have to do some snooping . . . and we found some stuff."

"What kind of stuff?"

Jane hesitated.

Kenny touched Jane's shoulder. "Laura, do you know a woman named Jenny?"

"Jenny Nardolillo?"

Kenny looked to Jane, then back to Laura. "Well, yes."

Laura's eyes wrinkled into a little smile. "Oh, bless your hearts," she said. "I knew all about her and Ozzie."

Jane raised her eyebrows. "You knew?"

"Honey, my Ozzie was a very sexy man. I can't lie to you, it's one of the reasons I married him." She shook her head. "We had some great times, him and me. But then this happened." She gestured to the wheelchair. "I've been in this damn thing for ten years. So, God bless Jenny. She helped save my marriage." She turned in her chair as if remembering something. "I should call her. She loved Ozzie, too."

A woman, another of Laura's sisters, stepped into the doorway with a young teenage girl. Jane and Kenny stood up and kissed Laura goodbye.

"Anything you need," Jane said.

Laura took Jane's hand and peered into her eyes. "You know what I need," she said. "Find him."

"We will," Jane said as Kenny slid the chairs together for the woman and her daughter.

The older woman sat across from Laura. *"Pobrecita,"* she said, and the two sisters and the girl held each other, crying softly.

Jane and Kenny worked their way back through the living room. Hank and Lieutenant Spielman were at the front door, sipping coffee.

"The Lexus kid was still in jail. So, nothing there," Hank said. "Kenny's notes said the shop owner mentioned something about Chinese kids in the neighborhood. I called the Chinatown gang unit for some help. I'm meeting with their guy later tonight."

"Thanks," Jane said.

"What about the ATM tapes?" Kenny asked.

"Locked away in the evidence room. Here's the receipt." He handed Kenny a blue slip of paper.

Lieutenant Spielman stepped aside to let a deliveryman with a huge bouquet of lilies pass by. "Did you talk with Laura?"

"Yeah," Kenny said.

"What'd you learn?"

Jane looked from Hank to Lieutenant Spielman. "That life's shitty, Ben."

She took Kenny's hand and they walked out.

24

THE NIGHT SHIFT had taken over by the time Jane and Kenny returned to Precinct Nineteen. A different civilian volunteer, an elderly man, sat at Roslyn Shapiro's reception desk. Someone else was at Cheryl Lomax's dispatch console, and other cops were at various stations in the bullpen.

"Okay, we're ready," Kenny said. He turned off the lights in Interrogation Room One and picked up the VCR remote.

Jane paced in front of the interior window, anxious to get under way. She stopped and put her palms flat on the table, leaning forward to watch the television.

Kenny clicked "play" and the blue screen flickered to a black-and-white image of a young couple making an ATM transaction.

"Meet Larry and Eileen Shaw," Kenny said. "Benjy interviewed them. Did a good job, too."

Jane studied the screen. "Let's concentrate on the background."

They looked past the Shaws to Jenny's Bride-To-Be across the street. Traffic was light, an occasional bus or truck momentarily blocking the camera.

Ozzie appeared at the doorway of the bridal shop. Jane drew a tiny shocked breath. "Oh God . . . Ozzie," she said softly. Ozzie turned back to say something then turned to his left. As he passed the display window, he smiled and gave a little wave inside.

Kenny looked over to Jane. She turned to him and saw the depth of the sadness on his face. "I know," she said.

Ozzie walked by the corner of the building and neared his squad car. He was about to get in when something caught his attention. He went toward the front of his car and out of camera range.

"Shit," Kenny said.

The couple at the ATM machine suddenly flinched. A moment later they whirled around.

"Damn it!" Jane whacked the table with her open hand. "We missed it!"

They watched as Jenny Nardolillo came out of her shop and walked toward the alley. She went around the front of Ozzie's car, passing beyond the right frame of the screen. A few seconds later, she ran back into frame. Her body heaving with distress, she raced into the store.

"Why didn't this couple go across to see what was up?" Jane asked.

Kenny turned the page on the incident report. "Benjy's notes say that the woman, Eileen, is seven months pregnant. They didn't want her to get upset."

"Okay, I buy that."

Kenny nodded. "They couldn't have helped Ozzie by then anyway."

On the screen, a police car whipped in from the left.

"That's Jensen and Melvoin," Kenny explained. "They were around the corner when the nine-one-one came in."

They watched as the car skidded up to the curb. The two officers, guns drawn, bolted from their seats, ran to the right and out of the picture.

Melvoin then hurried back to the squad car and spoke excitedly into his police radio. He threw the mike back on the seat and went out of frame again.

Moments later, other police cars came sliding up in ones and twos. A crowd was now gathering in front of the ATM machine. The crime-scene van pulled up, obscuring a corner of the picture.

Jane and Kenny saw the police spread out, their weapons unholstered. Then the Explorer arrived and they watched themselves get out.

"This is kind of weird," Kenny said.

"Yeah, I know," Jane said, still intent on the screen. "But it isn't giving us anything we need. The shooter did the deed offscreen and escaped offscreen."

"Think he knew about the camera?"

"I don't know. Maybe."

They watched themselves talk with Hank and Aaron. Then Kenny looked at Ozzie's body. When Jane tried to, Kenny put his hands on her shoulders and blocked her way.

Jane glanced at Kenny. "You were right. I'm sorry."

"Forget it."

On the screen, Jane and Kenny went into the bridal shop. Jane saw herself standing inside, looking out the display window.

By then Benjy was interviewing the young couple, the Shaws, in the foreground. Then he spoke with a man sitting on a fire hydrant, his back to the camera. The man lit a cigarette and looked over to Benjy for an instant, his face washed by the sun. He walked away when Benjy was interrupted by Larry Shaw.

Lieutenant Spielman's car pushed into the crowd and he got out. Then he went out of frame to look at Ozzie's body. Shaken, he came back into the picture and Benjy crossed over to him.

"Poor Ben," Jane whispered.

Jane saw herself come into the doorway of the shop and point to the security camera. Sitting in this darkened room, it was as if she were pointing at herself. Hank and Aaron looked toward the ATM and nodded. News vans arrived and began to set up for satellite transmission. "Becka Flynn," Kenny said when he recognized the reporter from KGO.

"Right." Jane watched herself and Kenny work their way through the police and the bystanders and get into the Explorer.

Benjy left his father and cleared a path for them. A Camaro, its color indistinguishable on the black-and-white video, stopped and let Kenny pull into traffic.

The fire truck came in from the right and settled near the ambulance, waiting to be called forward.

"That's enough," Jane said as she stood up. "The pisser is that once we get deeper into the case, something on this tape might make sense to us. And we have no way of knowing what that is yet."

"Part of the process."

"Since when do you think about process? I thought you were a results guy."

Kenny took the tape out of the deck. "Thanks to you, I'm getting in touch with my feminine side."

Jane stretched until she heard a satisfying pop high in her back. "C'mon, Inspector. Let's go to work."

As she turned to leave, she saw half a dozen cops standing at the window. They had been watching, silent and respectful, the death of one of their own.

25

JACQUES CARPENTER SAT on the roof of his building, smoking a cigarette and sipping Smirnoff from the bottle.

He had been up there for hours, reading the paper until the sun slipped behind the horizon. With the night had come the night sounds: salsa music, the Giants game on television, and, as always, a baby crying somewhere.

Carpenter held the vodka to his lips and let it slide down his throat, warming his chest. Across the way, on another roof, a match flared and the tip of a cigarette glowed. An orange dot in the night. Punky-Boy.

Taking his bottle, Carpenter rose and opened the roof access door. He wanted to watch the television he had stolen from the old lady in the apartment next to his.

The news should be interesting tonight.

He reached for the doorknob, still throwing off heat after another scorching day, and looked at his right hand. He could still feel the energy in it from the two shots he had fired into that cop's eyes.

In that energy was power.

He smiled.

It had begun.

Jane and Kenny had worked deep into the evening; poring over the on-scene incident reports from Ozzie's shooting. Follow-ups and forensics wouldn't be ready until tomorrow, and ballistics, even with a greased rush for a fallen cop, would take at least another day.

But still they stayed, feeling both numb and jangled, until Lieutenant Spielman had called and ordered them to go home. There would be plenty of midnight oil to burn, he had said, and plenty of midnights to burn it.

——

If a guitar could cry, then Stevie Ray Vaughan's Stratocaster was weeping hard as Kenny went through one of the moving boxes while talking on the portable phone.

The Giants and the Braves were on television, the sound muted. Chipper Jones hit a high fly ball to the deepest part of the stadium. "Hang on, Bobby," Kenny said as he leaned forward to watch the TV. "Okay, we got it. Anyway, let me talk to Jane and we'll figure out a night for you to sleep over. With the breeze off the water, it's a lot cooler down here. Say hi to your mom. See ya." He switched off the phone.

Jane came in from the kitchen with a homemade pizza. "What're you drinking?"

"How 'bout a beer?"

"Good thing, 'cause that's what I brought you."

She set the tray on the coffee table and sat next to him. "How's the prodigal nephew?"

"Didn't sound stoned for once. I invited him to come sleep over one night. Okay with you?"

Jane smiled. "It's your house, too. Anytime is fine with me." She nodded to the boxes. "You making a dent?"

"A tiny one." He held up a guitar pick. "Found this, though."

"Don't tell me, your first guitar pick."

"What's wrong with that?"

"Nothing." Jane laughed. "It's cute."

"I think I'm starting to hate that word."

On the TV, the Braves grounded into a double play and a promo for the local news came on. "Death of a street cop," the announcer said. "Tonight at eleven."

Kenny grabbed the remote and clicked the television off. "Christ."

Jane stood up, took the tray, and headed for the kitchen.

"Where you going?" Kenny called.

"You and I are gonna have a picnic on the dock."

"What about all this?"

Jane stopped in the doorway. "You decide: unpacking jock-straps and guitar paraphernalia, or an Italian picnic by the bay with the woman you love."

"I'll get my shoes."

— —

When they reached the end of the pier, Jane sat, as always, with her back to the Golden Gate Bridge.

Looking toward her house, she thought of how she was able to buy it just after the earthquake. She remembered how her father and uncles had helped her strip the walls and shore up its crooked skeleton. Sipping her beer, she saw a couple strolling with a baby carriage and a dog. They made sure to steer clear of the dusky shapes of the homeless people sleeping under the trees. Jane wondered which of those dark, motionless forms were Cito and his dog.

Above her house, far in the distance, was the spire of the Transamerica Building. Aglow with amber light, it was the focal point of the skyline it had changed forever.

Jane watched Kenny toss bits of pizza crust into the green-black water. A fish rose and took a piece, dimpling the surface with a perfect circle. Delighted, Kenny smiled at Jane, his boyish grin lighting up his face. She thought about her mother's ring and Jacob Turner, and she knew that one day soon she would go back to the Transamerica Building.

Next time she would take Kenny.

"How's the pizza?" she asked.

Kenny popped another beer and took a long pull. "Fish seem to like it." He put his arm around Jane's shoulder and kissed her hair.

"I can't stop thinking about Laura," Jane said. "She's going to wake up tomorrow and, for an instant, she's not going to remember that her husband is dead. Then it will all come crashing down on her again."

Kenny took her face in his hands and kissed her on the lips. They watched a sailboat slip across the harbor. Under power, it left a slim delta-shaped wake of white foam.

"Ken?"

"Mm?"

"Will we always be like this?" Jane kissed his fingertips. "Or are we going to start taking each other for granted?"

"I don't know," Kenny said. "But there's something safe and wonderful about being together long enough to take each other for granted."

"You are so sentimental."

"Told you."

They listened to the rhythmic sound of water moving over itself. The dock creaked with a swell from the sailboat's wake.

Jane turned in Kenny's arms. "Remember when I told Laura I was having a kind of midlife crisis?"

"Yeah. I thought I'd leave it till you wanted to bring it up again."

She kissed his hand. "I am."

"And?"

"And I think I want a different life. I mean, here we are on the brink of the incredible adventure of living together, and my brain is filled with dead people and killers."

"Comes with the territory."

"Only if you stay in the territory."

"So, what are you saying?" Kenny asked. "Are you talking about leaving the force?"

"Maybe."

"To do what?"

"I have no idea." Jane shook her head. "Except for working in Poppy's grocery store and waiting tables in college, being a cop is the only job I've ever had. I don't even know *how* to do anything else." She looked out over the water. Somewhere in the darkness a foghorn called. "What am I gonna do? Turn forty, become an ex-cop . . . and go job hunting? With what skills? And hunting for what job?"

Her cheeks flushed in frustration. "Shit, Ken. Just when I thought I had it all figured out, it all got so confusing." She wrapped her arms around herself. "I keep thinking about Hank. Did he wait too long? Will I wait too long?"

Kenny looped his arms around her waist. "Whatever you de-cide, whether it's to stay a cop for twenty more years or to get out tomorrow, you're stuck with me."

Jane touched her forehead to his. "Thank God."

Kenny pulled her to him. "If I told you you had a beautiful body," he said as he slid his hands down to her hips, "would you hold it against me?"

Jane laughed and took his hand. "C'mon," she said, tugging him along the dock. "Let's go do your favorite thing."

"Shopping?"

"Not a chance, buddy," Jane said as they headed back to the house.

26

SALLY BANKS STOOD on the first-floor landing, smoking a cigarette and sipping coffee from a Garfield mug.

Jane and Kenny entered the stairwell from the garage and started up the steps. "Hey, Sal," Kenny greeted her. "Get any sleep?"

"Not much."

Jane gave her arm a little squeeze. "I don't think any of us did."

Sally blew on her coffee, sending the steam sideways. "His desk is gone."

"What?" Jane asked.

"Ozzie's desk is gone. The lieutenant thought it would be best if we didn't have to look at it all the time."

"He might be right," Jane said. "Ben's got pretty good instincts about these things."

"Yeah," Sally said. She pulled on her cigarette. "Maybe."

"You take care," Jane said as she and Kenny went up the next flight and opened the bullpen door.

Two filing cabinets and a low table with an electric fan were in the corner where Ozzie's desk had been. A cardboard box under the table had CASTILLO written in felt marker on its side; the contents of his desk. Someone had put a coffee can on top of one of the filing cabinets with a sign that said FOR LAURA. It was already overflowing with money.

Finney sat in his cubicle eating an Egg McMuffin while talking on the phone with his wife. Cheryl Lomax was at the dispatch console, coordinating the movements of the precinct's patrol units. Roslyn Shapiro brought a cup of water to a very old man in reception. Lieutenant Spielman was working on his computer in his office.

"Life goes on, huh?" Kenny said.

The door to the evidence room opened and Benjy came out carrying a brown paper bag. He crossed the reception area, glanced at Roslyn Shapiro, and handed the bag to the old man. The man held it at his side and, head stooped, stepped into the elevator.

— —

Jane stood at the blackboard. She, Kenny, and Hank were briefing Lieutenant Spielman.

"Kenny sent the ATM video to the FBI Com Lab for magnification analysis."

"Those guys might be able to pull up a license plate," Kenny explained. "Or find somebody watching from a window the naked eye couldn't see."

"Hank met with a guy from the Asian Gang Task Force last night," Jane went on.

"Billy Ling," Hank said to Lieutenant Spielman. "Said to tell you hi." He checked his notes. "This kind of killing, Billy said, is inconsistent with the Tongs, Kowloon Furies, or any of the other Chinese gangs."

Lieutenant Spielman tapped the eraser of his pencil on his knee. "What about non-Asian gangs?"

"Still working on it," Hank said. "I've put the word out to my informants."

Through the interrogation-room window, Jane saw Sally pick up her gear bag and head for the stairwell door. She stopped at Cheryl's desk and, putting her hand on her shoulder, said something to her. Cheryl smiled weakly.

Talking about Ozzie, Jane thought.

Sally put an unlit cigarette in her mouth and went through the door toward the garage. Another cop going out on another patrol.

Jane turned back to Lieutenant Spielman. "We've got to go on the assumption that Ozzie's death wasn't a random act. Otherwise it's impossible to bite into the case. We're also looking for a link between Ozzie's murder and Skip Lacey." She slid a manila folder across to him. "Toward that end, Kenny and I have pulled up all of Ozzie's and Lacey's arrest records for the past ten years to see if anyone could have a grudge against them."

"We've been going over it all morning," Kenny said.

Lieutenant Spielman opened the folder and scanned the top page. "And?"

"And, nothing," Kenny said. "But there's a lot of stuff there and we'll look at everything."

"We've also called for records of any outstanding brutality or harassment suits against SFPD," Jane went on. "Maybe somebody has a hard-on against cops in general and Ozzie was just in the wrong place at the wrong time."

Lieutenant Spielman closed the folder. "Expand that to Oakland and Marin. Include Sheriff, CHP, and transit."

"Will do," Kenny said.

"We've got uniforms doing follow-ups with every name in the incident interview books," Hank offered.

"And," Jane said, "preliminary ME's report tells us Ozzie was killed with a twenty-two. Lots of street punks use little poppers like that. But so do professional hit men."

"Causes maximum damage at close range. And powder burns indicate this was extremely close range," Kenny said.

"Could this have been a professional hit?" Lieutenant Spielman asked.

"We're keeping all options open," Jane said.

"Any shells?" the lieutenant asked.

Jane shook her head. "No . . . none."

"So it was either a revolver," Kenny added, "or the killer picked them up."

"Probably a revolver," Hank said. "Perps don't want to have to clean up after themselves."

"One thing we have," Kenny said, "is usually, when something like this happens, it's one shot, bam, and the killer takes off."

"Right. But whoever shot Ozzie," Jane said, "took the time to shoot him twice. Once in each eye."

"What's that tell you?" Lieutenant Spielman asked.

"Maybe two things," Jane answered. "One: that the shooter was extremely angry. That plays into the grudge theory."

"And two?"

"Well, we're not sure, but the business with the eyes bugs the hell out of me. I still want to pursue a possible link to the Skip Lacey murder."

"May or may not be something there," Kenny said. "But it's a hunch worth listening to."

Lieutenant Spielman scraped back his chair and rose. "Good work, guys. Let's meet this afternoon to review—"

There was a knock at the door. Officer Finney stood there with a grey interdepartmental envelope.

"Great," Jane said, "the brutality-and-harassment stuff. Thanks, Mike." She held out her hand.

"It's for Inspector Pagano," Finney said.

Finney handed Hank the envelope. "Says here you have to sign for it."

Hank signed the receipt and handed it back to him. Finney lingered. "You guys talking about Ozzie?"

"That's right, Moby," Kenny said.

"Need anything?" Finney asked.

"We're fine, Mike," Jane said. "Thank you."

Finney gave a little bow and left.

Hank tore the envelope open, pulled out the single sheet of paper, and read it. Without a word, he dropped the page on the table and walked out of the room.

Jane looked first to Kenny, then to Lieutenant Spielman. She slid the letter to the edge of the table and read it.

"Goddamn it!"

Lieutenant Spielman leaned in to read it. "What is it?"

Jane spotted Hank just as he went through the stairwell door. "IA is going after him on the playground shooting."

She picked up the paper. "Says here, 'Lieutenant Jason Bloom of Internal Affairs has found just cause to open a formal investigation into the shooting-slash-killing of one Arthur Tyler by Inspector Henry Pagano."

"Motherfuckers," Kenny said.

27

SALLY BANKS PRESSED a lid onto her soda and walked out of the Dairy Queen. She hurried across the parking lot, wanting to get out of the heat. She unlocked her patrol car, number 425, and slipped inside. Turning the key, she started the engine and cranked the air-conditioning to maximum.

Sally picked up her mike. "3P240 to dispatch."

"Dispatch. Go, 3P240," Cheryl said back to her.

"3P240 requesting 10-7M."

"10-7M is a yes. Have a good lunch, girlfriend."

"Thanks, Cheryl. 3P240, out."

Sally put the black-and-white into gear and drove out of the lot.

Jacques Carpenter had been waiting for her to move. He touched the gas pedal of the Camaro and followed Sally Banks as she went west toward the freeway.

His fingers flexed on the steering wheel.

His heartbeat quickened in anticipation of the kill.

Kicking up dust as she went, Sally guided her patrol car through the vacant lot. She came to a stop in the shade of the Bayshore Freeway and turned off the ignition. With the windows rolled up and the air conditioner blasting, she unwrapped the turkey sandwich she had brought from home. She smiled as she took a bite, thinking of how her kitty, Vanilla, had snatched a piece of turkey from the package when she was making her lunch.

A shadow crossed her face and she looked up. She could see the torso of a man standing next to the car. He was wearing a white T-shirt and chinos. There was an unlit cigarette in his left hand.

Sally lowered her window and tilted her head outside. "Need a light?"

The last thing Sally Banks ever saw was the muzzle flash of the .22. She was dead before the second shot blew out her other eye.

— —

Jacques Carpenter pulled over to the right shoulder of the Bayshore Freeway and got out of the Camaro. He went to the emergency call box and pulled a handkerchief out of his pocket. He wrapped it around the receiver, picked it up, and dialed.

An operator answered on the first ring. "Nine-one-one. What is your emergency?"

"Yeah! Hello! I got out of my car to check my radiator. You know, with the heat and all?" Carpenter said breathlessly. "And I looked down under the freeway and I think I saw someone shoot into a police car! The car has the numbers four twenty-five on top!"

"What is your name, sir?"

Carpenter hung up the phone and went back to his car. He leaned against the front fender and looked down to SFPD patrol unit 425.

He lit a cigarette and waited for the show to begin.

— —

The emergency phone on Cheryl's console rang. She picked it up. "Nineteen."

"This is nine-one-one emergency dispatch. We have a call telling us that a police officer in unit four, two, five may have been shot. We put out an officer-down. Ambulance is en route."

"Oh my God!" Cheryl reflexively stood at her desk. "Thank you, nine-one-one." She toggled a button on her transmitter. "3P240," she said. "3P240, come in. This is dispatch." Trembling, she pressed the button again. "3P240! Do you copy?"

The other cops in the bullpen looked up as Cheryl, shouting now, repeated Sally Banks's call numbers. "3P240! Sally, do you copy?"

Cheryl wheeled around. "Finney!" she screamed. "Get the lieutenant."

Jane and Kenny came running in from the interrogation room.
"What is it?" Jane asked.

"Somebody called nine-one-one with an officer-down. Said it
was car four twenty-five." Her voice faltered. "That's Sally, and
now I can't raise her."

The speaker on her desk came alive with radio traffic. "2P418
responding to officer-down. CHP seven-seven-zero in vicinity and
responding. Transit nine responding to four-oh-six."

Lieutenant Spielman and Finney came racing up.

"We think Sally's in trouble," Jane said. She ran back to her desk
and grabbed her bag. Then she tossed Kenny his coat. "Let's go!"

Kenny ripped open the stairwell door and he and Jane tore
down the stairs.

28

Jacques Carpenter watched as, as if in a time-lapse movie, the police vehicles poured into the vacant lot where Sally Banks died.

The crime-scene van, its poster of the SFPD policeman gleaming in the relentless midday sun, rumbled to a stop. Two Highway Patrol motorcycle officers parked their bikes at the mouth of the driveway and directed traffic. News trucks and print reporters arrived and were shunted off to a holding area.

Carpenter looked up, squinting at the white-blue sky. Good, he thought, the sun would be at his back when he started shooting.

Jane and Kenny stood next to Sally Banks's squad car, looking in through the open driver's door. Sally lay with her head back and to the side, her mouth open. Her eye sockets were two disfigured black holes. Blood and brain matter trickled from exit wounds in the back of her head and ran down the headrest onto her shoulder.

"This sure as shit takes 'random' out of the equation," Jane said to Kenny, her body tense with rage.

Kenny chewed on the inside of his cheek. "We've got ourselves a serial killer."

"And he's killing cops." Jane nodded to the coroner's deputies and they raised the yellow sheet back over Sally's body.

Hank came up to them. "No shells."

"Then it's a revolver again," Jane said. She glanced at Kenny, then said to Hank, "We know about the IA thing and we'll do anything we can to help you."

"Don't let that fuckin' Bloom get you down," Kenny said.

"I'll be okay," Hank said. Then he nodded to Sally. "We got bigger fish."

Jane called to Aaron Clark-Weber. "How's the tire stuff coming?"

"Lots of different vehicles, including a bunch of ours. But we'll lift everything we can and take it in for laser analysis."

Jane took Kenny's elbow. "Let's take a walk. Make this scene talk to us."

As they started to traverse the lot, Jane noticed a couple of the younger uniformed cops nodding toward Hank. Worshiping the hero from afar.

"Inspector?"

Jane turned.

"Hi, I'm Becka Flynn, KGO News."

"I remember."

"Can I get a statement?"

"Not yet. This is still too active," Jane said. "You'd better check with the press officer."

"C'mon, Inspector, I don't need spin. I need facts."

Jane regarded her. "Not now," she said. "And especially not here."

"I'll call you, then," Becka Flynn said as she and her cameraman set up their remote broadcast.

Kenny lifted the crime-scene tape for Jane. "This is real bad."

"I'm just afraid it's gonna get worse," Jane said. "We've got to get this fucker before we lose anyone else."

"Yeah, I know." Kenny looked to Jane, but she was staring at something on the ground. There, in the dust, was a pebble-sized black dot.

Jane squatted down. "Motor oil," she said softly.

Kenny, immediately understanding the significance, cupped his hands to his mouth. "Aaron!"

Aaron Clark-Weber hurried over as fast as his bad knee would allow. "Find something?"

"Maybe," Jane answered.

Aaron leaned forward and peered into the dust. "Oil," he said.

"Looks fresh." He straightened up. "Hey, Tommy! Bring your kit and take some molds." He pointed at the two distinct tire tracks straddling the drop of oil. "Here and . . . here." As Tommy went to work, Aaron turned to Jane. "Anytime you want to move up to Forensics, give me a—"

"Aaron," Jane interrupted. She was shading her eyes, looking up to the freeway. "The nine-one-one came in from a freeway call box. Your guys been up there yet?"

"Already on top of it. Soon as I can release a team."

A black Chevy Suburban roared past the Highway Patrolmen at the driveway. It sped through the tangle of police vehicles and slid to a stop near the crime-scene van.

"Our fearless leaders," Kenny said as Chief Walker McDonald and Lieutenant Spielman climbed out. Becka Flynn and the other reporters converged on them.

"Chief, what can you tell us about—"

Two gunshots slammed into the side of the van, just above Chief McDonald's head. Lieutenant Spielman threw the chief to the ground as the news crews scurried for cover.

Police officers, their sidearms and shotguns drawn and ready, frantically scanned the area, searching for any sign of the shooter.

— —

Unseen by the police, Jacques Carpenter simply got into his car and, being careful not to speed, nudged it into the southbound traffic of the Bayshore Freeway. Within minutes, he was miles away.

He slowly balled his right hand into a fist as if to retain the energy.

Revenge was his sustenance, and he was still hungry.

— —

Chief McDonald's bodyguards hustled him into the Suburban. It sped away, churning up vast clouds of dust.

Lieutenant Spielman sat hunkered by the crime-scene van with Jane and Kenny while a SWAT team swept the area. "This is one nasty motherfucker, shooting at fifty cops."

"Take a look, Ben," Jane said. She pointed to the poster on the side of the van. Both of the handsome policeman's eyes had been shot out.

"Not only did this cocksucker kill two, maybe three cops," Kenny said. "He hung around long enough to send us a message."

Lieutenant Spielman looked up to the poster. "Saying what?"

Jane shook her head. "That he'll kill again." She went to the Explorer and picked up the radio microphone. "Dispatch, this is 3H58."

Cheryl came on, her voice anxious with worry. "3H58, go." She hesitated. "Jane, is it Sally?"

Jane looked to Kenny and Lieutenant Spielman. "Yes, it is. I'm so sorry." She raised an eyebrow at the lieutenant, silently asking him a question.

He nodded.

"Cheryl," Jane continued, "why don't you call Walter and have him come get you? We'll get someone from downtown to cover."

There was a pause on the other end. Then Cheryl said, "I don't know. We'll see."

"One more thing," Jane said quickly. "Please have the other dispatchers put the word out to all units in the field telling them to be careful. And, if you would, please call Benjy yourself."

"Will do, Jane . . . Dispatch out."

"3H58 out."

Lieutenant Spielman touched Jane's arm. "Thanks." He put his foot on the bottom step of the crime-scene van. "I've gotta call Sally's mother."

29

We have an extremely serious situation here." Lieutenant Spielman addressed his officers in the bullpen. "As you know, someone out there is killing cops. Two from this precinct." He paused, the hum of the electric fans filling the space. "As of now and until we catch this guy, all of San Francisco's law enforcement personnel are on full tactical alert. Extra caution is the rule of the day. Anything suspicious or potentially dangerous comes your way, call for backup. Unless a citizen's life is in danger, you wait until help gets there."

The elevator doors opened and Benjy came into the squad room carrying his shotgun and gear bag. Lieutenant Spielman nodded to him and continued. "Vests are to be worn by uniformed officers at all times. I don't care about the heat wave. Don't let me catch anyone without a vest."

He crossed to Jane's desk. "Inspector Candiotti is in charge of this investigation. Inspector Marks is her number two." Jane snuck a look at Kenny. "Any and all information pertaining to this case must be channeled through them. If you hear something, or suspect something, or even dream something that might help, bring it to Jane and Ken.

"One more thing. There's a department-wide directive coming down that all officers, uniformed and plainclothes, are to recertify with their weapons. Doesn't matter if you just passed last week, get to the range and get some shooting time in."

He looked around at the faces of the men and women in his command. "I only want two things here: all of you stay safe; and we take this asshole down."

––

" 'Yeah! Hello! I got out of my car to check my radiator. You know, with the heat and all? And I looked down under the freeway and I think I saw someone shoot into a police car! The car has the numbers four twenty-five on top!' "

" 'What is your name, sir?' "

There was the sound of someone hanging up a phone, and then a dial tone.

Jane turned off the tape recorder and looked to Kenny and Hank. "There's something about this guy's speech pattern I can't put my finger on." She sat on the table in Interrogation Room One. "Kenny, call FBI and run this tape by them."

Kenny looked up from his notepad. "Will do."

Jane thought she heard the slightest note of irritation in his voice. She decided to let it go.

"Sorry to interrupt," Chief McDonald said as he and Lieutenant Spielman strode in. "I know you have a lot of work to do, so I'll be brief." He turned to Hank. "Inspector Pagano, it's come to my attention, actually Ben brought it to my attention before Officer Banks was killed, that IA is filing on you over the school yard shooting."

"Yes sir, they are," Hank said, rising from his chair.

"Not anymore," the chief said. "We looked at what Jason Bloom had on you. It's all a mishmash of the same old stuff. Plus, I've reviewed the tapes and incident reports and I'm intervening on this one." He put a hand on Hank's shoulder. "Hank, this department owes you an apology. Jason Bloom is the worst kind of IA cop. He's an unprincipled zealot who has no imagination or compassion."

"To put it mildly," Kenny said.

Jane shot him a look.

"Perhaps," the chief said. "I've put Lieutenant Bloom on administrative leave pending further investigation from my office." He shook Hank's hand. "It's over."

"I'm very grateful, sir," Hank said. "Any other time . . ." He gestured toward the blackboard.

"I'll let you get back to work." Chief McDonald nodded to Jane and Kenny. "Inspectors," he said, and left the room.

Hank went up to Lieutenant Spielman. "Thanks for stepping in, Ben."

"We've got enough to worry about without Bloom's bullshit vendetta. Just catch me this killer." Lieutenant Spielman started for the door. "I've got the news guys setting up in my office. Just what I need right now."

As he left, Jane turned to Hank. She was about to congratulate him when he said, "I've been working on a possible non-Asian gang connection. But everyone I talk to says no way this is a gang deal. Last thing the San Francisco gangs want is for the cops to be this pissed off at them."

Jane could see that Hank didn't want to talk about what had just happened with Chief McDonald. She nodded. "Makes sense." She looked at the blackboard. Data on Skip Lacey, Ozzie Castillo, and Sally Banks filled the slate. "Why would somebody go to the trouble of shooting a cop in both eyes?"

"Not only is it barbaric," Kenny said, "it's risky, hanging around after the first shot."

"The shooter is definitely telling us something," Hank said.

Kenny turned to him. "Or telling his victims something."

Jane stared at the blackboard; at the circles representing each of the dead cops. Their heads. Their mouths. Their noses.

Their eyes.

And there it was. Kenny was right. The killer *was* telling them something.

"Goddamn it, that's it!" She jumped down from the table. "An eye for an eye. The ultimate revenge." She paced as she talked. "Somebody out there was fucked over by, or feels he was fucked over by, the police. Guys, we need to pursue the grudge theory hard. I want you to bring up the release records of the local prisons. See who might be harboring a grudge against cops."

Kenny sat forward in his chair. "Everybody in prison has a grudge against cops."

"There'll be hundreds of cons to check out," Hank said. "Maybe thousands."

"Then we'll get some help and do them all, one by one," Jane said. "Let's also hit the National Crime Computer in Atlanta. Someone could have gotten out of jail in Texas or Florida or someplace and come here to do his dirty work. Go back all the way back to ten years ago. See what you can find."

"It might be melodramatic," Kenny offered, "but I think we should call the mental hospitals, too. They might have had some lunatic escape. Or maybe they released some guy who wasn't as cured as they thought."

"For the sake of argument," Hank said, "are we sure it's a male we're after?"

"No, we're not," Jane said. "But the profile and the MO point that way."

"It's a guy," Aaron Clark-Weber said from the doorway.

Jane motioned for him to join her at the table.

"We have shoe prints from next to Sally's car that match shoe prints near the drop of oil," Aaron began. "Size twelve and a half. And . . . this is interesting . . . the mold of the bare foot found at Skip Lacey's murder scene is also twelve and a half. It's almost definitely a man, and a big one."

"Is it just me," Jane said, "or is it starting to look like Skip, Ozzie, and Sally were all killed by the same man."

"Seems so." Aaron opened his briefcase. "Tire molds from Sally's shooting indicate BF Goodrich model two-five-five, seven-oh, one-five. Wide-tread radials usually found on older muscle cars. GTOs, Camaros, Firebirds, that sort of thing."

"Did you cross-hit the data with FBI?" Jane asked.

"Yeah," Aaron said. "Nothing distinctive about the tires has turned up at any other crime scenes. But the same tread marks were also found on the soft shoulder of the freeway by the emergency call box."

"Prints?" Kenny asked.

"Wiped clean."

Jane looked to the blackboard. The names of the three dead people were like questions waiting for an answer. "What about ballistics?"

"Same twenty-two on both Ozzie and Sally. Also the trajectory paradigm shows the shots fired at the van originated in the vicinity of the call box."

Kenny whistled. "This guy is one hell of a shot."

Officer Finney stuck his head in the door. " 'Scuse me, Inspector Candiotti? Lieutenant Spielman needs you and Inspector Marks."

Jane turned and looked out the interior window. There were a dozen reporters and cameramen wedged into the lieutenant's office.

Kenny stood up. "This should be fun."

Jane joined him at the doorway. "Hank, will you bring up Sally's arrest records and cross them with Ozzie's and Lacey's?" She smiled at Aaron. "Tell your team we appreciate all the good work."

"Someone's killing our friends. We'll do whatever you need us to do."

Jane nodded solemnly. "Thanks, Aaron. See you after 'Meet the Press.' "

— —

"Sir, do we have a serial killer on the loose in San Francisco?" Anne Fleming of KFOX radio asked.

"Uh, we're still compiling information to that effect," Lieutenant Spielman said. Beads of sweat glistened on his upper lip. Clearly uncomfortable, he went on, "As of this point in time . . ."

The reporters groaned at his evasive response.

"Lieutenant, you've got two cops from this building murdered in exactly the same way," Becka Flynn began. "Maybe a third, if you count Steve Lacey. Doesn't that add up to a serial killer?"

Lieutenant Spielman squinted into the lights. "Senior Homicide Inspector Jane Candiotti here is lead investigator on this case. Frankly, she's more up-to-date on the facts than I am at this point in—"

"Inspector Candiotti . . ." Becka Flynn interjected, turning to Jane. "Do we or do we not have a serial killer in San Francisco?"

Jane scanned the room. The lights. The cameras. The faces. "Yes, we do," she said firmly.

Becka Flynn gave a little smile, acknowledging Jane's candor.

"Everything we know points to a serial murder sequence," Jane went on. "Similarity of method and of victims."

"Any suspects?" Cameron Sanders of the *Chronicle* asked.

"Not yet. But he's getting sloppy and we feel we're getting closer."

A young reporter in the back shouted out, "Will you describe the condition of the victims when they were found?"

"No, I will not," Jane said angrily. "These people who died were not only part of our law enforcement family. They were the children of someone and the brothers and sister and husband of someone. Their families don't need to have their loved ones' terrible last moments described to the public. Certainly not by me or anyone in this department."

There was a collective pause in the urgency of the questioning. Then Becka Flynn asked softly, "Inspector Candiotti, we know this is delicate, but can you tell us what you have on what the killer looks like? The citizens of San Francisco have the right to know that much."

Jane started to speak, then pulled it back. Choosing her words carefully, she went on. "All we know so far is the perpetrator is a male. He's big and he's very strong. He wears a size twelve and a half shoe and probably drives an older-model General Motors car . . . and he's soulless."

Jane looked into the KGO camera, knowing as she did that she was favoring Becka Flynn. "This killer is going to make a mistake. And when he does . . ." Jane narrowed her eyes. She could see a tiny reflection of herself in the lens. ". . . we'll hunt him down like the animal he is . . . and we'll put an end to this senseless tragedy."

— —

Jacques Carpenter sat in the open air-shaft window of his apartment. Naked, he smoked a cigarette, a faint downdraft cooling his back.

He was watching Jane on television. "If we have to, we will tear this city apart, street by street, building by building, brick by brick, until we find him . . ."

The bedroom door opened and Mickey Title came out. Pulling on his shirt, he put three hundred dollars on the kitchen counter. "Can I maybe take a shower? I worked up a hell of a sweat."

"No," Carpenter said, his eyes fixed on the TV. INSPECTOR JANE CANDIOTTI, NINETEENTH PRECINCT was supered across the bottom of the screen.

Title stepped into the living room and looked at the television. "That about those cops getting killed?"

"Yeah."

"Terrible, huh?"

"Heartbreaking."

— —

Jane's jaw bounced with indignation as she continued. "And he better pray to whichever god will still listen to a monster like him that, when we catch him . . ."

Kenny put his hand on Jane's arm. She pulled it away, determined to finish.

". . . that it isn't me."

Chastened, Kenny looked at the floor as Jane went on.

"That sounds like it's personal for you, Inspector," Becka Flynn said.

Jane looked at the constellation of faces and lights in front of her. Then she found Becka's camera again. "It is."

Lieutenant Spielman stepped between Jane and the reporters. "Okay, everyone. That's enough for now. We'll be releasing further information as it becomes available."

"One more question, Lieutenant," Cameron Sanders urged.

"Not gonna happen, guys. We have a lot of work to do. So can I please have my office back?"

Grumbling their displeasure, the journalists packed up their equipment and filed out. When she got to the doorway, Becka Flynn turned and caught Jane's eye. They exchanged a silent moment of connection before Lieutenant Spielman closed the door.

Jane took a bottled water from the mini-fridge and twisted off the cap. "God, Ben. Did I go too far?"

"Basically, you were credible and straightforward and—"

"And pissed off," Kenny said.

"I am pissed off, damn it!" Jane said. "Ozzie and Sally are dead." She pointed to the bullpen. "Someone out there could be next. And all we know is the shooter is big and strong and may be driving an old car!" She screwed the cap back on the water bottle and hurled it into the trash can. "Big fucking deal!"

There was a knock on the door and Finney pushed it open. "Inspector Candiotti? Your father's on line one."

"You can take it in here," Lieutenant Spielman said. He took Kenny by the elbow. "C'mon, Ken, let's give your partner a couple of minutes to cool her jets."

"Fine by me," Kenny said. "I've got something like a million mental hospitals to call."

Jane watched them go, then picked up the phone. "Poppy?"

"I just saw you on TV."

Jane drew a breath. "That was live?"

"I guess so."

"Jesus."

"Should I be worried about you, honey?"

"I'll be careful. I promise." Jane found herself relaxing, her father's voice soothing her. Next to the phone was a picture of Lieutenant Spielman and his son at Benjy's graduation. "How you doin' Poppy?"

"Kinda tired today," Poppy said. "Aunt Lucy's coming for dinner."

Through Lieutenant Spielman's window, Jane saw Jason Bloom walk up to the reception desk. Roslyn Shapiro pointed to Interrogation Room One. Bloom crossed the bullpen, ignoring the stares of the cops at their desks, and entered the interrogation room.

"That's good," Jane said, her curiosity rising.

"I think she still wants me to sell the house."

"Don't do it, Poppy," Jane said, surprising herself. "It means too much to you. If you need any help with money, I could—"

"Hey! I almost forgot," Poppy interrupted her, uneasy with what Jane was about to say. "Rosemary had her baby this morning. Margaret Grace."

Jane's eyes suddenly brimmed with tears. "Oh, Poppy, that's wonderful."

A sudden movement in the squad room caught her attention. Finney and a couple of other cops were running to the interrogation room window.

"I got peppers in the oven. I love you, honey."

"I love you, too, Poppy." She hung up and, wiping her eyes, hurried out of the office.

Jane ran past her desk and pushed her way through the small crowd at the doorway.

Hank and Jason Bloom were standing, chest to chest, in the middle of the room. The veins in Bloom's forehead were bulging with rage. "You and your fucking hero crap have ruined my life!"

"You ruined your own life, you Nazi fuck," Hank said, his blue eyes blazing with anger.

"Hank, Lieutenant!" Jane shouted. "We've got bigger things to—"

Jason Bloom whirled on Jane. "The chief busted me, Inspector. My career is over."

Kenny stepped in. "That's not exactly bad news around here."

"Ken," Jane said sharply. She turned to Bloom. "Two of my police officers are dead and you dare to come in here with your personal bullshit?" She pointed to the door. "Get the hell out of my precinct, Lieutenant!"

Lieutenant Bloom looked around the room. Unfriendly faces of every rank stared back at him. He took a step away from Hank and started to go. Then, abandoning caution, he turned and said, "You're always hiding behind a skirt, Pagano. First your wife and now Candiotti."

Bloom never saw Hank's fist crash into his cheek. He was sent sprawling backward over a chair and landed heavily on his side. His feet scrambling, he quickly stood up. Then he lunged for Hank, blood streaming from his cut face. Kenny and Aaron intercepted him and pinned his arms at his side.

"You are in really hostile territory," Kenny hissed into his ear. "How much trouble do you want in one day?"

Bloom shrugged himself out of their grasp and brought his fingers to the gash below his left eye. "You and I," he spit at Hank, "are not done yet."

Hank stood his ground, his fists clenched and ready. "You're damn right we're not."

Bloom turned on his heel and shouldered his way past Finney and the others.

"Okay, everyone," Jane said to the throng in the doorway. "We all have a lot of work to do, so . . ." She gestured for them to disperse.

Still excited by an IA cop being taken down by one of their own, they returned to their desks.

"Sorry about all this," Hank said. "But I've wanted to do that for years."

"He had it coming," Jane said. "If he comes after you again, you've got a station house full of witnesses."

Hank picked up the toppled chair. "Even he's not that stupid."

"C'mon, Kenny," Jane said as she grabbed her bag.

"Where we going?"

"Sally's apartment. Something might turn up." Jane started toward the stairwell door. "Besides, I need some air."

Kenny looked out to the street, cars whipping by in the blazing sun. News vans lined the curb in front of the lawn where the flag hung at half-mast. "Such as it is."

"Such as it is," Jane echoed as they went down the stairs.

When they came to the first landing, they both stopped and looked at the floor. The black smudges of Sally's cigarette butts stained the concrete surface along the far wall.

"I'll get somebody to clean that," Kenny said.

"Yeah," Jane said as she continued down the steps.

— —

30

Kenny guided the Explorer into the brilliant sunlight.

To the left, the news vans, their satellite arms stretching to the sky, sat idling in front of the police station. A produce delivery van slowed for him and Kenny turned right, drove to the corner, and turned right again.

Jane thought Kenny was quiet as he headed toward the freeway. "You okay?"

"Just a lot going on."

Jane slid her hand under his right thigh. "Yeah, I know."

Behind them, the delivery van pulled over to a Korean market and a primer-grey Camaro, keeping its distance, followed them up the on-ramp.

— —

"One of her mother's friends came by and took the cat," Mrs. Diamond, Sally Banks's landlord, said as she pushed open the door to her apartment. "You need anything, I'm down in One-A." Holding the railing, she started down the steps. "It's a shame, is what it is," she said, more to herself than anyone else. "Nice girl like that."

Jane and Kenny entered the small one-bedroom apartment.

"Whew," Kenny said. They were standing in the middle of the living room. The prefabricated bookshelves held pictures of Sally's nieces in various Halloween costumes. A cat poster hung over the brown couch. An unopened copy of the *Chronicle* was on the tiny dinette table.

Jane went to the bookshelf and pressed the play button on the answering machine. "Hi honey, it's Ma. Daddy and I want you to come up for dinner on Saturday. If you want, you can bring Vanilla and maybe stay over. Call us tonight. We love you."

The next call was a hang-up. The third and final call was Sally's mother again. ". . . (a sob) . . . honey? Please be there . . . oh God . . . They just called and said they thought you . . . (another sob) . . . oh God, honey, please be there . . . I don't know . . . (long pause) . . . honey? . . ."

Jane looked to Kenny.

"Yeah," he said softly.

They went down the hallway to the bedroom. Kenny opened a few drawers and stepped into the closet, but his instinct told him they weren't going to find anything useful. "Let's get out of here."

Jane was holding the official police-department portrait of a younger Sally. She was in her formal uniform, standing in front of an American flag with her pistol in her white-gloved hands. Her eyes were bright and hopeful, and her jaw was set in a tight, slightly embarrassed smile.

"It always gets me," Jane said. "No matter who it is. A junkie, that old guy who killed his wife on their fiftieth anniversary, Ozzie, Sally . . . anyone. They all were somebody's baby once." She shook her head. "Some mother gave them life, watched them cut their first teeth. Learn to crawl. Walk. Go off to school . . ."

Kenny put his arm around her and kissed her hair. "We'll get this guy, Jane."

Jane pressed into him, grateful for his tenderness and his resilience. They went down the hall and crossed the living room to the front door. "Let's go to the shooting range and get that out of the way. Maybe blow off a little steam."

"Only if you don't go getting all competitive on me."

"No promises," Jane said as she stepped outside.

— —

"Ready on the right. Ready on the left. Ready on the firing line!"

Top Gun was crowded.

Ordinarily, at this time of day, there would only be a handful of people at the indoor firing range. But, with the departmental directive that all police officers get some gun time in, the place was packed.

Jane and Kenny, wearing goggles and ear protectors, were in lanes ten and eleven. Jane fired her revolver steadily, methodically, its dull pop absorbed in the roar of forty weapons discharging simultaneously.

Kenny rapidly squeezed off round after round from his Glock 9-millimeter, firing seventeen shots in the time it took Jane to shoot six.

A whistle blew and the firing stopped. The human-form target cards rattled through the smoke to the firing line, where the shooters, mostly cops, but some civilians, inspected their marksmanship.

Kenny looked at Jane's target. "Good cluster." Four of the six shots were in the heart. The other two were less than half an inch outside the circle.

Jane took Kenny's card. "Not so bad yourself." The center of his card had been hit so many times, a large hole had been blown away.

"Sort of the Dresden theory of saturation sharpshooting."

At the far end of the firing line, in lane forty, Jacques Carpenter inspected his target card. He had fired twelve shots. There were two holes the size of quarters where the eyes had been.

He held the target up to his face, like a mask, and looked through the holes. Across the crowded shooting range, he spotted Jane.

"I see you," Carpenter said in a singsong lilt. He let the card fall to the floor and headed down the firing line.

Jane and Kenny were reloading when Carpenter came up behind them. His right hand flexed on the grip of his .22, the explosive energy still reverberating up his arm, a muscle memory of incomparable power. He stopped behind Jane.

Her dark hair, her slender shoulders.

It would be so easy.

— —

31

I⊤ WAS AFTER EIGHT in the evening when Jane and Kenny finished briefing Lieutenant Spielman.

For the time being, the investigation was still all process. Prison release records, mental-hospital patient routing, forensics reports, National Crime Computer hits, had all been requested and were on the way.

They had stopped to watch the local news on the television in the squad room. Photographs of Ozzie and Sally and a much-younger Skip Lacey played on the screen as Becka Flynn gave her in-studio report.

Jane's face came up on the TV, angry and resolute. She issued her warning to the killer, shrugging Kenny's hand off her arm as she became more incensed.

Then she and Kenny had typed up their notes and given them to Finney to distribute. Hank had left earlier, gone off to press his network of informants for shreds of information. Aaron Clark-Weber had long ago returned to his lab, sifting through the minutiae for any sort of clue. Cheryl Lomax's replacement, a His-panic woman in her late twenties, spoke softly into her headset, keeping tabs on the night patrols.

Bone-weary and unsettled, Jane and Kenny went down the stairs to the parking garage. The sooty smudges from Sally's cig-arettes were gone, scrubbed away by someone during the day.

— —

The Marina Green was teeming with people out beating the heat.

Couples sat on benches watching the passage of distant vessels across the bay. An elderly Japanese man sat cross-legged on a straw mat. Cito turned the faucet of the water fountain so his dog, up on his hind legs, could drink. Several college kids, racing the coming darkness, were trying to finish a game of Frisbee football. Two winos leaned against the chain-link fence passing a bottle of Thunderbird.

Kenny slid the Explorer up to the curb. Jane opened her door and stepped onto the sidewalk. A champagne cork popped and a ruckus of laughter erupted from the deck of one of the sailboats moored across the way.

"At least somebody's having a good time," Jane said as Kenny came around the car.

He put his arm around her. "C'mon, I'll make you some dinner. Pasta à la Marks."

"And that would be?"

"All I can tell you is the words 'Chef Boyardee' are involved."

"Tell you what," Jane said as they started up the path. "I'll do the cooking. You open us a bottle of—"

She stopped, tensing. In a dark corner of the porch, the tip of a cigarette glowed bright orange.

Kenny, responding to her look, reflexively reached inside his jacket. "Can I help you?" he called.

"It's me, Uncle Ken." Bobby moved forward into the soft yellow hue of the porch light.

"Hey, Bobby," Kenny said as he and Jane felt their tension subside. "What's up?"

Bobby flicked his cigarette into the street. "Just thought I'd come and hang. That okay?"

Jane unlocked the door. "You eat yet?"

"Uh-uh."

"Can you chop an onion?"

"I guess."

Jane leaned into the door until it opened. "Let's go, then." She turned to Bobby. "But no smoking."

"No smoking anything," Kenny added quickly.

"Real funny," Bobby said as they went inside.

——

Poppy Candiotti drizzled balsamic vinegar over the roasted peppers. Then he turned off the oven and placed the osso buco, the pan still sizzling and crackling, on top of the stove. He dropped the oven mitts onto the counter and reached up to take a bottle of Chianti from the cabinet over the refrigerator.

When he did, he suddenly felt himself flush. His face became hot and sweaty, and he heard a roar in his left ear, like listening to the inside of a huge seashell. Gripped with pain and fear, he fell to one knee. He looked about frantically, his ears still thundering, his breath coming in brittle gasps.

The phone was on the wall near the dining-room door. Too far away.

He put both his hands flat on the floor and waited, on all fours, his head bowed like a dog.

All he could think about was that he didn't want Lucy to be the one to find him.

"Not now," he whispered. "Not yet."

— —

Kenny sat on the couch absently picking at an unplugged electric guitar. Bobby was lying on the floor watching *Scream 2* on HBO.

"Uncle Ken, can I ask you something?"

"Yup."

Bobby gestured to an end table. "How come you got a picture of an old guitar in such a nice frame?"

"I knew I liked this kid," Jane said as she came in from the kitchen. She squatted down and went to muss Bobby's hair.

Bobby pulled back slightly, ducking his head.

Jane glanced to Kenny, and then asked Bobby, "How's the movie?"

"Awesome."

Kenny put down his guitar. "Hey, Bobby, Keb' Mo's at Heart and Soul next week. Wanna check it out with me?"

Bobby's eyes lit up. "For sure?"

"For sure."

"But I'm underage."

"And I'm a cop," Kenny said. "Anybody gives you shit, I bust his ass."

"Nice talk," Jane said. "Dinner's ready in five minutes, so—"

The phone rang.

Jane stood up. "I got it." She snatched the portable from the table next to the window seat. "Hello," she said, motioning for Bobby to turn down the volume on the TV. She listened for a moment. Then her hand went to her mouth as she choked back a sob.

"Oh God," she said. Kenny bolted from the couch and crossed to her. "We'll be right there." She let the phone drop from her fingers. "That was Aunt Lucy. Poppy's had a heart attack."

"How bad?"

"The doctors told her to gather the family." She started down the hall. "I'm gonna get my bag."

Kenny pulled a twenty-dollar bill from his wallet and thrust it at Bobby. "Here's some money for a cab."

Bobby picked the phone up off the floor. "I could maybe hang here till you get back."

Jane came running into the living room, her bag over her shoulder. "Let's go!"

"Thing is," Kenny said to Bobby, "we don't know when we're getting back. It's gonna be a long night."

Jane yanked the door open and ran outside.

"I'll call you," Kenny said as he hurried after Jane.

32

THE VIGIL.

The moment Jane had dreaded for years.

She sat on a beige Naugahyde couch, Kenny's arm over her shoulder. Aunt Lucy was across from her, sitting on the edge of a magazine-covered coffee table. She pulled a tissue from her sleeve and blew her nose. Timmy paced along the far wall of the family waiting room. Back and forth, back and forth, relentlessly like a bear trapped in a cage that was too small.

In the corner near the coffee machine, a doctor spoke in a low voice to a black family. There were two little girls, a mother, a father, and a grandfather. The father shook the doctor's hand and said, "Thank you, ma'am." He smiled to his wife and sat down again, relief flooding his face.

Jane watched the doctor go, knowing that no such good news would be coming her way this night.

She slid out from under Kenny's arm and went to the doorway. A young man sat on the floor next to the water fountain doing a crossword puzzle. Two women standing against the floor-to-ceiling windows talked about the heat wave.

Jane looked past them out the sixth-story window of Oakland's Kaiser Hospital. She and Kenny had raced over the Bay Bridge, the cherry dome light strobing on the roof of the Explorer. Aunt Lucy and Timmy had met them outside ICU and taken them to this waiting room.

The doctors were making Poppy comfortable, Lucy had said. Then they would come for them.

Aunt Lucy had summoned the courage to ask the unthinkable

question, and the doctors had said yes. It was time to call for a priest.

Jane leaned her forehead against the metal doorjamb, absorbing its coolness. She caught a flash of white to the left and turned. Poppy's doctor was heading toward her. Jane wanted to run to him, to beg him not to let her father die tonight. She'd make any bargain if only she could have Poppy for one more year. One more month. Until tomorrow.

Timmy had seen the doctor coming and joined Jane at the door. She took her brother's hand and noticed how cold it was. Aunt Lucy came up behind her. Jane glanced back into the room. Kenny stood there, solid and reliable, his hand on Lucy's shoulder.

Dr. Gandin reached between Jane and Timmy and took Lucy's hand. "Come, Lucy. It's time."

"For what?" Timmy asked.

Aunt Lucy turned to her nephew. "To say goodbye to Poppy." She stepped into the corridor. Dr. Gandin took her elbow. "Father Patricola is with your brother now."

They came to a room across from the nurses' station. Jane looked at the night nurse. The nurse looked back at Jane, compassion in her eyes.

Poppy lay in cardiac intensive care, his mouth open, his chest rising slightly with each meager breath. A bank of monitors hummed and glowed in the softly lit room.

Father Patricola stood over Poppy, holding his hand and praying in a rhythmic mumble. Feeling the family enter the room, he made the sign of the cross on Poppy's forehead and stepped back to the curtains. He nodded to Lucy as she stepped forward.

"Lucia," he said softly.

Lucy sat in a chair by her brother's head and touched her lips to his left ear. She whispered to him in Italian for a few minutes. Then she kissed him on the side of the head. "*Ciao, Paolino,*" she said, and went to stand with the priest.

Timmy, his head bent, held Poppy's hands in his and stood there with tears streaming down his face. Unable to say anything, he put his father's hands back on the bed. His shoulders racked with sobs, he sat in the bedside chair.

It took an eternity of three seconds for Jane to cross the room.

She put her hand flat on her father's chest, feeling his brave damaged heart beating faintly beneath her palm. She looked back to Kenny. He stood at a respectful distance in the doorway. Then she bent over her father's face to kiss him on the lips. When she did, she looked into his eyes, distant and unseeing, and saw tiny twin reflections of herself.

"It's okay, Poppy," she whispered. "You can go to Mommy now."

33

THE NEIGHBORS ALONG OAK STREET peered out their front windows as the cars arrived.

Hours ago, they had seen the ambulance take Poppy away. Now they knew he wouldn't be coming home.

Jane and Kenny stood in the kitchen doorway. The floor was littered with the wrappers of the cardiac kit the paramedics had left behind.

"I'll get this," Kenny said.

"Let's do it together."

Kenny knelt down and scooped up the debris of the futile struggle to save a man's life. He noticed the bottle of Chianti on its side beneath the footstool and picked it up.

Jane covered the osso buco and the peppers. She opened the refrigerator and looked inside. Anchovies and Parmesan, olives and Italian beer, prosciutto and calamari, empty promises of meals to come. She put the food away and was about to close the door when she saw Poppy's heart medicine on the shelf. *Paolo Candiotti, three times daily, with meals.*

Jane nudged the door closed with her hip and went into the living room.

Aunt Lucy sat in the corner of the couch dialing the phone. She looked up as Jane passed by. "I never thought I'd be the last."

Jane touched her cheek with the back of her hand. "There's a lot going on that we never thought about, Auntie." Lucy kissed her hand and Jane went up the stairs to her father's bedroom.

Poppy's rosary, Bible, and reading glasses were on the night table next to a two-week-old *Time* magazine.

The dresser was covered with framed photographs. His wedding picture. A favorite snapshot of Jane's mother taken on the beach one long ago summer. Baby pictures of Jane and Timmy. Timmy's high-school graduation photo. And the police portrait of Jane when she was a rookie cop. Like Sally Banks, she stood in front of an American flag, young and hopeful.

The doorbell chimed downstairs. Someone answered it and Jane could hear the muffled voices of those who had come to call.

Jane started to cross the room. She stopped at the bed. Poppy's slippers, worn and cracked, lay on a small embroidered rug. Jane knelt on one knee. She picked up her father's slippers, molded by time and wear, and held them to her cheek.

Then she kissed them.

Car doors closing outside. Footsteps on the porch. The doorbell. The door opening and closing. Shoes shuffling. Low voices. Someone crying. The doorbell again.

Jane rose and left the bedroom.

When she reached the top of the stairs, she paused to look below. Father Patricola was chatting with Mr. and Mrs. Tasca from next door. Jacob Turner sat on the couch, his hand on Aunt Lucy's arm while she talked on the phone. Timmy shook hands with one of his uncles and went down the hall.

Jane smelled coffee, and she knew that some of her aunts and cousins were already in the kitchen. Soon eggs would be cracking into frying pans and sausages would be on the griddle.

Jacob Turner saw Jane coming down the steps. He stood and held out his arms. "I'm so sorry, my darling."

Jane hugged him. "Thanks for coming, Jacob."

"Anything I can do, you let me know," he said. "You need help with the funeral or anything, you call me."

"I will."

". . . in 1925 in Napoli . . . uh, Naples . . . Italy," Aunt Lucy said into the phone. "He came to this country with his mother and three older brothers in . . ."

Jacob released her from their hug. "The *Chronicle*," he said softly, and went back to sit with Lucy.

Jane looked from Jacob to her aunt and realized that Aunt Lucy was calling in her brother's obituary.

The front door opened and one of Jane's cousins, Claudia,

came in with her five-year-old daughter. The girl, Lisa, was still in her pajamas. Claudia kissed Jane on the cheek. "Charlie's still at work. He'll come by later. He sends his love."

"Thank you," Jane said. She turned and saw Kenny coming out of the kitchen. He carried a baked ham to the dining-room table and set it down next to a basket of bread.

Jane went to him and put her head on his shoulder.

Kenny kissed her hair. "How're you feeling?"

"Heavy. Sad and heavy."

"I know." He looked around. "Your family is amazing. It's what, two-thirty in the morning and they all keep coming. And the food!"

"They loved my dad," Jane said, tears coming to her eyes in an unexpected rush.

Kenny held her close. "I had an idea."

Jane tilted back to see him. "What?"

"I don't want to step on any Italian traditions or anything. But how about for after your father's funeral, we throw him one last barbecue? Here, in the backyard."

"Oh, Kenny," Jane said. "Poppy would love it." She buried her face into his neck. "Thank you."

— —

Kenny turned the key in the lock and held the door open for Jane. Numb and exhausted, she stepped inside.

The message light was blinking on the answering machine. Jane went to the Parsons table, the photograph of Poppy prominent among the others, and pressed "play."

"Jane, it's Ben. Kenny called and told us about your father. Mary and I send our love. Take as much time as you need, both of you. Hank will handle your investigation until you get back. Take care."

The tape advanced. "Hi, it's Hank. Ben just told me. I'm so sorry. I'll cover the Ozzie and Sally stuff for as long as you need. My love to you."

There was one more. "Uh, Inspector Candiotti, it's Mike Finney. I heard about your dad and want to say . . . uh, Vicki and I hope you're doing okay. If you need anything, a ride or something picked up, I hope you'll call. Uh, hello to Inspector Marks, too. Okay then. Bye."

"He's a sweet man."

Kenny sniffed a little laugh. "Don't get me started." He handed Jane a piece of paper. "Bobby left you a note."

" 'I split around eleven,' " Jane read. " 'My mom wanted me home by midnight. I hope your dad's okay. I'm sure he'll be fine. Thanks for dinner. The pizza was great. Bobby.' "

Jane looked up. "Oh, Ken. Both my parents are gone and here I am . . . I don't know . . . feeling kind of exposed."

Kenny put his arms around her and she let go, her sobs coming in long, gulping tremors.

"I've got you," he whispered into her hair. "I've got you."

— —

Jane opened her eyes in the dark. Like a long-ago dream suddenly remembered, she understood that it was true.

Her father was dead.

Kenny slept next to her, his breathing strong and steady. Jane touched the scar on his chest with her fingertips and realized she had much to be grateful for.

She slipped out of bed and went down the hall to the living room. She sat on the window seat, pulling her knees to her chest, and looked outside.

The vaguely indistinct mounds of the sleeping homeless dotted the green. She knew that on a hot night like this, the cops wouldn't hassle them.

Someone had forgotten to take the flag down from the Harbor Office roof. It hung curled around its pole, still at half-mast because of the police killings.

Stars glimmered off the surface of the bay like diamond dust. Jane raised her eyes to the sky. She chose a star, a bright one, and stared at it. Then she closed her eyes, its afterimage a white dot behind her eyelids.

"Goodbye, Poppy," she said.

— —

"Open all night. Open all day," Punky-Boy said. "Who needs sleep anyway?" He was buzzing on a high he'd bartered from Marco. A fistful of bullets for his .357 in exchange for another night's worth of uncut magic.

"How much?" Carpenter asked, shirtless in the night.

"Way I see it," Punky-Boy said. "You come to me instead of a gun store 'cause you're a con. Am I right, or am I right?"

"You're a genius. How much?"

"One-fifty."

Carpenter nodded and thumbed seven twenties and a ten from the roll of bills he'd gotten from Mickey Title. He handed them over to Punky-Boy and picked up two boxes of .22-caliber shells and a silencer.

"You hear about them cops?" Punky-Boy asked as he folded the money into his sock.

"Me and everyone else."

"News said it was a twenty-two did it." Punky-Boy closed his suitcase. The sun was coming up and he didn't expect any more customers for a few hours. "And I'm all like thinkin', maybe it's one of my babies been doin' the damage." He grinned at Carpenter. "And I'm all like thinkin' maybe it's that big mean con doin' us all such a public service."

Carpenter dropped the silencer and the ammunition into the pocket of his chinos and lit a cigarette. The smoke wafted up to his eyes, stinging them. "And I'm thinking, you talk too fuckin' much."

Punky-Boy held up his hands. "I'm cool, brother. I'm cool. What you do with all them bullets is your business. Know what I mean?"

Carpenter turned and headed for the roof access door, his boots cracking the tar paper. He knew from prison that guys who talked too much ended up doing one of two things: talking to the wrong people, or getting themselves killed.

He knew that, before too long, he'd have to take care of Punky-Boy.

The cost of doing business.

34

E<small>VERYBODY CAME.</small>

The family. Extended now from Seattle to Florida. Even Cousin Guy came from Mexico City with his pretty young wife.

The neighbors.

Some of whom had lived on the same street as Poppy their whole lives. Some of whom had only just moved there.

The friends.

Two older men who were all that was left of the Thursday-night poker club. Jacob Turner sat with Aunt Lucy.

Rosemary brought her new baby daughter.

Poppy's casket was in front of the altar, sprays and wreaths dripping down its sides. There was a basket from Precinct Nineteen and a huge arrangement of Poppy's favorite flowers, bird of paradise, from Jacob.

When Father Patricola finished his sermon, he announced that there would be a barbecue for Poppy instead of the more traditional reception. Appreciative laughter murmured through the congregation.

"We were going to do maps," Father Patricola said, "but everybody knows where Paolo's house is."

— —

Jane sat on the railing of the back porch.

Kenny was at the grill, steam billowing as he cooked. She loved how easily he fit in, affable and confident, with her family. Aunt Lucy and Jacob were at the picnic table. Jacob started to pour her an iced tea. She held her hand up and took a sip from his beer instead.

Rosemary was breast-feeding little Margaret on the steps of the gazebo. She looked up and saw Jane watching her. Jane nodded, acknowledging that Rosemary, her closest cousin growing up, was now somehow different from her.

The screen door opened and Timmy, his camera around his neck, came out. "I've been looking all over for you," he said to Jane.

"I've been right here. What's up?"

"I wanted to give you this." He handed Jane a large grey envelope.

Curious, she took it from him and slid out an eight-by-ten photograph of Poppy and her that Timmy had taken at the last barbecue. In the picture, her head was resting on her father's shoulder. Poppy's dark eyes were blazing like black coals.

"Oh, Timmy . . . it's so beautiful."

"It's a good one, huh?" Timmy hugged his sister, holding on to the embrace a few seconds longer than Jane expected. When he pulled away, the side of his mouth twitched into an embarrassed smile. "Whew," he said, "Poppy's really gone."

Jane put her hand on his shoulder. "We need to talk about the house."

"What about it?"

"About what we should do with it," Jane said. "Do you want it?"

"Oh . . . I don't think I could . . ."

"Should we try to sell it?" Jane asked. "Would that be best?"

"I guess."

"Okay, then." Jane nodded tightly. "Maybe you could make some calls?"

"Okay, then," Timmy said. Looking at his feet, he shuffled down the stairs and waded into the crowded backyard.

Jane watched as, whenever someone came up to Timmy, either to console him or engage him in conversation, he would quickly raise his camera, snap a photo, and move on. A pane of glass always between himself and reality.

Jane slid the picture back into the envelope and swung her legs over the rail. She dropped down to the yard and joined Aunt Lucy and Jacob at the picnic table.

"How you doin', Auntie?"

"I'm fine, dear. You gonna take some time off?"

Jane shook her head. "Can't."

"But . . ."

"I know what you're going to say, Auntie, and you're right."
She looked from Lucy to Jacob. "There's death all around me.
My friends . . . Poppy. It's hard to explain, but a sort of wartime
mentality takes over, and we just do our jobs." She glanced to
the picnic table, where the cops from Precinct Nineteen had gathered. "There's a terrible person doing terrible things out there,
and if I worry only about myself . . . then I can't stop him."

Lucy smiled her understanding. "Well, if you can't worry about
yourself, then let your old Aunt Lucia do it for you."

Jane leaned over and kissed her. "Deal."

"As long as we're doing that," Jacob said, "there's something
we want to talk to you about."

"Does the word 'marriage' enter into it?"

"Actually," Jacob said, "the word was 'baby.' "

Lucy took her hand. "You know I'm the one who always
stopped the others from teasing you whenever the subject came
up. I knew how lonely you were and how much you wanted what
everyone else had." She squeezed Jane's hand, her eyes moist and
sincere. "It's time, Jane."

Jane let her head fall forward and she gave out a little laugh.
"I know it is, Auntie. But I'm just not sure about marriage yet. I
mean, Kenny and I are doing great and—"

"Then just have a baby," Lucy said.

Jane looked up. "Without being married?"

"You wouldn't be the first." Lucy's eyes gleamed with mischief.
She glanced over to Father Patricola, who stood under the oak
tree talking with a man she didn't know. "I won't tell the pope
if you won't."

Kenny and two of the cousins waded into the crowd, their arms
laden with heaping platters.

Lieutenant Spielman and his wife helped themselves, then
passed the platter to Benjy.

Jacques Carpenter waited for Father Patricola to take a piece of chicken from a tray. Then he helped himself to a spicy Italian sausage. He took a bite, his gaze drifting over to the part of the yard where the cops were eating. The young Spielman boy took some food and passed the platter over to a heavyset man.

Carpenter had seen the obituary in the *Chronicle*. "Survived by daughter Jane, son Timothy, and sister, Lucia," it had said. "A barbecue will be held at the family home at 314 Oak Street, San Leandro, to celebrate the life of Paolo Candiotti. All are welcome."

Carpenter slipped his hand into his pocket. His fingers closed around the grip of his .22. It felt solid and powerful in his hand, full of potential. Casually searching with his eyes, he found Jane sitting at the picnic table with an older man and woman.

Inspector Jane Candiotti had called him a coward. She had called him an animal.

She would die.

He would take her in time. But not today. He already knew who would be next.

There was a burst of laughter.

Jane looked up from the table. Mike Finney was pretending the huge tray of food was just for him. His wife, Vicki, nibbled on an ear of corn. Hank came up behind her and put his hand on her tummy, and Jane remembered that she, too, was pregnant.

"Hey, Mike," Hank said with a wink. "It's Vicki who's supposed to be eating for two."

Finney beamed, loving the attention.

Jane noticed some of her relatives watching Hank. A celebrity in their midst.

Behind the cops, at a respectful distance, was Martha Berry, an old roommate of Jane's from San Francisco State. She stood off to the side with her husband, whose name Jane had forgotten. She hadn't seen Martha for years and had been surprised when she walked into the church for Poppy's service. They had exchanged a hug made awkward by fifteen years of being apart, of living separate lives in separate worlds. Martha, tanned and obviously well-off, had whispered into Jane's ear that they must get together soon.

Stevie, one of Jane's cousins, came up and held a tray of barbecue out to Martha and her husband. They declined, and, after a few minutes, slipped out of the yard.

Father Patricola wiped his mouth and turned to Jacques Carpenter. "I'm going to visit with Paolo's sister. It's always nice talking with someone who is as devoted to the Bible as you."

"Goodbye, Father," Carpenter said. "God bless."

Kenny was heading back to the grill when Jane caught up to him. "You eat yet?"

"Not really."

Jane leaned into him. "Me either."

The gate creaked and a man in a white shirt and chinos, his back to Jane, held it open as Timmy carried in a cooler of soft drinks. The man nodded to Timmy and left.

"Amazing," Jane said, "I didn't know Poppy knew so many people."

Kenny put the platter on the table next to the grill. "It's the food," he said as he pulled her to him.

Two of the younger cousins climbed into Poppy's hammock and set it to rocking back and forth. It swung in wide arcs, almost tumbling them out several times as they squealed with delight.

Father Patricola arrived at the picnic table and sat across from Aunt Lucy and Jacob.

Jane caught Aunt Lucy watching her and Kenny, and she smiled.

35

Jane lay in the bubble bath, soaking away the day.

The barbecue had broken up late, after dark; people not wanting to leave. She and Timmy and Aunt Lucy had closed up Poppy's house while Kenny and some of the others cleaned up the yard.

Then, while Kenny retrieved the Explorer, Jane had pulled the front door closed and turned the dead bolt. She had put her hand flat on the leaded glass window above the doorbell.

The sounds, the smells, that had lived behind that door for so long had all come rushing back to her. Jane had touched her forehead to the glass, her breath fogging the window. A single lamp burned next to her father's reading chair.

"Oh, Poppy," she had whispered before turning away.

Jane smoothed down the mountain of bubbles before her with the back of her hand. She heard the floorboards creak in the hallway and Kenny came into the bathroom.

"Feeling better?"

"I'm okay. Just sad, is all."

"It's that kind of day."

"Thanks for being so terrific today."

Kenny shrugged. "The father of the woman I love died. It's what we do for each other, isn't it? Otherwise, what's the point?" He brought a package, wrapped in newspaper, from behind his back. "Here."

Jane shook the bubbles off her hands. "What is it?"

"Just something. Sorry 'bout the wrapping."

Jane tore the newspaper away. "Oh, Ken," she said, tears warming her eyes.

Kenny had taken Timmy's photograph of Jane and Poppy and put it in his antique silver frame.

"You like?"

"I love," Jane said. "It's so generous of you."

Kenny sat on the floor, his back against the radiator. "The woman I love," he said again.

Jane wiped the frame off with a hand towel and set it down on the bath mat. She looked to Kenny. He sat there, his forearms across his knees, his hands dangling, looking back at her.

"What?" she asked.

"I know it's couples protocol to wait at least a year before such conversations," he began. "But, I've been doing some thinking."

"About?"

"Let's get married."

Jane smiled warmly. "The thought's crossed my mind." She paused, knowing this was right. "So, this is how you propose? On your butt on the floor of a bathroom?"

"With you in a bubble bath. What could be better?"

"C'mere, you."

Kenny stood up and took off his clothes. "Room for one more?"

"In life, or in the tub?"

"How about both?"

"How about yes?" Jane scooted forward and Kenny slipped in behind her. She leaned back against his chest and he kissed her hair.

"This is one of those moments," Kenny said, "that we'll re-member forever."

"Good for us. We deserve it."

Kenny took Jane's left hand. "And your mother's ring goes"—he stroked her third finger—"here."

"What about you? What kind of ring do you want?"

"Simple and gold." He sat up a little straighter. "Maybe we should go see Jacob on the way in tomorrow."

"I'll call him later."

"I already did. We have an eight-thirty appointment."

Jane laughed. "Feeling a little sure of yourself, are you?"

"I've never been so sure of anything in my life."

Jane dropped her head back on his shoulder. "Oh, Ken."

"Hmm?"

"Poppy won't be there."

Kenny slid his arms around her waist. "Yes, he will."

— —

Union Square.

Surrounded by posh hotels and department stores, it was the last oasis of green in the heart of the city.

During the day it was a tourist attraction: musicians and food vendors, jugglers and souvenir peddlers.

At night everything changed.

Panhandlers slept on the low walls lining the crisscross walkways. Small-time drug deals took place in the open. A flash of money, a dime bag palmed and pocketed.

A couple of lost souls puffing spliff and tapping their bongos were driving the hotel patrons in the nearby tower suites crazy.

Small Joey, decked out in too many gold necklaces, leaned against the Naval Memorial in the middle of the park. He was fifty years old, as solid as a bank vault.

Union Square was his.

He checked his neon-green beeper. Seven messages and it wasn't even midnight. Another big night.

His internal radar sensed the young Chinese couple approaching him. He saw the girl, maybe eighty pounds, stop and hang back. The boy, not much taller than five feet, shuffled up. His eyes were glassed and his brain was blown. Small Joey liked this kid. He was a good customer.

When he paid.

"I need something, Joey," the boy said.

"So do I. It's called money." Small Joey felt his beeper vibrate. Jesus, he thought, what a night. Must be the heat.

"Just one bag." The kid fidgeted from foot to foot. "Me and Marci will split it."

"And I get paid when?"

The kid looked at his feet as if wondering why they were still moving. "Tomorrow. Maybe even tonight if I can get it together."

Small Joey leveled him with an icy stare. "What's the first thing I told you when you started buying shit from me?"

The kid swallowed, his mouth dry and hot. "You said you had two words for me."

"Being?"

"No credit."

"Way I see it, if I give you stuff now, you'll come back again."

The kid's eyes brightened. "Yeah, yeah! That's right. I'm definitely coming back. You're my man, Joey." He looked over his shoulder and smiled at Marci.

"What you don't understand, 'cause you spend your entire life all fucked up, is, if I don't give you the stuff . . . you'll still come back anyways." He spit at the base of the statue. "Only next time, you'll have money."

This was beyond the kid. "Are you gonna help me out or not?"

Small Joey smiled, his gold tooth with the diamond stud flashing in the light from a street lamp. "Not."

"Fuck you, asshole!" the kid yelled, so angry he drooled on himself.

"See you tomorrow," Small Joey said.

Marci grabbed her boyfriend's arm and dragged him away.

As Small Joey watched them go, he noticed someone light a cigarette on the park bench to his right. He was surprised. Small Joey thought he'd scoped the area pretty well and he hadn't seen this big guy sit down. He narrowed his eyes to check him out.

Jacques Carpenter sat on the back of the bench, rocking and smoking. Looking at Small Joey, and not looking at him. He watched as Small Joey pulled his bright green beeper from his belt. Then he pulled a cell phone from his back pocket and dialed a number, the beeps playing a melody above the bongo pulse.

Carpenter stepped down off the bench and started out of Union Square.

He flexed the fingers of his right hand.

Small Joey was already dead.

—·—

36

Every time I come here," Kenny said as he and Jane crossed the lobby of the Transamerica Building, "I hate it even more."

Jane stopped to let a UPS deliveryman push a four-wheeled cart toward the freight elevator. "It's not like we're going to live here. We're just coming to look at rings."

"Okay, but I still reserve the right to hate it."

"The record shall so reflect."

They went up to the security desk. The same burly guard, Lewis Parker, stood watching over the monitors. Jane smiled at him. "Jane Candiotti and Ken Marks for Jacob Turner Fine Jewels."

Parker regarded them. "Police business or personal?"

Kenny stiffened. "Whatever our business is, it's none of yours."

The top of Parker's bald head pinked up with a flush of anger. He leaned forward, his shoulder muscles bulging beneath his blue blazer. "All business in this building is mine."

Before Kenny could respond, Jane said in a soothing voice, "Jacob Turner is an old friend of the family. He's expecting us."

Parker looked from Kenny to Jane. Then he scribbled something on his clipboard. "Forty-fifth floor. Second set of elevators." He pointed to the elevators behind them and Jane noticed the serpentine tail of his tattoo at the edge of his shirt cuff. She glanced at Kenny. He had seen it, too. "Thank you very much."

Jane tugged at Kenny's jacket. "Here we go, dear." Kenny reluctantly broke eye contact with Parker and walked away with Jane. "That's a good boy."

"Guy like that could give the highly exalted position of security guard a bad name."

"God," Jane said as they entered the middle elevator, "do we really look that much like cops?"

They turned together to look at their reflections in the mirrored ceiling of the elevator car. Kenny shrugged. "I hate to say it, but—"

"Don't even *think* of finishing that sentence."

When they reached the forty-fifth floor, the elevator doors slid open and they stepped out.

"Why can't we just live in there?" Kenny asked, looking back into the elevator. "Wood paneling, big-deal carpeting . . . the mirrored ceiling."

"No windows."

"Speaking of windows," Kenny said as he took in the vista from the reception area, "look at this fucking view."

"Well put."

Jane approached Mitch, the gatekeeper for Jewelers' Corner. "We're—"

"Marks and Candiotti." He buzzed the lock on the thick glass door and Kenny held it open for Jane.

"These boys sure are efficient."

"I would hope so. There's a dozen jewel merchants up here."

"Inspectors!" Finney came out of Ahmet's Diamond Pavilion. He was wiping at a grease stain on his tie.

"Hey, Moby," Kenny said. "Nice outfit."

"Thanks." Finney lifted his tie to his mouth and sucked at the stain. "Ahmet's wife made lamb kebab. Want some?"

"It's eight-thirty in the morning," Kenny said.

Finney shrugged. "Couldn't wait." Jane and Kenny started to head down the hallway. "Uh, Inspector Candiotti," Finney said, "sorry about your dad." He etched a thick line in the carpeting with the side of his shoe. "Barbecue was great, though."

"Thanks, Mike. We're glad you were there."

They walked past the other showrooms, already busy with customers.

"Why so busy?" Jane asked.

"Everyone's cleaning out their old inventory. Should be some pretty good prices," Finney explained. "Making room for the big Christmas shipments."

They arrived at Jacob Turner Fine Jewels. Before Kenny could touch his finger to the doorbell, the lock buzzed open.

Jacob came out from the back room. "Ach. Welcome, welcome." He pulled Jane and Kenny into a vigorous hug. "I was so happy to hear from you." He nodded to Finney. "Hello, Michael."

Jane squeezed Jacob's hand. "Thanks for tearing yourself away from the *Today* show," she said, pointing to the television behind the display case.

"No matter. My Katie Couric's on vacation."

Jane was drawn to the window. She looked out and saw the Golden Gate Bridge cutting an orange swath from the bottom of the hill to the horizon. Jacob glanced at Kenny and a silent moment of understanding passed between them.

"This view is amazing, Jacob," Kenny said. "No wonder you like it here."

Finney was watching Jane as well. "This is only the forty-fifth floor, Inspector Marks. You should check out the view from the spire." He smiled with enthusiasm. "Wanna see?"

Jane looked to Kenny, knowing that his sense of adventure would override his inherent dislike of Finney. "Why not?"

Jane turned toward him. "Ken . . ."

"Five minutes."

——

"I'm not really supposed to do this," Finney said as he unlocked the gunmetal-grey door.

"Your secret is safe with us," Kenny said as he and Jane stepped into the cavernous chamber at the base of the spire.

"It's two hundred and twelve feet from here to the top," Finney said, his voice echoing in the vast space.

Jane and Kenny looked up. A series of steel staircases zigzagged up the wall to the apex of the spire.

Wind whistled through the louvered aluminum windows, and the floor thrummed with the vibration of a monstrous machine somewhere below.

Jane drifted to the east-facing wall and peered out through the slatted window. She saw the iron-grey tops of the Bay Bridge's towers. The next time she went over that bridge to San Leandro, to her childhood home, Poppy wouldn't be there.

"Where do these stairs go to?" Kenny asked.

"There's an airplane beacon at the top of the spire," Finney explained. "Those stairs are for the guys who service it."

Kenny started up the first flight of steps, the sound of his shoes on the steel tread echoing off the walls.

"Ken," Jane said.

He turned to her, a mock pout on his lips. "Aw please, Mom."

"You said five minutes."

Kenny hopped down. "You're no fun."

Jane slipped her arm around his waist and guided him to the exit door. "Yes, I am."

Finney, uneasy with this display of affection, averted his eyes as he tugged the door closed.

———

"I pulled some samples for you," Jacob said. "Just for an idea."

Jane and Kenny both reached for the same ring, a simple gold band.

Taking Kenny's hand in hers, Jane slipped the ring onto his finger. "What do you think?"

Kenny stared at the ring, then looked up to Jane. His lips parted, ready to speak. Then he glanced at Jacob. Finney stood by the door, watching the customers move from showroom to showroom.

"Uh . . ." Kenny began. "Uh . . ." He smiled sheepishly, unable to get the words out. "Well . . . uh . . ." He put his hand on top of the display case and moved his ring finger up and down. "I, uh, always thought . . . it's just that . . . uh . . ."

Jane and Jacob shared a knowing smile. "This is a huge thing we're doing, Kenny," Jane said gently. "It's okay to be nervous."

Kenny looked up quickly. "I'm not nervous."

"Tell you what," Jacob said, coming to Kenny's rescue. "Think about it during the week. Then come back this Friday. All of us up here are getting our Christmas shipments then. Diamonds, gold, everything. I'll pull some rings for you and you can have first choice of anything I have."

Finney turned from the window. "You talking about Friday?"
Jacob nodded.

"Hank told me all about it." Finney grinned like a child. "I can't wait."

"Okay," Kenny said as he slid the ring off his finger. "We'll come back. But only if Moby and his discerning taste will be here to help me choose."

Jane kicked the side of Kenny's shoe.

"Sure, Inspector," Finney said. "I'll help you out. Me and Vicki are kind of experts at this stuff."

Jane and Kenny glanced at Finney's wedding ring. It was an oversized gold-plated band with a gaudy inlaid pattern of silver.

"Oh God," Kenny said under his breath.

Jane tugged at his arm. "C'mon, Ken. The real world awaits."

Kenny met her eyes and they both grew serious. The real world meant the deaths of Ozzie and Sally, and the dismal work ahead of them.

"Yeah," Kenny said, the playfulness gone from his voice. "Let's go."

37

H ERE'S WHAT WE KNOW and what we don't," Hank said to Jane and Kenny.

They were in Interrogation Room One, cardboard boxes, accordion files, computer printouts stacked on every available surface.

"I got some Explorer Scouts to help with going through all this stuff and basically it's coming up zeroes."

"What about Atlanta?" Kenny asked. "Anything from the National Crime Computer?"

"More questions than answers so far. But we're doing second- and third-level scans. We'll probably hear from them later tonight."

Jane riffled through a box of files. "Anything with the FBI on the voice from the call box?"

Hank shook his head. "Until they get a better voice sample, all they can say is it's a nonspecific accent. Probably not California, but other than that they can't pinpoint it yet."

Jane slid the file box across the table. "On the off-chance we're wrong about the revenge angle—but I don't think we are—let's try coloring outside the lines." She looked to Hank. "Have someone check the full-moon paradigms, numerology on the dates of the murders, Zodiac stuff, the whole bit."

"We've done most of that while you were out," Hank said. "We even tried to see if there was a geographic pattern to the three murders. But it's too soon to tell."

Kenny swiveled in his chair. "We've investigated every police brutality or wrongful-death lawsuit verdict for the past decade."

Jane spotted Lieutenant Spielman making his way through the

bullpen. He stopped and motioned for her to join him in his office. She started for the door. "Two things: go back twenty, twenty-five years if you have to, and take a look at any cases that may have been thrown out of court. People like that can feel a double sense of being fucked over."

"We're on it," Kenny said.

Jane headed for the door. "Something else I've been thinking about." She stopped at the doorway. "Ozzie was killed at that bridal shop, a place he'd been visiting for years. Sally was killed at that underpass, a place where cops go all the time to chill out, smoke, whatever. It could be coincidence . . . or our bad guy might be stalking his victims, learning their habits, and then doing the deed."

Kenny looked to Hank. They both nodded as they chewed on this. "Might be something there," Kenny said.

"Might be," Jane said as she stepped into the squad room. Finney was just arriving from the Transamerica Building for the noon shift. Cheryl Lomax was back at her dispatch console. Although she was gamely trying to do her work, Jane could see that her spirit was gone. She had a picture of herself and Sally Banks, taken at a department softball game, taped to her monitor.

Someone had set a coffee can for Sally next to Ozzie's. Beneath it was a handwritten sign, LOVING CAT NEEDS LOVING HOME. There was a color Xerox of Vanilla sleeping in a wedge of sunlight on Sally's brown couch.

Lieutenant Spielman was on the phone when Jane came to his door. He gestured for her to come in.

"That's really considerate of you guys," Lieutenant Spielman said into the phone. "Tell your editors all of us here at the Nineteenth appreciate it." He hung up and looked to Jane. "That was Cameron Sanders from the *Chronicle*. They're going to run that story on Benjy and me in tomorrow's paper. The thinking is, some positive human-interest spin on cops might help department morale."

"I'm thinking they're right." Jane sat in the guest chair. "You wanted to see me?"

"I know we've all got a job to do, but I wanted to offer you a little time off, if you want it."

"I appreciate that. But I've got this case jumping up and down on my chest." Jane leaned forward, her gaze steady and grim. "Ben, I'm scared shitless this guy's going to kill again, and we have no real leads." She stood up, agitated. "I feel like we're playing Russian roulette here." She looked out to the bullpen. "Anyone could be next."

"What do you need? How can we help?"

"Main thing we need is manpower. Hank's pulled up a mountain range of files and—"

"You got it," Lieutenant Spielman said. "What else?"

"I need our bad guy to make a mistake before someone else dies."

Lieutenant Spielman pushed back from his desk and rose. "Jane, you're the best homicide cop in the city. Either you're going to crack this case, or he's going to fuck up and you'll pounce on him." He came around and put his hands on her shoulders. "I believe that, and I believe in you."

Jane nodded solemnly. "Thanks, Ben." She turned to go, then stopped.

"We're all good at what we do, but we sure could use a little luck."

Lieutenant Spielman picked up his phone. "Luck's a good thing," he said as he dialed.

Jane went to the door.

"Cheryl," Lieutenant Spielman said into the phone, his face creased with worry. "Find Benjy for me, would you please?"

Jane looked back to him.

He looked up.

Jane nodded and pulled the door closed.

38

THE MUCH-HATED L.A. Dodgers were coming to 3Com Park, and the head groundskeeper wanted his great lawns to be green and bright for tomorrow's game.

But the eighth consecutive day of triple-digit temperatures had sent one of his workers to the hospital and he had ordered the rest of the crew home before their shift was done. They had agreed to come in first thing in the morning, before the sun was high, to finish prepping the field. The last one out, like the captain leaving his ship, the head groundskeeper had set the field sprinklers on high for a good four-hour soaking and left the park early for the first time in his seventeen years working there.

Three men huddled in conversation behind home plate. The shade offered little relief and they looked longingly at the clouds of water rising from the sprinklers. Just the slightest breeze would carry the cooling mist their way, but even notoriously windy 3Com Park seemed to have yielded to the cruel heat. The air was as still as the inside of a closet.

The men spoke quickly in Vietnamese. The staccato rhythm of their language sounded like verbal machine-gun fire. Finally, an agreement was reached and Punky-Boy offered his hand.

The two others, twin brothers from the old country, shook his hand and sealed the deal. One of the brothers handed over an envelope bulging with cash. Punky-Boy pocketed it and shook hands with them again.

The twins nodded and descended the steps of the visitors' dugout. They hurried down the runway, past the visitors' locker room to a little-used door that emptied out to an area near one of the loading docks. Taking a handkerchief from his pants pocket, one of the men turned the knob and pushed the door open. They stepped into the brilliant sunlight. The driver of their Lincoln Town Car clicked the doors open. They climbed into the air-conditioned interior and were soon driving away across the shimmering blacktop.

Punky-Boy smiled.

He had just made three thousand dollars for an hour's work and there was more, a lot more, where that came from. No more nickel-and-dime, one-gun-at-a-time bullshit, he thought to himself as he watched the sprinklers ratchet off burst after burst of water.

Something caught his attention. Wiping the sweat from his eyes, he peered into the mist. Something in there was moving. Toward him.

A man.

Emerging from the vapor like a ghost coming out of a ground fog came Jacques Carpenter.

Punky-Boy started forward a half step. Then he stopped and waited as Carpenter, hands deep in his pockets, came fully out of the spray. Dripping, his clothes clinging to his powerful body, he crossed over home plate and passed into the shadows where Punky-Boy stood.

Punky-Boy slipped his hand behind him until he found the reassuring grip of his .45 automatic. He was glad he always kept a round chambered. Ready for anything. He let out a little laugh. "That's one way to stay cool, huh?" He hoped his laughter had covered the sound as he clicked the safety off with his thumb. "How'd you find me, big guy?"

"Nothing you do's a secret." Carpenter strode forward, his hands still in his pockets. " 'Cause you talk so fuckin' much."

Punky-Boy took two steps back. He didn't want to have to kill this man. "Hey," he said as he continued to yield ground, "you can't be out of ammo already. I ain't heard nothing about no more dead cops."

Carpenter was five feet away and still coming.

Slowly, he began to take his hands out of his pockets.

Punky-Boy watched carefully, waiting to see a weapon. No way this big ex-con fuck was going to take him out with the .22 he'd sold him. When Carpenter's hands were fully in view, Punky-Boy felt a spasm of fear deep in his gut.

Jacques Carpenter was wearing rubber gloves.

Punky-Boy pulled his .45 from his waistband.

And then Carpenter was upon him.

Punky-Boy crouched low and started to raise his pistol, leveling it at Carpenter's soaking chest.

In a motion so swift and so sure that Punky-Boy never saw it, Carpenter whipped his hand across the space between them and grabbed Punky-Boy's hand. Then he jerked down with such ferocity that he snapped the radius and ulna clean away from the wrist.

Punky-Boy was so startled at the sound of his own bones breaking that all he could do was stare at his useless hand as it dangled like a stone before him.

The pain came a half second later, and he howled in agony. It was then that he noticed that his .45 was now in Carpenter's gloved hand.

Panicked, Punky-Boy spun around and clambered over the low fence leading to the field boxes. Glancing behind, he saw that Carpenter was coming after him.

His damaged arm hanging like a dead man, he pounded up the steps toward the main concourse. His hope was to fling himself into the shadowy labyrinth of concession stands, rest rooms, and stairways until he could figure a way out of there.

Punky-Boy pulled out his cell phone. He yanked on the antenna with his teeth and dialed 911 with the thumb of his good hand.

It rang once, then a voice came on. "Nine-one-one. What is the nature of your emergency?"

"Yeah!" Punky-Boy screamed into the phone. "That guy killing all them cops is trying to kill me!" He crested the stairs and paused for a second to get his bearings. Out of the corner of his eye, he saw that Carpenter was only half a dozen steps below.

Punky-Boy tore across the concourse for the closest stairwell. "Hurry!" he gasped to the 911 operator. "He's crazy!"

"Sir," the dispatcher said, "what is your location?"

"Oh God!" Punky-Boy panted. "I'm at—"

Then the dispatcher heard a single gunshot, a curious echo seeming to wrap itself around the sound.

"Sir? Sir? . . . Are you there, sir?" She called her supervisor over and played back the tape. They heard a few more indistinguishable noises and realized that the caller's phone was still connected to them.

"Patch this through to Com Lab," the supervisor ordered. "Maybe they can triangulate the signal and get us a location." He started to hurry from the room. "I'm gonna put a trace on the line."

When the supervisor left, the 911 operator sat there for a moment, gathering her thoughts. She had, she believed, just heard someone die in her headset.

It was her second day on the job.

39

THE EXPLORER ROCKETED through the parking lot of 3Com Park and ground to a skidding stop next to the crime-scene van.

Jane, Kenny, and Hank threw their doors open and jumped out.

A young uniformed patrolman hustled up. Kenny started to speak, but the cop went past him and held out his hand to Hank. "Inspector Pagano, I'm Wade Levens. A pleasure, sir. A pleasure and an honor."

Hank shook his hand. "Thank you." He gestured to Jane and Kenny. "This is Inspector Candiotti and Inspector Marks. Inspector Candiotti is in charge."

Wade Levens seemed confused.

"The police-officer shootings," Hank went on, "belong to Inspector Candiotti. Inspector Marks is her number two. I'm just along for the ride."

Jane broke away and started for the gate. "Where's the victim?"

Levens ran ahead of her. "In a stairwell off the main concourse." He looked around and lowered his voice. "But, ma'am, he's all dead and everything. It's gross."

"I'm a homicide inspector, Officer Levens." She leaned in close to him. "I kinda get off on this stuff."

"Oh," Levens said. "Oh, okay!" He hurried down the gangway. "Let's go, then!"

They went through a tunnel and came out onto the field, back into the withering heat. Almost running now, being pulled along by the possibility of a crack in the case, Jane hustled past a forensics team taking shoeprint molds near home plate.

She led Kenny and Hank up the steps, her mood shifting, darkening. Above them a video team and a coroner's team worked in the shadows of the main concourse.

Aaron Clark-Weber straightened up from a water fountain and approached them. "This is a weird one." He led them to the stairwell behind a row of ticket booths. While their eyes adjusted to the light, a fingerprint tech stepped aside, and there was Punky-Boy.

Jane, Kenny, and Hank all squatted down. Aaron Clark-Weber, favoring his bad knee, sat on the second step next to the body.

There was a black hole the size of a grape in Punky-Boy's forehead. The entrance wound. The back of his head looked like somebody had punched his way out of Punky-Boy's skull with a sledgehammer. The exit wound. The wall behind and above him was splattered with hair, bone, and brain matter. His .45 was lying in a plastic bag at his feet.

But what drew their attention, more than the ravaged head of the victim, more than the gore dripping down the wall, was Punky-Boy's cell phone.

It had been rammed into his mouth.

It was seated there, half in and half out, in a muddle of broken teeth and blood. The phone's service light was on; the connection to the 911 dispatcher still active.

"Motherfuck," Kenny said under his breath.

"I would have to agree," Aaron said.

Jane pointed to the charred skin around the entry wound. "Powder burns?"

Aaron nodded. "And muzzle flash. This was one up-close-and-personal execution."

Kenny leaned in. "Witnesses?"

"Nothing," Aaron said. "Park's closed till tomorrow. Dodgers are coming."

A forensics man came up from the field. "Lieutenant," he said to Aaron, "we got some pretty good molds from the mud down there. They match up with some of the partials we got on the stairs."

"And?" Aaron asked.

"And he's a big guy. We haven't finished with the measurements yet, but I'd bet his shoe size is eleven and a half or twelve."

"Twelve and a half," Jane said as they rose.

"Yeah," Kenny agreed. "This is just angry and mean enough to be our guy."

"Brutal and excessive," Hank concurred. "Like the Skip Lacey killing."

Jane looked toward an upside-down Dixie cup. "The shell?"

"Yup. A forty-five."

"The shooter didn't bother to retrieve it," Kenny said, "because this one was different than the cop killings."

"Besides, the shell would only help us if we were looking for the murder weapon," Hank offered. "And we're not."

"But this is connected," Jane said. "Our dead friend here knew something or saw something or overheard something . . . and that's why he died."

Jane noticed Officer Levens hanging on the periphery of the cops who were securing the murder scene. "Hey, Levens," she called. "C'mere, would ya?"

Levens, puffing his chest just a little, came forward. "Yes, ma'am?"

"I need you to do me a favor," Jane said. "Take a couple of patrolmen and search this place. The stands, the bleachers, every nook, every cranny."

Levens's eyes widened. "You think the killer's still here?"

"No," Jane said. "But there may be a witness out there." She pointed to Punky-Boy. "He got in somehow. The killer got in somehow. Maybe someone else is in this place sleeping under the bleachers or something to beat the heat. Know what I mean?"

Levens flicked a look over to Hank, thrilled just to be standing in the inner circle. "You got it, ma'am." His right hand almost came up in a salute before he turned around and hurried off to recruit a couple of his friends.

Jane watched him go, then gestured to Punky-Boy's body. "So, Aaron, please tell me you know who he is."

Aaron sighed. "No ID yet. We found a bunch of money and a clip to a forty-five in his pockets. But that's all."

Kenny nudged the plastic bag containing the .45 with his toe. "Our bad guy probably shot him with his own gun."

"Looks that way," Aaron agreed.

"Prints?" Hank asked gesturing to Punky-Boy's ink-blackened fingers.

"Preliminaries show that the only prints on the weapon belonged to the deceased. Leads me to think that Mr. Twelve and a Half Shoes was wearing gloves."

Jane drew the men into a tight huddle. "We gotta ID this guy, Aaron," she said urgently.

"We put a name to the body," Kenny said, "then we get an address, then we get neighbors, then we get—"

Jane finished the sentence for him. "Then we get closer."

They watched as an investigator put a paper bag over Punky-Boy's left hand.

Jane looked up to Aaron. "Can we hot-fax his prints to Washington?"

Kenny nodded. "That big old crime-scene van has to be good for something."

"Already done," Aaron said.

"We hear back yet?" Jane asked, knowing the answer before Aaron spoke.

"No name, no address, no prints on file. The guy's probably an illegal." Aaron blew a huge exasperated sigh. "He's an orphan, Jane."

"So," Jane said, her frustration rising, "this body, this guy with a telephone shoved down his throat and half his head blown away . . . never existed?"

Aaron shook his head. "Not as far as the system is concerned."

"Then let's work outside the system," Jane said. "Hank, have this guy photographed and distribute the pictures to your friends over on the Asian Gang Task Force. I want the town papered with his photo."

Hank looked over to the police photographer and nodded. "You got it."

"Plus we need to—" Jane stopped when she noticed the crime-scene tech lift Punky-Boy's right arm in order to bag his hand. It flopped at an extreme, stomach-wrenching angle. "What the hell is that?"

"His right arm," Aaron explained, "is broken just above the wrist. Both bones snapped like Popsicle sticks."

"Could be," Kenny offered, "why he's no longer in possession of his own gun."

Aaron wiped the sweat from his forehead with his shirtsleeve. "That's what we were thinking."

"Then whoever did this," Jane said quietly, "is not only big and vicious. He's strong beyond all imagining."

40

JANE SPENT THE REST of the afternoon poring over the forensics reports from Punky-Boy's murder.

There had been only one set of fingerprints, the victim's, on the .45. The shooter, Jane agreed, must have been wearing gloves. A second call to the FBI fingerprint lab in Quantico had come up empty. The shoe prints taken from the molds near home plate at 3Com Park were a definitive match to those taken from the vacant lot where Sally Banks had been killed.

She read Officer Wade Levens's neatly typed crime-scene report. He and his men had found no other people in the park. Therefore, no possibilities of witnesses. Levens had, however, discovered an unlocked door near the visitors' locker room. He had secured the area and called in a crew from Aaron Clark-Weber's team to dust it for prints.

Good work, kid, Jane thought to herself.

She shook her head wearily. The relentless buzz of the electric fans was beginning to annoy her. She had a dead body positively linked to the murderer of Ozzie, Sally, and Skip Lacey. It was the mistake she had been hoping would turn up.

Or was it?

Why had the murderer been wearing gloves? If he was cautious and smart enough to wear gloves, then why had he repeatedly stepped in the mud, knowing that he was leaving behind such a distinctive clue? Why leave the murder weapon at the scene? Why jam the cell phone into the deceased's mouth? Why leave it on, still connected to 911?

Jane drew a quick breath of realization.

The killer was taunting the police.

Something about the murder at 3Com Park didn't fit. Something lingered deep in her gut. Something that made a difference. She'd had this feeling before, in other cases; and she knew that it would present itself in time.

Time was the one thing she didn't have.

Looking up from the paperwork, she let her gaze drift across the bullpen. Mike Finney was at the filing cabinets, looking for something, chewing on something. Lieutenant Spielman's office was unoccupied. He was down at the Hall of Justice briefing Chief McDonald. Kenny was in Interrogation Room One, working his way through the stacks of reports and inquiry follow-ups. Cheryl was at the dispatch console, talking quietly on the phone.

The stairwell door opened and Hank entered, returning from his meeting with the Asian Gang Task Force.

"Tell me something good," Jane said.

"Sorry," Hank said. "The victim's a new one to them. But the guys'll put the word out in a big way." He dropped the photos of Punky-Boy on her desk as he went by. "Something'll turn up."

"Yeah," Jane said softly. "Sure."

Sliding the photos so that they lay directly beneath her, she propped her chin in both hands and stared down at them. The horrific head wound. The bizarreness of the cell phone in the victim's mouth. The .45 in the plastic evidence bag.

Exasperated, she thought of going into Lieutenant Spielman's office to pilfer a soft drink from his mini-fridge, when something caught her eye.

In the fingerprint tech's photograph, the victim's right hand lay twisted at that disturbingly impossible angle.

Jane grabbed the preliminary medical report and scanned it. There, on page three, were the initial findings regarding the hand. As she read, her suspicions at the murder scene were confirmed. The breaking of the bones was not caused by a blow from some external object like a club or a crowbar. Rather, the radius and ulna showed evidence of having been fractured by a forceful downward twisting motion. The way one would break the neck of a chicken.

She looked up. "Hank," she said, and motioned for him to join her and Kenny in the interrogation room.

––

The first thing Jane noticed when she entered Interrogation Room
One was that Kenny had added the 3Com Park John Doe to the
blackboard. But, because that murder was different in so many
respects—there was no identity of the body, the lack of any mutilation to the eyes, the fact that the deceased was not a cop—he
had added the information below and to the side of the other
victims, a footnote to be drawn upon later.

Kenny and Hank listened intently as Jane recounted what she
had learned from the evidence so far.

They were in agreement that the killer of the 3Com Park John
Doe was almost certainly the killer of Ozzie, Sally, and Skip
Lacey.

Jane went on to read to them from the medical examiner's
report on the victim's right arm. "Remember how Aaron had said
that the bones in the deceased's arm had been broken like tooth-
picks."

Kenny turned his chair around backward and straddled the
seat. "Popsicle sticks."

"Huh?"

"Aaron said the 3Com Park victim's arm had been broken like
Popsicle sticks."

Jane shot him a look. "May I?"

Kenny smiled. "Please."

"Remember I was saying that not only was the killer vicious,
but that he was unbelievably strong?"

Kenny and Hank nodded, gesturing for her to go on.

"Then, when our killer broke that Asian kid's arm with his
bare hands, he finally made his first mistake." Jane began to pace
as she talked, trying to keep her thoughts in order. "Kenny,
you've got a mountain of paperwork on these tables. Rosters and
reports from mental hospitals and halfway houses from here to
hell and back. It could keep you busy for months."

Kenny and Hank seemed to catch on at the same moment.
"When was the last time," Kenny offered, "you saw someone
who's been in a mental hospital for any length of time in great
physical condition?"

Hank uncrossed his arms and rose. "Only about never."

Jane slapped her hand on the table. "So our guy, our killer, is a con. Has to be. That's all those guys do is work out. I mean, it's scary how strong we let them get in the name of rehabilitation." She turned to Kenny and Hank. "Look, guys, it's not much, but it's something. It means we can focus our efforts on prisoners, either paroled or escaped. It means we don't have to worry about chasing down thousands of mental patients out there . . . all of whom would have been dead ends."

Kenny closed the accordion file in front of him. "Thank God."

"And it means," Jane concluded, "that our killer has made his first mistake, and we're a little bit closer . . . which is closer than we've been before."

Kenny stood up and slid the chair under the table. "What if bigfoot is just some strong guy who works out and has never been in the joint?"

"I'd considered that," Jane said. "But the savagery of these murders and the fact that three of the victims were cops, adds up to a hard-ass con looking to settle some really ugly score."

"I agree," Hank said.

"Actually, so do I," Kenny said. "I was just floating a trial balloon here."

"So," Jane began, "let's put the mental-patient stuff aside for the time being and go over the release records of all the prisons on the West Coast. The lieutenant okayed some help in the manpower department for us. As soon as that happens, we'll broaden the search to include the whole country."

"We should probably start with cons arrested for violent crimes," Kenny said. "Murder, armed robbery, spousal abuse, the whole bit."

"Plus those whose arrests may have been particularly messy," Hank added. "Someone with a real hard-on for cops."

"I know we've covered this all before," Jane said, "but let's cross those with cons who have been suing the police departments, for wrongful arrests, brutality, whatever." She moved to the door. "I don't want to wait for this guy to make his next mistake."

She looked out to the bullpen, to the cops passing by the window. "Or worse."

It was well after nine in the evening when Lieutenant Spielman returned from the Hall of Justice.

Jane, with the help of Kenny and Hank, had brought him up-to-date on the 3Com Park John Doe and the fact that they'd probably never get an ID on him. Then she told him of her theory about the killer being an ex-con, and he had signed off on it.

Lieutenant Spielman told them that Chief McDonald had approved funds for extra manpower to help go through the avalanche of files.

"How 'bout some money to fix the damn air-conditioning?" Kenny had asked, only half joking.

Ben Spielman had smiled wearily and promised to see what he could do. Then he sent everyone home. "Until we catch this guy," he said, "the days'll be too long and the nights'll be too short. I want you all to rest up for the long haul."

Kenny took the cellular phone from the Explorer's console and dialed. "Hey, Bobby. It's your favorite uncle. Listen, I'm still planning to take you to Heart and Soul for a night of male bonding. But there's a lot of stuff happening at work and . . . well, there's a chance it might not happen." He listened for a moment as he stopped for a red light. "C'mon, Bobby, don't go getting all surly on me. There's some pretty drastic shit going on that's a lot bigger than you and me. Fine. See ya later."

Jane smiled at Kenny. "That went well." To her surprise, her eyes suddenly filled with tears.

Kenny looked to her. "What?"

"Poppy," Jane said softly. "His face sort of just flashed in my mind. That smile of his."

"I know. I think about him a lot, too."

Jane shifted in her seat. "Really?"

"Really."

As Jane turned to talk to Kenny, a primer-grey Camaro pulled up next to them at the intersection. Jacques Carpenter, a cigarette dangling from his lower lip, looked up at the Explorer. The back of Jane's head was three feet away from him, her dark hair wisping in the breeze from the air-conditioning.

The light turned green and Kenny gunned the engine, the Explorer leaping forward. Carpenter eased the Camaro into the wake of Kenny's exhaust and, maintaining his distance, followed Jane and Kenny to the Marina.

——

Kenny pulled up to the curb in front of the house.

Carpenter stopped at the near corner, his lights off.

Jane looked across to the Harbor Office. The flag had been taken in for the night. "Tell you what," Kenny said when she turned back to him. "How 'bout I cook us a late dinner?"

"But the cupboard's bare."

"Part of the offer is I go fill it while you go inside and have a bubble bath or some other girlie relaxation thing."

Jane leaned over and kissed him. "I accept." She opened her door. "You sure this isn't just an excuse for you to go shopping?"

Kenny feigned an injured look. "You do me wrong!"

"Get me some yogurt!" Jane called as Kenny drove away. Then she stood on the sidewalk and looked out across the bay. The Green was quiet tonight, not many people. The sound of low conversation and glasses clinking carried from a sailboat somewhere in the Marina.

Stretching her arms over her head, Jane turned and walked up the path to her house. She went inside and switched on the living-room light.

Carpenter parked the Camaro across the street from Jane's house and watched her through the bay window as she went down the hall.

He climbed out of his car and crossed the street. As he went up the steps to Jane's front door, he was aware of the weight of the .22 in his pants pocket.

He tried the doorknob. Locked. Then he glanced back to the street and, confident that he was unseen, unzipped his chinos.

Carpenter closed his eyes and let loose a strong stream of urine. It spattered against the doorjamb and puddled at the threshold near a flowerpot.

The feeling was rising in him again, from his chest to his throat. He swallowed back the faint nausea of anticipation.

And he knew that, this night, he would kill again.

Hurrying down the steps, filling with purpose, he was startled by a man walking with his dog. Carpenter slipped his hand into his pocket. But the man and dog just moved past without acknowledging him.

When they got to the corner and stopped, the man felt for the dog's neck with the back of his hand.

Carpenter, realizing that the man was blind, snorted a little laugh and crossed the street. Like a shark sensing blood in the water from miles away, he was being drawn back to the city by his next victim.

41

THE FRONT PAGE of the *Chronicle*'s Metro section had a large color photograph of Lieutenant Spielman and Benjy. Jane sat reading the paper and sipping a mug of tea.

"That the article from that day at the academy?" Kenny asked. He poured himself a cup of coffee.

"Yup." Jane sprinkled some granola over her yogurt.

"Anything interesting?"

"Just a puff piece." She held up the paper and read. " 'Rookie Patrol Officer Benjamin Spielman Junior, son of Lieutenant Benjamin Spielman of the Nineteenth Precinct, had always wanted to be on the force . . . blah, blah, blah . . . He loves helping people . . . et cetera, et cetera . . . We caught up with him on his lunch break at the docks near Pier Twelve. Watching the boats and feeding the seagulls is a great way to unwind, he says . . .' "

"Now that's some hard-hitting journalism." Kenny rubbed Jane's shoulders. "Sleep okay?"

"No." She tilted her head back and looked up to him. "You?"

"Nope. This case is just chewing on me."

"Kenny, the one thing we've learned after all this time is that although a murder case seems complicated—"

"And a serial-murder case even more so."

Jane nodded. "But no matter how complicated it seems, there's always something simple, almost pure, beneath it." She stood up. "That's what we have to find." She went to the sink and rinsed her dish. "Let's go to work."

"I was hoping you'd say that," Kenny said. "Who wants to spend a balmy morning down by the Marina when we can be sweating through our clothes at a police station?"

"Now you're talking." Jane tipped her mug and let the tea run into the sink. "I meant to tell you. When I got the paper this morning, I smelled something funny. I looked down and there was this pool of urine near the geranium pot."

"Either a dog or one of our homeless friends," Kenny said. "They should be moving on once the heat wave breaks."

"Disgusting, though."

"Look on the bright side."

"And that would be?"

"He only *peed* out there."

Jane grinned. "Yeah. We're the lucky—"

The phone rang. Jane reflexively looked at the clock on the stove. Six-thirty. She answered before the second ring. "Hello." She listened. "Hey, Hank."

Kenny put his coffee cup on the counter and moved closer to Jane.

"Shit," she said. "Okay, we're on our way." She hung up and looked to Kenny. "Someone found a body in Union Square."

"A cop?"

"Uh-uh."

"Then why call us?" Kenny asked. "Hank's rolling number one."

"The victim was shot in both eyes," Jane said, a quiver of dread creeping into her voice. "That makes it ours."

42

FIRST IT WAS THE SIRENS whooping to a stop below. Then the squawking of a dozen police radios. The guests of the St. Francis and the Grand Hyatt were drawn from the sanctuary of their air-conditioned suites to the rising heat of their balconies. Below them a squadron of homicide and forensics personnel swarmed over Union Square.

The hotel patrons focused on a dusty patch in the square's northwest corner. A group of uniformed and plainclothes cops mingled near a yellow plastic sheet. From the contour of the shape beneath it, everyone on the balconies understood that it covered a body.

Someone had been murdered, outside their rooms, while they slept.

In the heart of the city.

A crowd was gathering behind the police tape, pressing forward for a glimpse of the yellow sheet. Hank Pagano stood near the body, talking on his cell phone, scanning the faces of the onlookers. One of them recognized Hank and, grinning broadly, gave him the thumbs-up. Hank nodded curtly and turned away.

This wasn't the time or place.

Aaron Clark-Weber passed by Hank, a police video man close on his heel. "Get me a three-sixty of this whole area. Top to bottom."

The videographer shouldered his camera and went to work.

Kenny's black Explorer, its cherry dome light flashing on the roof, pulled up. He was about to get out when he looked to Jane. She sat still in the passenger seat, her hand flat against the glass of her window. Kenny touched her back. "What?"

Without turning, Jane said, "I got a bad feeling about this."

"If this is our guy again," Kenny said as he pushed open his door, "I'm right there with you in the bad-feeling department."

"Yeah." Jane climbed down from the Explorer. Kenny lifted the police tape and they scooched under.

"You hear anything on the street, I don't care how stupid you think it is," Hank said into the phone, "you call me. Day or night." He snapped the phone shut.

"Another one of your choirboys?" Kenny asked.

"Only takes one singing the right song."

Standing apart from them, Jane searched the faces in the crowd. A cable-car conductor, a couple of teenage tourists, a jogger, some city maintenance workers.

She turned to Hank. "Who called it in?"

"Male. Probably Caucasian. Didn't hang around."

Jane shielded her eyes and swept the surrounding buildings. "Security cameras?"

Aaron Clark-Weber came up. "Two from Tiffany's. One from the Hyatt. The St. Francis, which is closest, has one. But it's busted."

"Just our luck." Jane scraped the toe of her shoe in the dirt. "Aaron, please pull—"

"Already done," Aaron said. "The videos are on their way downtown. And the nine-one-one tape should be on your desk by the time you get back."

Kenny turned to Hank. "You see the body?"

"Yeah. Some drug dealer."

"Both eyes?" Jane asked.

"Both eyes."

"Shit," Kenny said. "A drug dealer? Doesn't make sense."

"Either our killer is expanding his horizons," Jane offered, "or we have a copycat out there."

She noticed a black-and-white patrol car arriving. Benjy Spielman got out. Slipping his nightstick into his utility belt, he went up to the uniformed sergeant-in-charge. Jane caught Kenny's eye. That sergeant should have been Ozzie.

"Let's take a look," Jane said. Aaron led her and Kenny to the yellow sheet. She glanced back to make sure that Hank would intercept Benjy and take him under his wing. Hank was already sending him to the St. Francis to begin his interviews.

Hank caught her looking at him and shrugged.

Benjy wove his way through the gathering crowd. He passed the city maintenance workers and the two tourists. Looking down to unbutton his shirt pocket and retrieve his notebook, he bumped into the jogger. " 'Scuse me."

The jogger looked at Benjy's name tag. "It's okay, Officer." Jacques Carpenter smiled, knowing that Benjy wouldn't recognize him in this context. "That fellow in there dead?"

" 'Fraid so," Benjy answered as he started across the street to the St. Francis.

Carpenter watched him go, the sense memory of killing Small Joey still resonating in his right forearm. "Soon enough, kid," he hissed toward Benjy's back. Then he stepped past the city maintenance workers and nudged against the perimeter tape. He watched as Jane knelt next to the plastic sheet.

Aaron Clark-Weber took a corner of the sheet in his fingers. "You sure?"

"Aaron, please," Jane said. She felt Kenny squatting down next to her.

Aaron lifted the sheet. "Meet John Doe number two."

Small Joey lay on his back, his large gold crucifix next to his ear. His head rested on a thin dark pillow of his own blood. His left eye was obliterated by a gunshot; his right eye hung from the socket on a grey tendril of muscle.

Jane drew in a breath. "Point-blank."

"Times two." Aaron started to lower the sheet. "And no shells."

Kenny grabbed his hand. "Wait a minute!" He got down on both knees and put his hand over Small Joey's eyes, studying his face. "Motherfuck."

Jane turned to him. "Motherfuck what?"

"I know this guy," Kenny said as he stood up, brushing the dirt off his pants. "Name's Joe Terrell—aka Small Joey."

"Since when," Jane asked, "are you so intimate with drug dealers?"

Kenny gestured for Jane, Hank, and Aaron to step in closer. Then he said in a low voice, "Joe Terrell is a cop."

Jane kicked at the ground, a tiny puff of dust rising. "Oh my God."

"He's undercover," Kenny continued. "Under deepest cover. He's busted more dealers and users than anyone on the force."

"Guy like him could have a lot of people wouldn't mind seeing him dead," Hank offered as Aaron let the sheet fall back over Small Joey's face. "Thing is, how did our shooter know how to find someone so far under cover?"

"That, plus what's the connection?" Kenny asked. "How's he fit in with Ozzie and Sally and Lacey? If he does."

Jane let a long worried sigh slip through her lips. "He does."

Kenny turned to her. "And we know that how?"

"We know that because nothing is telling us otherwise. We have five people dead. Four of them cops. All the cops with the same gruesome—"

She was interrupted by the insistent beeping of a pager. Jane checked hers on the strap of her bag while the others pulled theirs from their belts. Nothing. They looked around quizzically. Other police officers were taking their pagers out. But none of them was being called.

And still the beeping continued.

"Shit," Kenny said as he knelt next to the yellow sheet and lifted it up.

Small Joey's neon-green pager beeped three more times, then stopped.

Kenny pulled it from the dead man's waistband and examined the return number. "Some junkie's gonna need a new dealer." He tossed the pager to Aaron. "Might have a memory thingie. Who knows what dirty little secrets are hiding in there?"

Jane turned as the familiar clang of a cable car bounced off the surrounding buildings. Across the way, the doorman of the Grand Hyatt blew his whistle for a taxi. Music drifted in from a boom box somewhere. The city was waking up to another scalding day. Life going on as, there in a tiny patch of dirt in the corner of Union Square, she and Kenny broke away from the others and started to work the crowd.

Jane finished with the cable-car conductor and looked up. A fire truck sat idling near the entrance to the underground parking garage. With the sounds of the waking city growing around her, she hadn't heard it arrive.

The cable-car conductor and the city maintenance workers hadn't had much to offer. They had all arrived after the police, drawn by the radios and lights.

Jane glanced over to Kenny before moving on. He was too far away for her to catch his eye. Turning the page in her notebook, she approached her next interview. "Can you tell me your name, sir?" she asked the jogger.

Kenny was on the other side of the perimeter, questioning an emaciated black woman. She had given her name as Lana and her age as twenty-one. She looked fifty. "I know who killed that fella," she said as she poured six packets of sugar into a Styrofoam cup of coffee. The junkie's wake-me-up.

Kenny opened his notebook. "Will you share that information with me, Lana?"

"Hunnert bucks."

"Ain't gonna happen. So, just be a good citizen and—"

"Fifty."

"Ten."

"C'mon, man, I got serious expenses."

"Five."

"Shit, you a cold mothafucka." Lana swirled coffee over her grey teeth. "Show me my ten first."

Kenny dug in his pocket for his wallet.

Lana eyed the billfold. "Suck your cock for twenty."

"Well, you know, first date and all," Kenny said as he pulled out a ten-dollar bill. "You'd lose all respect for me."

"Fuckin' hysterical." Lana snatched the money from his hand.

—

N-o-r-m-a-n T-a-s-s-l-e-r.

Jane jotted down the name the jogger had given her. "So, Mr. Tassler, anything you can tell me, might help us out here?"

Jacques Carpenter reached into his fanny pack and pulled out a Marlboro. Somewhere in some unreachable place, the oddity of a jogger who smoked presented itself to Jane.

"Wish I could," Carpenter said as he lit the cigarette. "I only just got here after all those others." He nodded to the cable-car conductor and the maintenance workers.

"That yellow tape was already up," Carpenter continued, "and some young cop was tellin' us all to stay back." He shrugged. "So we all did." He looked to the plastic sheet. "Guy got shot, huh?"

Jane turned to where Hank was signing an evidence form and handing it over to Aaron Clark-Weber. " 'Fraid so." She flipped her book closed and dipped back under the tape. "Thanks for your time."

"Wish I coulda done more," Carpenter said, pushing twin trails of blue smoke through his nostrils.

Jane walked across the sidewalk to the patch of dirt where Small Joey lay. She noticed the coroner's people standing by, waiting to transport the body to the morgue. A uniformed cop stopped traffic, and Jane watched as Hank nudged his car into the street and headed up Powell. Probably off to work his informants, Jane thought.

She squatted next to Small Joey and looked around.

A cop, just stepping back onto the sidewalk, stomped the dust from his shoes.

The dust.

Jane glanced at her own shoes. A film of silky beige powder clung to the sides. Aaron Clark-Weber's shoes were also dirty. The police videographer's, too. She looked across the way.

Kenny was still talking to that skinny black woman. She lowered her gaze to his feet. More dust.

Rising, Jane scanned the shoes of the onlookers. The cable-car conductor, just now turning to leave. Clean. The maintenance workers. Clean. A businessman who had only then just stopped by. Clean.

The jogger.

Dust.

His shoes and socks were covered in dust.

Her heart pounding, Jane recalled that he had said he arrived after the police tape had been hung, that he had been instructed to stay back, and that he had complied.

A jogger who smokes.

Jane took a small step forward, not wanting to tip her hand. She looked across the square, desperate to get Kenny's attention. But he was too far away, still talking to that junkie.

Jane took another step toward the jogger. "Mr. Tassler, I'm sorry to bother you, but I forgot to get your—"

Jacques Carpenter dropped his cigarette and snuffed it out with his dusty running shoe. His lips twisted into a thin smile of understanding, and his eyes turned suddenly cold.

Jane, knowing now that the jogger was a moment away from bolting, reached into her bag and came up with her pistol. "Freeze!"

Carpenter yanked the .22 from his fanny pack and fired at Jane, its silenced muzzle sounding oddly like a sneeze. She was already instinctively turning her head when the bullet screamed past her ear, punching a hole in the windshield of a squad car.

In the instant it took for Jane to come back around, Carpenter was gone.

"Everybody down!" Jane yelled.

As the civilians hit the deck and the cops flinched into action, Jane glimpsed the jogger tearing across Stockton Street. Traffic screeched to a noisy halt as he raced into an alley of upscale beauty shops and coffeehouses called Maiden Lane.

Jane chased after him, breaking through the police tape.

Kenny, like everyone else, had reflexively crouched and pulled his weapon when he'd heard Jane shout. Now, as he rose, he spotted her running out of Union Square toward Maiden Lane. A few uniformed cops following her. He hurried across the square for the Explorer.

Lana pocketed her ten dollars. "It was Bill Gates kilt that fella!" she shouted. She turned to the man next to her. "I seen it."

——

Goddamn it, Jane thought to herself, these are the wrong shoes for this.

She ripped out her portable radio. "3H58 . . . in pursuit of male Caucasian!" She sidestepped through the traffic on Stockton Street and ran into Maiden Lane.

". . . six feet plus, brown hair . . . white T-shirt, black running shorts . . . black fanny pack . . . armed and dangerous."

Carpenter was near the far end of the alley when he glanced over his shoulder. He whirled and brought his gun up to shoulder level.

Jane dove into the doorway of a lingerie shop. Two bullets pinged off the marble siding, the ricochet of one of them dimpling a brass mailbox.

Jane poked her head out of the doorway. A shop owner lay sprawled on the ground, the hose he'd been using to wash down the alley gyrating wildly at his feet.

The jogger was just exiting Maiden Lane and turning left.

"Shots fired!" Jane called into her walkie-talkie. "Suspect heading up Grant."

Looking behind, Jane spotted a couple of uniforms entering the mouth of the alley. Behind them, Kenny's Explorer roared against the one-way traffic of Stockton Street, climbing the hill to intercept the jogger.

Jane leaped back into the alley and raced toward Grant Avenue.

The shop owner was just retrieving his hose when he saw a woman running toward him with a gun. He scurried into his pastry shop and slammed the door.

Jane sped by and threw herself around the corner. The jogger was a block and a half up the steep incline. The Dragon's Gates of Chinatown just beyond him.

"3H58 . . . to 3H61 . . . Kenny, he's headed for Chinatown!"

"Then so am I!" Kenny yelled into his mike.

Jane bent her body into the hill and struggled up the sharply sloping street.

Jacques Carpenter ran easily up Grant. Then, slowing, he let the lady cop begin to gain some ground on him.

Her lungs aching, her feet slapping the pavement in a steady one-two one-two, Jane felt the distance close between herself and her quarry.

Then the jogger simply accelerated, flying across Bush Street and into Chinatown.

As Jane strained up the last steep block, the awful awareness came to her that the jogger was toying with her.

"3H61 to 3H58. Stay on your radio and keep me posted as to your twenty at all times."

"Will do," Jane said. She tore across Bush Street and passed into the shadows of Dragon's Gate.

Unlike the rest of San Francisco, Chinatown had been up for hours. Delivery trucks lined the streets, dropping off their exotic cargoes. Produce and fish and flowers filled the open-air storefronts. Scores of people teemed from stall to stall, shopping early to beat the heat.

Jane exploded into the sunlight.

Momentarily disoriented, she stopped to get her bearings. The jogger was up ahead, pushing his way along the crowded sidewalk. Behind her, the uniformed cops were just working their way through the cross traffic of Bush Street.

When Jane looked back for the jogger, she couldn't find him. "Fuck!" she shouted. "Where are you?"

A commotion caught her eye. Some people were helping an elderly Chinese woman to her feet. Beyond them, the jogger. He had crossed the street when Jane wasn't looking.

Jane resumed the chase. "SFPD!" she screamed as she ran with her pistol up near her shoulder. The shoppers parted, clearing the sidewalk for Jane.

Jacques Carpenter plowed into a deliveryman, sending him and his two-wheel dolly flying. Caroming away, Carpenter burst into a tea shop. He bulled his way through the tiny shop and smashed through the screen door as he went out the back.

Kenny screeched around the corner of Sacramento and Grant and, two wheels on the sidewalk, forced the Explorer against the tide of one-way traffic. He spotted Jane just as she ran into the tea shop. "Shit, Jane. I'm a block away," he called into his mike. "Wait for me!"

"Can't. We'll lose him!"

She sidled along the wall, her eyes darting back and forth, her pistol waving in a tight arc before her. Someone rose from behind the counter. Jane whipped her weapon toward him.

It was a teenage boy, slim and frail. When he saw the gun

pointed at him, he took a sharp step backward and bumped into the shelves behind him. China pots and cups tinkled with the vibration.

"Where?" Jane demanded.

The boy turned toward the back door and nodded.

"3H61 . . . Kenny, I'm going out the rear of the tea shop."

Kenny's voice came crackling back. "Be careful . . ."

Jane braced herself against the doorjamb, her weapon tight against her chest. "Always," she said. Then she slipped through the screen door, back into the heat and light.

Squinting her eyes against the sudden glare, Jane swept her weapon from side to side. She moved in a half crouch as she peered behind a Dumpster, then a pile of loading palettes. When she reached an abandoned pickup truck, its wheels resting on cinder blocks, she squatted down and looked underneath.

Someone was under the truck.

Jane swiped at the sweat dripping into her eyes and inched forward. Then she saw a pair of grimy bare feet poking out from beneath a tattered cloth. Just a bum scavenging a little shade.

Jane moved on.

There was a storage shed next to the ten-foot-tall wooden fence. She scurried over to it and tested the door. Padlocked. Craning her neck, she looked up to the top of the fence. Coils of barbed wire stretched along its length. A dead end.

Cigarettes.

She smelled him before she saw him.

Just as she was about to bring her gun around, Jacques Carpenter, his dusty jogging shoes draped over his shoulders, grabbed her wrist. Jane's arm felt like it had been caught in a slamming door. Her hand jerked open and her pistol fell away. Then Carpenter swept her in against his body. His granitelike muscles closed around her arms and chest in a lethal embrace.

Completely outmatched, Jane felt the air rush out of her lungs as Carpenter squeezed even tighter. Roaring angrily in her ear, Carpenter lifted Jane off the ground and shook her violently like a lion trying to break the neck of its prey.

Jane searched the ground for her weapon and saw it lying next to the jogger's feet. He stood barefoot, oblivious to the heat, on the grease-stained cement. She realized as he applied even more pressure to her chest, that it had been him under the pickup truck the whole time.

"3H58, what's your twenty?" Kenny's voice scratched over her radio. "Jane, where are you? Jane!"

Carpenter raised his left hand and put it over Jane's mouth. Jane again noticed the stench of cigarettes on his fingers. Holding her still in his powerful grip, Carpenter pressed the muzzle of his .22 into Jane's left eye. The tip of the silencer was still hot from when he had fired at her in Maiden Lane.

Her mind blinded with terror, Jane frantically lashed out with her nails, her feet, anything, everything. Carpenter heaved her up again and viciously shook her until she stopped. Jane sagged in desolation, fighting now just to breathe. She remembered little Caitlin Sprague that day in the school yard, and understood that she was equally helpless.

"Jane! Talk to me!" Kenny's voice was desperate, fear becoming panic.

Carpenter put his lips to Jane's right ear. "Too bad about your father," he hissed.

Her body arching, Jane screamed into his hand. Her cries were muffled into silence.

Carpenter slid his finger onto the steel comma of the trigger. The sweet taste of revenge welled in his throat. His right forearm tingled in anticipation of the adrenaline surge that would come with the kill. His victim's agonized thrashing made it all the more satisfying.

His index finger flexed against the trigger and he swallowed to calm his breathing before he fired.

Just then, the wooden fence disintegrated as Kenny rammed the Explorer through it. Startled, Carpenter wheeled around. As he did, Jane yanked herself free of his grasp and lashed out with her walkie-talkie, catching him high on the head.

Carpenter staggered back, pawing at the spot where Jane had struck him. He raised his pistol and aimed it at her face.

The Explorer shuddered to a halt next to the Dumpster and Kenny leaped out with his shotgun. "Jane! Get down!" he shouted as he speed-chambered a round.

But Jane was paralyzed with fear and exhaustion. Her body simply would not respond.

"Jane!" Kenny screamed. "I can't get a shot!"

Realizing the odds were against him, Carpenter smiled at Jane. "Bang, bang," he said. Then he spun around and raced through the shattered wooden fence.

Kenny ran past Jane and, the shotgun level in front of him, hurried after Carpenter. When he got through the fence, he stopped. "Motherfuck!"

A maze of back alleys and side streets lay before him.

Jacques Carpenter was gone.

"3H61," Kenny said into his mike. "Suspect is at large. The alley behind Lao Chin Tea House. Requesting SWAT and helicopter." He lowered the shotgun and came back through the fence.

Jane stood where he had left her.

Kenny crossed to her. Then he laid the shotgun on the ground and took her in his arms. "I've got you," he cooed. "It's okay. I've got you."

With a cry, Jane collapsed into him, utterly spent.

"C'mon," Kenny said as he guided her back to the Explorer.

The two uniformed cops who had been following Jane burst through the screen door.

"What do we got?" the older one asked, gasping for breath.

The younger one bent over, hands on his knees, his thinning hair sweat-pasted to his scalp. Siren after siren pierced the air.

Kenny pointed toward the fence. "Bad guy went through there. Backup's on the way."

A SWAT muscle car, four helmeted men briefly visible, roared past the opening in the fence.

Soon the steady thrup of a helicopter drifted down to them. One by one, the sirens stopped, and in moments there were cops everywhere.

"Some fucking day, huh?" the older cop said to Kenny.

"Some fucking day," Kenny said. He opened the door to the Explorer and helped Jane inside. "Just sit and soak up some AC. I'm gonna get my shotgun."

He started to go.

Something deep in Jane's mind was screaming for attention. She closed her eyes, willing herself to push everything else away until it came forward. When, after a few seconds, it did, she jumped back out of the Explorer.

"Kenny!" she called as she ran across the lot.

Kenny turned to her.

"I know this guy! He was at Poppy's barbecue!"

"Jesus," Kenny said. "Are you sure?"

"Yes! He was talking to Father Patricola! I remember he left early."

She grabbed Kenny's hand and pulled him back to the car.

"Timmy was taking pictures at the barbecue! We've got to call him!"

She climbed into the Explorer and reached across to open Kenny's door. "C'mon, c'mon!"

The younger cop came up to her. " 'Scuse me, Inspector. Here's your weapon."

Jane turned at the voice, and saw for the first time that the younger cop was Benjy Spielman.

43

JANE TORE OPEN the pale grey envelope and dumped out Timmy's photographs from Poppy's barbecue.

Spreading them out on her desk, some of them spilling onto the floor, she quickly dismissed the ones she didn't need.

She slid one of Aunt Lucy sitting with Jacob Turner to the side . . . and there it was.

Jane sat staring, her teeth clenched in anger, at the picture of the man who had attacked her. He was in her father's backyard, at Poppy's wake, talking with Father Patricola.

He stood there, frozen in time, like a friend of the family paying his respects.

Like he belonged there.

The outrage, the sheer violation of it, boiled up inside her.

Incensed, Jane bolted from her chair and ran into the interrogation room.

Kenny and Hank were at the blackboard, adding information about Joe Terrell's murder, when they saw her coming.

"Son of a bitch!" She slapped the picture down on the table with such force the computer monitor shuddered.

An older man, with a fringe of wispy grey hair, looked up from a small table in the corner. He was wearing headphones and listening to an audiotape on a reel-to-reel player.

Jane glanced over to him. He nodded crisply and went back to work.

"FBI Com Lab," Kenny explained. "Going over the nine-one-one tapes."

"The tapes don't mean anything to us anymore," Jane said. "Neither do tire tracks, footprints, or any of the forensics stuff."

She poked a finger at the jogger's face. "He's showing his face. He's taking risks."

"But why?" Hank asked.

Jane gave voice to a feeling that had been nagging at her for hours. "He's getting ready for the endgame. Preparing himself for the inevitable . . . preparing us." She snatched the picture off the table. "I mean look at this fucker! What the hell's he doing there?"

"I hate to say it," Kenny began, "but maybe he's choosing his next victim."

Jane blew a low whistle. ". . . shit."

Hank hurried to the doorway. "Hey, Mike!"

Finney was on the phone in his cubicle. He turned to Hank.

"I need you to pull all the crowd photos from the police shootings. Right away!"

Finney nodded and quickly got off the phone. He pushed back in his chair and hustled into the interrogation room. "SWAT called in. The guy who attacked Inspector Candiotti got away." He yanked open a file drawer and took out a stack of folders. "There's something like a thousand pictures here."

Jane took the folders from him and dropped them on the table. "Then let's get to it." She took the top three from the stack and headed back to her desk. "This is priority one. Find every picture you can of this guy, no matter how obscure or seemingly insignificant. If he's hanging around the crime scenes of the cops he's killed, then he's telling us something." She started to go, then turned back. "I have the awful feeling we're running out of time."

— —

When SWAT had taken over the Chinatown crime scene, Benjy Spielman had gone back to the mobile field office at Union Square to file his report. His first one as a patrol officer. Afterward, hot and thirsty from the long foot chase through Chinatown, he had decided to break for lunch a little early.

Pier Twelve was a seldom-used loading facility on the northeast side of San Francisco Peninsula. Benjy had loved to come here when he was in college—to read, listen to music, whatever.

He had taken his first sweetheart here not too many summers ago.

Benjy drove his black-and-white slowly past the stacks of wrecked cars on their way to scrap-metal salvage. Dozens of seagulls opened their wings and allowed the faint updrafts off the harbor to lift them into the air. When he reached the shade of a huge shipping crane, he stopped the squad car and got out.

Benjy had been thinking about the leftover chicken from last night's dinner and the two diet Cokes all morning. His Igloo mini-cooler was in the trunk, next to the teddy bears that Ozzie had taught him to carry for calls involving children. He pulled out the cooler and a bag of old bread for the birds. Closing the trunk, he called in. "3P09 to Nineteen."

"Go, 3P09."

"Requesting 10-7M for thirty minutes."

"You got it, 3P09 . . . and, Benjy, good work today."

Benjy beamed as he set the Igloo on the car hood. "Thanks, Cheryl. 3P09 out."

After coming here for so many years, Benjy knew that if he fed the birds first, he'd be able to eat his meal in relative peace. He leaned against the front fender of his black-and-white and reached into the bread bag.

The seagulls squawked and dipped, gliding down in swooping arcs for the food. Other gulls, alerted by the clamor, lifted their wings and drifted over from the roofs of the abandoned warehouses. Benjy tossed more bread onto the calm harbor waters and opened the top of the cooler, anxious for a cool drink.

He grabbed the can in his right hand and, closing his eyes, ran the frosting metal across his cheeks and neck. What a day, he thought to himself. And I didn't do too bad either. Smiling, he popped the can and drank thirstily.

Unseen by Benjy, a primer-grey Camaro slipped along the pier.

Jacques Carpenter saw the cluster of seagulls and followed them with his eyes until he saw the SFPD patrol car. The article in the *Chronicle* had been right. This was where Benjy Spielman took his lunch break.

Carpenter parked the Camaro in the shadow of the scrap-metal wrecks. Then he stripped off his jogging clothes and pulled on a white T-shirt and chinos. He tapped the butt of a Marlboro on the steering wheel and watched as Benjy took a tinfoil-wrapped package from his cooler. Carpenter put the cigarette between his lips and lit it.

Drawing deeply, he let the smoke fill his lungs. He held it for a few extra seconds, feeling the pulse of his quickening heart beating behind his ears. Then he puffed his cheeks and blew a curling cloud of smoke against the inside of the windshield.

Without taking his eyes off Benjy, he reached to the floor behind the driver's seat and brought his fanny pack forward. He unzipped it and removed his .22. Off in the distance, in the shade of the loading crane, Benjy finished his first diet Coke and opened another.

Carpenter unscrewed the silencer and reloaded his gun.

He drew another deep drag from his cigarette and sat there, his pistol in his lap. Waiting.

Why not let the kid enjoy his last meal?

———

Jane tore through the photographs from the Skip Lacey murder site.

She paused for a second when she saw Penny and Randy Kinsella seated in the back of the crime-scene van, looking lost and afraid.

Quickly scanning the other pictures, she saw that their suspect wasn't in the photos. The next folder was from Sally Banks's killing. They weren't pertinent because there had been no crowd of onlookers in the vacant lot under the freeway.

She pushed them aside.

When she did, she noticed an envelope propped against her phone. It was square, large, and off-white; the familiar shape and size of a sympathy card.

Jane opened it.

> *Inspector Candiotti—*
> *Please accept my deepest sympathy on the loss of your father.*
> *We are poorer for his passing, but heaven is richer*
> *and God has a good man at his side.*
> *All best wishes, Becka Flynn*

Jane felt a warm flush in her cheeks. She opened her top middle drawer and dropped the card inside. When she looked up, Kenny was standing in the doorway.

"Got something," he said.

——

Jacques Carpenter snuffed out his cigarette in the ashtray. Then he pulled on his shoes and got out of the Camaro. The door creaked when he closed it, but Benjy, with the sounds coming off the bay, didn't hear.

Dropping the .22 into his pants pocket, Carpenter started walking toward the squad car.

Benjy noticed the shadow first and, not sensing any danger, turned around to greet his visitor. "How's it goin'?" he said through a mouth stuffed with chicken.

Carpenter allowed a smile to play across his face. "Not bad. You?"

"Doin' okay." Benjy watched as Carpenter came around the car and leaned on the fender next to him. "You want a drink or something? I got a cooler."

"Drink'd be great," Carpenter said as he lit another cigarette, the smoke floating away.

"All's I got left is water," Benjy said as he rummaged in the Igloo. "It's cold, though." He handed a bottle of Evian to Carpenter. "So, you taking a break?"

Carpenter twisted the cap off the plastic water bottle. "Not exactly." He took a long swallow, water dripping down his chin and throat. Then he looked out over the water. A freighter, its deck laden with cargo containers, pushed its way through the harbor.

Benjy looked at his watch. His meal break would be up in ten minutes. "What kind of work do you do gets you out here in the middle of the day?"

Carpenter squinted against the sun glare bouncing off the water. "I'm in extermination." He pulled at the Evian again.

"Interesting," Benjy said. "You hungry? I got some chicken left."

——

Lieutenant Spielman joined them as Kenny excitedly spread his pictures out on the floor. "Look at these." He pointed to the Union Square photos. "We believe this"—he indicated a man almost totally obscured by other bystanders—"is our guy. But we can't see his face."

He looked up to the others huddled around him. "But we've got lots better." He dropped another stack onto the floor. "Ozzie's murder scene."

Jane put her hands on her knees and peered at the pictures. There were photos of her and Kenny in front of Jennie's Bride-To-Be. There were a couple more of a young man standing with his pregnant wife by the ATM machine across the street. Larry and Eileen Shaw, she remembered.

"Forget these," Kenny said.

He pushed them aside and Jane gasped.

There was the jogger from Union Square, dressed in a white shirt and khaki pants, smoking a cigarette.

"That's him!" Jane cried. "That's the guy who shot at me!"

He was sitting on a fire hydrant, talking to Benjy.

They all turned to Lieutenant Spielman.

He straightened up and crossed to the door. "Cheryl," he called. "Where's my son?"

Cheryl looked up from her console. "He's taking his 10-7M. Should be back on in ten."

There was a moment of awkward silence.

Hank glanced at Jane and Kenny, then went over to Lieutenant Spielman. "Think I'll go out and shake down my informants." He pulled on his jacket. "I'll probably end up down at the docks if you need me."

Lieutenant Spielman sighed. "Thanks, Hank."

"It's what we do," Hank said as he left.

Lieutenant Spielman looked to Jane and Kenny. "I'll be in my office."

They watched him go. Then Jane grabbed up all the pictures with the suspect in them and turned to Finney. "Mike, I need you to hand-carry these to the photo lab and get us a bunch of different angles for distribution."

He took the photos from her. "Don't worry, Inspector," he said seriously. "I'll do a good job for you."

As Finney hurried from the room, Jane turned to Kenny. "We got a face. Now we need a name . . . and then we've got him!"

— —

"You got another paper towel?" Jacques Carpenter asked. "This chicken is great, but it's kinda messy." He and Benjy were sitting on the hood of the black-and-white.

"Here you go," Benjy said. He looked at his watch. Six more minutes left in his 10-7M. He watched as his visitor flung a piece of chicken skin into the air. A seagull dove, caught it in its beak, and gulped it down. "I love feeding the birds, too."

Carpenter wiped his fingertips, one by one, with the paper towel. "I know."

Benjy slid off the hood and stretched. Then he folded the tinfoil into neat squares and put them into the cooler. He'd use them for tomorrow's lunch.

It never occurred to him to ask how this man knew he loved to feed the birds.

— —

Jane paced furiously in the interrogation room.

"This guy's taking more and more chances. I don't like it." She stopped and turned to Kenny. "What are we missing? What haven't we thought of?"

Kenny sat on the table, his back against the boxes of case folders. "We're doing this right, Jane. We'll have some solid photos of this guy in every precinct house and squad car in an hour. Next time he shows his face . . . he's ours."

A chair scraped back in the corner and the elderly man pushed away from the table where he'd been working on the audiotapes. He dropped his headphones down to his shoulders and rose.

"Excuse me, Inspectors," he said. "I'm afraid we haven't been introduced." He crossed the room, limping slightly. "I'm Special

Agent Clay Frohman, FBI Com Lab." He nodded diffidently. "Sorry to bother. But I may have found something here."

Jane looked up, excited. "What?"

"Well, it may be significant or . . . not. But I think if . . . oh, hell, just listen." He flicked a switch and the reel-to-reel started turning.

". . . He's shot in the face!"

Frohman nodded to the tape recorder. "The nine-one-one tapes."

"What is your location?"

"Oh. Right. Sorry. Um, I'm in Union Square . . ."

Agent Frohman released the tape heads and rewound the reels with his hands. "I'm going to slow it down just a titch." He let the tape roll again.

"Oh . . . Right . . . Sor-ry . . . Um . . . I'm . . . in . . . Un-ion . . ."

He stopped the tape and looked to Jane and Kenny.

"Hear it?"

"Hear what?" Kenny asked.

"Wait a minute," Jane said. "There's something off in the way the guy talks. I noticed it before, from Sally's nine-one-one tape." She turned to Frohman. "But what is it?"

"He's a foreigner." Frohman turned off the recorder. "He's been living in this country so long, his accent is almost impercep-tible. But there is still what we call a residual telltale dialectic in his speech pattern. It came up when he said 'sorry.' That long 'o.' " Special Agent Frohman took half a step forward and said, "The man you're looking for is Canadian."

Jane clapped her hands. "That's it!" She hurried to the table. "Kenny, add 'Canada' to the data bank and let's see what it tells us."

Kenny jumped down from the table and went to the computer.

"Inputting Canada," Kenny said as he began typing. "Enter. Search. Enter." The computer clicked and whirred. In a few sec-onds the list of thousands of names—of escaped convicts, parol-ees, and mental patients—was reduced to three.

"Sandy Bennett," Kenny read. "Quebec City. Female. Sandra. That's not it." He brought up the next one. "Graham Yost. Ot-tawa. Born September fifth, 1958 . . ."

Jane started to jot down the information. "Wait, shit . . . *died* January second, 1994." He swiveled in his chair and looked up to Jane. "That leaves bachelor number three."

"Go for it."

"Going for it," Kenny said as he brought up the last name.

Jane stepped forward and read the name on the screen. "Jacques Yves Carpenter."

"I know that name," a voice said behind them.

They turned as one—Jane, Kenny, Agent Frohman—to see Lieutenant Spielman in the doorway.

He came into the room and held out his hand. "Let me see that picture."

44

IT'S HIM," Lieutenant Spielman said as he studied the photo. "He's older, more bulked up." He handed the picture back to Jane. "But it's him."

"Ben," Jane said. "How do you know this guy?"

"There was this case." Lieutenant Spielman pulled a chair away from the wall and sat down. "Years ago, in the Mission District, a liquor store holdup that went bad. A young cop happened by and shots were exchanged. Right there on the street."

Agent Frohman came closer, until he was standing just behind Jane and Kenny.

"People were scrambling, diving for cover like in the movies. The cop took a bullet in the forearm and returned fire. Shooting three times. The bad guy was hit twice and died on scene."

Kenny held up his hands palm out. "That would be a good thing."

"Not exactly," Lieutenant Spielman said. "The one bullet that missed went through the window of a Laundromat next door and struck a pregnant woman. She was killed instantly. They tried to save her unborn son, but he died at St. Alban's."

"My God," Jane whispered.

Lieutenant Spielman paused, gathering his thoughts. "The woman's husband was in prison at the time for some piddly drug thing. Needless to say, he was devastated . . . and extremely pissed off. He sued the department, the city, the state of California, everyone. And he lost every time. The courts determined that his wife's shooting, although tragic, was clearly accidental."

"And the guy in prison," Jane asked, "was Jacques Carpenter?"

"Yeah," Lieutenant Spielman said. "He got so out of control that he kept getting into more and more trouble. I think he fractured the skull of a prison guard in one incident. And they just kept tacking on the years to his sentence." He poured himself a glass of water, but left it untouched on the table. "So a kid doing small time for something like an ounce ends up in maximum security for half his life because some newbie cop killed his wife and baby while she was doing her wash."

"And he sat stewing in prison after prison for sixteen years, building up one huge hard-on full of hate for cops. All cops." Lieutenant Spielman gestured toward the computer with his chin. "Check it out. I'll bet he's only been on the streets a little while."

Kenny tapped the keyboard and read, "Jacques Yves Carpenter, paroled ten days ago."

"So," Jane asked, "who was that cop? Skip Lacey, Ozzie, Joe Terrell?"

Lieutenant Spielman unbuttoned his left sleeve and rolled it up. Just below the elbow was a narrow two-inch scar. "It was me."

"Jesus, Ben," Jane said.

"Then why," Kenny asked, "didn't this guy come up earlier in our databank searches?"

"Because," Jane said, "we were just looking for violent-crime arrests. Carpenter was busted on a minor drug charge."

Lieutenant Spielman's eyes reddened with tears. "Ozzie testified on my behalf at each of the trials."

"I get the Ozzie connection," Kenny said. "But what about Sally?"

Lieutenant Spielman shook his head. "I don't know."

"Wait a minute," Jane said. "Sally's murder scene was the one where the killer shot at the crime-scene van—at that poster of the cop—sending us a warning. What if that was why he killed Sally?"

"You mean," Kenny said, "he murdered Sally as bait? Just to get us all in one place, and send us a message?"

Jane nodded. "I wouldn't put anything past this guy."

Kenny looked out the window, not wanting to believe what he was hearing. "This is one sick fucker."

"No argument there," Jane said. She turned to Lieutenant

Spielman. "What about Joe Terrell and Skip Lacey? How do they fit the puzzle?"

"Years ago," Lieutenant Spielman said, "Joe Terrell was a by-the-book young narcotics cop. He was so zealous, he made Jason Bloom look like a slacker. It was Joe Terrell who busted a seventeen-year-old kid named Jacques Carpenter for possession with intent to sell."

Kenny turned away from the window. "The plot thins."

"Right. He could have let it go, but he didn't. He made every court appearance and hung tough on the case until Carpenter was sent away." He shook his head. "Hell, Joe Terrell was still like that till the day he died. Can you imagine? He was what, fifty? And still out there every night making undercover buys and sells."

"So young Jacques Carpenter," Jane said, "gets sent to jail on a nothing charge and that's the end of life as he knows it."

"The police department," Lieutenant Spielman said, "fucked him over big time. First with a bullshit prosecution . . . then . . ." He faltered, searching for the words. ". . . then when I killed his wife and unborn child." He sucked his lip in again and sat there, the rattling of the fans the only sound.

"And Skip Lacey?" Jane asked.

"Joe Terrell's partner back in the early narco days. They were this big-deal team. Called themselves Butch and Sundance. Skip Lacey testified against Carpenter. Maybe even embellished a thing or two. Then he developed a taste for the stuff himself and . . . well, you know how he ended up."

"Ben," Jane said, "listen to me for a second. Kenny and I've been talking about how this killer, Carpenter, has been taking more and more chances. Showing up at Poppy's wake, the Union Square and Chinatown thing . . ."

Kenny joined in. "We feel he's getting ready to do something big . . . something maybe . . . final."

Jane picked it up. "From what you're telling us . . . it could be you that he's coming after next. And . . ." She glanced at Kenny. "We'd like you to take all the appropriate precautions." Lieutenant Spielman started to protest, but Jane went on. "Now that we know who he is and what he looks like, we'll get him. But I want you under guard, full-time."

Lieutenant Spielman rose. "Jane, I don't think—"

"Ben!" Jane said forcefully. "This guy came after me. I've got Kenny to help me stay safe." She looked over to him. He nodded tightly. She took Lieutenant Spielman's hand and said softly, "Do it for Mary, Ben."

Lieutenant Spielman sighed, his shoulders slumping. "Okay, you're right. I'll go make the call." He started for the door, then turned back to Jane. "Thank you."

45

HANK PAGANO GUIDED his unmarked police sedan through the long shadows of the abandoned warehouses. He had entered the harbor complex at Pier Six. By counting the huge dock cranes to the north, he could tell how far away Pier Twelve was. A little over two miles, he figured, separated him from Benjy.

After almost thirty years on the force, Hank knew this area well. These warehouses, long ago fallen into disuse, provided refuge for the homeless, initiation grounds for the gangs, and an ideal location for all sorts of illegal transactions.

As Hank approached Pier Seven, he turned into one of the cavernous buildings, plunging himself into darkness. Driving slowly, his eyes adjusting to the murky dimness, he noticed an array of filthy mattresses and cooking utensils. Everyone's out panhandling, he thought to himself. Trying to get enough scratch for another night of Mickey Ds and T-Bird.

Hank came to the warehouse's huge barn doors and emerged into the blinding sunlight. Someone in silhouette stepped in front of his car. He stomped on the brake and twisted the steering wheel.

Hank slipped his hand under his arm and released the safety strap on his shoulder holster.

A man walked from in front of the sun to the side of the car. Then he bent down and peered into the driver's-side window.

"Thought that was you!" Silk Cullen said as he knuckle-tapped the glass. His rich disc jockey's voice echoed through the recesses of the warehouse.

Hank dropped his hand from his pistol and lowered the window. "This where you're crashing these days?"

"The finest in waterfront property."

Hank got out of the car. "Stayin' out of trouble?"

"Not exactly." Silk shrugged. "What kinda money you got?" His speech was slurred and his eyes unfocused. He'd been drinking hard for days.

"C'mon, Silk," Hank said, trying to keep it light. "You never have anything I can use."

"That was good information I give you that time," Silk Cullen said, the edge of a threat creeping into his voice. He was a big man, about the same size as Hank. But the ravages of vodka and dope had taken their toll; Hank knew he'd have little trouble controlling him if it came to that.

"It sure was." Hank grinned. He took a step backward. Just in case. "But, man, that was five years ago."

"It weren't no five years ago, Hank!" Silk shouted. "You fucked me then and you fuckin' me now! I need some cash!"

Hank had maybe half a minute of patience left. Then it would get messy.

— —

Benjy looked at his watch. His meal break had ended two minutes ago.

"Oops. Gotta go protect and serve," he said to Jacques Carpenter. He dropped the Igloo into the trunk. "Nice talkin' to you. Maybe I'll see you out here again."

Carpenter pushed away from the black-and-white. "Never know what might happen." He started to walk toward the stacks of wrecked cars.

Benjy closed the trunk and watched him for a moment. Then he came around the side of the squad car and opened the driver's door. When he did, he saw, reflected in the window, that Carpenter had stopped walking and stood facing him about thirty feet away.

Benjy turned around. "Forget something?"

Carpenter lit a cigarette. "Yeah, I did." He pulled the .22 from his pants pocket and leveled it at Benjy.

Benjy Spielman's entire body clenched in a spasm of panic. "Hey! What?" Fear thundering in his chest, his hands fluttered like birds on a string. "C'mon! Don't!"

The side of Carpenter's mouth curled into a grin as he raised his pistol and pointed it at Benjy's left eye.

Benjy cringed, his shoulders hunching as if he were trying to make himself smaller. "Oh God," he said as he finally understood who this man was. "You're him!" He grappled frantically to unstrap his holster.

"Don't," Carpenter said evenly. "It won't help."

He took a step forward, the .22 still trained on Benjy's left eye. Then he lowered it and slowly brought it down along Benjy's bulletproof vest.

Benjy trembled uncontrollably as he watched the black eye of the gun's muzzle move from his face, to his neck, and down his body. "Please, mister."

Carpenter inched forward another step and, without a word, fired a round into Benjy's groin. Hundreds of seagulls were sent squawking into the air as the shot echoed off the surrounding warehouses.

Benjy was thrown back against the car. He stood there a moment, his face frozen in openmouthed horror. Then his body slid down the side of the black-and-white and he ended up in a sitting position on the coal-hot blacktop. He reached down to touch his wound and brought his hand, covered in blood, up to his face.

The shock of being shot wore off and he gasped at the sudden rush of pain. "Why?" he screamed. "Why are you doing this to me?"

Carpenter, his pistol still trained on Benjy, took two more steps forward and squatted on his haunches. He bounced there for a few seconds and watched the seagulls drift back down. Then he finished his cigarette and flicked the butt away. A seagull dropped down from a piling and snatched it up.

"*Why!*" Benjy shrieked.

"Because," Carpenter said, the sun baking his back. "It's time."

— —

Hank thought he heard an odd noise, a pop from somewhere indistinct. The wind was blowing up the peninsula and he couldn't tell exactly what it was or where it had come from.

"Look, man," he said to Silk, trying to defuse any trouble before it began, "it's too hot to be getting all excited." He took a ten-dollar bill from his pocket and passed it into Silk's hand. "You go get yourself a couple of bottles of your stuff—Popov, right? And stay out of this heat, huh?"

Hank turned away and started to get into the car. He had spotted a swarm of seagulls circling to the north, where that popping sound may have come from. Somewhere between curious and anxious, he wanted to keep moving.

Silk slapped a hand on Hank's shoulder, stopping him.

"Ten fucking bucks!" he shouted, spittle flying. "After all I done for you? After all these years?"

Hank spun away from Silk's grasp, grabbed him from behind, and threw him, facedown, across the hood of the car.

Silk struggled for a moment, trying to lift his head. Then, realizing it was futile, he let his body go slack.

Hank looked to the north again. The seagulls were gone.

46

JANE AND KENNY STOOD in the doorway of the interrogation room as Roslyn Shapiro approached Lieutenant Spielman in the middle of the bullpen. She handed him a sealed manila envelope and returned to reception.

Jane pulled on the elbow of Kenny's shirt and said, "C'mon, I want to get that APB out so we can—"

She stopped when she saw Lieutenant Spielman turn to her, his face ashen, his mouth open in shock. A copy of that morning's *Chronicle* dangled in his trembling right hand.

Jane and Kenny ran to him. "Ben," Jane asked, "what is it?"

Lieutenant Spielman looked right through her. "Cheryl!" he bellowed. All the heads in the bullpen turned to him. "Find my son!" He shoved the paper at Jane and raced to the dispatch console. "Get Benjy on the radio, now!"

Jane held up the newspaper. It was the section with the picture of Lieutenant Spielman and Benjy. She let it fall open at the fold.

There were holes where Benjy's eyes had been.

Burned through with a cigarette.

"Shit," Kenny said under his breath.

They tore across the room and joined Lieutenant Spielman. Cheryl toggled the mike switch. "3P09, what's your twenty? 3P09? Patrol Officer Spielman, please report your twenty immediately."

Lieutenant Spielman put his hand on her shoulder. She stopped for a second so they could listen.

All that came back was silence; empty, hollow silence.

Lieutenant Spielman nodded for Cheryl to try again.

"3P09," Cheryl called, her voice beginning to quake. "Benjy, honey, you okay out there?"

They heard a faint click. Then another.

Cheryl punched a button and sent the incoming signal to the large speakers on top of her console. "3P09 . . . Benjy, is that you? If it is, click your radio twice for me."

There was a long, agonizing pause. Then . . . *click, click.*

Lieutenant Spielman brought his hand to his mouth. "Oh God."

He took the microphone from Cheryl's desk. "Benjy. This is Dad. Are you hurt?"

There was another click, followed by dry hissing air. Then the sound of difficult, tormented breathing. "3 . . . P . . . 0 . . . 9 . . . to . . . Nine . . . teen . . . officer . . . down . . ."

Lieutenant Spielman glanced at Jane for only an instant and, in his face, she saw the incarnation of perfect fear.

While Ben Spielman talked with his son, Cheryl grabbed up her dispatch phone. "Clear all channels for a Code thirty-three. Repeat. Code thirty-three. We have an officer down vicinity Pier Twelve. Give me channel three until further notice. All units report and respond."

Kenny wheeled around. "Moby, get us a chopper! Pier Twelve!"

Finney hustled to his cubicle.

As is always the case with a Code 33, a brotherhood of voices jammed the airwaves. "5P66 rolling from Embarcadero. Approximately eight minutes to . . . Paramedic unit niner, niner leaving Fire Six . . . CHP M, four, zero . . . Transit eleven . . . 1P772 . . ."

The speakers buzzed and rattled in the storm of radio traffic.

Lieutenant Spielman clutched the microphone so tightly, his knuckles lost all color. "Benjy . . . listen to me. Help is coming. Can you hear me?"

". . . yeah . . ."

Hank's voice came crackling through. "3H10 to Nineteen. Responding to Code three-three."

"Hank, this is Ben. It's Benjy. He's been shot. Hurry!"

"I'm two miles away. I'll be there in no time." The sound of Hank's siren came crying over the loudspeakers.

"Benjy, this is Dad. Stay with us, son."

Finney came running up. "Air One's down for repairs," he said breathlessly. "Two's working a burglary in North Beach . . . I . . ."

"Then, pull it off, damn it!" Kenny yelled in his face. "And get it to Pier Twelve!"

"Already did, Inspector," Finney said. "Should be there in three minutes."

Kenny shot him a look, surprised. "Good work . . . Mike."

Jane turned to say something to Kenny and noticed Special Agent Frohman in the doorway of Interrogation Room One. He watched at a respectful distance as the police officers of Precinct Nineteen tried to save one of their own, connected to the outside world by only a microphone and a speaker.

In a flash of random thought, it occurred to Jane that they were like the crew of an aircraft carrier listening over the radio to a dogfight being waged miles away.

Lieutenant Spielman absently ran his fingers through his thin hair, causing it to stand on end. "Benjy? . . . It's Dad. Keep talking to me, son . . ."

The labored breathing was more rapid now, taking on a machinelike rhythm, as Benjy struggled to speak. "He's . . . here . . ."

"Who is? Who's there?"

"The . . . man who . . . shot . . . me . . ."

Lieutenant Spielman slumped. "Jesus."

Jane ran around the dispatch console. "Cheryl, inform all units responding to the Code thirty-three that the shooter's still in the area."

Lieutenant Spielman thumbed the mike. "3H10. Hank, the shooter's still with Benjy!"

There was a moment of static, then the wail of Hank's siren in the speakers. "I'm there in ninety seconds!"

"Dad! He's coming back! . . . Grey Camaro . . . He's getting out. Help me!"

"Benjy, your weapon!"

". . . he . . . took it . . ."

Jane pressed the master switch. "Benjy, crawl under your car! Just lie down and crawl away!"

"... I can't ... too much ... blood ..."

Jane snapped a look at Lieutenant Spielman. Tears were streaming down his face. "Benjy, this is Dad ... all you have to do is ..."

"Oh God! ... He's pointing it at me ... No, mister ... please ... oh, shit ... Daddy!"

A shot.

Everyone in the squad room flinched at the same instant.

Another shot.

The line went dead.

For one suspended second, the only sound in the bullpen was the relentless whirring of the electric fans.

Then the silence was shattered. *"NO!"* Lieutenant Spielman shrieked. Unable to control his anguish, he grabbed the speaker closest to him and held it to his chest.

Without knowing why, Cheryl Lomax quickly stood up. Then she sat back down.

Roslyn Shapiro ran into the bathroom, her hand to her mouth.

Special Agent Frohman retreated into the interrogation room.

Mike Finney took two steps forward and, not knowing what to do, just stood there.

Jane put her hand on Cheryl's shoulder. "Get SWAT down there to seal off the area. Also send a medevac to Pier Twelve."

Cheryl looked up to Jane, thin black streams of mascara trailing down her cheeks. She started to say something, but couldn't.

"I know," Jane said softly.

While Cheryl dispatched SWAT and the medevac, Jane came around to Lieutenant Spielman and Kenny. "Ben, Hank will be there any second."

"We don't know for sure," Kenny added, "if anything ..."

The speaker in Lieutenant Spielman's hands suddenly came to life. "Name tag says Spielman ..." Jacques Carpenter's voice was laced with contempt. "Poor boy ... We're almost even ... *Daddy.*"

Horrified, Lieutenant Spielman dropped the speaker to the floor.

Jane gasped as she recognized the voice. "Carpenter."

They could hear the keening of Hank's siren as it grew closer.

"Uh-oh, gotta go," Carpenter said. "See you soon." There was a click; then another as Carpenter came back on for one last torment. "Sorry," he said, his Canadian accent thick and undisguised.

They heard the microphone fall to the ground. Then the sound of someone running. A car door slamming. An engine bursting to life. Hank's siren coming closer still. Tires screeching away.

An instant later, they heard another car skidding up. Hank called in. "3H10 to Nineteen. Ben, it's bad." A sizzle of static. "If you guys have me on the speakers, have someone take care of the lieutenant." Tires squealing. "I'm going after this guy. I'll keep my mike open."

Jane took Lieutenant Spielman's hand and held it in hers, rubbing her thumb along his index finger. He looked at her. The fear gone; complete and utter heartache in its place.

Kenny picked up the speaker and put it on Cheryl's desk. As he did, Hank came back on. "Heading north along the harbor. Just passing Pier Thirteen."

"Paramedic niner, niner to dispatch. Present location is Pier Eleven. We're on scene in one minute."

"CHP M, four, zero to dispatch. We're setting up an intercept at Pier Fifteen. Awaiting instructions."

Jane put her arm around Lieutenant Spielman's waist and Kenny put his arm over Ben's shoulder, keeping him between them. Holding him up.

The sound of an engine accelerating and tires squealing came over the speakers. Then the unmistakable *pop-pop-pop* of gunfire.

"3H . . . 10 to . . . dispatch. Damn it!" Hank breathed heavily, rapidly, over the airwaves. "I'm hit!"

Jane let go of Lieutenant Spielman and stepped forward. "Oh God, Hank. No."

She flicked the mike on Cheryl's console. "3H10. Hank, are you all right?"

"Not all right. I've taken two bullets in the—"

"Break off the chase, Hank," Jane pleaded. "Backup's on the way."

"Can't do it, Jane."

"Hank, please!"

"Losing control," Hank gasped over the radio. "Can't keep . . . wait . . ."

There was the squeal of tires losing their grip, then an abrupt crunching sound of metal on metal.

"Hank!" Jane screamed into the mike. "Hank, are you all right?"

Hank's voice came back in shallow gasps. "My legs . . . gasoline . . ."

Jane squeezed the microphone in her hand. "Hank, get out of—"

An explosion thundered through the speakers. There was a quick muffled scream, then another explosion, bigger than the first.

The connection was lost; the speakers settling back into a soft sizzling.

Cheryl bolted from her chair. "Hank!"

Kenny ran into the interrogation room to get his coat and Jane's bag.

"Jesus," Lieutenant Spielman said.

Jane took his head into her hands, bringing his eyes level with hers. "Ben," she said firmly, "someone has to call Mary before the news guys do."

Ben Spielman stared into her eyes, lost and defeated. Finally, he just shook his head and turned toward his office.

Everyone in the squad room parted for him, watching him pass. He went into his office and closed the door. He stood there for a moment looking at the telephone on his desk. Then he picked it up and dialed his wife to tell her of the death of their son.

Kenny dashed out of the interrogation room and tossed Jane her bag. They started for the stairwell door. Kenny ripped it open. Jane paused to look back at everyone watching her.

"Pray for us," she said hoarsely.

"Finney!" Kenny called. "Get someone from upstairs to come take care of the lieutenant."

"And send someone to their house!" Jane shouted. "Mary might be on this guy's list, too!" She hurried down the stairs. "C'mon, Ken!"

47

They sped along in silence.

Kenny maneuvered the Explorer up and around the hills of San Francisco, the red dome light cycling on the roof.

Jane looked out the window, watching the city pass. A Korean grocer was spraying his produce stand with water from a green hose. A teenager in a wheelchair waited for a bus in the shade of a street sign. A young father wiped ice cream from the mouth of his daughter. A panhandler shook his Styrofoam cup at all who passed.

A flag hung curled around a flagpole at half-staff in front of the post office.

Occasionally, an SFPD squad car or a CHP cruiser would blast by, light bars flashing, sirens screaming. Heading east, they were all going to the same place.

To the killing ground at Pier Twelve.

Jane turned to Kenny. He gripped the steering wheel with both hands, his jaw set. His lower lip quivered, and tears pooled in his eyes.

He felt her watching him and glanced over. ". . . shit . . ."

"I know," Jane said softly. She slid her hand under his right thigh. "They're gone . . . Benjy and Hank . . . just like that."

"It doesn't make it any better, and I'm not even sure if I believe it anymore," Kenny said, "but it's what we signed on for." He eased up on the gas and descended the last hill toward San Francisco Bay.

Jane let her head fall back against the seat and closed her eyes. The faces of the dead came to her, behind her eyelids, like afterimages from staring at the sun. Skip Lacey, Ozzie Castillo, Sally Banks, Joe Terrell, Benjy Spielman, Hank Pagano.

Poppy.

"Ken," she said, her voice hardly more than a whisper.

"Hmm?"

"After we get this guy . . ." she began, still formulating the thought as she spoke. ". . . I want out."

"Of?"

Two CHP motorcycle officers roared by. Then two more.

"Of the force," Jane said. "I want my life back."

— —

They saw the smoke first.

Then the helicopters, suspended like bugs in the perfect blue sky.

Kenny eased the Explorer to a stop outside the yellow tape perimeter at Pier Twelve. As Jane got out, she noticed two news photographers atop a stack of scrap-metal cars.

Aaron Clark-Weber came up to them, his face drawn and weary. "Jesus," he said softly.

Jane looked across to Benjy's car. His body, covered in a plastic sheet, was still in a sitting position against the door of his patrol car.

"He was shot once in the groin area," Aaron said. "Then the eyes." He spat on the sizzling hot asphalt. "The guys figure the killer's such an expert shot, that the groin wound was intended just to disable Benjy."

"To keep him alive . . ." Kenny began.

Jane finished his thought. "So Ben could hear him suffer."

"Looks that way," Aaron said. "One other thing. There's cigarette butts next to the car, and a bunch of empty drink bottles in Benjy's cooler. That, and two sets of chicken scraps, two wads of soiled paper towels, and—"

"Aaron," Jane interrupted, "what are you saying?"

Aaron turned to look back to Benjy's body. "I'm telling you it looks like the shooter sat and had a nice little lunch with Benjy before murdering him."

"Motherfuck," Kenny said.

Jane's gaze was drawn to the north. A mile away, the thick black smoke from Hank's car was turning white as the fire department extinguished the flames.

"More bad news," Aaron said. "The shooter got away."

Jane turned back to him. "Shit! How?"

"Don't know exactly. CHP set up an intercept at Pier Fifteen. But the car never showed. They did a sweep and found a Camaro behind a warehouse. They're pretty sure it belongs to the perp . . . But no bad guy."

"Damn it!" Jane said. "We got helicopters and CHP and SFPD all over the fucking place! This guy kills two cops under our noses and he gets away?"

"3P118 to 3H58."

Jane snapped up the radio. "Go, 3P118."

"Inspector," Mike Finney said, his voice clutching. "I'm just north of you. At Hank's car . . . it's so awful. His body . . . his body . . . is charred to . . ."

"Mike, listen to me. You were very brave to come down here, but we need you back at the precinct. Are you okay to drive?"

"Uh . . . yes."

"Good," Jane said. She saw Kenny and Aaron both looking to the west. She turned and was surprised to see Lieutenant Spielman just getting out of the back of a department car. "Mike, I want you to go back and set up a Com hotline. Will you do that for me?"

"Yes, Inspector. 3P118 out."

Jane tossed the mike back into the Explorer. She and Kenny started for Lieutenant Spielman. "What's he doing here?"

The patrol officers, the photographers, the forensics team, the coroner's deputies, all stopped to watch as Lieutenant Spielman approached.

"Ben, please." Jane touched his arm. "You don't have to be here."

He looked down at her, his eyes distant and empty. "Yes, I do."

Kenny gently nudged Lieutenant Spielman so that his back was to his son's body. "C'mon, Ben, we really should . . ."

An unmarked police car wove its way through the maze of vehicles and parked next to the Explorer. Mary Spielman climbed out of the back and, shielding her eyes from the glare off the windshields, searched for her husband.

They saw each other at the same time.

Ben Spielman pulled away from Jane and Kenny and started

toward his wife. Mary, gulping back a sob, raced into his arms. "Oh, my baby," Mary Spielman cried, her body going limp. "My poor . . . only . . . baby."

Lieutenant Spielman guided her, their heads down, to his car. The driver opened the back door for them and the lieutenant helped his wife inside. Ben turned back and beckoned for Jane and Kenny.

As they neared, he tried to speak. But it took him a few seconds to get the words past his quivering lips. Finally he said, "Find him," and joined his wife in the sedan.

"We will, Ben," Jane said, and closed the door.

A black Chevy Suburban with four motorcycles in escort came screeching up.

Before the Suburban came to a complete stop, Chief Walker McDonald bolted from the backseat and crossed to Lieutenant Spielman's car. Jane watched as Ben lowered the rear window and the chief stuck his head inside to talk. Then he reached across and said something to Mary.

After another few moments, he pulled back and patted the roof of the car. As it pulled away, Chief McDonald turned to face the murder scene. Every exposed inch of his skin was red with anger. His face, neck, ears, and hands all seemed to pulse with rage. "Who's in charge here?"

Jane took a step forward. "I am, sir. Inspector Marks is my number two."

Chief McDonald took off his coat and wiped his shirtsleeve across his forehead. "Candiotti, right?"

"Yes sir."

"Any leads?"

"Yes sir. We know who did this." She nodded toward Benjy's body. The coroner's deputies were just zipping up the body bag. "But we don't know where he is."

"Who is it?"

Kenny took out his field notebook. "Jacques Yves Carpenter. Just out of San Quentin."

"Jacques Carpenter," the chief repeated, mulling over the name. "He the one was always suing us over that accidental shooting?"

"That's him, sir."

"Of course . . . I remember now," the chief said. "It was Ben did the shooting." He paused to watch as Benjy's body was hefted onto a gurney, a reflective circle of dark blood staining the ground. "And it comes to this." He put his hands on Jane's shoulders. "Inspector, funds for anything you need are yours on my approval."

"Thank you, sir."

"Just get this cocksucker, you'll excuse my French, before any more of my cops are killed." He nodded to Kenny and the others. Then he turned on his heel and stormed back to the Suburban. His entourage scrambled behind him and within seconds all four doors had slammed and the chief and his escort were racing away.

It was then that Jane first smelled the smoke from Hank's fire. She looked at Kenny.

"Wind shifted," he said.

A grizzled old-timer of a sergeant headed for his cruiser. He took a Raiders water bottle from the dash and drank in long wet gulps. Then he picked up his radio mike. "5P601 to 5P330."

"5P330 to 5P601. Go, Sarge."

"Phil, when you guys finish at the Pagano scene, release me a fire truck, wouldya?"

Knowing that it was wrong even as it was happening, Jane felt herself being drawn to Benjy's car, to his blood. She started walking toward the black-and-white.

A photographer was crouched in front of where Benjy's body had fallen, obscuring the crimson stain on the asphalt. He started to rise, to clear the way for Jane as she came forward.

Just as the photographer was moving out of the way, Jane felt a hand on her back. She turned, and there was Kenny.

"C'mon," he said gently, "let's go break this case down and bust this guy."

They both knew that Kenny had saved Jane from whatever it was that had compelled her to look at Benjy's blood.

Jane leaned into him as they headed back to the Explorer.

"Thanks."

48

LOOK," JANE SAID as Kenny made the last turn to the station house.

Television news trucks, their satellite transmitters telescoping thirty feet in the air, lined the entire block. Jane spotted Becka Flynn's striking red hair among the reporters asking questions of a public-affairs officer.

As Kenny drove past, Becka Flynn turned and saw Jane looking at her. The two women nodded silently to each other.

"Check it out," Kenny said, and gestured to the front steps.

A half-dozen bouquets of flowers and several candles had been placed there. The beginnings of a makeshift memorial.

Kenny saw him first.

A SWAT-team member in full battle dress was stationed at the top of the stairs.

"I know it's a drag, sir," the SWAT officer said, "but no one gets in without showing his shield."

Jane caught up to Kenny. "Who set this up?"

"Chief McDonald. He wants your precinct under full tac alert 'round the clock."

Kenny turned to Jane. "Makes sense."

"Yeah," Jane said as she dug her badge out of her bag. "Guess it does."

"Thank you, Inspectors," the SWAT officer said, and opened the door for them.

Finney joined them as soon as they entered. "I've distributed photos of Jacques Carpenter throughout our department. Plus CHP, Sheriff's, and airport, bridges, and buses."

"Thanks, Mike," Jane said.

"Anything on the Camaro?" Kenny asked as they made their way through the bullpen.

"Yup," Finney said. "Plates came from a 1987 Toyota Tercel stolen from San Francisco State last March."

Jane shook her head and sat at her desk. "Surprise, surprise."

— —

The hours passed quickly.

Evening came, and with it, a slight respite from the heat.

The day shift, off the clock for hours now, stayed on into the night. Cheryl kept working the dispatch console alongside her late-shift counterpart. Finney called his wife to tell her he might not be home at all that night. One of the guys from SWAT made a run to the deli around the corner. "Old man behind the counter wouldn't let me pay for it," he said as he set up platters in the lunchroom.

Mayor Lucien Biggs held a televised news conference and offered a reward of $100,000 for information leading to the arrest and conviction of Jacques Yves Carpenter.

No one at Precinct Nineteen had time to watch.

Roslyn Shapiro approached Jane. "There's a Mr. Schultz here. Said you called for him."

Jane sipped a Coca-Cola. "Shouldn't you be getting home?"

Roslyn shrugged. "Thought I'd stay and help out."

"I appreciate that." Jane signaled Kenny. "Please have Mr. Schultz join us in Interrogation One."

— —

"I can assure you that everything was handled according to procedure," Larry Schultz said. "All the requisite forms were filled out and distributed within thirty minutes of Carpenter's failure to report."

Kenny bit into his corned beef sandwich. "As a parole officer in San—"

"Senior parole officer," Larry Schultz corrected him. He sat perfectly straight on the edge of his chair. A small island of order in the chaos of a full-blown police crisis.

"As a *senior* parole officer in San Francisco for the last seven years," Kenny went on, "and as the one person in the whole city most intimate with the details of Jacques Carpenter's file, did it ever occur to you that he might be—"

"I know what you're implying, Inspector," Larry Schultz said. "But such matters are simply not under the purview of my job description."

Jane finished her Coke and stood up. "Mr. Schultz, we have six police officers dead. We don't give a shit about what you think your job should be." She hurled the Coke can at the wastebasket. It hit the wall above it and clattered to the floor. "Is there anything you can tell us that can get us closer to Carpenter?"

Larry Schultz half rose from his seat. "Inspector Candiotti, I came here, after-hours mind you, because you called. But I certainly didn't come all this way to be . . ."

"Can you help us or not?" Jane said, cutting him off.

Larry Schultz closed his eyes for a second as if to compose himself. "I've already told you," he said, "that everything was done according to dep—"

Kenny reached across the table and pulled Larry Schultz to his feet. "Get the hell out of here."

Larry Schultz got up quickly. He took his briefcase from the table, snapped it shut, and strode across the room. When he got to the door, he turned back to Jane and Kenny. "I've served this city my entire career, and I really don't appreciate being treated—"

"Mr. Schultz!" Jane shouted. "If you don't get the fuck out of my station in two seconds, I'll shoot you dead myself!"

Larry Schultz opened his mouth to respond. Kenny took one step toward him and the senior parole officer thought better of it. He brushed past Mike Finney and stormed away.

Finney entered, looking haggard.

"What's up, Mike?" Jane asked as she willed herself to calm down.

"Prelim came back on Inspector Pagano." He started to speak

again, but hesitated, unable to go on. He handed the form to Kenny and left the room.

"Jesus," Kenny said as he scanned the report. He started to pass the report to Jane, but she held up her hand. "I don't need to go there right now."

They started to leave the room. Jane stopped and turned to Kenny. "What's it say about next of kin?"

Kenny checked the last page. "Nothing. It's blank."

Jane shook her head, thinking about a cop's life lived and lost without a family.

They crossed to their desks. "Remind me to call Aunt Lucy," Jane said. "I'm sure she's worried with all this stuff on television."

"Shit!" Kenny said. "I was supposed to go to that blues club with Bobby tonight." He snatched up the phone and dialed.

Jane crossed to the windows overlooking the street.

The lights from the news crews cast an eerie artificial glow on the front of the building. A SWAT car was parked by the entrance. There were now dozens of flower arrangements on the steps. Jane saw an old woman light a candle, its orange flame flickering, and place it next to the others. Too many to count now.

Someone had taken the flag in for the night.

"Inspector?"

Jane turned to see Roslyn Shapiro.

"There's a Mr. Title to see you."

"Don't know him," Jane said. "If he's a reporter, tell him to—"

Roslyn held up her hand. "He says he knows where Jacques Carpenter lives."

——

Mickey Title couldn't keep his hands still.

No matter how hard he tried, his fingers shook nervously.

"I'm not proud of what I did . . . or who I am. But I gotta get assurances that I can stay anonymous in all this."

"We'll do what we can to protect you," Jane said. "But no promises."

Mickey Title sighed heavily. His shirt was stained with sweat.

"I'm a teacher at a very exclusive private school in Marin. If this gets out, if *why* I know about Jacques Carpenter gets out, I'll be ruined."

"We appreciate your predicament, Mr. Title," Kenny said. "But, honestly, sir, if we make a deal with you that won't hold up in court, then this entire investigation could be compromised. And we're just not gonna let that happen."

"Mr. Title," Jane began, trying to find the right soothing tone for her voice. She'd dealt with reluctant, sometimes terrified, witnesses before. The way to get what you wanted out of them was to sublimate your own ego and let the witness feel he's in control. "Not only have we lost half a dozen cops, we have no indication that the killer is done with his dirty work." She put her hands flat on the table and leaned forward. "Anyone could be next. Anyone. Anytime. We need your help."

Mickey Title looked at his fidgeting fingers. "I . . . I don't know."

"The thing is, sir," Kenny said, "no one ever needs to know *why* you were acquainted with Jacques Carpenter."

Mickey Title sighed. "All my life I've made it a point to never get involved. It's a hard world out there and it's always been my policy to—"

To her surprise, Jane lost it. "Mr. Title!" She slapped the flat of her hand down on the table. Mickey Title was so startled, the rolls of fat around his waist jiggled like water in a bag.

"We tried kissing your ass, and that didn't work. But make no mistake, I'll do whatever I have to do to get you to talk." She pressed forward, closing in on him. "Even if that means breaking the law."

Mickey Title's lips parted, but he didn't speak. Just another part of his body he couldn't control.

"Here's the deal," Jane continued. "Listen carefully because I'm not going to repeat it . . . or change my mind." She glanced over to Kenny, then brought her eyes back to Title with such intensity, he sat back in his chair.

Title turned away and looked to Kenny. "I . . . I think I want a lawyer."

"Tough shit," Kenny said.

Jane reached over and brought Title's face back to hers. "If you don't tell us where Jacques Carpenter lives, I will go to the press. I will tell the newspapers and the television who you are and *what* you are. If another cop dies because you wouldn't lead us to Carpenter, I'll go to fuckin' CNN and tell the world."

She grabbed his mouth between her fingers and squeezed. "And you'll sue me. And you'll win. And we'll both be ruined." She let go of his face and grinned an odd, indifferent grin. "And you know what? . . . I don't care." She released his face and straightened up. "Let this be the night," she said evenly, "that you finally do something right with your life."

Mickey Title tried to stare back at her, but he just didn't have the nerve or the stamina. He looked away, his eyes flicking to the interior window, then over to Kenny. He nodded his head several times, very quickly. "Okay, okay . . . okay." He gripped the edge of the table to quiet his fingers. "He, uh . . . Carpenter lives in the Tenderloin. Eighty-two Ellis. Second floor, in back."

Kenny scribbled the address in his notebook. "Got it."

Jane grabbed her bag. "Let's roll!"

They hustled for the door.

"Hey!" Mickey Title called.

Kenny ran out of the room. "Finney, get me SWAT Command!"

Jane stopped and turned to Mickey Title.

He rose and shoved his hands under his armpits. "The TV said something about a reward."

49

MARCO KNEW THEY would be coming.

Ever since he had seen his Camaro on the news and the mug shot of that big ex-con, he knew it was only a matter of time before the cops figured it out and descended on the Tenderloin.

He sat on the lip of the roof across from 82 Ellis, legs dangling, smoking a cigarette. Since Punky-Boy disappeared, he'd taken over his business, selling guns and dope to all comers. Keeping the little ones happy with one-stop shopping. First it was the steady chop of the police helicopter hovering about a mile away. Then Marco saw the long line of headlights racing up Leavenworth.

Coming to the jungle.

Marco knew there were probably dozens of cons, busted parolees, and illegal aliens jumping out of windows and hauling ass out of the T-loin right now.

And then the street below was alive with skidding police vehicles of all sizes and descriptions. Two squads of SWAT jumped down from their vans and formed up, rifles ready, behind a black Explorer.

Jane adjusted the Velcro straps on her bulletproof vest. "Promise me," she said to Kenny. "No macho boy-stuff. You have more to live for than just yourself now."

Kenny switched off the engine. "You gonna deny me my God-given Y-chromosome right to—"

Jane cut him off. "I don't want any jokes. You go according to procedure and that's an order."

His face reddening, Kenny parted his lips to respond, but Jane was already opening her door.

The chief's Suburban, flanked by four motorcycles, ground to a stop.

Jane and Kenny climbed out of the Explorer and, avoiding a spreading puddle from the dripping fire hydrant, joined the SWAT teams. Chief McDonald stepped out of the Suburban and crossed to them. "You ready, Inspector?"

"Yes sir." Jane turned to address the SFPD and SWAT officers huddled around her. "This scene is to be considered hot. It now officially belongs to SWAT. I don't want any of my people playing cowboy out here." She stole a glance at Kenny. "The situation turns critical, stand down and call for SWAT."

Jane nodded to Hicks. "All yours, Scott."

"Thank you, ma'am." Hicks laid his M-16 on the hood of the Explorer and unfolded a diagram. "This is the floor plan of eighty-two Ellis. Right now the structure is surrounded. So if the suspect's in there, we're gonna get him—"

Suddenly, the street was illuminated from above. The Night Sun, suspended from the belly of the helicopter, washed the street with light. Jane and Kenny looked up at the thirty-million candlepower shaft of white cutting through the black sky. The SWAT teams never took their eyes off the floor plan.

". . . in the rear." Hicks tapped the diagram. "If he's in there, then he knows we're out here. Consider him armed and extremely dangerous." He slipped the action on his rifle. "Safeties off. Cameras on."

There was a rapid clacking of metal as the men prepped their rifles and switched on their miniature helmet-cams.

"Okay," Hicks shouted. "I want maximum firing discipline. This place is crawling with civilians, and they don't like cops. Plus there's kids in there." He held up a fist. "On my go." The men waited as Hicks turned to Jane and nodded. "Ma'am." Then he spun around, lowered his visor, and shouted, "Go! Go! Go!"

The SWAT teams fell into two lines and double-timed across the street. When they reached 82 Ellis, the line on the right fanned in two and set up a perimeter around the tenement house. The other line followed Scott Hicks up the stairs and through the front door.

Chief McDonald climbed the three steps to the SWAT command vehicle. "Let's have a look."

Jane started forward, then turned to Kenny. "You coming?"

Kenny, still angry over their earlier exchange, simply nodded and followed.

The interior of the van was bathed in the faint grey-blue glow of a dozen television monitors. A video tech sat at the console, adjusting the images transmitted from the helmet-cams.

They watched as the SWAT team switched on the high-powered flashlights mounted on their M-16s. The beams of light cut smoky white arcs in the dimly lit hallway. Racing past a baby carriage at the entrance, the team scurried up the stairs.

At the top, Hicks waited for the others to fall into place. Then he motioned his number two forward.

The video tech brought up another image as the second SWAT officer turned the corner at the top of the stairway. Another hallway came into focus as a half-dozen heavily armed men crouch-walked toward the rear of the building.

An apartment door to the right opened and closed, a heavyset black woman's face appearing for an instant. One of the SWAT commandos kicked the door in and raced inside.

"What's he doing?" Jane asked. "That's not Carpenter's apartment."

The video tech tweaked the picture. "Suspect might not be in his own apartment." He looked back to Jane. "Before we're done, we're going to visit every unit in the place." He brought up the team leader's transmission.

Hicks and his men were flanking the door to Carpenter's apartment. "Show time," the tech said as a SWAT member broke off the doorknob with a huge vise grip and shouldered the door open. The men piled in, their flashlight beams streaking the dusty room like a laser light show.

The team went into a precisely coordinated search of the living room, bathroom, and bedroom. One of the men looked up and down the air shaft while another checked the crawl space above the hall closet. Hicks pressed his radio mike. "No one home. Commencing door-to-door." The SWAT team scrambled out of the apartment and started pounding on the neighboring doors.

The speaker in the center of the monitors crackled. "Air One to Command. My FLIR is picking up something interesting on the rooftop across from eighty-two."

"FLIR?" Kenny asked.

"Forward-Looking Infrared," the tech said. "A night-vision thing."

They watched the center screen as a shadowy figure raced across the roof and tried to hide on the far side of the door housing.

Jane turned to Kenny, but he was already out the door. He jumped down the steps and, drawing his weapon, tore across the street.

Pulling her pistol from her bag, Jane ran out of the van. She jabbed her finger at three uniformed cops. "You, you, and you. Follow me!" With the others trailing, Jane bolted up the steps and burst through the front door. Kenny was just starting up the stairwell. "Kenny!"

Kenny stopped and turned to Jane.

"What the hell are you doing?" she hissed at him.

"SWAT's kind of occupied," Kenny said, keeping his voice low in front of the other cops. "What if it's Carpenter on the roof and we don't get up there fast enough?"

"And what if he takes out the first hotshot through the door because he went up there by himself?"

Kenny clenched his jaw and looked away.

Jane turned to the uniformed officers. "Everybody got vests?"

They all nodded.

She singled out the youngest cop; he was about Benjy's age. "You stay here in case there's another way down we don't know about." She thumbed the safety off her pistol. "Let's go."

Moving rapidly, Jane, Kenny, and the two patrolmen hustled up the three flights to the roof access. As they climbed, the pounding of the helicopter grew louder and louder, and they realized the upper door was open.

Jane nodded to Kenny and they hustled up the last run of stairs. Kenny and one of the patrolmen went through the door first, Jane close behind.

It was bright as day.

The Night Sun blasted a brilliant swath of light onto the rooftop. In the center of the beam, as if being pressed down by it, was a man lying spread-eagle on the tarpaper skin of the roof.

Jane, Kenny, and the two patrolmen moved forward in a cautious crouch, their weapons level in front of them.

As they closed in, Jane immediately saw that this man wasn't Carpenter. He was much smaller, about twenty years younger . . . and he was black.

Marco looked up, squinting into the blinding light.

"I ain't him."

— —

"Sorry, ma'am," Scott Hicks said as he and his men stripped down. "If he was in that building, we woulda got him." He peeled off his black leather gloves. "But he's gone. Could be anywhere by now."

"You and the guys were great," Jane said as she tore at the Velcro of her bulletproof vest. "Thanks, Scott."

Kenny tossed his gear bag into the back of the Explorer. Across the way the Suburban started up and, flanked by the four motorcycles, roared away.

"Chief's not too happy," Jane said as she put her vest on top of Kenny's bag.

Kenny slammed the hatch closed. "Nobody is." He strode to the driver's side and got in.

The helicopter switched off its Night Sun, abruptly returning this part of the Tenderloin to darkness.

As the SWAT vehicles pulled out, Jane took one last look up the street. She stood there, knowing without seeing, that the residents of Ellis Street were looking back at her, seething with hatred behind their windows.

"Where are you?" she shouted, her voice breaking.

Kenny started the Explorer and lowered his window. "You coming?"

Jane didn't move.

Kenny revved the engine. "Watched pot never boils."

Jane turned to him and said tightly, "Yes, it does." Finally, she climbed in and Kenny drove away, splashing through the puddle of water from the dripping hydrant.

The water trickled along the gutter and fell through a sewer grate cut into the high curb.

Two dark eyes stared out from behind the grate, as shiny as new coins.

Jacques Carpenter stood in the sewer, ankle-deep in water, watching the taillights of the Explorer move down the street. "Where am I, Inspector Candiotti? " he said under his breath. "I'm close by. I'm *always* close by."

He lit a cigarette to fight off the stench, turned to his left, and slipped into the darkness.

50

For the first time in what seemed like a lifetime, Jane was cold.

The air-conditioning in the media room of the Hall of Justice was on full blast, and the temperature was in the mid-sixties. With San Francisco awakening to yet another day of this unforgiving heat wave, Jane felt an odd pang of guilt as she fastened the top button of her blouse.

Mayor Lucien Biggs, with Chief McDonald just behind, approached the podium.

Jane scanned the crowd.

Becka Flynn, her red hair piled high on her head, caught her eye and nodded. Jane let her chin drop in response, and she reminded herself to thank her for the sympathy card. Cameron Sanders of the *Chronicle* tested his tape recorder, holding it close to his mouth and counting to ten. Other reporters, dozens of them, nudged their way forward, jockeying for advantage as the mayor prepared to speak.

"Ladies and gentlemen," Mayor Biggs began, "I will make a short statement for the local morning news outlets, and that will be all. There will be no Q and A; we're all too busy."

The mayor ignored the murmur of complaint and turned to the television cameras.

"Our city is being terrorized by a madman. Already five police officers and one former police officer have been taken from us. Murdered in cold blood."

"But now, thanks to the excellent and tireless work of our police department, we know who the killer is." He paused to glance at a monitor. "You may have already seen this photo last night or in this morning's papers. We'll be showing it to you every hour until we catch him. He's Jacques Yves Carpenter. Not only is he armed and dangerous . . . he's desperate. Desperate because he knows it's only a matter of time until we get him."

Jane looked over to Kenny. He was leaning against the wall at the foot of the stage. Ordinarily, he would have been up there with her. But since last night at the Tenderloin, he'd been uncommonly quiet. His pager beeped and he snapped it off his belt.

"The City Council," the mayor continued, "in an extraordinary session only a few hours ago, has approved the following: the one-hundred-thousand-dollar reward for information leading to the arrest and conviction of Jacques Carpenter has been raised to two hundred and fifty thousand dollars."

There was a ripple of surprise from the press.

Mayor Biggs waited for quiet.

"But, perhaps more important, there will be a joint ceremony for Inspector Hank Pagano and Patrol Officer Benjamin Spielman Junior at Grace Cathedral this Friday morning. Inspector Pagano, only recently awarded the Medal of Valor in this very building, was one of San Francisco's most beloved cops. Patrol Officer Spielman, the son of a San Francisco police lieutenant, was just a rookie on the force. He graduated from the Police Academy a little over a week ago. They gave their lives so that we may be safe from harm."

Chief McDonald said something into the mayor's ear. He nodded and went on.

"Law enforcement officers from all over Northern and Southern California, as well as from Oregon, Nevada, and Arizona will attend the memorial service. I promise you it will be the finest tribute to our fallen heroes this city has ever seen." He took a half step back from the podium. "Thank you," he said, and started for the steps.

"Mr. Mayor," Becka Flynn shouted. "Are we really safe?"

Mayor Biggs stopped and leaned back into the microphones. "Yes. Yes, you are safe. All of you. Because the San Francisco Police Department stands between you and the threat of danger; day and night, *every* day and night. Yes, you are safe."

He looked to Chief McDonald and the two men strode down the steps and out a side door.

As the press conference broke up, Jane noticed Kenny finishing a call on his cell phone. She crossed the stage and squatted down. "What's up?"

"Bobby called," Kenny said, his voice gripped with anger. "Fuckin' Lonnie hit him again and he wants to come over to the house." He dropped the phone into his pocket. "He was crying. You know what it takes to make a teenage boy cry?"

"You go on ahead." Jane moved to the side to let the other cops file by. "But I don't want you doing anything about Lonnie till I get home."

Kenny's jaw bounced with frustration.

"I mean it, Kenny."

Kenny narrowed his eyes at Jane and, shaking his head, stalked away.

"Ken!" Jane called after him.

Without looking back, he pushed his way through the crowd and disappeared out the front doors.

Jane jumped down from the stage and hurried up the aisle. When she emerged into the foyer, she spotted Kenny outside. He was just starting down the broad concrete steps when Jane came rushing out the doors.

The thick heat hit her like a bad memory and she undid the top button of her blouse. "Kenny! Stop!"

Kenny whirled around. "Is that an order, too?"

Jane scuttled down the steps. "What the hell is wrong with you?"

"After a while it just gets to me," he said, his eyes bright with temper.

"What does?"

"Everything. Simply fuckin' everything." Kenny let two plain-clothes cops pass. "Our relationship, our pecking order, is constantly being played out in public and I'm sick of it." He came up one step closer, hurling the words at her. "We live in *your* house. You're senior to me at work. Every fucking thing I say or do is scrutinized and second-guessed by you." He blew a long sigh. "And *always* in front of someone else."

Jane willed herself to keep her composure. "Look . . . yes, it's my house. We talked about that before we did this. And I'm senior to you at work because"—she tried for a laugh—"because I'm older. And, I'm sorry, but sometimes I do have better ideas about things. And sometimes you have better—"

"Just stop it!" Kenny hissed, surprising them both with his intensity. He held out his hands. "I don't want explanations. I only want you to tell me that you understand how I feel."

"Kenny, we—"

He cut her off. "Jane, you have to examine if you really want to ... if you really know *how* to ... be in a relationship." He kept his hands up, palms facing her, as if to ward off whatever she might say.

Jane stood there, struck by his words.

Finally, Kenny broke the impasse. "Bobby's coming over. I want to be there when he does."

Jane nodded tightly. "I'll catch a ride."

Without responding, Kenny went down the last few steps and climbed into the Explorer.

Jane watched as he peeled out, the back end fighting for traction. He ripped the Explorer into a hard right turn and was gone.

"Inspector?"

Jane turned to see Chief McDonald at the top of the steps. "My office, please," he said, and went back into the Hall of Justice.

Jane started up, but then stopped and looked back to the corner Kenny had taken. She half hoped the Explorer would reappear and he would come back.

She looked up to the pale blue sky. A plane was silently coursing through high thin clouds. It glinted a silver flash as it caught the morning sun and banked away. The clouds, Jane thought, were as white and frail as smoke.

A clutch of dread caught in her throat and Jane realized, for the first time, that she'd never actually been in a relationship that was this important to her.

And it came over her like a wave.

The fear.

As she went back up the steps, Jane was suddenly afraid that Kenny was right.

Maybe she didn't know how to do this.

51

JANE SAT ALONE in the back of Chief McDonald's Suburban with her arm over her eyes.

"More AC, Inspector?" the chief's driver asked as he curled past the Safeway and headed toward the Marina.

Jane let her arm fall to her lap. "I'm okay, thanks."

"What the chief said in that meeting? About how he's confident and such that you'll get this guy?" The driver caught her eye in the mirror. "Well, ma'am, we all of us feel that way." His blue eyes flashed a smile. "We know you're a good cop, Inspector." Feeling perhaps he had stepped over some invisible line, he broke eye contact.

"Thanks, Stan," Jane said as she gathered up her bag. "That means a lot to me."

"Lookit them kids," Stan said, changing the subject. "In this heat."

A group of college kids were playing soccer on the green. Beyond them, an old man sat in the shade of an elm tree. He had set up an easel and was painting some watercolor scene Jane couldn't quite make out. Three women in jogging clothes walked briskly along the path by the water, passing a plastic bottle of Gatorade between them. A bum rummaged in a trash bin, a Hefty bag bulging with soda cans at his feet.

"Pretty down here," Stan said as he swung into a U-turn and pulled up in front of Jane's house. He started to get out to open the rear door for her.

"I got it," Jane said as she stepped down to the sidewalk. "Thanks for the lift."

"Anytime, ma'am. See you around." He pulled on the gearshift and the Suburban slipped back into traffic.

The Explorer was parked right at the path leading up to the front steps. Jane smiled as she thought about how much Kenny loved it when he got a good parking space. Often, he would bring her to the bay window and, laughing, show her how his parking saint had once again smiled on him.

She wondered what his mood would be when she came in. Would he still be angry? Would he joke about his parking karma? Would they be able to wade through the tension and negotiate a truce?

Jane fished her keys out of her bag and started toward the house. As she did, she noticed Cito and his guide dog crossing the street two blocks up. Heading, as usual, for the Palace of Fine Arts and the coolness of the duck pond.

As she climbed the steps to the porch, Jane felt warm inside, a welling of something positive. She realized that Kenny had been right about them, about her. No matter how much she had thought she was ready for a permanent relationship, for marriage, she understood now that she still had a lot to learn.

She would begin by apologizing to him.

— —

"It's me!" Jane called as she pulled her key from the lock. The house was still, the only sound coming from the green across the way. "Kenny?" she called again. "Yo! Anybody home?"

Jane dropped her bag on the coffee table and noticed that the CD player wasn't on. Kenny was never home without the blues filling the living room. Maybe he walked to the market, she thought. She raised her hands over her head and stretched, chuckling at the notion of how much Kenny loved to go grocery shopping.

She suddenly dropped her arms and looked around the room.

Something was wrong.

Her heartbeat accelerated slightly as she tried to understand what was different in her home.

Then she noticed it.

The smell.

Cigarettes.

"Oh God," she whispered. She scooped up her bag and pulled out her pistol. Thumbing off the safety, she held the gun, elbows bent, at chest level. "Kenny!" she shouted as she walked down the hall in a half crouch. Her heart was racing now, every nerve ending fully alert.

She passed the Parsons table, the photograph of her and Poppy in Kenny's antique silver frame at the center of the others.

She leaned into the door of the guest bathroom and pushed it open with her shoulder.

Nothing.

As she stole toward the master bedroom, the image of Kenny lying there, his eyes . . .

She shook her head and chased the thought away.

Sucking in a deep breath, she hunkered by the doorknob and turned it. The bedroom door fell open. Her mind racing, Jane passed into the room. The ironing board peeked out from under the bed.

Kenny wasn't there.

The master bath was empty as well. That left the guest room and the kitchen.

Jane stuck her gun into the hallway and darted across to the second bedroom. Unpacked boxes and guitar cases.

As she made her way back down the hall toward the kitchen, she became aware of another odor. A pungent chemical smell.

She was just about to the door of the dining area when she saw it.

A cigarette ash, less than a quarter inch long, on the floor next to the throw rug.

Her breath coming in choking gulps, Jane stood with her back against the wall. She had her weapon up next to her cheek, gripping the butt with both hands.

She closed her eyes and, breathing through her nose, quickly counted to three. Then she opened her eyes and whipped around into the open doorway, her pistol pointed into the kitchen.

Kenny sat in the middle of the room.

He was bound with duct tape, hand and foot, to one of the

chrome chairs. There was a bandanna crammed into his mouth. He was trying to move, trying to say something, but all he could manage was a guttural grunt.

Jane started into the room, and Kenny intensified his struggle. He sounded like an injured animal as he thrashed his head from side to side.

Jane tore across the room, knelt on one knee, and pulled the bandanna from Kenny's mouth.

"He's still here!" Kenny gasped.

The pantry door flew open and Jacques Carpenter filled the doorway, his .22 aimed at Jane's face.

Jane started to raise her pistol.

Carpenter took one step forward and kicked the pistol out of her hand. It skittered along the linoleum and clanged off the bottom of the stove. Then he lashed out with his other foot and caught Jane just below the cheek. She fell back heavily, hitting her head on one of the table legs.

He was on her in a flash, his knee hard against her chest, holding her down. Then he jammed the muzzle of the .22 into her right eye socket, the sharp edge of the muzzle nicking the skin next to her nose.

"This should be fun," he said as he grabbed her by the hair and yanked her to her feet.

52

JANE LAY ON her left side, handcuffed to an elbow of pipe under the kitchen sink.

Kenny was still in a chair in the center of the room, immobilized by yards of strong grey duct tape.

Carpenter sat on the counter above Jane, smoking a cigarette and sipping a diet Coke he'd taken from the refrigerator.

Jane flexed her wrists against the cuffs and noticed that the crystal on her watch was shattered. Her pistol was on the floor across the room, by the stove. An impossible distance.

The drainpipe was cool, almost soothing, to the insides of Jane's wrists. Her eyes flicked around the cabinet space beneath the sink. Dishwasher detergent, Ivory soap, a blue plastic bucket with an old sponge, a plunger, silver polish, steel wool; nothing to use as a weapon.

"My mistake," Carpenter said as he crushed the diet Coke can and dropped it to the floor. It bounced once and came to rest near Jane's knee. "My mistake was killing the boy first. Now the lieutenant's under such heavy guard, I can't get to him." He took a deep drag from his cigarette and dropped an ash into the sink. "Pisses me off. I really wanted to kill him." He grinned, a crescent of yellow teeth showing behind the crease of his lips. "It was kind of the point."

Jane struggled until she was in a half-sitting position. It was uncomfortable, but she felt less vulnerable that way. "Hasn't there been enough killing?"

Kenny's back was to Carpenter. He strained to turn his head. "You've already killed six cops . . . plus that kid in 3Com Park."

"Why him?" Jane asked. "What was that about?"

"Knew too much. Talked too much. A bad mix." Carpenter lifted the front of his T-shirt to wipe the sweat from his face. His stomach muscles rippled like waves on a pond and Jane remembered how terribly strong he was. "Beautiful place like this and you don't have air-conditioning?"

"I'll put it on the list." Jane lifted her arms to take the pressure off her wrists. "What are you going to do with us?"

"Oh, I'm going to kill you, of course."

Jane stole a look to Kenny. His shoulders sagged. Then she turned back to Carpenter. "Why? Isn't it over yet?"

"That's what you don't understand," Carpenter said. He turned on the faucet and extinguished his cigarette. Jane could hear the water gurgling in the pipe by her ear. Then it stopped. "It'll never be over for me." He lit another cigarette, letting the match fall to the floor next to Jane. It flickered for an instant, then died.

"When your lieutenant took my wife and baby from me, he set something in motion. Something perfect and unstoppable. As inevitable as fate." He leaned forward and looked down at Jane. "And you, you go on TV and call me an animal." Suddenly furious, he kicked in the cabinet door next to her face, leaving a jagged hole. "Well, if I'm an animal, it's because you people turned me into one!"

"Fuck you!" Jane screamed at him. "There are plenty of people in the world who get dealt a shitty hand, and they don't go around shooting cops in the face!"

"Great," Kenny said. "That should calm him down."

Carpenter whipped his .22 out of his belt and trained it on Jane. With just the slightest motion, he moved it from her left eye to her right eye.

Jane recoiled, her face contorted into a tight grimace.

"Don't," Kenny pleaded. "Please."

Carpenter pointed the gun at the back of Kenny's head. "Are you begging me not to shoot her?"

Kenny looked at Jane. "Yes," he said. "I'm begging you not to shoot her."

"Okay." Carpenter jumped down from the counter. "Since you asked so nice." He slipped the pistol back into his belt. Then he reached into the sink and came up with a red gasoline can. "I'm willing to work with you."

He twisted the cap off the container and sprinkled gas along the counter. He crossed to the overstuffed chair and soaked it, splashing more of the flammable liquid onto the stacks of newspaper in the recycle bin.

A trickle of gasoline ran down the front of the cabinet beneath the sink and Jane realized that had been the chemical smell she'd noticed earlier. "Why are you doing this?" she demanded.

Carpenter swung a spray of gasoline into the dining area. "Because you're cops." He strode over to Kenny and held the can over his head. He looked at Jane, his eyes glinting with evil. "You called me an animal." He tilted the can until it was upside down. Two drops dribbled out. It was empty. "Just as well. We don't want this to be over too soon, do we?"

He flung the can against the far wall. It caromed off and banged to a stop in the corner. Then he squatted down next to Jane, his face so close she could feel his harsh breath on her cheek. "You called me an animal, Inspector," he repeated. "Know what? You're right. I'm an animal." He stood up, seething. "That's why I have to keep killing."

"But, why this way?" Jane asked, trying to steal a few more seconds before Carpenter made his final move.

"I suppose I could shoot you like the others," Carpenter said. "But a nice close-knit neighborhood like this? Somebody might hear." He flicked an ash on the floor. "So, I'm just gonna do this my way and walk out of the house. Calm as can be, like a friend come to visit." He sucked one last drag from his cigarette and tossed it onto the overstuffed chair. "Have a nice life."

He strode from the room. Jane and Kenny heard the front door open and close, and the sound of his footfall as he crossed the porch and went down the steps.

Jane strained to see the cigarette butt on the chair. A thin wisp of smoke spiraled upward from it. She turned to Kenny. "Can you move?"

He twisted and fought against the duct tape. "No. Can you?"

Jane yanked on the handcuffs. They held fast. "Not at all."

There was a small *pwoof* from the overstuffed chair and a tiny explosion of flame erupted on the gasoline-soaked fabric.

Kenny wrenched his body around to face the spreading fire. "We're totally fucked." A spark fell onto the recycle bin and it immediately burst into flames. In seconds the fire was eating its way up the curtains toward the ceiling.

"Do you have your cell phone?" Jane asked.

"In my pants pocket. No way I can get to it."

Jane snapped at the cuffs. Then again. "Shit!"

There was another whooshing explosion from the overstuffed chair and then it was completely involved. Thick black smoke reached toward the ceiling. It hung there for a moment, a building cloud of choking soot, then it banked back on itself and began to fill the room.

Frantic, Jane tried to grab the can of silver polish to throw through a window. But it was too far back and Carpenter had clasped the handcuffs too tightly. She couldn't reach it.

When the curtains were completely consumed, burning fragments of fabric floated down like little deadly parachutes. One of them landed on the counter and, in moments, flames were licking at the cabinets.

Other smoldering bits landed on the floor. Jane and Kenny desperately began stomping them out with their feet, flailing wildly at any they could reach.

And still they fell.

There was a sudden rush of bright orange as the fire ignited the trail of gasoline. In no time, the dining area was crackling with flame, sending even more black smoke into the kitchen.

Jane watched helplessly as the fire clawed its way across the hallway and into the living room. The couch nearest to her caught. Then the cushion in the bay window. The curtains. The bookshelves. The other couch and Aunt Lucy's pillows. The rocker. The lamp shades. Kenny's guitars.

The Parsons table.

Poppy's picture.

The paint on the kitchen wall bubbled and the crackling of the fire turned into something resembling the sound of wind.

"Try to knock your chair over!" Jane yelled. "There's more oxygen down here!"

Kenny bounced on his toes, struggling to topple the chair. The smoke was now curling back down the walls and was only a few feet above the floor. The bubbling paint ruptured with a staccato sequence of tiny pops.

Finally, Kenny was able to tilt his chair partway over. Jane struck out with both feet and sent him crashing down, landing heavily on his side. He had fallen at such an angle that he was facing Jane, about a foot away from her. Still bound to the chair.

Knowing it was futile, Jane pulled and pulled at the handcuffs, scraping and rattling them over the pipe. They held fast.

"The key!" she shouted through the smoke. "Where's the key?"

"Back . . . pocket!"

Using his feet and shoulders, Kenny tried to maneuver the chair around so Jane could reach his pocket. A flaming bit of debris fell on his pants. Jane threw her legs over him and extinguished it.

The smoke was now only a foot off the floor.

Kenny looked to Jane, his eyes watery and sad. For a moment, time stood still. "I love you," he said.

"Oh, Ken . . . I love you. I'm so sorry for—"

"No, don't . . . I love you's good enough . . ." He dissolved into a racking cough as the smoke pressed inexorably downward, sucking away the oxygen and slowly smothering them.

Exhausted and seconds away from losing consciousness, Jane touched her right foot to Kenny's chest. He lowered his chin and kissed the toe of her shoe. "Shit," he said. "I didn't want to—"

The kitchen door exploded inward. It hung on one hinge and fell across the doorway. A boot appeared from outside and kicked the door into the room. Then the shape of a body emerged from the smoke.

Bobby.

Crawling on the floor, his T-shirt wrapped around his mouth, Bobby scurried to Kenny. "Tell me what to do!" he shouted, his voice cracking with fear.

"A knife!" Kenny yelled. "Get a knife and cut me loose!"

Bobby gulped a lungful of air and jumped to his feet. He went to grab a knife from its slot in the smoldering butcher block, but the handle was too hot. Tearing the T-shirt away from his face, he used it to grasp the knife and, choking on the smoke, sawed away at the duct tape holding Kenny's hands.

As soon as one hand was free, Kenny thrust it into his back pocket and came up with his keys. He gave them to Bobby and took the knife. While Kenny finished cutting away the last of the duct tape, Bobby lunged over to Jane and unlocked the cuff on her right wrist.

The weight of her body sent her crashing down onto her shoulder.

Fighting to breathe, fighting to see, she felt two pairs of hands around her ankles and suddenly she was being pulled across the floor.

And then she was outside. Brilliant, searing sunlight slicing through the smoke.

The three of them sat on the grass by the side door, coughing and spitting; battling to soothe their tortured lungs with fresh air.

Jane brought her hand up to push the hair back from her face. She still had one handcuff locked around her left wrist.

"Jesus, Uncle Ken," Bobby said when he could manage a breath. "What happened?"

Before Kenny could answer, the window over the kitchen sink blew out, showering them with white-hot bits of glass.

Kenny put his arms around Jane and Bobby. "Let's get to the street!"

As they scrambled to their feet, Jane heard, cutting through the roar of the fire that was destroying her home, the thin wail of the first fire engine racing toward the Marina.

It sounded, she thought, like a woman in pain.

53

By the time Jane, Kenny, and Bobby reached the sidewalk, the house was almost completely consumed by flame.

As she watched, Jane became aware of the noise. The whooshing of the fire, the crackling of the wood, the scream of the sirens as they grew closer.

Kenny drew her to him. "Your beautiful home," he shouted over the din.

She looked up to him. "*Our* beautiful home," she shouted back.

The bay window gave way, sending shards of glass onto the porch. Jane turned her back on her burning house and looked across the street.

A crowd of nearly a hundred people lined the green. The fire trucks were almost upon them now, their sirens throwing a deafening blare.

Jane turned back for a last look at her house, and was surprised to see a small hole suddenly appear in her mailbox. Then the left taillight of the Explorer exploded, little rubies of glass spraying everywhere.

Someone was shooting at them.

Jane shoved Kenny and Bobby aside. "Get down!" she shrieked.

Kenny threw himself on top of Bobby and they fell to the ground.

Jane spun around and yelled to the onlookers, "Get back! Get back!" But the bystanders couldn't hear the gunfire over the wail of the sirens. They stood there, transfixed.

Grabbing Kenny's keys from her pocket, she thumbed the remote and unlocked the Explorer. Then she ripped open the door and dove inside, just as a bullet ricocheted off the sidewalk and sliced into Kenny's side.

"Shit!" she heard him cry.

Jane snatched up the radio. "3H58 to Nineteen."

"Go, 3H58."

"Cheryl! I've got a four, oh, six. My house is burning and we're taking gunfire. It's Jacques Carpenter!"

"Help is on the way, Jane. Stay low and stay safe."

"Listen to me. You've got to have the fire department stand down. It's too dangerous."

"Will do."

"And send an ambulance. I think Kenny's been shot."

"Oh no . . ."

Jane didn't wait for Cheryl's response. She tossed the radio onto the dash and reached under the seat for the shotgun. As she did, a bullet whistled through the back window and struck the windshield. Because it was a .22, the windshield didn't shatter. A small hole surrounded by a concave oval was carved out of the glass.

Jane dropped back to the street and crawled to Kenny. "You hit?"

He was lying prone over Bobby, covering him with his own body. "I think I got a punctured . . . love handle. But I'm okay."

Jane chambered a round into the shotgun. "I'm gonna get this fucker." She started to go.

"Jane," Kenny said. She looked back. Kenny grimaced. "Don't go getting all macho on me now."

"Not my style," Jane said. Then she rose into a crouch and fired the shotgun into the air. As she had hoped, the crowd in the green scrambled for cover.

A block and a half up the street, Carpenter leaped out from behind a parked van and bolted away.

Jane quick-chambered a shell and snapped the shotgun into the firing position. She drew a bead on Carpenter's retreating back. But, at the last instant, he broke to his left and disappeared down a side street. Jane lowered the shotgun and called back over her shoulder, "He's heading toward the Palace!"

Holding his side, Kenny started to get up. "I'll call it in."

"Give the all-clear to the fire department, too!"

Bobby pushed himself up off the grass and watched as Jane gripped the shotgun in her right hand and started running up Marina Boulevard.

As she ran, Jane ticked off the possibilities of what could happen next.

Carpenter could simply keep on going and try to get away.

Maybe.

Or he could be lying in ambush behind any parked car, any building.

Not likely.

Or he could be luring her onward into some kind of trap like he did that day in Chinatown.

Probably.

Her lungs aching from the smoke and from the exertion, Jane turned left on Baker Street and crossed over to the park that fringed the Palace of Fine Arts. She stopped to get her bearings.

The area around the duck pond was nearly empty. Usually on such a hot summer day it was crowded with families and joggers and homeless. They're all down the street, Jane realized, drawn by the smoke and the sirens, watching my house burn.

She scurried down the slope to the walkway and tried to decide whether to go right or left. Then she noticed Cito and his Seeing Eye dog sitting at the edge of the pond, a cluster of ducks paddling nearby. Jane hurried up to him and saw that he was breaking off pieces of sourdough from a small loaf and tossing them into the water.

"Cito," she said breathlessly, "it's me, Jane."

Cito lifted his head, tilting it toward her. "I know." He flared his nostrils. "There's a fire somewheres."

"I'm looking for someone. Someone dangerous. You hear anything?"

"Guy ran by before." He stroked his dog's neck. "Wrong shoes for running. Smelled like cigarettes."

"Which way?"

Cito gestured with his chin. "That way."

"Thanks," Jane said as she rose. "You should get out of here. If you bump into anyone, have them call for help."

The shotgun level before her, Jane started up the path toward a small copse of trees.

A young Chinese woman lay on a towel, Walkman earphones on her head. When Jane's shadow fell over her, she opened her eyes and saw the shotgun. Panicking, she scrambled to her feet and tore away, leaving her towel and sandals behind.

Two men in tight cutoff jeans, tank tops, and work boots rounded the far curve of the pond. One of them stopped when he saw Jane's soot-covered face and shotgun. He elbowed his friend.

"I'm a cop," Jane said. "You seen a tall, muscular guy in khaki pants and a tight white T-shirt?"

"I wish," one of the men said.

Jane waved the gun. "Get out of the park. Now!"

The two men looked at each other, their mouths open. Then they clambered up the slope and raced away.

Jane approached the stand of trees. There were some soiled blankets and cheap wine bottles in a small clearing. A bum lay under a flattened cardboard box, a Hefty bag of soda cans near his head.

Crouching low, Jane moved forward, ready for anything. "Hey, mister," she hissed at the sleeping bum. He didn't stir. She kept going, moving toward the next clearing. When she reached the line of trees, she slipped behind the largest one and looked back.

The sleeping bum threw off his cardboard cover and drew himself up to his knees. Then he shrugged off the filthy blanket and looked around.

Satisfied that he was alone, Jacques Carpenter stood up and started back toward the duck pond.

Jane stepped out from the protection of the tree. She was about to train the shotgun on Carpenter when a young teenage boy blasted by on a skateboard. Carpenter turned at the sound and saw Jane.

As soon as the boy cleared her line of fire, Jane whipped the shotgun at Carpenter. "Freeze!"

But Carpenter kept turning his torso toward her.

"I said . . . *don't move!*"

Carpenter stared at the shotgun, the black hole in the muzzle. Just like an eye, he thought to himself. Funny.

Then he saw the handcuff dangling from Jane's left wrist. "I thought I killed all the heroes."

Jane took a step forward, the shotgun pointed at Carpenter's chest. "No one can. Not even you." She waggled the shotgun. "On the ground. Facedown."

Carpenter's face fell slack, all the tension draining away. Then his lips furrowed into a sick grin. "As inevitable as fate. Remember?" His hand moved toward his belt, toward the .22.

"Don't," Jane warned.

He stopped, his hand inches away from his pistol. His gaze moved from the shotgun to Jane's face, his eyes boring into hers with such ferocity, Jane almost looked away.

"Don't," Jane said again.

Carpenter closed his eyes and slowly shook his head. Then he opened his eyes again and said softly, "I have to."

His hand slapped at his belt and he gripped the butt of the .22.

"*No!*" Jane shouted as she squeezed back on the trigger.

The shotgun jumped in her hands and Carpenter's chest exploded into a thick red vapor.

Then came the sound, a deep booming report. All through the park, birds erupted, squawking, from the trees. The ducks ran along the top of the pond and took the air, their wings beating in terror.

Jane yanked back on the action, ready to fire again.

Carpenter stumbled backward a couple of steps. He lowered his head, his face wrenched in disbelief, to look at his mangled chest. Then he looked at Jane, his trembling hand still trying for his gun.

Jane's finger tensed on the trigger. She raised the barrel for a head shot.

But Carpenter sucked in a last gurgling breath and died as he stood.

His knees collapsed and he fell backward into the pond, his blood infusing the water with bright crimson clouds.

Carpenter's body floated there for a few seconds, the rosy water lapping over it. Then it sank, coming to rest on the slimy shallow bottom. The water at the edge of the pond was less than two feet deep and the body, still draining red puffs of blood, stayed clearly visible.

Something disengaged itself from the right front pocket of his chinos. A pack of Marlboros bobbed to the surface, stayed there a moment, and then, waterlogged, drifted back down, landing on Carpenter's thigh.

Jane felt her heartbeat slowing; not nearly to normal, but finally slowing. She became aware of the shotgun. Its weight was suddenly unbearable. Holding it by the trigger guard, she let it swing down until the butt was touching the ground.

She stared at the man she had killed until she heard the sound of running footsteps behind her. Kenny and Bobby were just coming down the little slope, a couple of patrolmen behind them.

Jane quickly shook her head at Kenny and he stopped, motioning for Bobby to stay behind. The body of a killer, his chest torn away, lying in two feet of bloody water, was the last thing the boy needed to see.

Kenny came up. "You okay?"

Jane let the shotgun fall and sagged into his chest. Kenny caught her, pulling her close with both arms.

"I killed him, Ken," she said. "I gave him every chance. He didn't want them . . . and I killed him."

"It's a shitty thing."

Jane pulled back and looked into his eyes. "Not this time," she said evenly. "Not this time."

—–

"It's crazy," Kenny said as he gingerly stepped down from the back of the ambulance. "Bobby comes to us for protection from the lunacy of his home life, and he almost gets burned to death. Then, as if that isn't enough for one kid in one day, he almost gets shot to death, too."

Jane stood at the curb watching the firemen dousing the last hot spots in her house. The roof had burned through and the side wall had collapsed. Her home and everything in it was a total loss.

She turned to Kenny. "Bobby was amazing today." She nodded toward the charred skeleton of her home, her eyes filling with tears. "All I have left is you."

Kenny put his arm around her shoulder.

Jane leaned her head against him. "I need you to help me so I don't screw it up."

"Screw what up?"

Jane looked up to him. ". . . Us."

Kenny smiled and kissed her hair. "And you help me, too."

A fireman with a chain saw sliced through a smoldering section of roof. It crashed down into the living room, sending a cloud of smoky dust shooting out through the opening where the bay window had been.

Kenny brushed a tear away from the corner of Jane's eye with the back of his hand. "I knew I shoulda kept my apartment."

54

Usually, when a cop in Homicide took down a killer, there was a small celebration as his name was erased from the murder board.

Not this day.

The mood in Precinct Nineteen was somber, and the deletion of Jacques Carpenter's name from the board was greeted with a grim sense of closure.

Jane sat at her desk.

She had written her report and briefed Lieutenant Dytman, who was temporarily assigned to their station until Ben Spielman felt up to returning to duty. Now she felt exhausted and alone, sliding down the back side of a steady diet of adrenaline.

Kenny was at San Francisco General, having his wound dressed. Jane looked over to his desk. She loved his stuff. A baseball, signed by Willie Mays, sat in a clear Plexi box. An army-surplus hand grenade held down his papers from the breeze thrown off by the fans. Coupons. She shook her head and smiled. The man she loved clipped coupons.

The copier whirred to life and Jane looked up. Mike Finney was busy trying to coax the ancient machine to work.

Roslyn Shapiro crossed over and handed her a note. "Becka Flynn's here. Says you called for her."

"Thanks. I'll meet her in Interrogation One."

Roslyn started to go, then turned back. "Jane . . ." she began, her voice catching with emotion, "we're all so proud of you."

Before Jane could respond, Roslyn was already walking back to reception.

Jane looked at the note. "Penny Kinsella called. WCB." She

shook her head. WCB was "Will Call Back." She wondered why she had called, and if she'd ever hear from her again.

Jane stood up. Mike Finney came over with a stack of paper. He handed the top sheet to Jane. It was an announcement for Hank Pagano and Benjy Spielman's ceremony the following morning at Grace Cathedral.

"I can't go," Finney said, his voice hardly more than a disappointed whisper.

"What do you mean?"

"I gotta work for Mr. Turner. One of the guys already took his vacation time." He started off to distribute the flyers. "After all he's done for me, no way I can let him down."

"Want me to call him?" Jane offered. "I'd be happy to."

Finney pulled his lips tight across his teeth. "Thanks, Inspector. But I gotta be there for him." He lowered his eyes. "Besides, I don't think I could handle it . . . being in that church with Hank and Benjy . . . y'know?"

Jane nodded. "I know."

Finney walked away, utterly defeated.

— —

"Yes, I caught Jacques Carpenter. And yes, I had to kill him. But he came after me, came to my house . . . and I did what I had to do . . . I'm no hero." Jane shrugged to Becka Flynn. "That's why I agreed to this interview. I know you're going to do a story for tonight's news and I just wanted it all to be in perspective."

Becka Flynn poured the rest of her iced tea into a Styrofoam cup. "You've been straight with me all along. I'll find an angle that will be respectful to your wishes."

"Your producer will let you do that?"

"Fuck him." She grinned, her green eyes flashing. "I'm the hot new babe at the station. New York's been calling. Right now he needs me more than I need him."

Jane leaned back in her chair. The interrogation room was overflowing with files and maps and research reports from the Jacques Carpenter investigation. Someone had turned the blackboard and its grisly gallery of murder victims against the wall. Tomorrow, after the ceremonies, she and Kenny and Finney would begin to break it all down. By Monday or Tuesday, it would all be gone and they'd be on to other things.

"How old are you, Inspector?"

Jane tilted her head. "Idle curiosity or probing journalistic inquiry?"

"I'm a reporter. There's no such thing as idle curiosity."

"Forty this winter."

"You wear it well."

"Maybe not today." Jane nodded with her eyes. "But, thanks." She saw Kenny passing through the stairwell door. "How old are you?"

Becka Flynn blushed behind her freckles. "Twenty-eight."

"And your friends. What do they do?"

Becka Flynn looked across the table, intrigued. "Most of them are from the station. Some from when I was at the *Chronicle*."

Jane understood why she'd been drawn to this woman. Becka Flynn was where Jane was, *who* Jane was, ten years ago. She hoped the young reporter wouldn't wait another decade like Jane had before she asked herself if the ambition and isolation were all worth it.

She pushed back her chair and rose. "I gotta get back to work."

Becka Flynn stood. "I appreciate the one-on-one. You'll be happy with tonight's story."

Jane started for the door. "Oh, I almost forgot. Thank you for the card about my father. For your kind words."

"My dad died four years ago," Becka Flynn said. "I think about him all the time. I just wanted to . . . I don't know . . . reach you in the middle of all this."

She offered her hand. "Maybe we could have a drink sometime, off the clock and off the record."

"That'd be great," Jane said as she shook her hand.

She watched her cross to the elevators. When they opened, a news crew stepped out and approached Roslyn Shapiro at the reception desk.

Becka Flynn looked back to Jane and shrugged a smile. Then she entered the elevator and was gone.

Kenny stepped up with Jane's bag. "Let's get out of here before the reporters start their feeding frenzy."

"What'd the doctor say?"

"Couple more bullet wounds and they'll play connect-the-dots with me." He slipped his arm around her waist and nudged her toward the stairwell.

Jane began to go with him, then stopped. "Wait a minute. Where are we going?"

"Home," Kenny said. "I'm taking you home."

55

THERE WAS A FOR SALE sign in the lawn in front of Poppy's house, across the yard from the oak tree with the tire swing.

The refrigerator was filled with dishes Aunt Lucy had made: lasagna, fried calamari, baked ziti, sausages and peppers, a chicken pie.

Clothes from Rosemary and Timmy lined the closet in the guest room. Jane's old room.

"Your family is amazing," Kenny said as he pulled a platter of antipasto from the refrigerator. "Beer?"

Jane stood at the sink, washing her hands. She scrubbed vigorously at them, trying to wash the day away. The grime of her burning house, the surge of the shotgun.

Kenny came up behind her. "Want a beer?" he asked again.

All Jane could do was shake her head. All that had happened that day—of losing her home, of killing a man, of being in Poppy's house—came raining down on her in an emotional downpour.

She turned to Kenny, weary beyond all imagining. "I need to take a shower."

Kenny kissed her high on the forehead. "I'm going to unwind a little. I'll come up in a bit."

Stinging needles of hot water massaged Jane's back as she stood, her hands against the tiled wall and her head bowed, in her father's shower. It was a delicious pain, and Jane half wished it would never end.

Steam billowed over the shower door, filling the bathroom.

Jane reached for the soap. The bar of Ivory was worn down, curved to the contours of Poppy's body.

Weeping now, Jane held the soap to her face and breathed in her father's familiar scent. She lathered her body over and over again. Washing her aching body, her wounded soul, in the pounding hot water.

And then it ran out, the water abruptly turning cold.

Twisting the faucets off, Jane opened the shower door and stepped into the clouds of steam. She picked up a hand towel and swiped at the mirror until she could see herself.

She stood there, naked and pink, and looked at her reflection. Then she took a towel from the rack over the toilet and, wrapping it around her waist, padded into the bedroom.

Poppy's slippers were still on the floor next to the bed, his rosary still on the nightstand.

Jane lay on the bed, on her mother's side, her wet hair cooling her shoulders. The vague sounds of the evening news drifted up from the television downstairs. Kenny was probably flaked out on the couch, in Timmy's sweats, devouring Aunt Lucy's cooking, drinking Poppy's beer.

Smiling at the thought, Jane pulled her father's pillow over her face and breathed in the lingering sweetness of his Old Spice. The sweet fragrance of her childhood.

In less than a minute, she was asleep on the bed in which she was conceived.

56

Jane awoke in pieces, sense by sense.

She heard the mockingbirds quizzing each other in the oak tree outside the window. She felt the towel still wrapped around her waist. She had a dry, slightly salty taste in her mouth from going to bed hungry.

She smelled her father.

She opened her eyes.

Kenny stood at the dresser, tying his tie.

"Hey you," Jane said, her voice husky with sleep.

"Hey, Sleeping Beauty." Kenny turned to her and held out his hands. "What do you think?"

"That's Timmy's best suit." She propped herself on her elbows. "You look great."

"It's really generous of him." Kenny sat on the bed and put his hand on the flat of her chest, above her breasts. "How are you?"

"Better." She sat up, stretching her back. "Boy, did I need that sleep."

"Tell me about it." Kenny started to get up.

"Ken?"

"Yum?"

Jane took his hand and pulled him back to the bed. "Let's get married."

Kenny broke into his boyish grin. "I thought we were pretty much in agreement in that department. The only issue is when."

They listened as a delivery van cruised down the street. A newspaper hit in the driveway next door. The van drove past Poppy's house. Then a paper hit in the driveway on the other side.

Jane touched his face with the back of her hand. "How about next week?"

"Are you serious?"

"Absolutely." She took his hands in hers and kissed them. "I was thinking about it all night. I love you so much and I want it all to feel . . . complete."

Kenny put his hands on her shoulders and pushed her back on the bed. Jane opened her mouth as he came down to kiss her. Their lips met, gently at first, then more intensely. Their tongues played against each other, searching, reassuring.

Finally, Jane broke off the kiss. "What time is it?"

"Little after eight."

"Shit." Jane wriggled out from under him. "We can't be late." She swung her legs over the side of the bed. "I'm gonna see what Rosemary left for me to wear."

"While you do that," Kenny said, straightening his belt, "I'm gonna call Jacob. Maybe we can stop by and get our rings before we head back to the station."

Jane pulled Poppy's slippers onto her feet. She was surprised at how snug they were, and she smiled at the memory of her father's slender feet. "Isn't he kind of busy today?"

"Worst he can do is say no."

"Yuh, right." Jane laughed. "Like he'd say no to this."

Kenny pulled her up and kissed her. "My point exactly."

— —

Jane lowered the visor against the slanting morning sun as Kenny drove the Explorer up Nob Hill. "What'd Jacob say?"

"Mazel tov." Kenny slowed in traffic at the last turn before Grace Cathedral. "Then he said he'd drop everything if we wanted to come by after the service. He's expecting us around noon."

Jane slipped her hand under Kenny's right leg. "He's a sweet man."

"He also wanted me to tell you . . . your mother's ring is ready."

"Great," Jane said. "Let's get it."

Kenny crested the hill and stopped. "Wow."

Jane followed his gaze. "My God."

A sea of police cars, motorcycles, and limousines filled the street, their windshields sparkling in the sun. News vans from CNN, KGO, and other networks were parked across the way, their satellite dishes pointing to the sky like metal sunflowers. The sidewalks were jammed with onlookers pressing against wooden barricades. Police officers in varying combinations of black, blue, grey, brown, and beige were filing into the church, representatives of over fifty police departments come to pay tribute to two members of the brotherhood.

A traffic cop recognized Kenny and directed him to a space near Chief McDonald's limousine. Kenny tilted his head. "Check it out."

Mayor Lucien Biggs removed his trademark black fedora and passed into the church. Farther down the steps, a tall man with greying blond hair paused for the photographers before being escorted inside.

"The governor?" Jane asked.

"Himself."

Jane checked her makeup in the sun-visor mirror, then raised it back up. When she did, she saw the bullet hole in the windshield. A scar from her gun battle with Jacques Carpenter.

Kenny saw her notice it and squeezed her hand. "We're all right," he said softly.

"Yeah," Jane said as she opened her door. "I know."

Cheryl Lomax was just ahead of them as they stepped up to the sidewalk.

"Where's Walter?" Kenny asked.

Cheryl shook her head. "Damn phone company wouldn't give him time off."

Jane took her arm. "Then sit with us."

They reached the bottom of the stairs leading up to the cathedral and stopped.

At the top, just in the shade of the great oak doors, Ben Spielman clutched Mary to him, his arm trembling across her back, and guided her inside.

Jane looked to Kenny and Cheryl. They had seen it, too.

"Let's go," Kenny said, and they started up the stairs.

There was a sudden flurry from the right as the newspeople recognized Jane. They pushed against the barricades, camera flashes strobing. Through it all, they remained eerily silent, understanding that this wasn't the setting to be shouting questions.

Kenny put his arms over Jane and Cheryl's shoulders and hurried them up the steps. When they reached the doors, Jane stole a look back.

She caught a glimpse of Becka Flynn's red hair before she was hustled inside.

——

It was cool inside Grace Cathedral. Cool, and given the number of people already there, remarkably quiet.

The shuffling of feet as the mourners took their seats was the principal sound in the huge hall. That and the occasional whisper.

An usher led Jane, Kenny, and Cheryl to a blue-padded pew on the left side of the center aisle. At the top of the aisle, in the transept, two coffins lay side by side. They were draped in American flags and wreathed in sprays of lilies.

A gold-framed picture of Benjy Spielman was propped on the coffin on the right. It was his Police Academy portrait, taken only two weeks ago. His smile was a little self-conscious and his eyes shone with promise. After the ceremony, his body would be transported to Temple Beth Shalom for a private Jewish burial service.

Ben and Mary Spielman sat in the first row on the right, a few feet from their son. Chief McDonald leaned forward and whispered something to them. When Lieutenant Spielman turned to answer, Jane saw the devastation in his eyes.

The coffin on the left, Hank Pagano's coffin, was flanked by six tall candles, their flames shimmering in the dim light. His official photograph, taken three years ago when he had come over to Homicide, rested against the framed citation from his Medal of Valor ceremony.

Cardinal Dennis Regan sat on the dais conferring with Alan Eisner, the rabbi from Beth Shalom. Police officers in their dress uniforms and white gloves stood shoulder to shoulder around the entire nave of the church.

Through the muffled silence, a single bagpipe hummed the first strains of "Danny Boy" from the choir loft.

Kenny touched Jane's hand and she turned to watch as a group of children from Clark Street Elementary School were led down the side aisle.

Jane noticed that the church was still less than half-full, with hundreds more mourners queued up outside.

Cheryl dabbed at her eyes and said, "There's so many people, they're going to start late." She indicated the program in the pew-back in front of her. "If the bagpipe is just now playing and the choir isn't even in place, they're going to be hours behind." She folded the program and put it in her purse. "For Finney," she said. "I'm sure he'd want it."

"We're here for the long run," Kenny said. He nodded to the dais. Next to the bishop and rabbi were four unoccupied red velvet chairs. The governor, the mayor, Chief McDonald, and the police chaplain had yet to take their seats.

"What time is Jacob expecting us?" Jane asked.

"Noonish."

"And what time is it now?"

Kenny checked his watch. "Little before ten."

"Gimme your phone."

"Why?"

"I'm gonna call Jacob."

Kenny started to protest. Jane held up her hand. "Ken, it's Friday. If we miss him, he won't be open again till Tuesday. I want my mother's ring . . . and I want you to have yours."

Kenny reached into his pocket and handed her his cell phone.

"Back in a sec." Jane rose and worked her way up the aisle, sidestepping through the stream of arriving mourners.

When she reached the vestibule, she turned left and ducked into an alcove. She dialed Jacob Turner's number, holding her hand over the phone to dampen the beeping. Pressing the phone to her ear, she listened as it rang four, five, then six times. She let it continue. When she had counted twenty rings, she pressed the off button with her thumb. Then she reentered the nave and went back down the aisle.

Kenny looked up when she arrived. "What'd he say?"

"No answer."

"Well"—Kenny shrugged—"he is kind of busy today."

"Jacob always answers his phone." Jane looked across Kenny. "Cheryl, do you have Mike Finney's cell number?"

"Yeah, somewheres." Cheryl rummaged through her purse and came up with a small dark green phone book. She took a miniature gold-plated pen and wrote down the number for Jane.

Jane took the paper. "Thanks." She started to go, then stopped and turned to Kenny. "Come with me, will ya?"

Kenny could see that this was important to her. He tilted his head to Cheryl. "Save our seats."

Jane took his hand and led him back up the aisle to the vestibule. She turned left again and guided him to the same alcove as before. Then she dialed Mike Finney's cell number and listened as it rang and rang. Twenty times. She flipped the phone closed. "Nothing."

"What do you want to do?"

Jane watched the people file past, crossing the vestibule into the nave. Another group of police officers from someplace out of state came in. Then Roslyn Shapiro passed through. Jane had never seen her out of the context of Precinct Nineteen. She looked small and frail and deeply sad. Roslyn waited patiently behind Scott Hicks and his SWAT team, and moved forward when they did.

Jane pulled Kenny deeper into the alcove. "Bear with me on this." She lowered her voice. "I don't like the fact that Jacob, on the biggest day of the year, isn't answering his phone."

Kenny nodded, gesturing for her to go on.

"And I *really* don't like the fact that Finney isn't picking up. You know he's been completely neurotic about answering his phone since Vicki got pregnant." Jane paused to gather her thoughts. "Either one of them alone, and it's no big deal. But both of them . . ."

"Might be something there," Kenny said. "I never mentioned it to you, but I keep coming back to that jerk-off security guard at the Transamerica Building who made us for cops. What was his name, Parker? Only two kinds of people spot cops like that: other cops . . . and ex-cons."

Jane raised her eyebrows. "Did you see his tattoo?"

"Yeah, and for an older guy, he was built like a Clydesdale. He's a con plain as day."

A couple of rookie cops from Benjy Spielman's graduating class came in out of the blistering sun. They looked like teenagers.

"Okay," Jane said. "Let's break this down so we're not talking ourselves into anything." She ticked the items off on her fingers. "One, Jacob isn't answering. Two, Finney also isn't answering. Three, the head of security for the Transamerica Building is an ex-con. Four, Jewelers' Corner is receiving millions of dollars' worth of gems and precious metals as we speak."

"Five, six, seven," Kenny said, "every cop in America is in this church!"

Jane grabbed his hands. "You're right! If I'm gonna pull a big job like ripping off a zillion dollars in diamonds, what better time than—" She tugged at Kenny's hands. "Let's go!"

"Wait," Kenny said. "What if we're wrong?"

"Then we're assholes." She caught Kenny's eyes with hers. "But, Kenny, what if we're right?" She dropped the phone into his pocket. "You with me?"

Kenny squeezed her hands. "I'm with you."

Jane started toward the main doors of Grace Cathedral. Kenny pulled her up short. "Reporters."

"Good point. C'mon."

They went back into the church just as the governor and Mayor Biggs were mounting the dais. Jane took Kenny's hand and they walked briskly past the honor guard of police officers until they got to a side altar. A statue of the Blessed Virgin smiled into the middle distance.

"We can cut through the sacristy and out the parking-lot door." Jane parted the thick velvet curtain.

"A good Catholic girl," Kenny said as he went through.

"Used to be." Jane crossed herself and hurried after him.

57

Everything seemed normal.

Well-dressed men and women, deep in conversation, were crossing the plush lobby of the Transamerica Building in every direction. FedEx and UPS drivers pushed two-wheel dollies laden with boxes. Visitors and tourists kept the revolving doors in constant motion with their comings and goings.

Jane and Kenny rounded a corner and looked to the main security desk. An older black man, his hair gone grey and his eyes gone yellow, was giving directions to a bicycle messenger.

"Shit," Jane said. "Our friend Parker isn't at his usual post."

Kenny nodded. "Not a good sign."

A younger security guard in a blue blazer was standing at the head of the elevator banks, blocking their way. Jane and Kenny started toward him.

"Name tag says 'Simms,'" Jane said out of the side of her mouth. "And he's wearing a wedding ring."

"Got it."

They headed for the elevators, looking to all the world like a couple of crisply dressed executives.

"But here's how we win," Kenny said to Jane in a self-important voice. "Precedence was clearly established in California versus General Motors when the court found that the aggrieved parties could . . ."

Jane smiled to the guard. "Morning, Mr. Simms. How's the wife?"

"Same ol', same ol'," the young guard said as he stepped aside.

". . . could submit a writ of mandamus," Kenny continued, "and that any multinational corporation found liable for negligence whether knowingly or . . ." They stepped into the last elevator. There was a quiet ping and the doors slid closed.

Jane caught Kenny's eye in the mirrored ceiling. " 'Writ of mandamus'?"

"Thank you, Court TV." Kenny pointed to the numbered panel. "Forty-five, right?"

"Maybe we should get off at forty-four and take the stairs up a flight, just in case."

Kenny pressed forty-four and the elevator began its ascent. "Sounds like a plan."

—–—

Jane clutched the knob of the forty-fifth-floor stairway door.

It turned easily in her hand. But when she tried to push it open, it wouldn't budge.

"Let me." Kenny twisted the knob and leaned into the door. Something on the other side was keeping it closed. Something heavy.

Kenny bent his knees and dug his shoulder into the door. It moved grudgingly about six inches, enough for Jane to peek through.

The lifeless body of a UPS deliveryman, his brown uniform soaked in blood, lay against the door. Beyond him was Ahmet's showroom. The glass was blown out, and Jane could see the body of Ahmet's wife lying in the hallway. There was another body, partially hidden, next to her. By the black socks and brown leather sandals, Jane could tell it was Ahmet.

She strained to look up the corridor to Jacob's showroom, but couldn't get a good angle. Suddenly, a black-clad figure raced from one door to another, an AK-47 assault rifle under his arm.

Jane pulled Kenny away from the door. "It's a slaughterhouse in there. Three bodies right away. Probably more. Plus there was a guy in black with an AK-47."

"Jesus."

"It gets worse. I think he was wearing body armor."

Kenny pulled out his cell phone and dialed. "Carla," he said in an urgent whisper, "this is 3H60, Marks from Nineteen. We've got a robbery-in-progress at the Transamerica Building, and we've got bodies. Unknown number of suspects. Heavily armed, possibly body armor. Jewelers' Corner, forty-fifth floor. I need SWAT, EMS, anything you can throw at it. Plus the building has to be evacuated." He listened. "Do what you can and do it fast!"

He flipped the phone closed and looked at Jane, his face betraying his worry.

"What?"

"Everyone's shorthanded because of the memorial service. Plus, there's a hostage thing going down over in the Castro District. Too soon to even determine response time." He yanked the Glock out of his shoulder holster. "Your call."

Jane reached into her bag and pulled out her revolver. "Jacob's in there." She leaned into the door. "Finney, too."

Kenny snapped the slide back on his pistol, chambering a round. "So this is us going in."

Jane held her weapon up next to her chin and flicked the safety. "This is us."

Kenny pressed his back against the door and pushed. When it had opened about a foot, he looked to Jane. She nodded tightly, and the two of them slipped into the devastation of Jewelers' Corner.

Crawling forward on their hands and knees, Jane and Kenny came to the reception desk near the elevators. The closest elevator was propped open with a thick steel bar. They were surprised to see a FedEx man huddled in the space beneath the desk.

"We're cops," Kenny said. "How many robbers are there?"

The FedEx man shook his head violently, his eyes darting back and forth.

Jane pointed back toward the stairwell. "You can get out that way."

He stayed where he was, clutching a package to his chest, seemingly paralyzed by fear.

Up ahead, another figure decked out like a commando in black Kevlar body armor hurried down the hall. He had slung his assault rifle over his shoulder and was dragging a large satchel behind him.

"If that thing's filled with jewels," Kenny whispered, "this is one big payday for some very bad guys."

"Bad and well armed," Jane said. "C'mon." Staying low and close to the wall, they scurried down the corridor, passing the bodies of two more diamond merchants, until they reached Jacob's showroom. The glass was shattered, hanging dangerously in large jagged triangles.

As they closed in, they could hear Jacob's television. ". . . may seem like a senseless tragedy . . ." Mayor Biggs said from Hank and Benjy's memorial service, ". . . but these two brave police officers fell in the line of duty, protecting the city they loved . . ."

With Jane in the lead, they crept over the broken glass and into the showroom. Jane flicked her eyes to the left and right, desperately hoping that Jacob hadn't met the same fate as Ahmet and his wife. She signaled Kenny forward as she worked her way behind the main display case.

Mike Finney sat in a widening pool of blood, his breath coming in rapid shallow gasps. He had a bullet wound high on the right side of his chest.

Jane looked at Kenny and pointed two fingers at her own eyes, indicating for him to keep watch. Then she scooted up to Finney's side. Kneeling on one knee beside him, her pants leg soaking in his blood, she whispered into his ear. "Mike, it's me. Help is coming."

Finney nodded.

"Mike. How many are there?"

Finney took three quick breaths. ". . . I . . . don't . . . know . . ." He swallowed hard. ". . . three . . . maybe four . . ." His head fell back against the display case. The sliding-glass door rattled slightly.

Kenny reached up and raised the volume on the television to cover the noise. A choir was singing "Amazing Grace."

Jane touched Finney's face. He turned his head to the touch. "Mike, where's Jacob?"

Finney's eyes found Jane and he struggled to answer. ". . . don't know . . ."

"Okay, Mike. You're doing great. We're gonna get you some

help." She nodded to Kenny and they crept out of the showroom. They scurried in a low crouch back toward the stairwell. When they reached the reception desk by the elevators, Kenny hissed to the FedEx man, "Let's go, buddy. We'll get you out of here."

Pushing his box before him, the FedEx man started to crawl out from beneath the desk. Kenny had turned away to open the stairwell door, when Jane noticed something odd.

The FedEx man was wearing a jacket, in this heat wave; and beneath it bulged the telltale outline of a bulletproof vest.

"Ken!" she yelled, just as the FedEx man shook away the cardboard box and came up with an AK-47.

Jane fired once, her only option being a head shot.

The slug tore into the FedEx man above the right ear. He dropped like a slaughtered cow, blood pumping from his wound, and landed heavily on top of his assault rifle.

The wall above their heads disintegrated as dozens of bullets tore into it. Kenny leaped across the dead FedEx man and tackled Jane just as another burst riddled the glass wall behind her. It exploded, sending daggers of glass everywhere. Kenny pulled Jane under him and peeked around the corner.

Three commando-clad men, every inch of flesh protected by Kevlar, advanced on them with AK-47s blazing.

Kenny squeezed off three quick rounds at the closest assailant, striking him repeatedly in the chest. The man shook off the hits like they were a child's punches and kept coming.

"Shit!" Kenny yelled. "I can't get through their body armor!"

Jane lay beneath him, looking into the eyes of the man she had just killed. She wriggled free and wrenched the assault rifle from under the FedEx man. "Try this," she said, and slid it over to Kenny.

Kenny jammed his Glock into his waistband and cranked back on the bolt action of the AK-47. A torrent of bullets destroyed the doorjamb next to him, peppering him with shrapnel. He drew a quick breath, spun around, and fired, the AK-47 erupting in his hands.

The lead robber took hits in the groin, stomach, and chest. He was catapulted back against the far wall, stood there for a moment, then slid down to the floor. As he fell, he left trails of dark blood on the bullet-pocked wall behind him. The slugs from Kenny's rifle had not only pierced his body armor, they had gone clear through.

Kenny sprayed another burst and the remaining assailants dove for cover.

"Hey, assholes!" he shouted. "How do you like a level playing field?"

"Kenny!" Jane grabbed his elbow and pulled him down.

"What, they're gonna get more agitated?"

The two gunmen jumped to their feet and opened up, obliterating the ceiling directly above Jane and Kenny and showering them with bits of gypsum and metal. A fluorescent light fixture was torn from its frame and fell, live wires crackling, across Jane's feet. Kenny pushed her under the reception desk.

"They're laying down cover fire! They're gonna try something!"

The robbers made their break. One going for the stairwell. One going for the elevators. Both shooting from the hip.

Kenny rolled across the narrow opening and came up firing, spent cartridges cascading away.

The first commando took a slug above the knee, stumbled, and threw himself through the stairwell doorway.

Kenny kept blazing away at the wall next to the door, his AK-47 shredding the plasterboard and metal struts at ten rounds per second. Then his rifle abruptly stopped firing. "Shit, I'm out!"

Jane dug into the jacket of the FedEx man and came up with another clip.

Kenny tossed the rifle to her. "FedEx, when it absolutely, positively—"

A burst of automatic-rifle fire from the stairwell took out another glass wall behind him. The commando appeared in the doorway. Staggering from several bullet wounds to both his arms, he struggled to draw a bead on Kenny.

Knowing his part in the game was over, the robber advanced on Kenny, shooting wildly as he came.

Kenny whipped out his Glock and emptied it at his attacker, the sharp cracking of the pistol dwarfed by the roar of the AK-47.

Still the gunman came on, his wild firing closing in on Kenny.

When he was only a few feet away, he leaned against the wall to steady his right arm. Then he brought the muzzle of his rifle to bear on Kenny's chest. He grinned a twisted grin, his white lips snarling in the mouth hole of the black Kevlar ski mask, and tightened his finger on the trigger.

As he did, a full burst of AK-47 fire ravaged his chest and he slumped to his knees, dead before he hit.

Jane raised the AK-47, smoke curling from the muzzle. "Did he get you?"

"Almost." He crawled over to Jane. "Thanks." He took the rifle from her. "Here's the deal: we're here. The other bad guy's somewhere over there. And he wants to get to that elevator in the worst way." He ejected the clip and checked it. Half-full. He slammed it home again and turned to Jane. "And we . . . ?"

Jane nodded grimly. "Are going to stop him."

Kenny pulled out his Glock and reloaded it. Then he snapped the action on the AK-47 and called over his shoulder, "We're cops! SFPD! You've got five seconds to give yourself up!"

A torrent of rifle fire cut the air right over their heads. "Fuck you!" the last commando yelled, his voice deep and angry.

Kenny raised his eyebrows in recognition. "Sound familiar?"

"Yeah, who is it?"

"Parker, that dickhead security guard from downstairs."

Another short burst sliced into the wall above them and Parker made his move.

Kenny leaped to his feet and pulled back on the trigger. His rifle fired twice, then jammed.

Shooting as he ran, Parker raced for the elevators.

Frustrated, Kenny tossed his rifle aside, pulled out his Glock, and went after him.

Parker kicked away the thick metal bar holding the elevator open and dove inside. He punched the lobby button and, as the doors began to close, started to remove his ski mask.

Kenny flung himself across the reception area and grabbed at the elevator doors just before they shut.

Parker, unable to bring his AK-47 into firing position in time, grasped Kenny by both hands and, falling backward, pulled him inside.

"Kenny!" Jane shrieked as the doors closed and the elevator began its descent. Frantic, she pounded on the doors. "Kenny!"

Out of the corner of her eye, Jane saw a flicker of movement reflected in the high-gloss finish of the elevator doors. Before she could react, the hot steel of a rifle muzzle was pressed against her neck. Holding her hands out before her, she slowly turned to face another black-clad commando. His pockets were stuffed with ammunition clips and he had a large satchel slung over his shoulder.

"You exposed yourself without securing the crime scene," he said as he slid the muzzle up under her chin, raising her head with it. "Very sloppy . . . Jane."

Jane gasped at the sound of his voice.

58

DROP YOUR WEAPON," the commando said, motioning with his AK-47.

Jane let her pistol fall to the floor.

The gunman tucked his assault rifle under his arm, the barrel still pointed at Jane. Then, with his left hand, he reached up and rolled his ski mask to the top of his head.

"I hate these things," Hank Pagano said. "Too fucking hot."

"Hank," Jane said. "My God, what have you done?" She noticed that the elevator Kenny and Parker were on had stopped at the twentieth floor, one floor before it would have gone into express mode down to the lobby.

"Just move away from the elevator."

"Why?"

"Because someone's going to lose in there," Hank said as he nudged Jane back to the reception area. "And the winner's going to come back up here. If it's my guy, we're gone. If it's Ken . . ." He paused and shook his head. "Then, sadly, I'll have to kill him."

"Jesus, Hank, this isn't you."

The corner of Hank's mouth rose in a sad grin. "Yes, it is."

Jane crossed to the reception area and looked around. The FedEx man was at her feet. Two commandos lay dead. As did Ahmet, his wife, a UPS deliveryman, and two other merchants. "Then, it isn't the best of you."

"Don't you get it, Jane?" Hank said as he kicked her gun into a corner and joined her at the desk. "The best of me died a long time ago."

The television in Jacob's showroom droned on. ". . . Inspector Hank Pagano will be buried at Our Lady of the Pasture Cemetery, next to his beloved wife, Irene," Chief McDonald was saying. "Hank was a cop who made San Francisco proud; who helped us, in this day of cop-bashing, love the men and women of our police force . . . Most of you know about his courage that day at the school yard, about his Medal of Valor. But long before that, Hank had served the citizens of our . . ."

Hank dropped his satchel onto the desk with a weighty thud. "I begged them," he said. "I begged anyone, everyone, I could find to help me. To not let Irene die like that. And no one came forward. *No one!*" He sat on the edge of the desk, the AK-47 pointed at Jane's gut. "Do you know what it's like for a man like me to beg?"

There came the hollow report of a gunshot from the elevator.

Jane drew a breath and took a step toward it.

"Don't," Hank said softly. "Whichever way this is going has already been determined."

The situation was almost surreal to Jane. Here was Hank Pagano being eulogized on live television while she stood across a gun barrel from him. Here were Kenny and Parker fighting, probably to the death, in an elevator only a few feet away; and she couldn't help the man she loved.

"Irene," Hank went on, pulling Jane out of her thoughts, "died in such excruciating pain . . . that we actually talked about my killing her." He shook off the memory. "She died bit by bit, Jane. Her system shutting down. First her kidneys, then her liver. Her bowels, her brain . . ." He let out a long, anguished sigh. "Then her poor heart."

Hank swiped a bead of sweat from his eyebrow. "Do you know what her last words were to me?"

Jane just looked at him.

"She said, with her last breath on this earth . . . she said . . . 'I'm sorry.' "

Jane started to take a step toward him, but he stood up from the desk and leveled the rifle at her. She stopped and said, "What happened to Irene was awful. But nobody killed her. Fate, maybe some bad luck, that's what took her from you."

"It wasn't *that* she died," Hank said, his voice rising in anger. "It was *how* she died. Jason Bloom and his sick little vendetta took away the only thing she had left, her dignity . . . and mine."

Jane stole a look at the elevator. The numbers above the elevator changed as it began to ascend. It was at the twenty-fifth floor and rising.

"So, you planned this all along?"

"For years. Once Irene died, it was just a matter of when. Did you really think I was going to retire on some shit pension? The lonely widower ex-cop drinking himself to death in some stinking bar with all the other lonely ex-cops." He glanced up to check on the elevator's progress. "Then Carpenter starts killing cops and I saw my chance."

"But the chase down at the docks? What about that?"

"Never happened," Hank said. "I was never even close to Carpenter."

Jane shook her head. "So you crashed your car and faked your own death."

Hank nodded. "Opportunity knocked."

"And the body?"

"Informant of mine. Silk Cullen. Guy had a knack for being in the wrong place at the wrong time." Hank shrugged a little laugh. "I had always wanted it to be Jason Bloom, but it didn't work out that way. Heh, the symmetry would have been beautiful."

The shock of seeing Hank had worn off, and now Jane was feeling active, hot contempt for him. She wished she'd carried a drop weapon. She would have shot him in the face.

"And Benjy? You let him die like that so you could pull off your little caper?"

"I know you won't believe me, Jane. But I really tried to save Benjy."

"Yeah," Jane spit at him, "you're a saint."

The elevator was passing from thirty-two to thirty-three.

"After my"—Hank made quotation marks with two fingers of his left hand—"death . . . I was going to lay low for a year. Maybe hit Jewelers' Corner next summer. But once it was announced that the memorial service was going to coincide with the diamond delivery, I saw my chance. It was a scramble, but it had to be today."

Jane looked around at the killing zone that was Jewelers' Corner. "You sure fucked this up, Hank."

"It didn't exactly go as smoothly as I had planned." Hank looked down the corridor toward Jacob's showroom. "I even tried to recruit Mike Finney this morning. Offered him a fortune. But he wouldn't get on board."

"Sometimes," Jane said, "people surprise you." She let the irony hang between them like an echo.

Hank nodded his understanding. "Finney panicked and pulled his gun. Regrettably, there was some shooting."

The elevator was at the fortieth floor and climbing.

Hank shifted the AK-47 in his hands and grabbed Jane by the collar. He yanked her forward and swung the rifle muzzle toward the elevator doors. "Damn it, Jane, what the hell are you doing here?"

"Playing a hunch."

"You've always been the smart one."

The elevator passed forty-three.

"Wait a minute," Jane said, struggling to free herself from Hank's grip. "What did you do with Jacob Turner?"

The numbers above the elevator changed from forty-four to forty-five, then stopped.

"Let's just say," Hank said as he stepped toward the elevator bank, "that Jacob won't be getting in my way."

There was a soft *ping* as the elevator arrived at their floor.

Hank shoved Jane closer. As he did, she could see their distorted images in the reflective surface of the elevator doors. It was wavy and out of proportion, like the mirrors in a fun house . . . a huge man and a very small woman.

Jane knew one thing above all.

If, when the doors opened, Kenny was still alive, there was no way she would let Hank kill him.

Her eyes darted about, looking for a weapon, a distraction, anything.

Her pistol was too far away, lying on its side in the corner near the windows. The jammed AK-47 was all the way over on the other side of the reception area.

The elevator doors began to part, splitting her reflection from Hank's.

Jane held her breath and said a silent prayer.

As the doors separated, a figure began to come into view.

Kenny stood there, leaning against the door support, his face, shoulders, and chest covered in blood.

"Thank God," Jane whispered.

Kenny looked up and his eyes met Hank's.

Hank raised his rifle.

In one swift, desperate motion, Jane twisted out of Hank's grasp, fell to the floor, and kicked with all her strength. Her heel crashed into the side of Hank's knee, buckling it.

Roaring with pain, Hank opened fire on Kenny.

Just as he did, Kenny reached to his right and pulled Lewis Parker's dead body in front of him. As a fusillade of high-caliber slugs tore into the body, Kenny rolled out of the elevator and squeezed off a burst from Parker's AK-47.

Hank took a bullet in the upper arm, the impact whirling him around. Screaming in rage, he rattled off a burst of covering fire. Then he ripped open the door to the spire and dove through.

Kenny turned to Jane, incredulous. "Was that the asshole formerly known as Hank?"

"Yeah." Jane pulled him into a hug. "How badly are you hurt?"

He wiped his face. "This isn't my blood."

"What happened in there?"

"Let's just say he didn't fight fair." Kenny gestured toward Parker's bullet-torn body. "And he didn't die easily."

"But how . . . ?"

Kenny took her face in his hands. "I didn't fight fair either," he said softly. "That's all you need to know right now." He gave her a quick kiss on the forehead. "Maybe I had more to live for than he did."

He looked to the spire access door. "Fucking Hank Pagano." He turned to Jane. "Lucy, you got a lot of 'splainin' to do."

"Later," Jane said as they scrambled to their feet.

Kenny reloaded his rifle and pulled back on the action. "Why'd he go up instead of down?"

"Only one reason." Jane retrieved her pistol, cocked it, and started for the door. "He's got a plan."

59

THE BLOOD TRAIL pulled them forward.

Jane and Kenny raced up the access stairs, past the throbbing machine rooms, to the spire.

They came to the heavy steel door. It had been propped open with a thick metal bar similar to the one the gunmen had used to keep the elevator doors from closing.

Thick dark teardrops of blood marked Hank's progress from the top of the stairs, through the door, and into the interior of the spire.

"Why'd he leave the door open?" Kenny asked, his AK-47 tight against his chest.

"Maybe he's already made good on his escape and it doesn't matter." Jane looked across the doorway to Kenny. "Or maybe he wants us to follow him."

"And either way?"

"And either way . . . we're going in." Jane flexed her knees. "On my three."

Kenny lowered the rifle to his hip and nodded.

"One . . . two . . ." Jane gripped her pistol with both hands. "Three!"

They dove through the door and separated; Jane to the right, Kenny to the left.

Almost immediately, the floor in front of them churned up bits of concrete as the deafening roar of Hank's AK-47 boomed through the cavernous spire.

Hank stood at the third landing of the zigzag metal stairway that hugged the inner wall. He had pulled his Kevlar ski mask back down. The black satchel, bulging with jewels, hung from his left shoulder.

Kenny dropped into a prone firing position and, nursing his ammunition, squeezed off a short burst. The bullets sparked off the iron railing in front of Hank, sending him farther up the stairs.

Jane fired three shots, each hitting Hank in the torso, each deflecting harmlessly off his body armor.

Hank reached the next landing and ducked behind a broad steel electrical junction box. Jane and Kenny kept shooting, their bullets caroming off the box and slashing into the spire's windows, shattering them.

Shafts of hot white light poured through the broken windows, slicing the heavy smoke-filled air.

"I'm low," Kenny called to Jane.

Jane flipped open her revolver and speed-loaded a fresh six-pack. "I'm down to my last six!" she yelled back.

The spire erupted with the earsplitting pounding of Hank's weapon. Bullets ricocheted like laser beams, whistling within inches of Jane and Kenny.

Kenny scooted back from his original position and emptied his clip at Hank. He dropped the assault rifle and jerked the Glock out of his shoulder holster.

Another storm of bullets forced them to hug the floor, cringing as lead fragments zipped through the air, whizzing by their faces.

Hank stopped to reload. He released his spent clip, sending it clanging down the stairs, and with his good hand, struggled to seat a fresh one.

Jane and Kenny realized they had a critical window of only a few seconds. "Forget trying to shoot him," Jane called. "Go for his rifle!"

Rising to their knees at the same time, Jane and Kenny came up firing. Bullet after bullet smashed into Hank's AK-47, ripping it from his hands.

He lunged to retrieve it, but it fell, toppling end over end, to the concrete floor of the spire.

"Damn you!" Hank bellowed, and raced up the zigzag staircase. He rounded another landing and disappeared into the shadows near the narrowing top.

Jane and Kenny tore up the stairs, taking them two at a time, until they reached the third landing. Hank's blood was everywhere. They could hear him above them, but at this steep angle, they couldn't see him.

Closing in, they advanced cautiously, their pistols level in front of them as they crept up another flight.

They cleared the last step before the fourth landing.

And there was Hank.

Perspiring profusely, he had rolled his Kevlar ski mask back to the top of his head. His short grey hair was dark with sweat. His chest heaved with exhaustion. Blood from his wounded arm dripped onto his combat boots.

"It's over, Hank," Jane said, her pistol trained on his face.

Hank drew his lips into a tight, laconic smile.

Then he reached behind the turn in the stairs and pulled Jacob Turner forward. The old man's hands were bound with duct tape, the faded blue numbers on the inside of his left arm partially covered with the taut grey tape.

Hank plunged his hand into his Kevlar jumpsuit and came up with a .45. He held the gun to Jacob's temple.

Jacob, his eyes filled with hatred and resolve, didn't flinch.

Suddenly, the heavy chop of a helicopter filled the vast space. The air and smoke churned and whipped as a sleek black helicopter swooped by the shattered windows behind Hank and rose to the top of the spire.

Hank glanced at his watch. "Right on time!" he shouted over the din.

Jane and Kenny stood in place, their weapons still pointed at Hank's face.

"Don't make me kill him!" Hank jammed the .45 into Jacob's hair. "Just lay them down!"

The helicopter rotor beat above them, concussing the space with an almost unbearable pressure.

"Ain't gonna happen, Hank!" Jane yelled.

"Thought you might say that," Hank said. He swung his pistol away from Jacob and pointed it at Kenny's face. "Three seconds, Jane."

Jane looked to Kenny. He stood there, furious and helpless. "Don't do it!" he called to her.

"Your heroism is touching, but I don't have time for this!" Hank's finger pressed on the trigger. "One . . . two . . ."

"Shit!" Jane said as she bent down and laid her pistol on the top step.

"Excellent," Hank said. He whipped the gun to the right and thrust it at Jane's face. "Your turn, Ken. You have *one* second!"

"I hate this!" Kenny yelled as he, too, put his weapon down.

Hank shoved Jacob at them. He stumbled down a couple of steps, unable to stop himself because of his bound hands. Jane and Kenny caught him before he hit the railing.

Clutching the satchel to his chest, Hank backed up a few more steps. Then he raised his .45 and pointed it at Kenny. "I've got no choice."

Kenny stood there, his arms half-raised, his gaze focused on the gun's muzzle.

Jane took a step forward. "Hank, don't do this."

"And what, Jane? You're gonna let me turn my back on you and just walk out of here?"

"So instead," Jane said, "you'd kill all three of us?"

"Regrettably, yes." Hank tilted his head and nodded tightly. "You and your damn hunches, Jane. You sit back and mind your own business . . . this doesn't happen."

"We're cops, Hank. Cops live by hunches."

Hank swung the .45 over to Jane. "And die by them."

Out of the corner of her eye, Jane saw Kenny, almost imperceptibly, begin to lower his arms. She had to keep Hank distracted for as long as possible.

"Fuck you!" Jane shrieked above the jarring noise of the helicopter. She flicked a look over to Kenny. She knew he was going to dive for his gun.

It was all they had left.

"Fuck you, Hank!" she screamed again, desperately trying to steal a few more seconds. "Fuck you and your fucked-up sense of right and wrong! You're a goddamn parasite! Living off the memory of your dead wife!"

"Shut up!" Hank yelled. Incensed, he came down one step and jabbed the .45 at Jane. "How dare you talk about Irene! You don't have the right to . . ."

Jane, pretending to cringe, turned her head away from the muzzle and looked across Jacob to Kenny. Their eyes touched and a silent signal passed between them. As Hank thumbed back the hammer of his pistol, Kenny threw himself to the ground and grabbed frantically for his Glock.

Before he could reach his gun, the air was split with a sharp crackling sound that pierced the racket of the helicopter.

Hank convulsed as a line of deep black holes was stitched up his body, from his hip to his neck.

The impact sent him hurtling backward. A grimace somewhere between shock and dismay clouded his face even as the holes in his body welled, then spilled over with blood.

He crashed into the broken windows behind him and his upper body fell through, sending shards of amber glass tumbling into the air. At the last possible instant, the combat boot on his left foot caught in a wedge of window frame, stopping his fall.

Hank hung there, upside down, suspended outside the Transamerica Building; a thousand feet above the ground, fifteen feet below the waiting escape chopper.

Before Jane and Kenny could react, Hank, gurgling mists of blood, tugged on the black satchel, struggling to bring it to his chest. The bag, heavy with diamonds and jewels, slid down his body toward his head. Its shifting mass caused Hank to lose his foothold and he fell completely through the opening, his body plummeting down the side of the building.

His lungs were so damaged, he couldn't even scream as his body thudded awkwardly, again and again, into the side of the pyramid-shaped Transamerica Building. It finally landed, demolishing his skeleton and bursting his internal organs, on the sidewalk at the corner of Clay and Montgomery.

Even before Hank's body hit the ground, the helicopter veered away, banking hard toward the north. As the sound of its engines subsided, the cries of a dozen sirens sliced the air.

Jane and Kenny and Jacob stood, their chests heaving, in the broad beam of light streaming in through the broken windows.

They turned to look down to the spire floor, to where the shots that had killed Hank and saved their lives had come from.

Mike Finney stood amid the debris, Hank's smoking AK-47 hanging loosely at his side. He raised his head and found Jane. "Inspector . . ." he began to say. Then he collapsed to his knees. Weak from loss of blood, he teetered there for a second, and fell backward.

Even as he lost consciousness, he understood that he had just killed his hero.

60

JANE WATCHED FROM HER DESK as Jessica, the sandwich lady, put a small basket of muffins on Mike Finney's desk.

"He's gonna be okay," Jane said softly as Jessica passed with her cart. "Should be eating us all out of house and home in a month."

"That's great," Jessica said. "Tell him hi for me."

"You got it."

The late-afternoon sun poured into the squad room, filling the bullpen with a warm golden glow. A cloud passed in front of it and, for a moment, everything was in shadow.

Jane, her clothes still soiled from the gun battle at the Transamerica Building, leaned back in her chair. She raised her arms over her head and stretched. As she did, she felt a cool breath of air on her face and she realized the station's air-conditioning had finally come on.

She looked around as others in the station noticed it, too. For the first time in weeks, the electric fans were turned off. With their constant whirring now gone, Jane began once again to hear the sounds of Precinct Nineteen. The typewriters and telephones, the elevator bong and the traffic outside, the muffled conversations.

But not laughter.

Laughter would come again; after time, after memory loosened its grip.

Jane rocked forward and pulled the report from her typewriter. The body count at Jewelers' Corner had been horrendous. Ten dead, including Hank Pagano.

The helicopter pilot who had come for Hank had been intercepted just south of the Oregon border and arrested.

Most of Jacob's jewels had been recovered. But even as Jane and Kenny drove him home, he was already talking about selling the business and retiring.

Jane hoped he would. She wanted him to spend more time with Aunt Lucy.

Roslyn Shapiro, still in the dark dress she had worn to the memorial service, crossed the reception area to close the windows. A Japanese woman in her early twenties sat on one of the chairs, waiting for a patrol officer to bring her the personal belongings of her father, killed the night before in an ATM shooting.

Jane shook her head sadly.

Death goes on.

Kenny emerged from the locker room in a borrowed white shirt. "Okay if we make a little stop before we head home?"

Jane put her hands against the desk and pushed back. "Sure."

As she stood up, Kenny put his arm around her and she melted into his body, the exhaustion of a brutal day finally catching up to her.

Holding her close, Kenny led her across the bullpen to the stairwell door.

Jane stopped to look outside. A young uniformed cop, probably from upstairs, was raising the American flag back to full staff.

It caught a breeze, the first breeze in a long time, and fluttered open. A passing taxi honked, its driver waving in support.

The elevator arrived and Becka Flynn stepped out. She scanned the squad room and spotted Jane.

Kenny opened the stairwell door and, still holding Jane close, guided her through.

"Want me to get them?" Roslyn Shapiro offered.

Becka Flynn watched the door click closed. "Nah," she said. "Let her go."

61

F~OG~.

Thick soothing fog, the first since summer began, drifted in off the bay. Pushing the heat away.

The windshield of the Explorer was covered in a fine mist and Kenny had to turn on the wipers. He looked over to Jane.

She lay back in the passenger seat, her feet on the dash, her forearm across her eyes.

"Think it's over?" Kenny asked.

"Think what's over?"

"Heat wave."

Jane lowered her arm and looked outside. "Fog," she said softly. "Wow."

Kenny braked to let the car in front of him turn into the driveway of a modest house. "Way I see it, if the AC's working at the station, then the heat wave's definitely over."

"I guess."

"Hey," Kenny said gently. "Where are you?"

Jane turned to him, her eyes heavy with weariness. "That's just it, Ken. I don't know where I am." She reached down with her right hand and brought her seat up. "My house is gone . . . everything I own. I've got a big midlife crisis brewing in the career department." She shook her head. "My brain is filled with dead people. Every time I close my eyes, I—"

Kenny reached across and took her hand. Jane felt something pressing against her palm and looked down.

Her mother's ring.

She turned in the seat to face Kenny. "How?"

"When the shit hit the fan, Jacob slipped some stuff into his pockets. You don't live the life he's lived without learning a couple of things." He touched her face. "We're getting married next week, remember? That's something."

"Yeah." Jane took his hand and kissed it. "That sure is."

——

Kenny eased the Explorer to the curb across from his sister's house. He put it into park and switched off the ignition. Then he grabbed the door handle.

Jane put her hand on his arm. "How ugly is this going to be?"

"Ugly." He opened the door. "The guy hit my nephew."

Lonnie was just pulling his pickup truck into the garage when Kenny came up. He got out of the truck and grinned. "You believe this? The one day I wash the truck and it fuckin' rains."

Kenny shoved Lonnie in the chest, sending him stumbling back into his truck.

"The fuck you doin', man?" Lonnie yelled.

He started to regain his footing, when Kenny shoved him again, harder. He fell back over the hood and Kenny was on him.

"I told you before, Lonnie," Kenny hissed, "don't *ever* lay a finger on Bobby!"

"Hey, wait a minute," Lonnie protested. "You know what that kid said to me?"

"I don't give a fuck," Kenny seethed. "No one, *no one*, has the right to hit a kid. Especially a low-life piece of shit like you!"

Lonnie twisted his body, trying frantically to get away from Kenny. He stopped squirming when he felt the muzzle of the Glock pressed against his windpipe.

"You are going to disappear, Lonnie," Kenny said through clenched teeth. "You don't go inside. You don't pick up your things. You don't call Andrea." He jammed the pistol deeper into Lonnie's neck. "And you don't even think of even *looking* at Bobby again!" He pulled Lonnie up until their faces were only inches apart. "You do, and I'll fucking kill you."

Kenny released his grip on Lonnie's shirt and straightened up.

Lonnie slid off the hood of the pickup. He opened his mouth

to say something. Kenny took a half step forward. "Don't talk!" he said. "Just go away."

Kenny tossed something to him. Lonnie snatched it out of the air.

A bullet.

"Tell me you understand, Lonnie."

"I . . . I understand." He got into his truck, started it, and tore out of the garage. When he hit the street, he yanked the pickup into a rough left turn and peeled away.

Kenny stepped into the rain and watched him go. Then he slipped his pistol into his shoulder holster and crossed the street.

In the rain-speckled windshield of the Explorer, Kenny could see the reflection of Bobby watching from an upstairs window. He turned to him and nodded.

Bobby nodded back, a smile playing at the corners of his mouth.

Kenny yanked open the door and climbed inside.

"That went well," Jane said.

Kenny started the car. "You don't fuck with family." He put the Explorer into gear and pulled away from the curb. "Christ," he said. "What have you done to me?" He laughed, his eyes sparkling. "I'm starting to sound Italian."

62

JANE SAT IN POPPY'S reading chair, sipping a glass of Chianti and listening to the rain. A red sauce bubbled on the stove, filling the house with a wonderfully familiar smell.

She looked at the letter folded in her lap. It had come to her by messenger from Chief McDonald. She opened it again and re-read it.

Dear Inspector Candiotti:

I called you at the station, but they said you'd gone home. I know you're going to take a few days off—well deserved—to get your life back in order.

While you do, I'd like you to consider something.

Ben Spielman isn't going to come back. Under the circumstances, I know you join me in appreciating his decision.

He and I spoke, and we came to the conclusion that you'd be the best person to replace him at Precinct Nineteen.

So, Inspector, I'm offering you his command and his rank.

I'm sure you know that, if you accept, it will make you the first female homicide lieutenant in the history of the San Francisco Police Department.

But it's more than just an honor.

It's recognition, perhaps overdue, of your excellent record as a police officer for almost twenty years.

Call me anytime; either with your decision or if you want to talk further about this.

I hope you'll say yes.

Respectfully,
Walker McDonald
Chief of Police, SFPD

There it was.

The culmination of years of ambition. The final door, the door to power and respect and a sense of finally belonging, being held open for her.

Jane put the letter on the small table next to the chair.

Tucking her feet under her, she looked around the living room.

She looked to the couch where she had first put her hand on her mother's stomach and felt Timmy move inside.

To the piano where, her feet dangling, she had taken lessons from Mrs. Grad for all those years.

To the fireplace where the four red-and-green flannel stockings had hung, lumpy with secrets, every Christmas morning.

To the stairs where, chasing Timmy, she had fallen and broken her collarbone.

To the rocker by the window where her mother would sit with her *Reader's Digest;* reading every word of every story, struggling with her new language, until the next issue came in the mail.

She touched the arm of Poppy's chair, the fabric worn thin by his elbows.

The front door opened and a cool rush of wind pushed into the room. Kenny came in, his hair plastered down by the rain.

He crossed the room, took Jane's wineglass, and put it on the side table, next to the letter. "Been thinking about the chief's offer?"

"That, and other things."

"And?"

Jane looked up to him. "And . . . I just don't know."

"That's okay, too." Kenny reached down and grabbed her hand. "C'mon, I need your help." He tugged her to her feet.

"What are you doing?"

Kenny pulled her to the front door and took Poppy's yellow rain slicker from the coatrack. He slipped it over her shoulders and opened the door. "Just shut up and come with me."

They raced down the steps and across the yard, hand in hand, until they reached the oak tree. They huddled there, next to the tire swing, the rain falling on the umbrella of leaves over their heads.

The side door of the house next door flew open, a splash of light falling onto the driveway. Davey Tasca, home from college, dashed out into the rain, picked up his little sister's bike, and ran back inside.

"I've got it, Ma. Jeez!" he cried as she slammed the door.

"He wasn't even born when I moved away," Jane said. "He got so big."

"Shh," Kenny said as he opened Jane's raincoat and pulled her to him. He held her close, about to speak, but deciding not to.

Then he kissed her, deeply.

Jane felt the urgency, the promise, in his kiss and put her arms around his neck. She folded herself into him, drawing his warmth, his strength.

Finally, she pulled away and looked into his eyes. "Oh, Ken," she said. "We're gonna be great."

"You bet we are." Kenny took her hand and led her away from the shelter of the broad oak. They crossed the wet grass, their shoes squishing, toward the FOR SALE sign.

Kenny stopped.

Jane stopped and saw the light dancing in his eyes.

And then she knew.

"Really?" she said.

Kenny nodded. "Really."

"You're sure?"

"I'm sure," Kenny said. "But could we hurry up and do it? It's kind of wet out here."

"C'mon!" Jane yelled, and they ran to the sign.

Leaning their shoulders into the post, they rocked it back and forth. When it finally came loose, they wrapped their arms around it and heaved.

It slid out of the wet ground and they let it fall on its side.

They stood there in the rain, looking at it.

After a moment, Jane turned to Kenny. "I've got a sauce cooking."

She took his hand and led him back to the house.